Worth Any Price

Books by Jacqueline DeGroot

Climax
The Secret of the Kindred Spirit
What Dreams Are Made Of
Barefoot Beaches
For the Love of Amanda
Shipwrecked at Sunset
Worth Any Price
Father Steve's Dilemma
The Widows of Sea Trail—Book One
Catalina of Live Oaks
The Widows of Sea Trail—Book Two
Tessa of Crooked Gulley
The Widows of Sea Trail—Book Three
Vivienne of Sugar Sands
Running into Temptation
with Peggy Grich
Running up the Score
with Peggy Grich
Running into a Brick Wall
with Peggy Grich
Tales of the Silver Coast—*A Secret History of*
Brunswick County
with Miller Pope
Sunset Beach—*A History*
with Miller Pope
Flash Drive

Worth Any Price

Three Women, One Nightmare

by
Jacqueline DeGroot

Dedicated to mothers
everywhere
who believe
that their children
are worth any price.

Acknowledgments

Thanking all the proofreaders who made my story better:

Kathy Blaine
Arlene Cook
Deb Coyte
Bill DeGroot
Peggy Grich
Nicki Leone
Martha Murphy
Nikki Smith
Leslie Ulrich

And the help of my writing groups:

Author's Ink
Hemingwaifs
Writer's Bloc

My Editor:
Nicki Smith

&
Kristi and her daughter, KiLee for being the models
for the cover

&
Jim and Peggy Grich
Who made this happen when no one else could.

I couldn't have done it without all of you.

Jack

Worth Any Price

Introduction

As firefighters carried the child's body up the steep slope of the river embankment, Detective Kel Vain couldn't help thinking one horrible thought: That this child's mother hadn't loved him enough. She hadn't loved him enough to do what was necessary to get him back from a deviant sexual predator, a monster that was terrorizing the city with a whole new kind of crime.

As water steadily dripped from the boy's blond head draped over the arm of the rescue diver, Kel's stomach churned. This one was only four-years-old, his body so tiny it might never have been found in the creek, except for the light yellow hair that had drawn a boater's attention.

As he stood and watched the small body being loaded into the medical examiner's van, Kel's mind reverted to his earlier thought and he amended it. He'd already met the mother, so he knew she loved the boy—loved him to distraction. She just hadn't been strong enough.

His hands thrust deep into his pockets, his lips a hard firm line, he turned to walk back up the hill to his squad car. He wouldn't have to make the official notification on this one. The press was already here and he'd never get all the way across town before this went live. He could stop them of course, but it wouldn't make any difference. His mother had to already know. She was, after all, the one who had sealed the little boy's fate.

He shook his head in disgust and trudged up the hill. He was more than just a little frustrated, he was beside himself with guilt. God, he had picked the absolute worst time to be off from work. When he had left three weeks ago, the port city of Wilmington was preparing for the Azalea Festival. Nothing was going on crime-wise other than the incessant drug dealing, the never-ending domestic disturbances, and biweekly car thefts. This Southern coastal town was not at all prepared for the deviant crimes one man was now perpetrating.

Four so far. Two women had done his bidding and had their children back. Two had not, and so lost them forever. Was it because of self-consciousness? Denial? Shame or ignorance? Fear, for sure, but that was a given for all of the women.

The monster called himself The Voyeur, and so far the meager clues he'd left hadn't amounted to enough to establish anything other than an M.O., which was to snatch the child, leaving a note for the mother to find. In the note there would be a list of three things she had to do to get her child back. And it always included a stern admonition; "If you fail to perform, you'll never see your child again." And of course, the obligatory, "Do not inform the authorities," accompanied each missive, and it was always tagged with something cavalier like, "not that it'll do any good."

The first woman, shocked with her "to-do list," had ignored the careful instructions and instead, had offered the man money when he called to remind her that time was running out. That little boy had been found three days later in the Intracoastal Waterway.

The second woman, made aware of the man's seriousness by the media coverage on the death of the first kidnapped child, had complied. She did as specified and performed all three of the disgusting and humiliating scenarios that had been outlined for her. She stripped naked and allowed herself to be photographed in lewd positions, then sent the digital pictures to an online photo web site account so the man holding her child could view her. For her second task, she walked into a crowded strip club, made her way to the stage and removed all of her clothing—and ironically got arrested by a vice officer for not wearing a G-string. Then as the final dictate, she went to a tattoo parlor and had a heart with a banner across it that said "Mom," tattooed on her right buttock. The tattoo had to be photographed and the picture relayed to the photo web site. Six hours later, her five-year-old daughter was found stumbling, blindfolded, all alone in the parking lot of Westfield Mall. Only then had she gone to the police with her bizarre tale.

With their help, the photo web site was temporarily shut down, but not before pornographic pictures of her were viewed all over the world; saved on hard drives and printed by the thousands. In less than a week someone recognized her and circulated the pictures. Unable to stand the scrutiny and the humiliation of her friends, family, and coworkers seeing her exposed in such a blatant way, she made preparations to move with her child and to change their identities.

The third woman panicked as soon as she discovered her child was missing and notified the police before she found the directives from the kidnapper. The window had been open and the ransom note had blown under the child's bed. The police found the note, but The Voyeur wasn't happy about their involvement. The little girl's body was found under a private pier in Futch's Creek just hours after the note was discovered.

The fourth woman did exactly as the note specified, and now had her son back. She did as The Voyeur had commanded — she robbed a liquor store, being sure to show her breasts to the security camera before running out of the store; she videotaped herself masturbating and left the video on a shelf in the New Hanover Public Library; and she went to a bar, propositioned two men and then let them take her, one after the other, on the back seat of her car while each videotaped the other. Her seven-year-old son fell against her door just four hours after that video tape had been left in a pew at St. Mark's Church, his eyes swollen half-shut by the adhesive left from the duct tape that was used to blindfold him.

In each case, the children had been blindfolded with duct tape the entire time they were held captive. From the moment they were abducted, they were securely bound, blindfolded, and gagged. They had not seen the man, yet they were fairly certain that it was a man, even though he never spoke to them. They had been given no food, no water, and were not permitted to go to the bathroom, so they had relieved themselves in their clothing. It seemed he had no feelings for them whatsoever. They were only pawns. Pawns in a game. A game of power he held over women; women who had no choice because he had their children.

Kel could find no connection between the women, except that they were all single mothers, working in the city, relying on childcare, nannies, or baby sitters while they worked. All of the children had been taken from their home, either while they were napping in the afternoon or after they were put to bed for the night. None of the homes had been particularly secure, but none had been all that inviting either. Yet the man had come unseen, picked the lock or had a key, and stolen off with the sleeping child.

It was more than scary. It was the worst kind of terrorism. And it was his job to put an end to it.

Chapter One

Kel Vain dropped the morning paper onto the kitchen table, turned to the counter, and poured a big mug of coffee. He had just come from an exhausting morning run; the exhausting part was courtesy of the repeated Jack Daniel's shots he'd tossed down last night. He took a bracing sip of the coffee as he walked back to the table and blinked as he swallowed the strong, acidic brew.

Sliding onto the padded seat of the nook, he took note of the cardinals feeding at the window tray just inches from where he sat. It was a beautiful spring morning, he just wasn't eager for the full bright sunshine to pierce his fuzzy eyes. It was his own fault, he told himself. He knew better than this—liquor didn't help. No amount of it could erase the memory of seeing a child's lifeless body carried out of the woods or pulled from a river.

He wet his fingertips on the condensation from his orange juice glass and then used his dampened fingers to separate the sections of the morning paper. It was his habit to organize the paper before reading it: Sports page first, Money next, Local, then National. Classifieds and sales flyers were immediately tossed into the trash.

In the course of shifting the papers to the proper order, his eye was drawn to a picture on the front page of the Local Section. He blinked twice. Then his eyes opened wide with shock. He knew that woman. Without the benefit of having to read the tag line under the photo, he knew her to be Laura Wyndham, a classy Wilmington socialite whose family donated millions to local foundations and charities. He had adored this woman from afar for more years than he cared to count. And here she was, posing, regal as could be in a floor length gown, standing in the middle of a stage.

Nothing unusual about that, except that she was topless. The halter part of her gown had been undone and hung down in front of the full skirt of her ball gown. The newspaper, keeping with rigorous community standards, had placed black bars over the center of each of her breasts covering her nipples. His eyes remained wide as his sculpted, arrogant, dark brows lifted to meet the dark curl that fell across his forehead as he examined the picture. Then he forced his eyes lower to read the terse caption: "Socialite Laura Wyndham had an apparent 'costume failure' at last night's Gala Fashion Show." In the body of the accompanying article he read, "According to Sheila Barnstable who was sitting at a front table, 'It was apparent to anyone sitting down front that she was purposely flaunting herself. She stood right in front of us, then she reached behind her neck and unclasped the top of her gown, letting it fall forward. We could all see her lips, those who cared to look away from her chest that is, as she slowly counted to ten. Then she cupped her breasts with her hands, turned and strode quickly off the stage. It was the strangest thing. I would never have expected that of her! Not in a million, zillion years.'"

Kel dropped the paper onto the table and jumped off the bench. He strode to the end of the counter and jerked open a drawer. He grabbed his holstered gun and badge case and ran to the garage. As usual, in his haste, he rapped his head on the doorjamb getting into his new cruiser and it hurt

6

like a son-of-a-bitch. These unmarked cruisers were getting downsized with every model year and he practically had to fold himself in half just to get in the damn things! He had to remember to ask the motor pool to give him one of the older ones.

He was snaking his way through traffic and speeding across town before he realized he was still in his sweaty jogging shorts and tank top. But it didn't matter. He had to find her, and he had to find her right away. Because he knew, without a doubt, what would cause a woman as well bred as Laura Wyndham to do something as drastic and as foreign to her nature as exposing herself like that.

And his heart went out to her. How hard it must have been for her to get up the nerve to stand before her friends and neighbors, as well as the general public filling that huge ballroom, and stand completely topless. She was such a lovely woman, and to have to bare her breasts like that . . .. The thought sickened him. But with the next thought, an unwelcome prurient one, he had to briefly close his eyes and grimace. He was disgusted with himself when his mind recalled the picture, his imagination trying desperately to fill in the details the newspaper had tastefully covered.

He had thrown his blue light onto the roof of his unmarked car as soon as he'd pulled out of his driveway, and now, as he swerved around a pickup truck and ran a red light on South College, he cringed. *God I hope it's not too late.* He stopped at the next intersection, thought for a moment, got his bearings, and jerked the wheel to the right. After a few more turns, he was headed down Masonboro Loop, his blue light flashing and siren whelping. It was quite a coincidence that he knew exactly where she lived now. But he did, since he was the officer who'd had the dubious honor of fingerprinting her and writing her up just two days ago when she'd been brought in for shoplifting. He'd been covering the desk while some street officers were qualifying at the firing range.

He should have known it then! Damn! He hit his fist on the steering wheel hard enough to crack the Lincoln insignia imbedded in the plastic. He'd known she wasn't capable of shoplifting! He'd known something was off kilter, it just hadn't dawned on him what. She wasn't just some spoiled socialite—she was Laura, and she was above that kind of thing. He knew it. Deep down, he knew it. He'd been two years ahead of Laura when they'd attended Laney High School, and even though they hadn't run in the same circles, he'd had plenty of opportunity to idolize her from afar. He watched her when she was with her friends chatting in the halls, cheerleading in front of the bleachers at basketball games, and speaking at assemblies as her class president. Once, he'd even gotten close enough to pick up a book she'd dropped. Her soft blue eyes and ready smile had mesmerized him then, and he'd envied the boys who were confident enough in their status to ask her out.

He remembered one Christmas concert when she'd sang a solo. It was Shubert's version of "Ave Maria." He had watched her from six rows back, constantly craning his neck to keep her in view as two girls in front of him jostled each other. Her eyes had sparkled and her lips had shone with a deep cherry gloss as she stood, hands clasped with fingers interlaced, looking up as if the words were written on the auditorium ceiling. She had looked like a dark-haired angel. The song still haunted him; he couldn't hear the melody without remembering how lovely she'd looked that day. His Laura was special, always had been.

As he read the numbers on the mailboxes and realized he was getting close, he shut off the siren and removed the light. Then, at a customized, bricked-in mailbox, he pulled off the road and followed the long, winding, gravel driveway.

The narrow drive twisted several times and even reversed itself before he finally emerged in a large clearing.

Her house on the Intracoastal Waterway sat back from the lane, thirty feet beyond where the circular drive ended. He could just make out the green water of the Intracoastal behind the house through the trees along the sides. It was definitely a spectacular house, set high off the ground with massive double front doors at the top of a curving brick staircase. The same brick had been used to encase the mailbox at the road and provide a low wall around the landscaped lawn and flowerbeds. He stomped on the brakes, shoved the gearshift into park, and pulled out the keys. He slid his gun from the holster, shoved it into the waistband of his shorts, and grabbed his badge before forcing the car door open with his elbow. With the efficient moves of a man who'd done these maneuvers countless times, he scanned the area as he ran while clipping his badge to the waistband of his shorts. He banged on the solid wooden door. The sound reverberated off the triple-sized wooden porch, echoing in the high rafters as it wrapped around the sides of the house. He waited a few seconds and banged again, this time much harder.

He could smell the sweet perfume from the wisteria that was clinging to a decorative light pole leading to a walkway bordering the house. He noted that the carriage light had erroneously been left on. He stepped back a few feet and saw that all the outside lights were also on. On each corner, flood lights aimed out to the lawn and burned bright in the early morning sun. As Kel walked back to the door he spied a light for a doorbell peeking out behind an ivy planter. He punched it four times. Then he saw movement through the glass side panel, a shadow moved in the back part of the house. He continued to ring the bell repeatedly; over and over again, eight times, nine times, ten times . . . . He saw the darkened image move once more. Now the figure was leaning on a wall at the end of a long hallway, its head tipped all the way back, standing, waiting. Waiting for him to go away.

"I'm not leaving until I talk to you, Mrs. Wyndham! You remember me, I'm Detective Vain. I saw you at the station this week. I'm the one who read you your rights and fingerprinted you for shoplifting. Now open this door!"

He watched through the glass as the slim woman, wearing what appeared to be a terry cloth bathrobe, slowly made her way to the foyer.

"I don't want to talk to anybody. Please leave me alone." Her voice was cultured and cool, but he could hear her falter on the word "alone." He recognized the fear trembling in her voice and he was sickened with concern.

"You need to let me in. And you need to do it now before he sees me."

Instantly, the figure in the darkness covered the remaining distance to the door. He heard the bolts click as they unlocked and the door abruptly opened. He pushed his way in, forcing her away from the opening. Then he quickly closed the door behind him and leaned back against it.

"Mrs. Wyndham, where is your daughter?"

Her eyes flew to his, saw understanding there, and she lost every ounce of the composure she had been trying to maintain for two days.

As tears came to her eyes, her hands flew to her cheeks. "He has her," she whispered. Completely out of control now, she broke down. Hysterically sobbing, she screamed over and over. "He has her! Oh God, he has her! That monster has my baby!"

Kel reached for her and pulled her into his arms. He held her close and tried to comfort her by rubbing his hands up and down her back. He couldn't help but notice the soft, powder-fresh fragrance that enveloped her and he was reminded of his own not-so-fresh redolence. He set her from him and gently wrapped his big hands around her upper arms as he ducked his head to look into her face. The tears streaming down her cheeks just about broke his heart. She was too beautiful a woman to cry; she looked like an angel who should have nothing more to worry about than playing a harp. He used his thumbs to wipe away the tears. But it didn't do any good, they kept coming.

"We'll get her back. Shhh, shhh. We'll get her back, we will." Then stupidly, he added, "I swear we will."

He led her into a darkened part of the house, away from the sunny kitchen to a huge room on the right, toward what he assumed was the living room. The sun was on the back of the house, but here in the front it was all shadows and quiet coolness.

"You can't be here," she sobbed. "He said if I called the police, he'd kill her. You have to leave! Now!"

He continued to hold her by his side as he led her over to a comfortable-looking leather sofa. She felt warm and soft, and small, snuggled against his large body. He drew her powder-soft fresh scent deep into his lungs.

"There's no way he'd know I'm a cop, my car's an unmarked Lincoln and I'm wearing a sweaty jogging outfit for crying out loud!" He didn't mention that he'd come brandishing a gun and a badge. He forced her to sit on the sofa, then sat beside her on the sectional where it turned so he could face her.

"Tell me what happened. Start at the beginning. I need to know everything if I'm going to be able to find her."

"H . . . h-how did you know?" she stammered.

"I saw your picture in the paper this morning." He watched as fresh tears filled her eyes and overflowed her lashes. She flushed scarlet with the memory of what she had done. Her hands covered her face as she dropped it into her lap.

"I could just die."

"I knew the minute I saw the picture what had happened. A woman like you . . . well, there'd be no reason . . ."

"I'd do anything for Kayla. Anything. But that was so hard. I don't honestly know how I did it. I just knew I had to. I . . . I . . ." Then the tears started again.

"I should have known something was wrong when they picked you up at the mall!" he slammed his fist into his palm. "A woman like you just doesn't do that! Shoplifting lingerie! Did you want to get caught?"

"Actually, those were his instructions, I had to get caught." Tears continued to stream down her face. She was swiping at them with the meager belt of her robe. "What am I going to do?"

He slid around beside her and took her hands in his.

"Start at the beginning. Tell me everything. When did you notice Kayla was missing and where is the note?"

A worried look creased her brow. If she gave it to him everyone would know what she'd had to do. She remembered the media releases about the other notes, nothing was held back. He knew there was a note, she wouldn't be able to lie to him. And now, she wasn't sure she even wanted to.

He could see by her wariness that she needed some encouragement, "I'm one of the detectives assigned to this case, I'm in charge. I've seen all the notes from the other kidnappings. I was out of town for the last few weeks, but I've read all the reports. I came back early when I heard what was happening. Now answer my questions."

She sniffed and then let out a deep breath. "It was Tuesday morning. I went into Kayla's room to wake her for school and she wasn't there. There was a note on her dresser, pinned to the front of one of her dolls."

"Where's the note now?"

She sniffed again, blinked her eyes, reached into her pocket, and drew out the much-maligned note. He took it from her by the edges. Then he looked around for a box of tissues. He saw one on the sofa table behind him and reached for it. He handed her a wad of tissues and instructed her to, "Blow."

Using just the barest touch on the corners, he unfolded the note. "Have you been carrying this around with you?"

"Yes, I didn't want to lose it or have anyone find it."

He scanned the note then read it again. He leaned his head back against the sofa bolster and closed his eyes.

"Still got one more to go, huh?" he said to the ceiling.

"Uh, yeah. One more. Tonight." Her voice was so soft now that he could barely hear her.

He sat up, leaned forward, then with the note open between his knees he read the note aloud:

Laura Wyndham: I have your daughter. If you want her back do these three things and DON'T involve the authorities, for all the good they'd do. You should know by now that I'm not fooling around.

First: Go to Victoria's Secret at Westfield Mall. Shoplift six Wonder Bras. Size 38 D, something with lots of lace. And get caught. If you don't get caught, it won't count.

Second: Wednesday, the night of the big fashion show, the one at the Waterfront Hilton. I know you're scheduled to model a Karan halter-style ball gown. Once you're on stage, drop the top and let all of Wilmington see your titties. For at least ten seconds, or it won't count.

Third: Pick up a man. Take your pick of any man in Motley's Bar and Grille this Thursday night. Then go with him to the Jefferson Motel next door any time after eight and request room 12. Have sex with him there. There's a hidden camera behind the TV that feeds to the Internet. I want to see him toy with your breasts and I want to see his fingers buried deep inside you before he fucks you. After I've watched your performance, I'll return the girl. Oh, and the guy must pull out and come like they do in the porno flicks—on your belly or in the crack of your ass. Or it won't count. And live dangerously, no rubbers. Here's a bonus: get him to eat you, and your daughter comes home a virgin.

Kel let out a long sigh while Laura sobbed quietly, staring at the paper in his hands. "The man is incredibly brutal and crude," she spat out.

And quite imaginative, Kel thought. "Any idea how he could know you were in the show and what you'd be wearing?"

"It wouldn't be hard to find out. Lots of people knew. I've had six fittings and three dress rehearsals; anyone at the Hilton, or a clerk at the dress shop could tell someone what I'd be wearing if they'd asked. It might even have been published in a publicity ad."

"This is despicable what he's demanding. What kind of man does this to a woman?" He was thinking out loud as he shook his head against the soft leather, his thick brown waves getting mussed.

"He wants me to be a stripper."

"And a porn star for Christ sake! The man is a pervert of the worst order," Kel's lips pursed and when he sat up, she could see fury blazing in his dark steely eyes.

"I have to do it, you know that," she whispered.

14

He took her hand and covered it with his. She lifted her head until their eyes met. "I know you do. I know exactly what it would mean if you didn't."

There was silence for a full minute as they both stared into each other's eyes. The clock ticking on the mantel was the only sound that intruded into their somber thoughts. Then Laura slipped her hand from his and sat back against the cushions. Her head fell back and she closed her eyes tightly, trying to keep the tears from overflowing yet again. Kel sat back and stared fixedly at the burl coffee table, taking in the cut-glass crystal ashtray, William Mangum's exquisite picture book of North Carolina, and the pile of damp tissues Laura was building on the edge. Good God, what the hell could he say to this woman? What should he say? Jesus! Some man was going to have to have sex with her in front of a camera for her to get her daughter back! Just where was the definitive police manual when you needed it? What would the repercussions be? Being recorded . . . damn! I could lose my fucking job!

Into the quiet morning, he barked, "I'll do it. You'll meet me at Motley's."

"What?"

"I'll be the stranger you meet. You'll meet me at the bar, we'll have a few drinks, and then we'll go to the Jefferson and give him the show he wants so you can get your daughter back. And, yes, I'll make damned sure she comes back a virgin."

She blinked her eyes wide and sat straight up. "Can you do that?"

"Do you have someone else who can do it?" He'd made his decision and now it bothered the hell out of him that she was questioning it. And he couldn't pinpoint what his feelings would be if she answered his question in the affirmative.

15

"No! No. I just . . . . God, this is so strange."

"Tell me about it."

"I don't do this kind of thing . . . ."

"Neither do I."

"I'm scared. Really scared."

To keep from wrapping his arms around her and soothing her, as he wanted to, he leaned back against the sofa and spread his arms out along the top cushions. He casually crossed his ankle over his knee and let out a big sigh. He was forcing his ankle not to shake. He was as unnerved as she was, but damned if he was going to show her.

"I know you are, but you really don't have much choice if you want her back. The mothers that didn't do his bidding gambled with their kids' lives and lost. Ordinarily we don't advocate submitting to this type of terrorism, but we aren't able to stop him yet. We have remarkably little to go on. So far, he's calling the shots, as horrible as that is."

"I'll do anything to get her back."

"I know. And I'll try not to make it any worse than it has to be. I'll use my body to shield yours from the camera whenever I can."

"This is the strangest conversation I've ever had. Especially with a man I've just met."

"Want to take a chance on what you'll find at Motley's?" he quipped, raising one dark eyebrow.

She met his steadfast gaze. "Not a chance. At least you're a known quantity." Besides, I doubt I could do better in a hundred bars. She blushed from her errant thought and ducked her face. "In any event, I don't have anybody else I can ask." She looked him up and down then managed to get the words out. "I haven't had sex in over three years, and I'm not using any birth control. I won't be protected."

"I'll be pulling out, remember?"

The thought of exactly what he was referring to

caused her to shiver. "How am I going to get through this?" she whispered.

"We'll get through it together. Just make sure you don't do or say anything that might let on that we've met before. In the meantime, I'm going to go see what I can find out about this motel. Like how the hell he knows room twelve is going to be available after eight."

"You won't . . . ."

"Don't worry, I won't tip our hand. I know the consequences this man deals out. We'll play it his way, because we have to. But when this is finished, I'm going to get the sick bastard! He'll be sent to a prison where the inmates will cut his balls off with a rusty shiv."

He stood. "I'll see you at Motley's around seven. You go straight to the bar, order a drink, and I'll sidle up to you. Then you can come on to me in case he's in the bar watching. After a few drinks, we'll walk over to the motel. Then I'll take over and you just follow my lead. I know this will be extremely difficult for you, but if you can relax and trust me it'll fare better for you. I'll try not to hurt you and I'll make sure to position us so the camera gets more of me than you while still satisfying this pervert's demands."

"I can't believe this is happening to me. I can't believe he was able to just waltz in and steal my baby!" She had turned the waterworks on again, and it tore into his heart.

"After we get her back, we'll find out how he did it and make sure he can never do it again."

Kel turned to leave, then pulled her up with him, keeping her hands in his. "I need to go to work. I have to set a few things in motion."

"You won't . . . ."

He wanted to put his fingers on her trembling lips to still them, but instead, squeezed her fingertips, "Don't worry. I won't jeopardize Kayla, that you can count on. She's the most important thing in my world until we get her back."

"Won't you be jeopardizing your job?"

"No, I don't think so. But even if it did, it wouldn't matter. Kayla's all that matters now."

"Thank you so much Detective Vain. I didn't know how I was going to handle this. I was actually bracing myself to go to bed with the first man who sat beside me tonight."

"Well, that'll be me. And you can call me Kel. We're going to get to know each other really well in a very short space of time. And Laura?"

"Yes?"

"When we're in the room, you're going to have to beg me to go down on you. It just wouldn't be a man's normal inclination to do that at a time like this. He'd be more into pleasing himself. It's not something normally done in this kind of situation—one-night stands are not usually about satisfying the woman that way. Right at about the time I'm fingering you would be a good time, okay? Start begging then."

Her cheeks turned fire engine red. She simply nodded.

They walked silently to the door. "And you can turn all those outside flood lights off, they might have helped before, but now that he has her, we certainly don't want to discourage him from bringing her back." He reached down and squeezed her hand. "It's going to be okay. We'll get her back."

Then he was gone.

Chapter Two

*L*ord what had he gotten himself into now? Kel stood in front of the triple mirror over the long vanity in his spacious bathroom. He was a big man and he liked to have plenty of room to move around. He'd picked this house primarily because he liked the generous master bedroom and bath. At six foot four he didn't like the closeness of eight-foot ceilings. His house had ten-foot ceilings with the main rooms featuring recessed trays. In addition to the high walls, all the counters in the bathrooms were raised so he wouldn't have to bend low and kill his back.

With both hands he slapped aftershave on his smooth-shaven cheeks, gingerly rubbing the abrasive tingle past his jaw and down his throat. He'd been especially careful to shave close tonight, as if he was going out on a date. His knuckles brushed the skin under his bottom lip where he'd abraded it with one upward swipe too many; he knew from experience that once the sting wore off, the redness would, too.

He focused on the devilish visage reflecting back at him as he envisioned his mouth between Laura Wyndham's thighs and he chided himself. That was no way to think. The woman was desperate, distraught, and in the most serious straits of her life. How could he possibly be having such vile and despicable thoughts?

However, she was definitely a beauty and he knew that any man with testosterone running in his veins would gladly step into his place. It was only natural for him to think ahead and prepare his mind and body for the upcoming assignment. As difficult a situation as this was, he couldn't help but think of her as a woman, a lovely, soft woman. Just think, tonight, I'm going to have my lips and mouth wrapped around Laura Wyndham's snatch, savoring the musky smell of her, inhaling her special woman's essence. He slapped his cheek, hard. He had to curb these thoughts. They were piling up and bumping into each other in his brain, one graphic image of her after the other. Like flip cards in a bawdy deck of cards, his imagination was filling in all the places he would soon be touching and tasting.

All day he'd managed to avoid prurient thoughts like this because of the seriousness of the kidnapping, but they couldn't be held back; the male animal in him was awakened and heightened by the thought of Laura, naked in front of him. And even though there would be no emotional attachment involved in their coupling, he couldn't help but be excited and aroused even as he was a touch apprehensive.

Man oh man! If the guys only knew! Then a sobering thought occurred to him. They surely would know. Once Kayla was returned the case would be fully workable. All the evidence would be collected and examined. The investigation would turn up the kidnap note, it would have to—he was leading the investigation. And no matter how hard he tried to keep this matter private, he knew it would soon be a part of the public record, possibly even reported by the press. The public would want to know, in their sick, curiosity-filled minds, what the pristine Laura Wyndham had had to do to get her child back. They already knew of the others and what they'd had to do.

His mind flitted back two days to when he had actually met her after so many years of watching her walking down high school corridors and ogling her at school events. The last decade, like many of her classmates, he'd kept track of her only through the media.

The picture of a regal topless enchantress warred with the vision of the docile and polite woman daubing at the smudges of fingerprint ink on her fingertips as she had apologized for shoplifting the bras. She had been so contrite and so polite, apologizing over and over for her actions. Her attorney had been in the courthouse on another case and within minutes he had arrived and arranged for her release. He had made her stop talking and had quickly escorted her out a back door well before the press could line up on the front steps. And it hadn't clicked. The incongruity of it all still hadn't clicked in his detective's mind. Where had that special sixth sense he prided himself on having gone? Why hadn't he put it all together then?

Laura, Laura, why did this have to happen to you? You are such a sweet lady, and so damned beautiful.

He alternated between being thrilled that he would see the breasts the elite of Wilmington had viewed just the night before, and horrified that she'd have to bare them against her will again. The idea that he would soon be touching and caressing them hardened him, but then just as quickly, he remembered the reason why he was being placed in that position, and he replaced his lustful desires with an angry passion.

How had this monster managed to get to a woman such as Laura? He almost envied the control The Voyeur had at this moment over the woman he admired so much. But as the image of a sick pervert leering at Laura's naked body grew in his mind, he vowed he would catch him. This was one son-of-a-bitch that was going into the North Carolina penal system and never coming out. He envisioned himself pummeling a faceless man until there was nothing left but a bony skull. He grabbed his coffee cup from the counter and took a long swig.

Then the image of Laura's finely sculpted face floated in front of him and he envisioned himself tasting her lips with his. Other places his lips would wander came to mind and he wondered how he'd react when everyone he worked with knew where his lips had been, where his tongue, and yes, even where his penis had been, all in the line of duty of course. The duty that just might get him fired. He was going against police procedure. He wasn't even sure how many official rules he was breaking. Insubordination for one — after getting a break on a case like this, he should definitely be telling someone higher up in the chain of command. But he just couldn't risk it right now, there just wasn't enough time to get a team in place. He wouldn't even be sending any officers to Laura's house tonight in the event the killer returned Kayla to the house — he simply wasn't going to take the chance. Laura would never forgive him if something went wrong. He'd never forgive himself. He'd deal with the repercussions as they came; certainly no one could fault him for stepping in. A quick smile spread over his face before he could stop it. Yeah, no one, certainly no one he knew on the force.

Being videotaped was the part that quirked all this. Should it become known, he had no idea how the department would handle this kind of thing. He wouldn't exactly be doing anything illegal, but they had pretty strong ethics and moral codes in place for their officers in the South, and he was sure that making your own porn, regardless of the circumstances, would be highly frowned upon. But he wasn't a rookie. He was a highly trained, multi-commended master detective. He figured the worst they could do was suspend him without pay, unless of course things got really hinky, and the child died. That would be a whole other scenario, and with the pull of her family in this community, he'd be out on his ass.

How the hell would Laura handle all this? How would she face her family, her friends and the press? Thankfully, it would be years before her daughter would know what her mother had sacrificed for her. How she had put the life of her child before everything. Just how the hell was Laura going to deal with this, he wondered.

Raised as a woman of privilege, Laura was confident and trained in the social graces. Anyone desiring her attentions would have to treat her with respect; would have to show her ladylike care, be unceasingly gentle and proper. Except that now this monster had her attention, and he was treating her like . . . like he owned her, like she was his. The blood in Kel's veins came quickly to a boil and the rage behind his eyes was almost palpable. He didn't like having these feelings. The intense anger warped his thinking. He had to calm down. He closed his eyes and tried to envision Laura smiling and holding her daughter tightly in her arms. It was not hard for him to imagine the scenario, he'd seen it in print. And now he was determined to make it a reality again, he was determined to help her get her child back.

During such a crucial time in her life, Kel was proud to be the one offering assistance to Laura Wyndham—honored to be the one coming to her rescue. She was handling herself regally despite having to whore herself for the despicable excuse of humanity who had stolen her child.

Kel, like most of the boys in high school, had always felt he was light years out of Laura's league, and had only admired her from afar. For whatever reason, she had never seemed approachable, and the boys he knew, like him, just drooled over her pictures and fought for a spot on a curb whenever she was in the Azalea Festival Parade. Over the years he had seen her picture appear in *The Wilmington Star News* on the society pages at least a hundred times. First, as she posed in sweet cotillion dresses, then later in sophisticated prom dresses, and finally in an elegant wedding gown. Even after her marriage to Ryan Vardella, the up-and-coming state representative had failed, she still made the local section, decked out in regal refinery for one charity event after another. That Kel knew so much about her life was no oddity; she was a well-known public figure in Wilmington that he, along with many others, respected and admired. Being from a wealthy family made her prominent, being poised and unaffected by it, made her popular.

He was whimsically amused that over the years he'd conjured up an image of her as some sort of fairy tale princess. And now, the sweet, lovely young princess was in trouble. She needed rescuing from the tower, where an ugly ogre had her cornered, and he desperately wanted to kick that ogre to kingdom come and back.

Idly he stroked his bare chest, casually examining his torso in the mirror. He scratched at the fur pelt generously sprinkled on his pecs. He had a big body. His tall, muscled frame with wide, full shoulders could easily shield Laura's diminutive body from the camera. He could lay on top of her, wrap his arms around her and plunge deeply into her without revealing anything of her secret womanly parts. But even the possibility of allowing her that small modicum of modesty had been taken away from her. The Voyeur's explicit instructions called for her blatant defiling. The bastard wanted to view her. That's how he got his jollies; controlling women and making them humiliate themselves for him. What kind of man got off watching a woman being taken by a man when it wasn't her will?

As soon as he found a free minute, he was going to call the profiler in New York City who was already working up a report for him. The man was renowned for breaking down the inner sadistic tendencies of rapists and serial killers into likely physical and emotional characteristics. He needed all the help he could get to capture this vile creature; this filthy vermin whose leering, lusty eyes would soon have his fill of one of the most gracious women Kel had ever known. He would get in touch with his friend tomorrow and find out more about this creature who all but wanted Laura publicly raped.

Good God, rape. Was that what he was about to do? Rape Laura Wyndham? He fisted both hands and pounded them brutally on his hard thighs. Yes, that was exactly what this was going to be—rape. He would be taking her by force, against her will. Sure, he wasn't the one commanding the act, but he would be the one taking her, using his flesh as a weapon to torture and dishonor her. So, now he was a rapist by proxy. Wonderful. Just fucking wonderful. A lifetime of upholding the law only to break it in the most profound and demeaning way possible. He looked down at the hair curling at the juncture of his thighs. Then why the hell was he as hard as an anvil? The strength of his erection scared him; it was so rigid he felt he could balance a hammer on it. Dear God, I hope I don't have any tendencies for enjoying manhandling a woman; especially a woman like Laura—as gentle as Laura. He felt a sticky wetness oozing from the tip of his penis. Shit. Usually he loved his work, but not this way.

Chapter Three

*L*aura forced her red-rimmed eyes to look up. She had been clutching the edge of the sink so tightly that her knuckles were white. She took stock of herself in the mirror and quickly covered her face with her hands. How was she going to get through this? Her hands fisted in her hair, the curls tight and damp from her shower. I can't do this. I just can't do this!

Then she thought of Kayla, her dear sweet Kayla, and realized that she had no choice. She had to do it. She reached for her brush and roughly ran it through her hair and the knots in it until her burning scalp rebelled. Then she threw the brush as hard as she could at the mirror.

It surprised her that it didn't break. *Get hold of yourself. You are the only one who can get her back. Just get through it! See the end result, not the means.*

She picked up the brush and ran it slowly through her hair. She didn't have the energy to do anything with it, so she just let it fall over her shoulders. Normally she wore her long hair back from her face, usually in a fancy chignon or French-braided twists. Now gathered at the crown and loose, it fell in waves, randomly parting itself on the left side. She didn't look at all like herself. Her face had a haunted look. Her normally pale, translucent skin was allowing faint purple shadows to show under her red eyes. Her high cheekbones, the apples normally accented by a natural blush, now looked sallow from her despair. The twinkle was gone from her azure eyes, the window to her soul was now a dull, flat, vacant wasteland. There was hope, deep, deep inside, but you couldn't see it—she was afraid to let it show.

With luck, maybe no one would know who she was. Except of course, Detective Kel Vain. He'd certainly know who she was. Hell in a few hours, he'd know more about her than anyone, save her ex-husband. Well, that wasn't entirely true, she thought; Kel would know more. He would know what it was like to taste her in her most feminine folds. Putting his mouth down there was something her husband had loathed doing. On their honeymoon, he tried it once, but his obvious discomfort unsettled her. He kept gagging on hair and then complained about it so much that it ruined the whole mood of their lovemaking. It was an experience neither had found enjoyable, so it had never been repeated. Yet he had insisted she service him in that intimate manner. Until the night she had walked into his office and found his aide-de-camp kneeling at his feet taking over the chore for her. The man hadn't thought her strong enough to withstand the public humiliation of a divorce. Well, he had been wrong hadn't he? Good God, talk about public humiliation. The divorce had been a cakewalk compared to what last night's repercussions were going to be for her.

The thought almost caused her knees to buckle. She forced herself to stand tall and to hold her head up as her mother had always taught her. Her mother. She was going to have a fit. Tonight her daughter was going to become a prostitute. Tonight, Laura would sell her body. Not for money, mind you, but for the life of her own daughter. That was the only thought that kept her going as she reached for deodorant, then powders and creams. When she lifted the can of feminine hygiene spray, she burst out with hysterical laughter. Would the good detective prefer Strawberry Spring or Gardenia Blossoms?

She was the type of woman who usually knew a lot about a man before even letting him venture a kiss. She put the can back on the counter. She'd better not use either; the man could be allergic to fragrance for all she knew. Besides, how bad could she get in an hour or two even sweating from every pore as she battled fear and embarrassment? God, what if he didn't even like cunnilingus? The thought that he might find both her and the act as disgusting as her husband had, caused her to shiver.

Then she thought of the man holding her little girl and she didn't really care about the detective's preferences. Her fists clenched so tightly into her palms that her nails created half moons in them. When this was over they were going to get him. She didn't care if it took every last penny she had, she wanted to see this man die for what he was doing to her. Doing to her daughter. She knew that somewhere her daughter was bound, gagged, and blindfolded with duct tape, that she wouldn't be given anything to eat or drink, and that in all likelihood she was soaked to the skin in her own urine. That had been the pattern, the press had covered that part pretty thoroughly each time a child had been discovered. The kidnapper was very consistent in how he treated the children. He apparently neglected and ignored them the whole time he had them. The uncompassionate bastard! She sobbed as she thought about Kayla and how badly she was being treated. Her baby was hungry and scared and not able to even call out for her mommy. The tears flowed from her eyes and she had to hurry and blot them before she had to redo her makeup, again. But she couldn't stem the flow, she just couldn't seem to stop crying, she hurt so much.

She collapsed onto the bathroom throw rug and said

a prayer. God, please give Detective Vain the strength to do what he must to bring my baby home, safe and unharmed. I promise if you can get us through this, I'll do everything in my power to keep this evil monster from ever doing this again.

After pulling herself back to her feet, Laura repaired the damage then gave great thought to dressing. She selected her lingerie very carefully with ease of removal in mind. A front-opening bra would allow her breasts to be bared, while she still kept it on; a skirt would make it unnecessary to remove all her clothing. A blouse would allow her to cover herself quickly once the requirements were met. She didn't bother with hose or stockings and opted for bikini underpants instead of the thong type that she usually wore. When she was as happy with her appearance as she could be, given the circumstances, she grabbed a sweater and her purse and went down to the garage.

As she passed by the phone she wished for just a moment that she could call her mother. But nobody could know, especially her mother. It would only make things harder for them all. And her father, almost as emotional, would insist on getting the authorities involved, and he would be furious that she hadn't already. The fact that they were away at their house in Italy was fortuitous. But certainly, after last night's stunt, there would be a lot of questions to answer. As soon as they got back she'd find out how supportive they truly were. Up until now, they had been ideal parents. This would be a true test for her family. And her brother . . . Lord, when he got wind of this he'd have what her mother used to call a "conniption fit." He was always overly concerned with appearances.

The message light was blinking on the phone. Since last night's debacle many people had phoned—the curious, the concerned, the shocked, and the indignant. She pushed the button to see how many messages were stored. Last night at midnight, there had been forty-two. The red L.E.D. number flashed—eighty-six. Among them, she was sure, were several heated ones from her ex. She knew he still had ties to Wilmington, and surely the phone lines had buzzed way into the night with the news of his ex-wife's shocking behavior. Knowing him, he would have used a few choice words to describe her despicable display, accused her of being drunk out of her mind, and then he would have expounded on the fact that he didn't need this kind of publicity during an election year. The only thing he wouldn't mention is her being an unfit mother, because he certainly didn't want Kayla thrust into his life; he'd leave well enough alone on that score.

She wanted to press delete and send all the messages into oblivion before listening to them, but she couldn't. She had to quickly run through each one, skipping to the next as soon as she recognized a voice. She was listening for an unfamiliar voice, the voice of the man who had her daughter. But in her heart she knew the man wouldn't call. He would just do as he said, depending on what she did. It was a well-established pattern—he didn't deviate. He made it a point not to. It was where all her fear came from—his horrible crimes of the past weeks, his despicable dirty mind and his evil, cold soul.

She listened as familiar voices said, "Laura, I just can't believe . . . "; "Laura, are you out of your . . ."; "Laura, what the hell is . . . "; "You fucking bitch . . . "; "Laura, call me . . . ." Once Kayla was home, she would force herself to listen to each chastising message, it would be a form of punishment she would make herself endure. She deserved it. All the harsh words in the world she deserved and much, much more. But if she got Kayla back, she could deal with it. She could deal with her mother and her father, her brother and her friends. She could even deal with her ex. The sad thing was that he was Kayla's father. When he did finally hear all that had happened, he still wouldn't have any compassion or understanding for what she'd had to do or for what his daughter had been through. She knew without a doubt that he was too involved in his own little world to care about anything except his political career.

She went through the pantry and mudroom to the garage entrance and pushed the button for the automatic garage door opener. Once in the car, she bemoaned the leather interior of her Lexus. Her hands were already sweaty and now so were her bare thighs. She longed for something cool and soft, something not quite so sticky. Even though the sun was on its way down, it was hot, unbelievably hot. Was that just her body working overtime? It was after all, only spring, the most beautiful season for this coastal city, a time of the year she loved.

She thought of all the places she took Kayla in the spring: Orton Gardens; The Airlie Arts Festival; Greenfield Park where they rented a paddle boat; Hugh McCrae Park where they listened to wonderful concerts; the Arboretum on Oleander where they sniffed the orchids, and Kohl's for strawberry cheesecake ice cream. A sob took her and she had to blink hard to keep the tears at bay so she could see to drive. She forced her mind away from thoughts of Kayla and how happy her life was just taking care of her and attending the obligatory family social events. She was nervous to the point of distraction as she drove down Masonboro Loop and made her way through the city to Market Street and to the north end of the city.

She knew exactly where the bar was where she was supposed to "pick up" a complete stranger to take to bed. She'd passed it many times on her trips to Porter's Neck and the nursing home there that she'd championed over the years. She pulled into the gravel parking lot on the side of the weather-beaten, ramshackle building and watched as people went in and out. She was early, so she pretended to touch up her makeup in the vanity mirror while admonishing her heart to slow down.

It was indeed the kind of place where she knew she'd have a varied selection of men to choose from, but none quite her type. Not that she was a snob, but the men going in and out seemed more countrified than citified, most wearing jeans and work boots, some in construction clothes still wearing their tool belts on their hips. They must think that looks sexy or something, she thought. Surely Kel Vain, even in his Adidas running shorts and Nikes would be in the upper echelon here. There had been something about his bearing, or maybe it was the cut of his hair. As a detective he was probably more educated, more sophisticated, even more cautious and thoughtful than the people she was now watching. She was unaccountably thankful for the providence that had brought him to her this morning, and if her mind hadn't been automatically reverting to Kayla every ten seconds, causing her heart to plummet and almost fail, she would have been intrigued by the man, who like a knight on a steed, was coming to her rescue.

Gallant knight. Hmmm. His part was surely not going to be as gruesome as hers. Unless the man was gay or . . . a thought suddenly occurred to her—what if he was married! Oh, good God, what was she asking him to do? And if she were his wife, how would she feel about what he was doing "in the line of duty?" The irony hit her and she winced into the mirror—Undercover Man. You had to love having a sense of humor at a time like this, she said to herself as she opened the door and stepped out. It was the first time she'd had a hint of a smile since she'd discovered her daughter missing, and she felt guilty for it.

Chapter Four

She walked into the dimly lit bar and took a moment to let her eyes adjust before she scanned the room, trying to be unobtrusive. But she was too pretty a woman to go unnoticed, especially in a tavern like this. She slowly made her way to the bar. The tables scattered around the perimeter were filled with men and women laughing and talking. It was a noisy place, full of activity and camaraderie. Waitresses were bustling about with trays loaded with pitchers of beer, and groups of people were gathered around tables, overflowing them as they chatted and hoisted their mugs. Two bartenders were moving up and down the bar in perfect synchrony, emptying ashtrays, refilling popcorn bowls and replacing drinks. She noticed several patrons sitting at the crowded tables looking her up and down quite thoroughly. She was careful not to smile—it would not do to encourage anyone to approach her.

She kept her sunglasses on and lowered her head as she made her way over to the bar. She knew she would be easily recognized downtown, but maybe not here, not this far north, away from the cultural centers, the waterfront and the river. Her long dark tresses had always been one of her most remarkable features, and with a wince, she bemoaned the fact that she hadn't thought to wear a big floppy beach hat to minimize her chances of being recognized. But rarely did she wear it loose like this, so she felt somewhat safe.

Idly, she lifted the bulk of it off her neck where it was sticking, one of the reasons she usually wore it off her face and neck. At the bar, she pulled out a stool and tried to lift herself onto it. She'd never really sat at a bar like this and was surprised that the stool was so high. It was not an easy feat for her to get her petite body up on the stool, she had to make a second attempt. Suddenly, two hands gripped her waist and she was lifted onto the seat.

"Hey sweetheart, let me help you with that," a man drawled and she turned to look into the most reassuring blue eyes she'd ever seen. Kel. She almost wept with relief to see him there.

"Why, thank you," she replied. Fortunately her innate manners were on autopilot because her mind was now mush.

"You new 'round here?" he asked as he slid onto the barstool beside her.

"Uh, yes. I just came in to get a drink," she whispered.

Then taking a deep breath, she repeated. "Got a mite thirsty, this looked like a right-friendly sort of place."

In the blink of an instant she had turned from a shy dilettante with proper spacing and structure to her words to a Dixie belle with a put-on, sweet-as-pecan-pie Southern accent. She was even slurring her words slightly.

What a trooper, Kel thought. "Well, what are you drinkin, darlin'? It's on me."

She could see his eyes trying to lead her.

"I don't know, what do you suggest?"

He smiled a devastatingly wicked smile and she noticed how rugged his face looked and how white and straight his teeth were. "Are you in the mood for something potent or something exotic?"

"Surprise me."

Kel looked over at the bartender and the bartender nodded and came over. "A Sex on the Beach for the lady and I'll have the same," he said in a husky voice. It was apparent the reason he chose that particular drink was because it gave him an opening to flirt, his wink to the bartender confirmed it.

"Sand's too gritty. Unless you want to be the one on the bottom," She countered, never missing a beat.

He roared with laughter and it sounded so genuine that Laura thought maybe Kel had some acting experience in his past. She'd had some in college and even enjoyed it, but when she became engaged to Ryan, he had discouraged her from trying out for any parts.

"I'll be anywhere you tell me to be sweetheart, but I prefer cool crisp sheets, myself. Where're you from?"

"All over. I travel a lot."

He nodded as if to say, *Good, you're being vague. That's the way a woman who just wants a one-nighter would be.* "Are you here on business or for pleasure?"

"Definitely pleasure," she said as she picked up one of the drinks the bartender placed before them. She removed the decorative stirrer after giving it a quick circle around the glass. It was a slim piece of pink plastic with a green palm tree molded into it at the top. He watched as her dainty tongue darted out and licked it along the edge, then with a mischievous smile, she plunked it into his glass before picking her drink up to clink it with his.

Man, she was a natural at this. "You married?" he asked as he adroitly moved the stirrer aside with his thumb. That was a standard question. Every man wanted to know what he was dealing with in that department when he hooked up with a lady at a bar.

"Was."

"What happened?" he asked conversationally. "But if it's too new, we don't have to go there."

"It's not new, it's old news now. It broke. I couldn't fix it."

"I'm sorry to hear that. How long ago?"

"Over two years. I'm over it. He was a sleaze."

"Really?"

"Yeah. Caught him sleeping around."

"On you? That's hard to believe. You're gorgeous. How could he think he could possibly do better?"

"Well, that's certainly very nice of you, Mr. . . . .?"

"My friends call me Dylan."

"Am I your friend, Dylan?"

God, she was good. She must have taken some acting classes when she was at UNCW. "Do you want to be?" he whispered, bending low to her ear.

"Maybe," she said evasively, trying to be coy.

A soft ballad came over the ancient jukebox in the corner and a few couples across the room got up to dance on the small wooden dance floor.

"C'mon, come dance with me," he said in a low throaty murmur as he slid off the stool and took her by the arm.

She didn't say anything, she just slid off her stool and took his other hand. It felt warm and firm wrapped around hers and he squeezed it gently. Her eyes met his and she had to fight back tears. His were sharp and piercing, and she doubted that there was a movement in the room that he wasn't aware of. She blinked her eyes hard and forced them to soften, then she halfway smiled.

When they reached the dance floor, he turned and in one swift, graceful movement he pulled her into his arms. As they moved to the soft strains of "Are You Lonesome

Tonight?" he gingerly stroked her back and ran his fingertips
up the sides of her bare arms while whispering encouraging
words. He took more and more liberties with his hands as
the song wound down and a new one began. Then bending
to kiss her on the temple, he admonished her to put some
feeling into her dancing so it looked liked she was trying to
convince him that she was up for a good time. He told her to
put her hands in his hair at the nape, to stroke her fingertips
down his jaw line and to meet her eyes with his while smiling
beguilingly.

She did as he suggested and it was all he could do
to keep his concentration. Her fingers touching him felt
exquisite, very feminine and very soft. Then her soft voice
broke through the sensual fog she was putting him in.

"I hate that word, it always reminds me of that stupid
movie with Clint Eastwood."

"The Beguiled?"

"Yes, the one where they—"

"Yes, I remember," he said, putting a finger to her
lips. "Don't say it, you'll spoil the mood I'm working on
here."

His lips brushed her temple again, then slid through
her hair to her ear. "Move your body in closer to mine,
gyrate your hips a bit and make it look like you're coming on
to me so we can get out of here." His warm breath tickling
her ear made his request easy to comply with. She slid her
foot between his and pressed her thigh against his.

"Ahh . . ." he moaned as she settled her pelvis into
him. It was a reaction that he didn't even try to hold back.
The woman was doing incredible things to him. As she was
well and truly supposed to be.

She could feel the hard ridge of him and for a
terrifying moment realized what a truly large man he was.

When the song was over, he led her back to the bar

where they finished their drinks before ordering another round. Just as the bartender moved to clear his empty glass, Kel plucked up the palm tree stirrer. As he looked at her seductively, he ran his tongue down the length of it. Then he tucked it into the pocket of his sport coat.

As he repeatedly stroked away the condensation on the outside of his glass, he continued to look her up and down and openly admire her. If anyone were watching, it would certainly look like he was taken with her. "You got a name?"

"Kelly. Yeah, that's a nice name."

He whooped with laughter again. *Man she had this down pat.* "Well, 'Kelly,' tell me, what do you do?"

"What do you want me to do?" she breathed. Her voice had picked up a sultry air and he had to admire her for being able to call up all her wiles at a time like this.

"I meant for a living, but I think you know that."

"I . . . I'm a stock broker."

Good choice. Almost anybody could talk about stocks for a few minutes. "Ah, the ups and downs."

"Mmmm, the ins and out," she murmured.

Sweet Jesus. This woman is not as naive as I thought. "Would you like another drink or should I just accompany you to a place where we can discuss the raging bull?"

"I'm game. No beach though."

"No beach."

"Well come on then, time's a wastin'." She was all Southern and flirty now. Hell she was even smiling at him. He had to hand it to her, she was a natural, or he had totally mistaken her true nature all these years. He should never have built an image of her in his mind just by reading what was written about her in the social pages. For all he knew, she could really be a hellcat. But there was something about her that made him think otherwise, something that made him believe she was the genuine article, that she hadn't changed that much since high school. Her smell maybe—it was regal and refined and made him want to stop and bask in it while he tried to pinpoint all the separate essences. Yes, she had the ultimate essence of woman and it stirred him greatly.

"Yes, ma'am," he said as he threw a twenty and a five on the bar and winked at the bartender. Then he put his arm around her shoulders and led her out of the bar. Outside on the small stoop, he pretended to stumble and she reached out to steady him.

"You look like an out-of-town business man who's had one too many." Peripherally her eyes swept him up and down as he walked. "A successful one. In more ways than one," she added with a wicked smile.

She was still in character and it occurred to him that maybe she had decided it would help to stay that way to get through the next part.

"Thanks. You look like a tourist, all summery and up for a good time. Out for a one-nighter," he said with a smile. "You did really good. I'm amazed. You didn't even appear to be nervous. And the Southern thing along with the blotto thing was a nice touch."

"I wanted to get that part over with. I figured if I came in already tipsy it would be plausible to get out of there with you a little sooner."

"Well, if the rest goes as well as your performance in there . . ." He didn't finish his thought, they were heading into the parking lot of the Jefferson Motel and there were people in the cars they walked alongside. Kel wasn't obvious about it, but he took everything in.

"Do you think he was in the bar?" she whispered.

"I didn't see anyone who would foot the bill, but it's hard to say for sure. He could certainly have been there. Ready?"

She let out a huge sigh. They were at the motel.

"I'm going to try to shield you with my body as much as I can and I will try not to hurt you, but remember I still have a part to play in this as well; this is not my favorite scenario for getting off. I haven't had a one-night stand since college."

"I would hope not. But I never have, so you're ahead of the game where I'm concerned."

"You gonna be okay?"

"I'll be all right. I have to be, don't I? I have no choice. Let's just get it over with."

"Okay. Let's go register. Room 12, remember?"

"Yes."

"Hey," he said as he stopped her by touching her hand, "I've got to get into this, and we need to get this part over with anyway." He grabbed her by the back of her waist and pulled her into his chest. Her soft, yielding breasts came up against the muscled bands of his broad chest and desire spiked through him. He could feel her tremble as he tilted her chin, see her sparkling eyes lose their focus as she looked into his.

"What part?" she stammered.

"This part." He leaned down and gently brushed his lips against hers, not caring if he smudged her dark lipstick. He let his lips linger, savoring the feel of her softening and warming to his kiss. His hand moved up to cup her cheek as he slanted his lips and claimed her mouth. He tasted her lipstick, it was slick and sweet like cherries. Kissing Laura was the most pleasurable sensation he'd had in a long time and he didn't want it to end. He wanted to hold her in his arms like this and caress her until she made him stop. He wanted more, much more. When her tongue touched his, he nearly lost his mind.

He chased it with his and licked at her inner lip where

he found the taste of her drink and popcorn. His control slipped as his hunger for her increased maddeningly; he couldn't stop the groan that moved up his throat, the guttural sound that filled the air spoke of his urgency.

He should be acting, but he wasn't, he didn't need to. Kissing her was the most natural thing he could imagine doing right now. Her blatant reaction to his kiss was heady. He was a man intoxicated by the touch and feel of this woman's response to him, her surrender to his kiss.

She was enticing him with her tongue, so much so, that he had to hold back his desire to thrust into her pelvis, to let her know of his body's pressing need to penetrate her, to be inside her. In an effort to regain some restraint, he slowed his lips, letting them languorously close over her bottom lip which he sucked and pulled lightly on as his hand moved to cup her head. Her upper lip got the same treatment ending with him allowing his teeth to lightly graze the part he had turned out before letting it go. He ended the kiss, but then quickly went back for another. He couldn't help himself, he had to kiss her one more time, as he might never get another chance at the ecstasy that kissing this woman brought.

This time he kissed her deeply, angling his head to allow his tongue better access, to let his tongue tangle with hers inside her mouth where it frantically wanted to be. There was no resistance in her body as he pulled her closer to his and let his passion take them away. She enraptured him by her taste, by her scent, by the feel of her just being in his arms. He kissed her as if to possess her, as if he was entitled simply because she needed him right now. Plunging and retreating, renewing a fevered hunger in them both, he meshed lips with hers. Desire streaked through him and he gloried in the feel of his rigid member swelling and nudging against her soft, yielding pelvis. For a small woman, her female center met his almost perfectly, he figured it had to be because of her heels. As his penis probed the curve of her hip, a surge of heat flashed under his skin and it took him off guard. With the power of a careening comet, he realized that he wanted her as badly as he'd ever wanted any woman. Not in the way he was going to be forced to have her, though. Abruptly, he pulled away and whispered, "Remember, you've got to beg."

She licked her lips and nodded. *Mmmmm. That was nice.* She wouldn't mind just doing that for a while. She looked him up and down as he walked ahead of her into the office. He was several inches over six foot, had thick brown hair that was almost black that tended to curl at his collar, and shoulders so broad that he filled the old-time cottage doorway. His torso tapered to slim hips and his jeans encased a firm, well put together butt. If only they'd met some other way.

Together they went into the dingy office, waited for the desk clerk to get up from his dinner and come to the counter so they could register. Laura was acting a little woozy again and Kel wondered if this time it might be for real. He had purposely asked for a drink with several liquors hoping that the added belt of the complex drink would relax her some. But it hadn't occurred to him that maybe she wasn't a drinker.

Feigning sentimentality, he asked for room twelve, and winked at the desk clerk as he handed over the money, hoping to get a rise from him, some indication that he might know what went on in that particular motel room. The young man opened a drawer, fished through some keys, and produced one attached to a long plastic tag that had a big "12," handwritten in black marker. He handed it to Kel and with a lackluster demeanor, turned to go back to his dinner, acting as if he did this a hundred times a night.

Kel walked with Laura to the room, used the key to

open the door, and waited for her to enter before following her in and locking the door behind them.

Her look of distress upon entering the room momentarily startled him. In the blink of an eye, she had become timid, unsure and scared. He could see it in her eyes, in the way they flitted around not liking anything that they saw. Not allowing her any time to think about what had to happen next, he grabbed her and pulled her into his chest. His strong arms enfolded her and then his head dipped and he began ravishing her, acting like a man who'd had a few drinks; like a man getting free sex with a beautiful woman; like a man possessed who was holding a gorgeous creature that he was most ardently desirous of. He definitely was the latter that was for sure. He wanted this woman—very, very much. And had they been truly private, there was no doubt he would have had her naked in less than a minute. As it was, he had to remember his promise to her. He backed her up to the side of the bed until her knees touched, then eased her onto the bed and followed her down, climbing on top like a sleek, long, cat.

He'd noticed the typical placement of the TV, sitting on a dresser across from the foot of the bed, as soon as they'd entered the room. With its hidden camera, it would give the optimum view of unsuspecting lovers. Placing her sideways on the bed as he had, he hoped to find a way to cover all the bases without exposing her too much.

He kept kissing her lips and her throat, fighting against the incredible delicious taste of her as he positioned his body on top of hers. She felt incredible lying under him and as he moved his groin suggestively in circles over her pelvis, his eagerness became bold and evident.

She gasped as she felt the hard ridge of him, erect and rubbing firmly into her as he repeatedly pushed his hips into her belly. Her body started to respond to his and he felt her begin to gyrate with him. "Careful," he whispered in her ear before letting his tongue circle the inner whorls. She shivered and he smiled to himself. He could swear he was affecting her, managing somehow to arouse her when she had to be absolutely terrified to death.

He propped his head on one elbow, his back to the TV, and looked down at her as she lay facing the peeling ceiling. He ran his hand over her breasts from the outside of her blouse, carefully avoiding grazing her nipples. He knew it was time for things to progress in order for this encounter to be believable, yet it infuriated him to no end to have to showcase her for the camera. For this alone, he vowed to make somebody pay. He allowed his hands to wander freely over her body so he could figure out her clothing and plan accordingly and he had to smile at her foresight.

He had initially noted the front opening of her blouse and the easy-to-deal-with skirt instead of more complicated pants, now he was finding out about the front clasp of her bra, and realizing that her panties were the only barrier to her sex.

As his hand roved and lingered over her bra cups, he could feel her nipples becoming hard under his palm. He went light headed for a split second as his lust spiked. He was becoming totally enthralled with her and he knew he had to mentally step away from what his body was doing or he'd blow it. He concentrated on her buttons, the size and shape of them and then the texture of her blouse before taking several deep breaths and starting to unbutton her shirt. Her hand reached up to still his, it trembled as it gripped his wrist. She turned her head to his and their eyes met, and for a brief moment he had serious doubts as to whether she was going to be able to go through with this. Then she shuddered slightly and started unbuttoning her blouse for him. When she spread the shirt wide and he saw her breasts encased

in only lace, his penis jumped and even more blood surged
to flow into his groin. He moaned his pleasure and gently
plucked at the dusky nipples visible through the thin lace.

She tossed her head back and forth on the bed and
moaned. The moan was followed by kittenish mewling and
there was no doubt in Kel's mind that her distress was caused
by the genuine pleasure he was giving her, not just her
ability to act. It thrilled him immensely because he knew
she was having to fight against her rational inclinations and
go with these surges of passion, just as he was; not be able
to truly give in to the moment and forget about playing the
part—forget she was a lady, forget she was supposed to be a
woman doing this as a means to an end. Right now, he was
having a hard time forgetting that he was a gentleman and
she was his lady, his damsel in distress. He wanted her as
badly as he'd ever wanted any woman and it was killing him
to remember just why they were here doing what they were
doing in the first place.

Toy with her naked breasts. It was time to take care
of one of the terrorist's demands. Expertly his fingers flicked
the front closure, and the elastic band holding the bra cups
together sprang open. Before the cups could fall away,
revealing her, his mouth was there to claim a breast while
his hand claimed the other. As he greedily suckled her and
outwardly roughly palmed her, he fought the incredible urge
to uncover her and let his own eyes feast. He hadn't seen
her breasts yet, and neither had the camera. Yet here he was
holding them, caressing them, kneading them. Bracing on an
elbow, he wrapped his arms around her and dug his elbows
into the mattress, then he flipped, taking her with him so her
back was now facing the camera. Now he could look at her
as he so desperately wanted to, but instead, he looked into
her face to see how she was doing.

She was scared, he could see that, but he could also

see trust, and something else. Was that desire? He smiled and let his eyes fall to her kiss-swollen lips, fighting the urge to let them drift lower, then he moved in and kissed her thoroughly. He lingered as long as he dared, mating his tongue with hers and enjoying the way their mouths joined and communicated so completely. But after the kiss he had to see; had to let the camera see that he was looking at her. He pulled away and his eyes lowered until he was looking at her creamy, pale breasts. They were flushed from his touch with rosy-tips proudly jutting out. They were dainty and lovelier than he could have imagined; pale and smooth with dusky centers, now swollen from his attentions.

"Beautiful," he whispered. Then his mouth returned to pay homage again as his hand insinuated itself under her skirts. From the camera's angle you could tell where his hand was going. Her skirt rose proportionately but not higher than the back of her thighs. He reached under her skirt and pulled her panties down to her knees. Then stroking his fingers along her outer thigh, he inched his hand up until it was under her skirt, and quite obviously, from the constant shifting of the fabric, he knew it would appear that he was fingering her. And indeed, he was.

She was so wet that it shocked him. He hadn't expected that, not under the circumstances. His long fingers glided up and down and in and out of her slick channel and he thought he was going to absolutely lose it. He was bursting with the need to be inside her. He had to force himself to focus on Kayla and the case and the madman who had her before he was out of control and unable to do what needed to be done.

I want to see his fingers buried deep inside you before he fucks you. As wonderful as this felt and even though he was actually, most definitely, fingering her, he wasn't sure he was following the directive to the letter.

"Sorry, honey," he whispered as he slowly used his hand and allowed the skirt to climb up the back of her smooth thighs. If he let the camera see her from the backside, the view would certainly be of his fingers buried deep inside her, but it wouldn't be one of her genitalia. His fingers probed deeper, then he used them to quickly do a few in and out thrusts as he leaned in close to her and whispered, "Time to beg, sweetheart, and make it good."

"Dylan! Oh, Dylan! Kiss me, suck me, there, there where your fingers are! Lick me please! Please, please, I need your mouth on me. I need your tongue on me! Right now! Pleeeease!" she ended the last plea on a whimper and he prayed it was from passion, and not from disgust.

Other than using his fake name, her plea was perfect and if he hadn't already been as hard as the Rock of Gibraltar, he certainly would be now.

"Well certainly little darlin', it would be my pleasure," he cooed. He shifted her and his hand came out from under her skirt, coincidentally pulling it partially down. Taking her by the hips, he adjusted her around on the bed before pulling two pillows from the headboard. He firmly tucked them behind her back, forcing her to sit up facing the head of the bed. Her back was again in view of the TV, only this time she faced a different direction. He stood beside a night stand and removed his shirt while looking appreciatively at her bared breasts. Breasts that he had strategically made sure were facing the opposite side of the room from the camera, sheltered from view by her body and the pile of pillows. He undid his belt, the fastener for his trousers, and pulled his zipper partially down so he could get some relief for his straining member. He didn't allow it to seek its way out of the opening though, he had some modesty and wasn't quite ready to be the porn star yet.

Kneeling at the head of the bed, he grabbed both

her and the pillows and pulled them as one to him until he had her at the angle he wanted her. He removed her panties and threw them over her shoulder making sure they floated through the air in front of the camera, then he pushed her knees up until her feet were flat on the bed. Her skirt was tented over her lap, but it couldn't hide the most feminine part of her. He could see her dark curls and a glistening pink gash in the deep shadowy tunnel made by her upraised thighs. Because he had to have a reason for facing her in this more awkward position, he reached over and flicked on the night stand lamp. "There, ummm, I can see you a lot better now. You've got great tits. And what a nice juicy cunt."

He watched as her face blanched at his words and surreptitiously, he moved his hand on the sheet and pinched her big toe, hard. He had to make sure she understood, and that she trusted him.

He looked over her raised legs to her face. He wanted to reassure her but he couldn't conceal the hot lust in his eyes. In a husky voice he said, "Pull your skirt up and spread your thighs for me. I want to see all of you, then I want to taste you. Badly. I can't wait to taste you on my tongue." Even to his own ears it sounded as sincere as could be.

Her eyes went wide, then she shut them tightly. He squeezed her toe again and she complied. She inched her skirt up until it was at her waist.

"Now spread your legs wide so I can feast on you."

Her eyes met his and she saw that he was trying to give her some control in all this by having her open herself up to him, but honestly, it wasn't working out that way; this was so much worse. She wished he would just do whatever it was he had to do and leave her out of it. She knew that she'd have to submit to this, but not that she'd have to be the one extending this blatant suggestion. He was looking at the juncture between her thighs, and granted she wasn't as wide spread as he wanted her to be, but still, she knew from where he knelt that he could see plenty. And the stark yellow glow coming from the night stand lamp wasn't helping matters. She bit her bottom lip and spread her knees wider for him, giving him the view the camera was supposed to be seeing; her completely open womanhood.

She watched his face as his eyes took in her nakedness. His nostrils flared, his pupils became dark with passion, and his Adam's apple moved first up, then down as he swallowed. Then almost reverently, his hands slid on the sheets going under her body until he was able to grip her buttocks and pull her toward him. His mouth lowered and he kissed her.

The second his mouth touched her she sobbed and he didn't know if it was because of the denigration she was experiencing or if it was the extreme pleasure her senses were conveying to her nerve centers.

She closed her eyes and tried to ignore the wonderful things his mouth was doing to her, there at her core.

Kel was in Heaven, mesmerized by her scent, her velvety slickness and her unique taste. This, the most intimate of all caresses, as a man kissed a woman between her legs, was what many women had told him was the ultimate in lovemaking. Nothing gratified like this, nothing was this sensual or this intimate. This selfless act of a man going down on a woman was adoration personified, the male kissing the rosebud of his mate, and he'd had more than his fair share of devoted fans screaming into the night because of his efforts.

Deciding he was going to make sure something about this experience was positive for her, he used every technique he could think of to pleasure her. He sucked on her labial lips, he lapped at her wet gash trying to take the essence of her into his body by way of his tongue, he nibbled lightly around the outer edge of her lips while reaching up and fondling her breasts, pulling on her nipples, and then when she was close to the edge, he flicked her swollen nubbin with rapid-fire licks of his tongue until it was fully distended and ready to burst. Holding her open with his thumbs, he gently took her precious, throbbing pearl between his lips and sucked possessively on it. A split second later she shuddered wildly and spent into his mouth. He stayed with her until the aftershocks died, then he closed her legs, allowing enough room for his hand so his fingers could stroke and calm her as he climbed atop her body to kiss her.

Even through glazed eyes he saw the fear and the questions. Still foggy and leaden from her orgasm, she knew what was next. He kissed her thoroughly, trying to reassure her and calm her, letting her taste her own sweet essence as he tried to plan out the final outrage in his mind.

He fucks you. Oh, and the guy must pull out and come like they do in the porno flicks—on your belly or in the crack of your ass. How the hell was he going to do that without exposing her to the camera? Then he had an idea.

If he knelt at the head of the bed, facing the television, the camera wouldn't be able to see his lower body. He could actually pretend to be fucking her. He could situate himself against her mons and lean into her as if he was thrusting into her very core. When he made himself ready to come, he could pretend he was pulling out when he'd never actually been in. Then he could quickly straddle her, move up and come on her belly, moving the pillow prop for the camera to catch the spurting action. Her head would be blocking her breasts, so she would be minimally exposed to the camera that way. And he'd make sure he was high enough over her so the camera would get his cum pumping out of him. So much for modesty—his anyway.

But before he could put his plan into action, she wrapped her hand around his penis and led him to her. The boss part of his body, which right now certainly wasn't his brain, obviously liked this plan better and before he could do otherwise, he was positioned at her opening, and practically sucked inside. He gritted his teeth and hissed at the intense pleasure of being inside her. As he dealt with his guilty conscious, his body savored the sensations. God, this was incredible! She was tight and hot and pulsing around him. His body took control while his mind staged a futile battle. He finally forced himself to slowly retreat and plunge, reseating himself tightly against her several times before he noticed her movements were matching his. She should hate this, but her hips arching off the bed told him a totally different story. His irrational mind tried to convince him that she was just eager to get this over with, but her body was responding in ways that were exciting him beyond his power to control.

His hands fisted in her hair as his large body pummeled her petite one, and as her hands came up to clench his shoulders, her nails dug into his straining muscles. There was no way, even if she had been in the frame of mind to receive it, that he could last long enough for her to reach climax this way. He moved his mouth from her neck, where he had been alternately kissing and licking her, to her ear. "Nggnh. Uhhh. Tell me to pull out! Damn it! Tell me now!" he hissed low and with great urgency.

"You have to pull out! You can't come inside me. I'm not on the pill!" she called out and the panic in her voice was very real.

"Nngh!" He moaned, followed by a loud, "Shit!"

He immediately pulled out and flipped her over, purposely causing the pillows blocking them to fall down and opening the view for the camera. He pulled her bottom up, causing a long sleek sway to her back, then he reinserted himself. He gave a few good, hard thrusts for the camera then pulled out and held his penis in his hand as he pumped his

51

seed in the curve of her backside where her cleft started. His roar was guttural and anguished; every cell in his body had wanted to stay inside of her for this, yet he knew he could not. His ejaculate pooled in the little hollow at the small of her back and he knew without a doubt that the camera trained on them could see it.

Deliberately flattening his hand, he coated his palm with his ejaculate and rubbed small circles at the base of her spine. Then he wrapped an arm around her waist and lifted her higher off the bed. With his other hand he reached under her and caressed her smooth, flat stomach with his slick, coated palm.

It was the most erotic thing he had ever done. He had taken his seed and symbolically placed it over her womb. It spoke of how cherished she was to him at this moment. And how taken he had been by her. He smeared the proof of his climax on her belly to comply, to make sure they met the requirement, but the gesture was more his way of communicating to her his extreme pleasure. As a man, she had satisfied him wholly, to his very core. She had to know that, he was telling her so by this most intimate gesture. He sure as hell would never be able to tell her any other way.

After a few moments of leaning over her, he nipped her on the shoulder, grabbed the bed cover and flipped it over onto her, ostensibly so he could reach for the sheet under it to wipe at himself.

The note had said belly, or the crack of her ass, surely that would do. After all, the man wasn't supposed to have read the note, as he had. He stood up and leisurely strolled across the room. Then he stood right in front of the TV, his backside almost up against it. He smiled at her as she lay on her belly looking at him with a questioning frown. He cocked his head and told her with his eyes to get up and get out of camera range while he was shielding her.

Immediately she scrambled out of the bed, and taking the sheet with her, she made her way to the bathroom. He moved around the room picking up their clothes then he cracked the bathroom door and tossed hers in. He sat on the edge of the bed dressing, shaking slightly as he fastened his belt. His nerves were frayed and he was upset about his performance. She had shattered the rigid control he always managed to maintain. He had never felt so drained in his life. But this wasn't exhaustion; it was dealing with the aftermath of the stormy electrical charges that had consumed him as he'd pulled out of her, and then sprang erratically from him, as he had emptied himself on her pale, smooth skin.

His eyes drifted over the rumpled bedclothes as he recalled everything they had done on the faded, threadbare sheets. A small, light blue scrap of ribbon caught his attention and he reached over to pick it up. He recognized it as one of the tiny bows from her panties. He sat fingering the soft symmetrical loops, letting his thumb graze over the smooth satiny knot in the center, then he carefully tucked it into his jacket pocket with the palm tree stirrer.

When she came out of the bathroom, everything was back in place and except for her reddened eyes, she looked fresh and untouched. In his put-on drawl he said, "Hope you don't mind me running out on you like this. But I told my wife I was going to the bar for a quick one. This wasn't exactly the type of quick one I'd had in mind though, or I'd have angled for more time."

"Wife!" She didn't have to feign being indignant. She was truly mortified.

"Yeah, I never said I wasn't married."

"How could you!"

"How could I what? This?" he asked nonchalantly, waving his hand toward the bed. "She'll never find out and you were just too beautiful to resist, babe. When can I see you again?"

"Never! You're married! Ugh!" she said as she stomped across the room, making her way to the door.

He came over to stand beside her. Suggestively, he pulled her pelvis into his hips several times. She could feel that he was either still hard or hard again.

"It doesn't make any difference to me, so it shouldn't to you."

"Well it does! Get the hell out of here!"

"Whatever you say, little lady. But my, you are one fine piece of ass, sure you won't reconsider and give me your number, I know you enjoyed my tongue." He stuck the pointed end of his tongue out and let the tip slide suggestively around his lips.

"Not on your life. I don't do married men."

"Well don't look now, darling, but ya just did. And ya did me mighty fine. 'Course you had some fun there, too. Good God you taste good! Had me worried at first though, I thought you was crying for a while there."

"Get out! No, on second thought, I'll get out!"

She picked up her sweater and purse where she'd left them on the chair, shoved her sunglasses in place, and after unlocking the door, she jerked it open. He could hear her take a deep breath as she crossed the threshold. He followed behind her, firmly closing the door in their wake. She stalked over to her car and after watching her ass wiggle for a few moments, he sauntered like the prick he was pretending to be, to his.

Neither said a word. She walked briskly across both parking lots to her car and never looked back as he walked behind her then veered off to hop into a nondescript sedan. He followed her for several blocks then turned into a parking lot in front of a grocery store when she turned in. He pulled his car alongside hers and his breath caught when he saw the tears streaming down her face. He got out of his car and walked over to hers as she rolled down her window. And of all the things she could have said, she shocked him with, "You're not really married are you?"

He smiled down at her, put his hand over hers where it rested on the door frame, and squeezed it. "No. Not married. Not engaged, not attached in any way."

"You scared me there."

She had just gone through probably the most traumatizing hour of her life, yet her first thought had been of him and how his marriage would hold together after something like this. Her humility almost brought him to his knees.

"Would you have done this anyway if you were?" she asked.

"Hard question. One I don't have to answer to right now, thank God. You did really well. Everything went off without a hitch. We hit on all the perversities he demanded and I managed to shield most of you from the camera in the process."

"Thank you, Detective. Thank you, very, very much."

"I think you can call me Kel, now. We certainly know each other well enough to use first names."

She blushed crimson from the base of her neck to her temples. "Yes, well . . . ."

"The clip could be uplinked to the website within minutes so Kayla could be released anytime. You go home, I'll go to the station and wait to hear from you. I'll have people patrolling the mall in case he releases her there. He did that once before."

"Yes. I know."

"See if she's hurt, but don't take off her clothing. Don't clean her up in anyway. It's important, Laura. We need to catch this bastard, and we're going to need every clue we can get from her and her clothing."

Her worried mother face was back. He bent and kissed her softly on the cheek then walked back to his car. He waited for her to pull away, all the while looking around for anything unusual. Nothing. The parking lot was packed with tourists and locals hurrying to get either their milk and bread or their beer and pretzels. He drove to his office reliving segments of the last hour in his mind while continually fingering the palm tree stirrer and ribbon rose in his pocket. It had been the most unusual hour of his life. And damn! He'd have given a year's pay to have done it differently. To have been able to come inside her warm, soft body and whisper words of encouragement for her to come with him.

Chapter Five

$\mathcal{L}$aura pulled out of the busy parking lot and made her way across town trying hard not to let the tears falling from her eyes blur her vision. Her body shuddered as she sobbed, and she recognized the utter fatigue flagging her system. The last two days had been hell. Since finding Kayla missing she hadn't eaten and she definitely hadn't slept.

Her days had been filled with worry. Worry so pervasive she thought she would drown in it. And pretense. All the time pretending things were all right when they were really the worst they could possibly be. Then the embarrassment and the humiliation. God, dealing with humiliation. And there was plenty more of that still to come. The anxiety over that alone would surely keep her from sleeping for the rest of her life!

She swiped at the wetness pooling at her chin and could smell him on her hand, the sex of him. She had held him and led him into her. Oh good God, how was she going to deal with all this! Well, soon the hard part would be over. The worry. Kayla would be home soon. She had done everything asked of her. Every . . . despicable . . . thing.

At a stoplight she closed her eyes and stared at the bright stars bursting against her tightly closed lids. Things that were despicable, degrading, criminal, and all irreversible.

She could never undo the damage from all this. She would have a felony record for the shoplifting unless her lawyer had some favors to call in; she would have to go into seclusion for who knew how long—people just didn't forget the kind of thing that happened at The Hilton all that quickly. The snide comments would never die, men would always look at her differently and she would wonder, had he been there that night? Had he seen her bared breasts? People who didn't know about the event would be told, even years from now the gossip would still linger. Christ, she still heard stories of the caught-in-the-act, clubhouse locker room trysting between Babs Sherland and the new Australian tennis pro. And they'd been caught in flagrante delicto eight years ago! This year's topless fashion show would be fodder forever. She groaned out loud and then jumped as a car behind her honked its horn.

And now her latest stunt. Kel had been wonderful, but there would still be a lot to see if anyone cared to look, and she was sure that the prurient interests in this city were no different from any other. Sex scandals of this magnitude were what spiced up the monotony of life. And she could laugh and titter like the best of them—when it wasn't her life that was being shattered.

Kel . . . God, he was sweet. What a very, very nice man. And oh, how he had stirred things in her that had been simmering on the back burner for years. He had taken her to full boil when he shouldn't even have been able to warm her up. She recalled the touch of his lips on her nether ones and unbidden, a shimmer of pleasure went through her at the recollection. Ironically, she had just had the best sex she'd ever had, on one of the worst nights of her life.

She pulled off the main road and onto her long private drive. As soon as her headlights flashed on the house she noticed the light in Kayla's bedroom window. Not bothering to drive to the garage, she pulled abruptly up beside the steps leading to the front door, shifting into park so hard that the car lurched before settling. She pulled the keys out of the ignition, all the while keeping her eyes on the light in the window as she tried to remember whether she had left it on or not.

No, she was pretty sure that she hadn't. She quickly threw open the car door and ran up the brick steps. Fumbling with her keys, she tried to unlock the door but her hand on the knob opened it before she had turned the key even part way. It was unlocked. She had left by the garage, but she knew for certain that the front door had been locked. She had locked it when Detective Vain left that morning, and she hadn't opened it since.

Fear unlike any she'd ever known raced up her spine but then she thought of Kayla, and hope surged. She remembered the other children that had come home and she pushed open the door and ran through the entranceway to the stairs. She took them two-by-two, heedless of where she'd thrown her keys and her purse but aware that things were clattering down the heart-of-pine wooden stairs. Reaching the top, she grabbed the newel and used it to reverse her direction towards Kayla's room. She ran into the room, and instantly fell to her knees when she saw Kayla in her bed, tears streaming from under an opening in the dirty duct tape that covered her eyes and running onto the tape that covered her mouth.

With one trembling hand covering her own mouth she sobbed her relief, with the other, she reached out as if blindly feeling for her daughter as she crawled on her knees over to the bed. Reaching Kayla, she gathered her into her arms and rocked her as she cried and sobbed out her joy.

"Oh, my baby! My baby!" she sobbed as she stroked Kayla's grimy, matted hair. Then she held her own tear-filled face away from her daughter's as she gingerly tried to pull the duct tape from her eyes and lips. Kayla's nose was running with mucus and was so caked with it underneath that it was a wonder she could breathe, but the full rise of her chest and the pink color of her skin showed that she was breathing. Kayla's pitiful moans stopped Laura's plucking fingers. She wasn't making much headway with the gooey mass and she decided to take Kayla into the bathroom where she had some baby oil that she thought might help. It was then that she saw the note pinned to Kayla's tattered overalls.

Congratulations Laura. You passed the test. It seems you love your daughter more than yourself. So few do. I will enjoy my memories of you, clothed or naked you are a very beautiful woman. And now, a proven mother.

There was no way, even before reading the note that she was going to leave Kayla, not even for the scant time it would take for her to run to her bathroom and get the oil. But now, after finding the note, she was afraid to leave her alone for even one moment.

She lifted Kayla into her arms and carried her into the adjoining bathroom where she attempted to sit her on the toilet. But Kayla would not let go of her. The tiny arms wrapped around her neck were pinching like a vice and Laura was fearful for a moment that her own daughter was going to choke her to death.

"Not so tight honey, Mommy's here. I'm not going to leave you. Ever, ever again. C'mon honey, loosen up so I can get the tape off your mouth." She was frantically searching the cabinets for the baby oil she kept there while holding the full weight of Kayla against her side.

Then the phone rang. She turned her head to listen but made no attempt to run for the extension in her room.

Whoever it was, it was certainly not important enough for her to stop attending to her daughter. It finally stopped ringing as her hand found the plastic bottle it was seeking under the cabinet.

Pulling a washcloth from the towel rack she slopped the mineral oil on it and coated the area around Kayla's mouth and forehead. With diligent care she was able to slowly peel the offending gag and blindfold from her daughter's face. She watched her daughter's eyes cloud from the unavoidable pain when she was finally able to pull the last bit from the skin around her mouth. The word she was rewarded with as soon as the gag was completely removed from Kayla's lips was a heartfelt, albeit croaky, "Mommy!"

Her arms went back around her mother's neck and she sobbed into the hollow at its base. Her words were indistinguishable through the harsh sobbing. Laura, on her knees in front of the sink, held her daughter tightly then slumped to the floor, taking Kayla with her onto her lap. She rocked her as she held her and crooned soft words while Kayla continued to sob heartbrokenly as only children feel free enough to do.

"It'll be okay baby. It will be. You're gonna be just fine. It's all over now. You're home. You're safe again. Shh. Shh, now."

Realizing she had no idea how to handle whatever trauma her daughter had faced, and what she would need to do to deal with it, she lifted her high into her arms and managed with the help of the vanity to stand. She knew she wasn't supposed to clean Kayla up, but she'd had to get the tape off, and now she had to give Kayla some water, regardless of the evidence destroyed by doing so. She filled a cup from the dispenser and helped Kayla drink it slowly. Then cradling Kayla in both arms, she made her way halfway down the steps to where the contents of her purse had spilled

61

out. Spotting Kel's card, she grabbed the banister and lowered herself until she could pick it up. Then she righted both her and Kayla and went back up the stairs to the master bedroom.

Using the phone on her night table, she punched in the series of numbers Kel had scribbled under the main number. It rang and was instantly picked up.

"Detective Vain."

"I have her Kel. He brought her back."

She had punctuated her terse words with a long sob and it was everything Kel could do not to break the cell phone he clutched in his hand into pieces.

"Is she all right, Laura?"

"I think so. She's filthy. I just got the tape off of her mouth and eyes."

"We'll be right there. Don't touch anything else, don't clean her up. We can get prints from that tape so leave it where it is, don't do anything with it. And try not to touch her shoes or her clothing. And don't talk to her about what happened. I have a child psychologist standing by to question her properly and to help her deal with this. My team will be there in less than twenty minutes. I'll be a few minutes behind them, I have a lead on the video. I think I can get it off the web before too many people see it."

"Thank you, Kel." Her words were heartfelt and sincere. The woman was truly grateful; grateful that he had taken her body and used it for his pleasure. He was humbled.

He managed to choke out, "Hey, the worst is over. We'll deal with the rest." Then he disconnected and bolted out of his chair. In three minutes he was directing twenty men and coordinating the investigation.

ঔ๕

It was four in the morning before things settled

down. Kayla had been given a sedative and the crime scene investigators had carefully photographed her before removing her clothing and bagging it for the lab. Kayla's doctor had been summoned to the house as Laura refused to let Kayla be taken to the hospital. She had been checked by the doctor and found intact and unharmed, although moderately dehydrated and chafed where her wet clothing had been in contact with her skin for so long. The doctor recommended that Kayla spend a few days in the hospital to recover, but again, Laura refused. She knew what the press was like, and she knew what was truly best for her daughter, and that was to be at home with her.

After Kayla had been examined, her mother rushed to bathe her and remove the excrement that caked her from her waist to well past her knees. An I.V. drip was started and now hung on a stand high above her head as she slept. The clear liquid would replenish fluids and nutrients to her depleted system. The drugs needed to calm her and allow for a full examination had taken their full effect. She was blissfully asleep, looking very much like a clown baby due to the red marks the tape had left around her mouth. Cuts and scrapes shone in the semidarkness where ointments had been liberally applied. And her once-long hair had been modified to just above her shoulders; the lab wanted samples, and it had been impossible to detangle anyway.

Two cruisers were patrolling this particular section of Masonboro Loop while an undercover team was staked out around the perimeter of the house. The crime scene techs had been all over the place photographing and fingerprinting, doing electronic sweeps, but finally all the questions had been asked and everything picked through. The note that had been pinned to Kayla, and the scraps of tape, had been bagged and sent out and Kayla's bedroom had been thoroughly gone over. They also had the ransom note Laura had thoroughly compromised. At first she hadn't wanted to give it to them, but then she remembered the promise she had made. That she would do anything in her power to catch this madman and keep this horror from happening to someone else. But she did ask that they keep its contents private. Kel assured her that his department would, but realizing how many would have access, he stopped short of promising her.

Kel could see the exhaustion on Laura's face as they stood in the doorway of the master bedroom. Kayla was curled into herself in a tight ball, one hand tucked under her cheek, looking like the angel that she was. Kel knew that there was no way Kayla would be sleeping anywhere other than in her mother's bed for quite some time, maybe even up until the day she was sent off to college.

Kel stroked his finger down Laura's arm to get her attention. She had changed and was wearing a white velour robe, she looked like a sad angel who hadn't earned her wings. She looked up at him and he saw the glistening tears clinging to her lashes. She looked fragile and he wanted desperately to fold her into his arms and hold her.

"You're exhausted. You need to get some sleep yourself. I'll let myself out. Don't worry, nobody's going to get in here again. We'll see to it."

"They can't stay here forever, Kel. Eventually they'll have other places they have to patrol."

"For now, they'll be here. Tomorrow I'll arrange to have a friend who's a security expert drop by and design a security system."

"I'm just going to sell the house." Then after a moment's hesitation, she added, "I was thinking about it anyway, it's too isolated back here."

His eyes blinked wide and he took a step away as if to sidestep the Pinocchio-style peg that should be growing from her nose. "C'mon, you're a Wyndham. You have more backbone than that. You love this house. I read all about it when you gave the tour the year you renovated it. It was your grandparents' house and their parents' before that." His hand waved, encompassing the long hallway with its grand entrance foyer visible at the end. "You ordered the tile and the chandelier from Italy. I remember reading about the Murano panels and how long they took to make. You don't want to sell the house. We both know that. Just make it more secure, get some alarms, a coded gate out at the road, better lighting, a few big dogs."

"I'll talk to my brother, he owns a security company. But I don't know when that'll be, I don't want to talk to him right now. He certainly is not going to be pleased with me. Neither are my parents."

"You got Kayla back. Nothing else matters. If you don't want to ask your brother, I'll get my friend to design and install a system for you. He owes me a few favors—I kept him from getting his ass in a sling quite a few times when we were in college."

"Thank you," she whispered, her voice husky from emotion. "Thank you for everything you've done for me."

He gathered her into his arms and with great tenderness, pulled her close. She wasn't wearing heels and his chin rested on top of her head. He chuckled, "Either way I answer that is liable to get me slapped. I could say you're certainly welcome . . . anytime. Or I could say thank you!"

She pushed softly against his chest and looked up into his eyes. Her wry smile charmed him. "You'll be the first one I call if I ever need anyone to come to my rescue again."

He almost hooted out loud, but he bit his lip instead. She didn't even realize what she'd just said, "come" to my rescue. He had certainly done that! He bent to kiss her on the cheek. "Get some sleep. By morning there'll be reporters hanging out all over the place."

The instantaneous look of panic that flashed across her face made him want to pull her close again and shelter her from the inevitable. "We'll keep them from coming up to the house. But whenever you decide to leave, they're probably going to hound you, at least until you give a statement or agree to an interview. You might want to consider staying in and ordering your groceries delivered for a while."

"And what about you, what are you going to tell the press?"

"Certainly no details involving us. And unless you tell them, it could be weeks before they find out what went down." *Ouch, I hope she doesn't think that was a pun!* "Me, I'm going to track down the owner of that website. I managed to get us off the Internet pretty quickly but only because I know some great hackers, and fortunately I knew just where to find them in the middle of the night—they're trustees in the New Hanover County Jail. I think we might get lucky on that score." *Damn, pun again!* "Maybe only a few people have seen our show and hopefully they didn't download anything to their hard drives."

She cringed at the thought of anyone seeing their performance, but she had already braced herself for it to go all over the world before anything might be done. It would truly be a bonus if Kel could stop it before that happened. "Whatever you're doing, I really appreciate it. That video is not something I want my family and friends viewing if it can be helped."

"Mine, either." He hesitated for a minute before turning away, then bent and brushed his lips lightly over hers. He was walking down the stairs before she could register the fact that he had just kissed her. A quick, fleeting kiss that said maybe things were not over between them. At the door he called up to her. "Lock the door behind me and try to get some sleep."

She walked into the bedroom just to touch Kayla's face and to press a kiss on her cheek before going down to lock the door and turn off all the lights. The blue and white lights from the police cars were bouncing off the walls on the lower level and it was comforting to see them.

A few minutes later when she slipped off her robe and climbed into bed, she noticed a little slip of paper by the base of the lamp. It said simply: "In the drawer, just in case. Kel."

She lifted herself up on one arm and pulled open the drawer. There on top of her romance books was a gun with another note. "Loaded. Safety off. Shoot to kill."

Chapter Six

Kel drove straight to the motel where they'd had surveillance since early the previous afternoon. He had actually done one thing right according to his angry supervisor. He hadn't been dismissed, suspended, or even taken off the case when he'd come clean with him. But other than the maid, no one had gone into room twelve until he and Laura had, which had been shortly after eight.

It was now four-thirty in the morning and still no action. Kel gave the signal for the stake out team to go in. They were instructed to confiscate the TV and the camera, any tapes they could find, and to do a full electronics sweep of the area, being very careful to preserve any fingerprints on the casings of the equipment.

While they were unhooking and unbolting the items, he sat in his cruiser and punched in the number and then the extension of the department's computer genius, and his good friend, Mark Twiller. He'd spoken with Mark many times over the afternoon and then again in the evening. Just prior to arriving at the station, after having left Laura at the grocery store parking lot, he learned from Mark that the contents of the tape had been uploaded by remote to a website the kidnapper had standing by.

Through a series of trial and error searches and with

some assistance through intuition and dumb luck, along with a few of Kel's trustee friends in prison, Mark had finally stumbled onto the website displaying the amorous action between Kel and the very lovely and shapely Laura Wyndham.

Interestingly, the search perimeter "Room 12" had netted the final link that had led to the website and the feed. A pop-up labeled Green Door Videos had flashed on the screen, and just coincidentally, Mark had remembered that all the doors at the Jefferson motel were a different color. And sure enough, the door of room twelve was indeed green.

The temptation to view the sordid scenes before erasing them from the web had been more than he could bear, but realizing he couldn't afford to be caught watching the feed by Kel or anyone else for that matter, he had downloaded a copy to the hard drive and to his home unit using his deft finger magic. When Mark had received the signal from Kel telling him that Kayla had been safely returned, it took only a few minutes to delete Laura and Kel's pornographic acting debut from the world wide web.

When the phone on his desk began to ring, he knew it could only be one person.

"Yes, Kel. I know I did a good job. Thank you. I told you that it would be child's play once we found the link. But what a shame, hubba hubba, you two certainly did look fine!"

"Get rid of it!" the voice on the other end of the line snarled.

"I told you, I did."

"I mean the one you downloaded to the hard drive."

"Oh, Kel!"

"Do it!"

There were a few moments when neither said anything, but the click of computer keys could be heard over the line.

"I did. It's gone. Zapped into a trillion pieces and floating out there in cyberspace somewhere."

"I owe you, Mark. I owe you big time. Thanks for staying up for me all night and doing this for me. And for the department, of course."

"You're welcome. I'll put in for a pay back one day. Plus overtime, of course."

"Now give me the website info so I can track it to the owner."

"It won't do you any good. It's a camp-on site out of Vegas. Multiple owners, something like a co-op. Anybody with a charge card can upload to it. Once, twice, as many times as they want as long as everything can be shared. A lot of wankers upload images of women using beaver cams hidden in shopping bags, briefcases, and the like."

"You mean I have to worry about others having made copies?"

"Yeah, but it's the middle of the damn night, and there's an awful lot out there to sift through. We probably pulled it fast enough. Though time will tell. But you can be sure he's downloaded a copy."

"So there's at least two."

"Two?"

"You can't fool me you sleaze bag. I know you have one."

"How can you say that?" Mark's voice sounded wounded.

"Because I know you, and because I know human nature. As easy as you could do it, it would have been too much of a temptation to delete it blind. Now just tell me I'm right."

"Aren't you always?"

"I want that file deleted."

"Damn!"

"And I'm coming over there now to escort you home so I can watch you do it."

"You don't trust me not to watch it?"

"No, I most certainly do not. Get your shit ready, I'll be there in three minutes."

"You're a hard man."

"You have the evidence that I was. Hey, by the way, I got you a case of Dewar's."

"You knew you'd have to have something to exchange?" Again his feelings sounded wounded.

"Hell, I know you've got terrific blackmail material there and I really wouldn't care so much if it were just me on that tape, but it's not. So just consider the booze a gift, and a way for you to steer clear of any nefarious intentions down the road."

"I can't believe you said that," Mark said with a fake sniff as his fingers flew over the keys in an attempt to get his home unit to clone a duplicate of the file he'd already sent. The sudden loud pop coming from a can of soda being opened scared him out of his seat, and he turned to see Kel leaning in the doorway.

"Three minutes, huh?" he asked with a raised brow.

"Three minutes until I'm going to beat your sorry ass into pulp!" Kel said with a huge grin as he snapped his phone closed.

"You win. Damn! I can never outsmart you."

Kel took a long sip of his drink and ambled into the room. "So, can you figure out from all this," he indicated the electronic equipment piled all over the room, "if the particular scenario we're interested in was downloaded to anyone and if so, just who that might be?"

"I don't think so. It's like file sharing, but it's not a closed loop. If I hadn't deleted it, the next time someone wanted to download it, they would have had to get it from someone else who'd already downloaded it."

"Why didn't you tell me that before?"

"Because you emphatically stated that my mission was to find it and get it off there tonight! And, it wouldn't have mattered anyway. He surely has downloaded it or at least seen it—after all, he returned the kid for Christ's sake! And my home system is so well protected that they couldn't get it from me, they wouldn't have been able to get in there to leave a trail."

"So . . . when you downloaded it, did your system search and find his download?"

"I don't know. It could have."

"Jesus, Mark! We have a serial murderer here, wake up! I shouldn't have to make these connections for you! Do your job!"

"You're right! You're right!" he said as he swung his chair around and dropped into it. "Fucking A, just like I just said, you're always right."

His curved fingers flew over the keyboard again as he alternately clicked the mouse and changed screens before letting out a loud sigh that made his lips rumble. "Nah, can't get it. Whoever he is, he's well protected, too. Shit. This could have been so easy if he wasn't a geek."

"I wasn't counting on it being easy. C'mon. Let's go get that download off your machine. I'd hate for you to come up on charges for having porn on your system."

"It's not illegal unless the victims are underage. Child porn this ain't."

Kel put his arm around his friend's shoulders as he led him out of the room. "Okay, I'll put this another way. Let's go to your house, where I'll sit down with you and Jill, and we'll all watch tonight's drama unfold. I guarantee you that once she's seen me in action, no matter who's currently 'entertaining' her, I'll have top billing in her fantasies from then on."

"Ah, c'mon. That's not so."

"When was the last time you did more than diddle her before plowing her?"

"Got a point there. I really should watch your performance. I could use some pointers."

"Not a chance Bud, not a chance. Get a book and a vibrator."

They were clomping down the main steps now, heading for Kel's car at the curb.

"So, how did you know what to do? You know, to make the video?"

"Unfortunately, I had a list," Kel said with remembered anguish. "A fucking to-do list."

Chapter Seven

 $\mathcal{L}$ aura woke to the sounds of car doors slamming in the circular drive and then she heard the raised voices of people arguing. Her sleep-fogged eyes immediately went to the child sleeping tucked into her side, and she drew Kayla's warm body against her. Kayla, her baby. She was safe and she was here. And she really didn't care who was in the driveway. Unless, oh God . . . it couldn't possibly be her parents or her brother yet, could it?

She scooted on her side to the edge of the bed, careful not to wake Kayla or disturb her I.V., then she eased out of the bed and went to the window that looked out over the front lawn. As soon as she parted the curtains, she saw cameras raise to capture the action. Immediately she let the filmy sheer curtains fall back into place and then she reached for the long rods that drew the drapes together. The room became dark and the only thing she could make out was shadows. She brushed the touch lamp on one of the night stands and a soft glow illuminated the room.

She heard an angry voice using a bullhorn telling the reporters that they were trespassing and that if they didn't get back into their cars and vacate the premises immediately they would be arrested. Moments later she heard car doors slamming again and then she heard tires crunching on the

74

gravel drive. She peaked through the drapes in time to see two news vans and several trucks disappearing between the trees. Her eyes moved down to the drive by the front door and she spotted two police cruisers, their doors open, effectively blocking the entrance to the house. She looked at the officers hoping to spot Kel, but he wasn't among them.

She looked over at Kayla and bent to brush a kiss on her soft cheek, then went into the master bath to freshen up. She couldn't bring herself to close the connecting door. Regardless of what she was doing, she wanted to keep her eye on Kayla. She knew that eventually, she'd have to leave Kayla's side, but that day wasn't going to come for quite a while.

She grabbed a pair of jeans and a sweater from her closet and dressed in the bathroom. She desperately wanted a shower, but today, she wasn't going to let Kayla out of her sight. She'd get one when Kayla woke, when she could sit her on the floor of the bathroom with some toys. At the dresser she ran a brush through her hair and quickly twisted it up into a bun. Then she gently woke Kayla and unhooked the empty I.V. bag the way she had been shown the night before. She picked her up and carried her down to the sofa in the family room. Sunshine was streaming in through the tall windows, lighting up the wood flooring and creating gossamer shafts for the dust particles to ride.

She was on her way to the kitchen when she heard another car pull up out front. Confident the police would dispatch whoever it was, she jumped at a soft tap on the front door. She turned and looked at the glass side panel and saw Kel leaning over to peer in. Her bare feet flew across the foyer and she hurried to unlock the door.

His smiling face greeted her and she gave him a glorious smile back. Then she stepped back and let him in. God, he was tall. Or was it just that she was in her bare feet and was shorter than usual? The top of her head barely came to his chin and she was conscious of having to look up into his ruggedly handsome face. His grin was so wide that she became instantly aware of deep-set dimples in unshaven cheeks and eye crinkles at the corners of twinkling blue eyes—blue eyes red with fatigue.

"I have great news!"

His smile was contagious and she couldn't help smiling back. "You got the tape!"

He grabbed her in a bear hug, lifted her off her feet, and spun her around. "I got the tape!"

Her hands were on his shoulders and she was looking down into his ecstatic face. It seemed the most natural thing in the world to wrap her arms around his neck and hug him back.

"Mommy? Who's that man, Mommy?"

Kel turned his head at the same time that Laura turned in his arms to look down at a very sleepy Kayla. Kel set Laura down, enjoying the lingering feeling her warm body sliding slowly down his had left in its wake. He watched as Laura knelt to gather her daughter into her arms.

"This is Detective Vain, sweetheart. He helped Mommy get you back. Don't you remember him from last night?" The little girl in her nightgown shook her head and laid it on Laura's shoulder. Laura carried her into the kitchen. She set Kayla on a bar stool at the counter, kissed her cheek, and stroked her hair. Her face still bore the red streaks from the tape, although they were fading.

"Would you like some breakfast, sweetie?"

Kayla nodded and pointed at the cabinet across from them. "O's."

"Cheerios it is!" Laura practically sang as she grabbed the box of cereal from the cabinet and began pouring it into a bowl. She was so happy to have her daughter safe at home that she couldn't contain her joy.

"I was just getting ready to make some coffee, would you like some?" she asked Kel.

"I would love some. I haven't been home yet. I had to tell you I got the tape off the Internet before I did anything else."

"Do you know if there were any copies made?"

"I don't think we're ever going to know that. All we can hope for is that whoever has seen it hasn't downloaded it, or if they have, that they have no idea who you are."

"This is going to be like waiting for the other shoe to drop . . . forever."

"I know and I'm sorry. A full report will shield you from any moral recriminations later, when and if it ever becomes public, or you can try to hide it and hope for the best."

"What do you recommend?"

"Honesty while avoiding specifics, since there's no telling what the media will eventually turn up. I probably wouldn't alert them just yet though, they'd only knock themselves out trying to find our little peep show if it's still out there somewhere."

Kayla sat at the counter, holding her little spoon and crunching on the cereal that managed to make it into her mouth. She was watching Kel as he paced the kitchen.

On one of his passes, he stopped by her chair and ran his fingers through her curls. "You're quite a Cheerios fan I see. I used to eat Cheerios when I was your age. I wonder, do they still taste the same?"

Without any hesitation, Kayla took her loaded spoonful and offered it to him. He smiled at her and helped himself to two Cheerios with his fingers. He popped them into his mouth and grinned at her. "Mmm mmm. Boy, are they ever good. I had forgotten how good they were."

"Would you like your own bowl?" she asked in a soft, sweet voice.

Kel looked down into her face and studied the red marks where the tape had been beside her mouth, and at the cuts at the corners of her mouth. He wanted to hurt somebody over what they'd done to her.

"Are you sure that would be all right with your mom?"

"Mom, can 'tective Vain have some O's, too?"

"Of course he can."

"He can use my Barney bowl."

"Would you like that 'tective Vain?" Laura asked with a brilliant smile.

"I surely would!"

Laura and Kayla sat while Kel stood on the other side of the counter. All were munching on Cheerios. Kel watched Kayla as she carefully pushed the Cheerios onto the tiny Minnie Mouse spoon. He marveled at the miracle of her and how unaffected she seemed right now despite what she had been through.

Then Kayla asked to be excused and crawled down off the stool to go watch TV in the family room. Kel took Kayla's seat and he and Laura sipped their coffee in silence, listening to the cartoon sounds and watching Kayla's curls bounce whenever she clapped her hands.

"She needs counseling," Kel stated.

"I know. I'll make some calls today."

"The department can make some recommendations."

"I'm sure her grandfather will insist on doctors he knows."

"Be that as it may, you're her mother and this isn't something to mess with. She needs someone who has experience with this kind of thing. She seems fine right now, but that only means she's dealing with it some other way."

"You're right and I know that."

"You could use some help in that department, too."

"And just what would I call my problem?"

"I'm not saying you have a problem. You just need someone to talk to, someone who can keep it all in perspective for you when the shit hits the fan."

"And when's that going to happen?"

"My men can stay on for a few days to keep the media away, but sooner or later you're going to have to go out and Kayla needs to go back to school."

"No. It's just pre-K, she doesn't have to go back."

"Isn't she going to miss it?"

"I don't care. I'm not taking any chances, I'm not letting her out of my sight."

"Laura . . . don't let him win."

She looked over at him and her eyes were sad. Was there anything sadder than doleful baby blues, stripped of their confidence?

"You did everything you had to. You were perfect. You were strong, don't let him beat you now."

He watched as she gathered and began to rinse their breakfast dishes, admiring her slim figure as she stood at the sink. Then as she stooped to place the bowls in the lower rack of the dishwasher, he watched her rounded bottom. He remembered his hands touching her there and he had to clench his fingers into his thighs under the counter to keep from jumping up and grabbing her.

He stood and tucked the stools under the counter. "I have to go write my report and tear down that motel room to see if there's anything else there. The child psychologist the department's using, the lady Kayla spoke with last night, will call this morning to see if Kayla remembers anything more. I'm going to check out Victoria's Secret at the mall and question some people at the Hilton. Will your parents be here soon?"

"I have no idea. I have hundreds of messages on the answering machine. For all I know they could be on their way here from the airport now."

"I don't like leaving you alone like this."

"I have Kayla now, I'll be just fine." She walked him to the door and smiled up at him. "Besides, I think I'd rather be alone than deal with them, or my brother. Or my ex for that matter, he's bound to show up."

"No one is going to be harder on you than you."

"You don't know my family."

"They always appear to be charitable."

"Looks are deceiving."

"Charity doesn't begin at home?" he asked.

"Let's just say, I don't expect them to be very 'charitable.' They're going to rake me over the coals."

"Don't let them. Just remember one thing."

"What's that?"

"You're my hero. And the most devoted mother I know." He playfully tapped the end of her nose and then opened the door. There was a young officer standing at the door ready to ring the bell.

"Detective Vain?"

"Yes?"

"We found this in a bush down by the water." He was holding up a lilac lace bra by a pen threaded through the shoulder strap. It looked fairly new except that there was a grayish-white stain in one of the soft cups that any man would recognize as semen.

Kel turned to Laura. "Is that one of yours?" His eyes told her that he knew it was.

Laura's face paled. "Yes," she whispered.

He turned to face her and she saw his expression

grow hard. His eyes closed tightly and his lips thinned as his rugged jaw set firmly—the planes of his face had instantly grown harsh. In clipped tones, he barked an order to the officer about getting an evidence bag for the bra and sending it to the lab. When the young man skittishly ran back to the cruiser, Kel turned and looked at Laura.

"You get a security company over here to install an alarm system this afternoon or I will."

She just nodded.

"That looked like the one you wore last night."

"It was."

Chapter Eight

Kel and Laura stood staring into a half-filled laundry basket that was sitting on the cement floor at the end of a laundry chute. The last time Laura had seen that bra, she had been pushing it through the little swinging door in the master bathroom wall. It had ended its journey in this basket in the utility room. That had been at four something in the morning. The utility room was on the ground level, sandwiched between the double garages on both sides of the house, two levels down from the master bedroom. It was a room designed for storage but it also housed the washer and dryer. The maid was the only person other than Laura who had access to the storage area. As it did not connect into the house, Laura honestly didn't know if the outside door had been locked or not.

"So why didn't he take your panties?" he asked as they stared at a scrap of material on top of the pile that was the exact same color as the bra.

"They weren't there for him to take," she murmured. Then turned from him and stared at the wall behind the washing machine.

"Why not?"

"The panties had some blood on them, I was soaking them in the sink. I just put them down the chute a little while ago."

"Why was there blood on them?" he asked, concern etching his face as he turned her back to look at him. "Did I hurt you?"

She lifted her head and met his piercing blue eyes with hers. "No, it's just been a long time."

He cursed as he ran his fingers through his hair, then he turned from her and hit his fist on one of the wooden pilings holding up the house.

Neither said anything. When the silence grew unbearable, he ground out, "He was here. He was here when I fucking left!" His fist hit the piling again. This time it made a cracking sound from the impact, but it was too significant a piece of timber to be structurally affected by the blow. Still, Laura blinked.

"He was here. And I left," he whispered in horror.

"Kel, don't do this to yourself. You left your men. They checked everything twice, once before you left and then again after. Nothing happened, we're still safe."

He was so angry that he barely managed to grit the words out between his clenched teeth. "He got your bra, he took it and then he masturbated in it, probably right here in this very room. And then he left it in a bush for us to find so we'd know he was here watching you."

"I'll take Kayla and I'll leave."

"You shouldn't have to do that!" His voice was strained and she could see the frustration in his eyes.

After another stretch of silence, he said, "But I have to agree with you and say that's probably a good idea at this point. I don't have a handle on this pervert. Not a single clue as to who he might be or what he's capable of next. Unless we get a DNA match, which could take weeks, we're stymied. And the fact that he so purposefully left his 'sample' for us, tells me he's probably not in any registry."

"My parents have several rental properties on Wrightsville. I'll just pack a few things and go live on the beach until you find him."

He turned to face her, his angry eyes flashing as they roamed over her face before settling on her parted lips. He couldn't believe the incredible urge he had to kiss her. He blinked his eyes hard and when he opened them again he forced his attention on the tiny frown lines that were forming between her brows. "Don't tell anyone where you are. Except me. I have to know. I will have to keep assuring myself that you're safe, especially after this. God, Laura, I'm so sorry."

She touched his arm. "Kel, don't do this. It's not your fault."

"The hell it's not!" He spun on his heel and opened the door before turning back to say, "Let me know when you're settled. And don't forget to pack the O's," he managed as an aside. Then he shrugged and flashed her a lopsided, self-deprecating grin.

Laura stood staring down at the tiny purple scrap on top of the pile of laundry. Then she began rubbing her hands up and down her arms. Goose bumps rose along her pale skin. He could have taken Kayla again, she thought. Then her mind instantly flitted to the gun Kel had left in her night stand drawer, and she shook her head. No. No, he couldn't have taken her again. She wouldn't have let him.

She flicked off the light and left the dark little room and went back to the family room. Kayla was still sitting on the sofa watching cartoons with a policeman, another policeman standing by the front door could be seen smoking a cigarette through the glass side panel.

"C'mon pumpkin, let's go get packed. We're going on holiday to one of Poppy's beach houses. Do you want to go to THE LAUGHING GULL or to the TUMBLING TURTLE?"

84

"I want to go to TIDE'S AWASTIN', it has a slide in the pool! And a swing in the back!"

"Okay, I'll make some calls and see what I can do. You go get dressed. And keep the door open."

At two o'clock, she, along with several police officers, loaded suitcases into her car. Then she locked the front door behind her. Earlier in the day she had met with a security specialist, given him a key, and arranged for a security system to be installed. She ordered groceries at Lowe's Foods that she was going to pick up curbside on the way to Wrightsville Beach, and notified her father's rental agency that she was booking the TIDE'S A WASTIN' beach house for a few weeks to some out-of-town friends. She had keys to all her father's beach houses, so she wouldn't have to pick them up. When Velma, the office manager asked if they would require maid service, she said no. Velma probably knew what was going on since news of Kayla's kidnapping and return was on every TV channel, but Laura knew that she could be trusted, Velma had worked for her father for as long as she could remember. Then she called Kayla's school and told them she wouldn't be returning, listened to all her phone messages, and even held an impromptu press conference on her front porch in hopes of getting the press out of the way for a while.

She wasn't answering her phone but did listen to the messages being left. There were a few terse words from her father using an airfone, telling her that they were on their way back from Europe, and would be home later that night. Her brother had called and said he was going to try to come over if he could get away from the office, and her ex was driving in from Raleigh to find out, "What the fuck is between your ears, for it sure isn't brains!"

She was glad she was getting out before the showdown. She hadn't bothered to call and tell her ex that she was relocating this afternoon. Kel, well . . . she thought about calling him several times. But she needed some distance there, too. She was missing him, and it surprised her. No way should she be having feelings for this man, he was just a means to an end.

The drive over the bridge improved her mood. It was exhilarating, she opened the sunroof and lowered all the windows. The ocean breeze ruffled her hair and swept to the back seat to toss Kayla's curls. The salty tang coming off the ocean made them both raise their heads and sniff. Kayla smiled and sang words from "Under the Sea" and Laura laughed delightedly at her. Kayla was here. She was safe. And she seemed not to remember the misery of the past few days.

Chapter Nine

Kel caught the six o'clock news. One of his officers had relayed the information that Mrs. Wyndham had granted a press interview of sorts a few hours before moving out of the house on Masonboro. He could not imagine why she had consented to do that, and just shook his head as the announcer began the intro teaser that would hold everyone's attention until they returned from a commercial.

"Did she leave a number or an address?" he asked the officer who was just now reporting in.

"No sir. I did hear her tell someone that she'd be at the rental unit sometime before three, but that was all. It might have been her father, she had a conciliatory tone."

The news anchor returned and then the shot switched to an onsite reporter who said a few things about Laura before climbing the steps to the porch of the Masonboro house and shoving a microphone in Laura's face.

Laura stepped away and in doing so, expertly made the newswoman defer to her. Laura's sweetly cultured voice rang out as she thanked everyone for their concern and confirmed that Kayla had been kidnapped and now was safe at home.

"Mrs. Wyndham, because of the Hilton incident, are we to assume that Kayla was a victim of The Voyeur?"

Laura flushed, her coloring reddening from a combination of anger and embarrassment, yet she remained in control and looked straight into the camera.

"Kayla and I were both victims of this horrible man, and although I am not proud of my actions, neither am I ashamed of them. I did what I had to because that is what we do for love. I had no choice. Getting Kayla back was my only concern and I will not apologize for any of it. Ever."

"Mrs. Wyndham, we know the kidnapper has set requirements for each parent, in your case it was a shoplifting episode and the Hilton confrontation. What others were there?"

"I asked that the ransom requirements be kept private. It is disconcerting that everyone is so intent on finding out how I had to suffer in order to save my daughter's life. Curiosity is fine to a point, but when satisfied, if it's only going to be destructive, why can't people be more compassionate? I don't need to share my suffering with the world. I only need you to celebrate my victory with me. A monster has not perpetuated his evil in the ways that he could have. Yes, the last few days have been hard, unbelievably difficult. But everything I did, I did with Kayla's welfare in mind. She is worth any denigration, worth any price, any humbling thing I had to do. I am a mother after all, and from the day I gave birth to Kayla, she came first. If the people of this city could find it in their hearts to give me and my family some space and some time to recover from this horrible ordeal, it would truly be appreciated."

"Have the police been involved the whole time? Are there any leads?"

"I involved the police when I was able to. I don't know what they have discovered, but I feel confident that in time, they will find the man who took my child."

"What has been your parents' reaction to all this?"

She gave a tiny, sideways smile and pursed her lips slightly. "I expect to find out soon, as they are due back later this afternoon. But I am sure they will be greatly relieved to know that their granddaughter is safe and unharmed. Everything else, we will deal with."

"Are you going to be attending the opening ceremony of the Wilmington Summer Symphony this weekend, and the UNCW graduation next week as you usually do?"

"I haven't decided, I doubt it though. My family will be my first priority for the next few weeks. This year's season shows great promise, and even if I am not present, you can be assured of my continued support behind the scenes. And let me take this opportunity to congratulate the Wyndham Scholarship recipient in the event I'm not there to do it in person next Saturday. Now if you'll excuse me, I'd like to get back to my daughter. I promised I'd watch *The Little Mermaid* with her. Again," she said with an enigmatic smile.

Laura went back into the house and the camera zoomed out, giving a panoramic view of the house and the woods along each side.

Well, he had to hand it to her. She did a fine job. She didn't give them any information they didn't already have, and she put them in their place to boot. What a woman, he thought as he spun back around to his desk to read some reports. But thoughts of her and her panties kept crossing his mind, at first making him angry with himself, and then making him hard. He remembered that they had been the bikini type and that when he had removed them, he had been pleased to discover that though skimpy, they did cover her luscious bottom. He didn't care much for the thong-type. There was no mystery there, and to tell the truth, he loved seeing panty lines through a woman's clothing—to him, it was sexier than all-get-out. But his main reason for his preference was that he wanted to feel the soft spongy, pliant bottom of a woman before he saw it. And then when he did see it, he would rather it not have a dark line from the red or black thong, emphasizing the separation. He thought of a woman's derriere as one entity, one pleasingly plump, enticing little ass. Most people were unaware that the symbol of a heart was derived fom the shape of a woman's derriere when presented to her lover.

He had to get his mind back on the reports—the woman had completely taken over his thoughts and he did not know what to do about it. He dated frequently, but rarely did a woman remain in his thoughts, especially while he was working. And never in his life had thoughts of a woman caused this nervous, jittery feeling in the pit of his stomach.

Chapter Ten

So far as they could determine, The Voyeur had come by way of water via a small boat that he probably kept tethered in the marsh. The tide constantly slapping against and over the bulkheads had erased any footprints within minutes, but one of the officers had found a chaw of tobacco sitting in a clump of reeds. It was on its way to the lab for analysis, even though the officer who had found it felt certain it had been there for quite some time. Kel was on his way to check out some security agencies. It stood to reason that this man had some experience with surveillance techniques, so while the motel TV was being taken apart, he decided to check with some of his friends in the security field.

Steven McCall, a friend from his rookie days, was a private detective specializing in industrial espionage. He'd been all over the world sweeping board rooms and laboratories to keep corporate secrets out of the wrong hands, and if anyone had the answers to his questions, Steve did.

"Unfortunately Kel, this sort of thing is commonplace now. You can buy miniature cameras almost anywhere. Radio Shack, Best Buy, heck, most of the stuff I need I get at Wal-Mart. You're going to have a real problem identifying any one person from whatever he's left behind, unless you have fingerprints, DNA, or voice patterns. And your guy may not ever have even been in that motel room or touched that television. There are clubs now that you can belong to. One person sets everything up, and for a fee, everyone shares in the action."

"There's nothing hi-tech or specialized in any of this?"

"Nothing you can't pick up from any science magazine. Popular Science goes over this every other month. The only thing you've mentioned that narrows it down at all is the ease with computers the man seems to have. He's confident and he knows what can be done with them."

"But how does he know the women have the same knowledge?"

"Either he doesn't care and leaves it to them to find someone to help them get this stuff on line to him, or he's picked them because he knows they're capable of it themselves."

"Good point. And one I really hadn't thought about."

"Stands to reason if he knows so much about their personal lives, the kids and all, that he probably knows about their careers and interests."

"Yeah . . . ."

"But you know this information is really not going to help you all that much."

"Why not?"

"Because even in a city this size, there must be tens of thousands of people—both men and women—capable of this. Think of your own friends. How many would be able to tap a few keys and click a mouse and do this?"

Kel thought for a moment. "You're right, quite a few. This isn't going to help."

"No similarities in the victims, no common denominator?"

"Not that I can see."

"I feel for you Kel, this is a tough one. Go back to the kids. Maybe you've missed something."

Kel ran his fingers through his hair and expelled a hard breath. "I feel like I'm spinning my wheels while I wait to see if the lab has anything we can go on."

"This guy's too careful. If you've got prints or DNA, I'll bet they're not even in a data base."

"That's what I'm beginning to suspect, too." The despair in Kel's voice was almost palpable.

"Back to the chalkboard."

"Nah, I'm on my way to the psych ward."

"Ben Atkinson?"

"Yeah. I contacted him earlier this week. I'm supposed to call him this afternoon."

"Maybe he can help."

"I'm hoping."

"Call me if there's anything else," Steve said.

"I will. And thanks."

"For what?"

"You saved me a lot of time. I was going to go to every security agency in the book."

"That would be like opening a phone book and trying to divine the perp."

"Seems I'm no further ahead than that."

"Something'll break, it always does."

"I just need to get a handle on this before another kid is taken."

As Kel walked through the doorway and into the hall, Steve called after him. "You're not going to do it without any sleep!"

"Yeah, yeah . . . ."

Chapter Eleven

*B*en Atkinson had agreed to meet Kel halfway between Wilmington and Raleigh, where he was attending a conference. The profiler was in demand across the country, both as a speaker and as a consultant as serial killers of all kinds continued to jump out of the woodwork across the nation. There was a great deal of confusion in the world of law enforcement as to exactly how many serial killers were in operation at any given time. Some said twenty, some said thirty, and some estimated the number to be in the hundreds. Ben believed that there was at least one in every major city — either one in the field or one in training.

"Damn! I was hoping for more than this Ben."

"With what you sent me Kel, you're lucky to have that. Most serial killers are usually on the street for years before we can even pull this much together."

"Contempt of cops or authority figures?"

"Yeah, he doesn't think you guys are good enough to catch him. He's not really all that threatened by the idea of these women calling in the troops, he just doesn't want anyone detaining them or talking them out of performing for him. By the time he's picked up a kid, he's anxious to see a show. He's probably been waiting too long when the urge hits to set everything in motion."

"Why do you say that?"

"The impatience comes through. The instructions are implicit. His methods for compliance are immediate. He doesn't like the waiting game. And it's either because he's on a rigid time schedule himself, or he needs to prove that he's the one in control."

"Could it be that he's just uncomfortable once he has the kid and knows that everything has to come to fruition fast?"

"Maybe. We are definitely looking at the shortest time spans I've ever heard of for the victims being returned, and they're all relatively unscathed."

"So, he doesn't want to hurt the kids?"

"I don't think he cares one way or another. They're a nuisance for sure, but he seems concerned about keeping his end of the bargain if the women do as he instructs. He's cultivating a clientele with the help of the media, and his new victims have to know his word is good or they might not do as he demands. And then the game will be over."

"A serial killer with a conscience? C'mon Ben, where you going with this?"

"It's just that I see him as a man with some pride. He gets in, he gets his reward, and he gets out. It's almost like these women are his private harem. A club of sorts—women he has controlled, women who have bared themselves for him, shown him their deepest, darkest secrets. Maybe he even fantasizes that they like it, that they're willingly stripping as a way of trying to seduce him."

Kel took in a deep breath and then slowly blew it out, his exasperation evident. "So we know what? What do we know that I can use to narrow this search down some?"

"He's smart, very educated. He's older, probably in his forties, possibly not all that attractive; he was raised under a woman's thumb or is currently under one's now.

And he has visual fixations and fantasies that control his sex drive. The kind of fantasies that men in college have."

"Whoa! Whoa! Whoa! Let's take this one at a time," Kel said as he looked up from the notebook he was hastily scribbling in. "Older . . . in his forties? Why?"

"The words he uses and the way he uses them, hardly any slang. His grammar is impeccable, the punctuation, too. And some of the things he says just aren't said in that exact way anymore. For instance, he says 'titties' instead of tits, boobs, or hooters, 'toy with her breasts' instead of fondle her, 'have sex with a man' instead of simply saying fuck him. He has some respect for these women. At least in his mind, they're something special. In essence what he's saying here is that women get fucked by men, that they don't fuck men. The man has to be taking her on his own terms. And that's the way he wants it. So he's an older guy, a crass older guy. He's sensitive, but he wants what he wants, and he wants their bodies in the only way he can have them. If he were good looking, he could have them for the price of a few drinks, maybe not the absolute stunners he's been picking, but women decent looking enough, I would think."

"Whew! It's amazing how you get all this from those simple notes."

"It's years of training and files full of data, and hard-earned experience. Plus a lot of guesswork."

"So, how about the men in college thing? What do you mean by that?"

"You remember, college boys like to show off any prize they have. Be it cars, tech equipment, or a girl. If you had a good lookin' babe on your arm, and she had great tits, you'd want to share them with your best buds, show her off some. It's the reason for all those free beer parties."

"Oh yeah, I remember. You get your girl to take off her top and show her tits to the crowd and all the beer you and she could drink was free."

"Something like that. There's a different version at every school. The groups that pass the women—who are drunk out of their minds—around for everyone to sample; the ones who like to put on a porn show for their buddies to watch; and the ones who specialize in the girls gone wild theme with video cameras. You ever do any of that yourself?"

"I saw it all the time, but I was too busy studying. I had to get in and get out, my family didn't have the money for me to party."

"Yeah, mine either. But I did manage to find the time to do a few things I wish I hadn't."

"Well, I didn't say I didn't have any regrets about my actions," Kel said with a hearty laugh. "There was this hot chick in one of my criminal justice study groups . . . mmm, if library walls could talk."

Ben snickered. "Tame. If that's your wildest time to date, your sex life is pretty tame."

Kel looked down at his drink, closed his eyes, and quietly sighed. *Oh, no, that definitely wasn't his wildest time to date.* He could have told Ben about Laura, but something in his heart kept their time together sacred.

"Hey, I did think of another thing I wanted to mention to you."

Kel snapped out of his memories of the moments he'd spent with Laura in that motel room and looked over at Ben. "Yeah, what's that?"

"The guy you're looking for is probably pathetic in bed. He's focusing on looking at women, not touching them. And, as I said, he can't be too attractive or he wouldn't have to go to these lengths to get a woman interested enough to disrobe for him. His self confidence may have taken a bashing somewhere along the line, I'm betting on a mother, as that's usually the case, but it could be an old girlfriend or wife. This guy's got loser written all over him."

Kel sat and thought about that as Ben stood. "Hey wait, I almost forgot," Kel said as he handed over a copy of the note that had been pinned to Kayla's overalls when she was returned. "We just got this yesterday. It was attached to the child who was returned."

Ben took the paper in his hand and sat down again. Kel watched as his eyes scanned the page, then went back and scanned it again.

Congratulations Laura. You passed the test. It seems you love your daughter more than yourself. So few do. I will enjoy my memories of you, clothed or naked you are a very beautiful woman. And now, a proven mother.

He slapped the page with the back of his hand. "I knew it! They all have problems with their mothers! Why are there so many bad mothers out there?"

"What's it mean?"

"It means his mother didn't love him or didn't show him love in any real way. Now he's challenging the mothers of his victims to pay what he deems the ultimate price, or choose to be selfish and only concerned with themselves."

"So his mother was not a good mother."

"No, she probably wasn't, and maybe he believes that there aren't any perfect mothers. This may be his way of finding out who they are, if in fact there are any."

"Well according to this, he thinks Laura is."

"Yeah. I'd be especially careful with her. He's liable to try to get to her again. In his mind, she and the other women who complied are perfect women and mothers, a combination he may have doubted existed before all this began. He might want to substitute them for his, either in his mind or physically somehow. I just don't know, this one is weird."

98

"He masturbated in her bra and left it behind."

"Oh shit, Kel. He wants her. And I don't think he just wants to look at her."

They were both silent, staring at the sports memorabilia on the restaurant walls.

Kel fingered the palm tree stirrer that he continued to carry in his jacket pocket. The ribbon rose that had come from Laura's panties had started to show some wear from his attentions, so he had placed it in his night stand drawer. "I fucking hate this," he whispered. "I feel absolutely helpless. He's going to keep doing this, and I can't stop him."

"Something will break Kel, with these kinds of cases, it always does."

"Yeah, well, from what I've read that can take ten or twenty years sometimes."

"It can. But this time I don't think that will happen."

"And why the hell not?" Kel asked sarcastically.

"He's doing it too often. And, The City of Wilmington has you, you won't give up. You'll see a pattern, discover a clue, or pick him up on a traffic violation with a kid in the back seat."

Kel scoffed and then smiled. "Thanks for the encouragement. I think I needed that more than anything."

"Well, I have to go. Let me know how this pans out. And good luck to you Kel. I know this can't be easy for you. Christ, killing kids for sex, ugh. What a miserable job we have."

Kel ran his thumb over the etched design in his glass and simply nodded as Ben walked off.

"Yeah," he said to himself a full two minutes later.

Chapter Twelve

*I*t was late in the afternoon and Kel was wondering why the hell she hadn't called as he'd requested. Called to let him know she and Kayla were all right. Called to let him know where the hell she was.

He spoke to each officer that was on shift when she'd left the house on Masonboro. None of them knew where she'd gone, only that she had headed north after pulling out of her drive and onto the main road. One officer, the one sitting beside Kayla watching cartoons this morning, had heard her mention the names of a few beach houses, but he couldn't recall any of their names now.

He finally remembered that one of the officers had mentioned that he'd heard her half of a phone conversation. Something about having her own keys for a rental unit and nixing maid service. She had told him this morning that she could arrange to stay at one of her parents' rental houses on Wrightsville Beach. Would she have done that the way she was feeling about her family, or would she have just found a place on her own? He knew she had the means to do whatever she wanted. She could easily get on a plane and get far away from the nightmare her life had become. Part of him hoped that she had, the part that was now worried for her safety, hers and Kayla's. The other part wasn't ready for her to walk out of his life, and if protection was something she needed, he wanted to be the one to provide it.

There were over a hundred rental agencies in this beach town, too many some said. Everybody would know her though, especially now. Would she risk moving from one place where she was being hounded to another just as bad? No, she was a smart woman. She'd go with daddy's firm, at least there would be the promise of anonymity, if not in actual reality.

He flipped through the phone book and found the main office of Wyndham Realty. It was over on Wrightsville Beach, about twenty minutes away. He grabbed the keys to his cruiser and went out to the parking lot through the back door. There was still a contingent of reporters hanging around out front, hoping for a break in the case or a one-on-one with the lead investigator. And he had zip. The best lead so far was probably Laura's bra, and the press didn't even know anything about that yet. But DNA testing was slow and the databases to cross-reference were insufficient at best.

On the way over to the beach he visualized Laura's bra again. He had seen it on her, appreciated how her breasts were displayed above the lacy cups. He had touched it, pushed it aside, and if memory served, he had even licked it once or twice around the edges for effect. Wouldn't that be a kick? His DNA on the damn thing! How was he going to explain that to the press? But as far as he knew, his DNA wasn't on file anywhere.

His thoughts mellowed and soon all he could envision was her smooth white breast poking over the satin edging, her budded nipple beckoning. He wanted desperately to hold her in his arms again, and the intensity of that feeling scared him. The feeling that he needed to be with her and that he wanted to hold her was shamefully foreign because he'd never needed a woman before, at least not for anything other than the most basic requirements. He didn't even like hanging around when those were dispatched with. He was the original Wham-Bam kind of guy. Oh, he wined them and dined them and usually took three or four dates to bed them, but once there, he rarely opted to return more than a few times. He didn't need or want any attachments.

So why the hell was he so gung ho on this one? Hell, he hadn't even really bedded this one, at least not in the usual way. Their joining hadn't been marked by time standing still; nothing existing in the universe but them; the release of tension and the quick trip to oblivion; the rejuvenation of mind and body. Their lovemaking, if that's what you wanted to call it, had been none of those. Well, to be honest, it could have been all of those—if they hadn't had so many other things to think about at the time.

And just maybe, that's what this was all about. Maybe he wanted another chance. A chance to do it right. To go from the meet and greet to the trip to the moon without an audience or a play book. But that was stupid, and irreverent. He didn't even really know Laura Wyndham and here he was thinking of her as just some bimbo he'd met at a bar or a bike rally. He was thinking of her as some sort of physical event occurring in his life, and only a possible physical event at that. Under other circumstances, she probably would never even have gone out with him and he knew it.

So why the hell did he feel like enfolding her in his arms and crushing her to him? Inhaling her sweet fragrance and lazily assaulting her sexy mouth?

He turned into the realty company and somewhere between slamming his car door and going into the office he dared anyone to give him a hard time about where the hell she was.

The middle-aged woman at the counter had a haggard look. A pencil was rammed into her bleached and frizzed, over-teased bouffant, and her lipstick had disappeared hours ago, leaving only the dark outline penciled in around the edge. Her eyes were bloodshot and weary, and she acted as if she was the most overworked person in the universe.

"I'm sorry sir, for the third time, I can't give you that information. And I really don't care who you are."

"Lady, you have two choices here. Either you tell me what I need to know," he pointed to his badge case open on the counter, "knowing full well I don't have a nefarious intent, or I call for a warrant, take over your computer, and bring the whole damned department down here to go through each and every unit until I find her!"

To her credit she didn't flinch. "You don't even know if she's in any of these units."

"Well, I sure as hell have to start somewhere, don't I?" he gritted out as he brought his police mobile unit to his lips. He had just pressed the button to speak when she closed her eyes tightly at something she saw over his shoulder through the window. Instantly her lips firmed and her color rose. He turned to see what she was looking at and saw a tall, thin, rakish looking man stepping out of a black Mercedes sedan. He looked familiar, but Kel couldn't place him.

Suddenly she threw a set of keys at him. "Number's on the keys, it's a mile and a half down on the left. Hurry and get there and tell Laura her ex just pulled in, looking meaner than I ever did see. He's a partner. He'll just come in and check the computer, if he doesn't already know where she is."

"Thanks. I'll take care of her."

෨෪

And now why had he said that? I'll take care of her. Like that was his job? His right? His duty? Well, he smiled to himself, he was a cop, and his duty was to protect and to serve. And regardless of whether Laura knew it or not, she needed someone to take care of her right now. That frazzled lady at the real estate office thought Laura needed protection from her ex. Why was that?

After all that had happened, it would only be natural for Ryan Vardella to come check on his daughter. Kel's first thought was that he would be intruding on a family matter, a reunion of sorts, if he stepped in. But because the lady in the office had changed her tune so quickly upon seeing Vardella pull up, he had an uneasy feeling in his gut about this. And not all of it had been caused by the receptionist's icy reaction to the man who signed her paychecks.

He found the house, but didn't pull into the drive. Instead he drove up past a few more houses and pulled to the side of the road. He quickly got out of his car and used a beach access to approach the house from the back side. As soon as he turned the corner of the house, he saw Laura and Kayla sitting at a table on the top deck. At almost the same instant he saw her, she saw him. After a moment of uncertainty, and some confusion, she waved.

He saw the look of puzzlement on her face, but when he smiled, she smiled. Then she stood and went to the rail and called down to him. "Come on up!"

"You have company coming in about two minutes. The prickly lady at the real estate office sent me to warn you!"

"Who?" she asked, and then she realized who he must mean. She'd already talked to her parents, and her brother had called to say he couldn't get by. It was Ryan's turn.

"Oh no," he heard her moan.

"I'll come up."

"No! No! That would only make things worse."

"How's that?" he asked with a raised brow.

"I can't explain right now. He's at the door." She

turned and grabbed Kayla from her seat and carried her into the house. From two floors below he saw the French door being pulled to, but he didn't hear it close, and no lock clicked in place. He strained to see and noticed that it hadn't been shut. It stood ajar by about six inches.

Well, no decision here, he thought. He was going to see what this was all about. It wouldn't be breaking and entering, after all, she had invited him up. He walked away from the worn beach pathway, stepped over some low bushes and onto the bricked-in walkway that led to the stairs going up to the deck. On the right he saw a built-in pool with a slide. Stepping softly, he climbed the series of steps to each deck, ending with the one he had seen them on. He made his way to the door, and hearing faint voices, eased his way in, allowing the breadth of his chest to slowly expand the opening.

He could hear the voices better now, Mr. Vardella was doing most of the talking. Kel inched his way into the room and realized he was standing on a loft overlooking the main part of the house. The voices were coming from below. He looked over the edge and saw Laura standing a few feet from her ex, who from this angle was missing a small patch of dark hair at the top of his head. Kel looked down the hallway to the left and saw several doors. One of them was closed and he assumed Kayla was in the room behind it, as he didn't see her anywhere below.

"I can't believe you did this!" There was a smacking sound and Kel leaned forward to see the man smacking his hand against a newspaper.

"I had no choice! Kayla had been kidnapped! That was the ransom! I had no choice!"

"You could have called the police!"

"It wouldn't have made any difference, and in a way I did."

"What that's supposed to mean?" The man had a snarl that made him look like a ferret, otherwise he had a gaunt, Clark Gable kind of appeal.

"I had some police help getting her back."

"I haven't read that in the papers or seen that in the police reports."

"If God is with me, you won't. Anyway, I did what I had to. I got her back and that's all that matters. I don't care about any stupid pictures!"

"Well I do! This little escapade of yours is all they're talking about in Raleigh. This could cost me the election!"

"Escapade! Escapade! How can you call what happened to our daughter an escapade? She could have been killed!"

"I just think you handled it all wrong, this wasn't necessary." Again, he tapped the paper. "And how the hell did you let her get taken in the first place? What were you doing? Why weren't you watching her?"

"I was sleeping! In my room!"

"Alone?" he asked with some sadistic curiosity.

"Of course alone, but why is that any of your business? You're the one with the raging hormones, not me!"

"Well as far as I'm concerned that's your fault, too. You neglected your wifely duties and I had to seek fulfillment elsewhere. Don't you dare try to pin this on me. You were pitiful in bed! And if this comes back to haunt me in the election," he stepped closer to Laura and grabbed her by the forearm, "if this costs me my seat in the House, you'll pay, Laura, you'll pay."

"She'll pay what?" Kel called from above. "And take your hands off her. Now!"

A shocked Ryan Vardella looked up at him and Kel drew his gun. He aimed it at Vardella's head. "I don't like your hesitation," Kel snapped.

The man dropped Laura's arm and jumped back.

"Who the hell is he?" he asked Laura, stunned that they'd had an audience he hadn't been aware of.

"I'm her bodyguard and next time you touch her you're going to lose a hand."

"You can't talk to me like that! Do you know who I am?"

"I don't care who you are. Touch her again and we'll see who wins in court." He flashed his badge and leaned over the rail. "I carry a bit of weight in this town and they like me in Raleigh, too. Now I suggest you leave before I see a bruise come up on her arm."

Vardella looked at Laura. "Are you going to let him talk to me like that?"

"Yes," was all she said. Then because she liked the way it made her feel, she said it again. "Yes."

Vardella flung the paper across the room, spun on his heel, and stomped out of the house, not even bothering to close the door behind him.

Kel was walking down the steps when they heard the car start, and they could hear the sound of the car losing traction in the gravel drive before screeching when the tires met asphalt.

"Did he even ask to see his daughter?" Kel asked as he walked over to close the door.

"No," she whispered. "He never does."

"Then why even let the bastard in?" He was walking over to her now and as she slumped and dropped her head so she could rub the back of her neck, his fingers itched to do it for her. He wanted to touch her, to feel her skin under his fingers again.

"I don't know. I guess because of Kayla I thought I had to."

"You don't have to put up with that, and it's sure not

107

doing Kayla any good hearing it."

"I make her wear headphones and listen to her music whenever he comes. We have a system."

"Geez! Is he always like this?"

"Yes."

"I'm sorry Laura. I probably shouldn't have intruded."

She lifted her head and gave him a tiny smile. "Then I would have missed seeing him jump like that."

Kel smiled back at her and then looked up when he heard a door open and soft padded footsteps coming down the carpeted hall. Kayla, eyes wide and face pale, looked down at them. She had a small smile for Kel.

"Hey, Kayla. Is that your pool out back? I saw some big dolphin floats out there, are they yours?"

"Yes," she whispered. "Mine and Mommy's."

"Would you invite me to come swim with you one day?"

Kayla looked over at her mother questioningly. Laura nodded.

Kayla walked slowly down the stairs, took his hand, and started leading him out the door.

"Not now! I don't have a suit with me."

She was still clutching his hand and looking up at him with sad eyes. Either she'd heard the argument after all, or she was starting to deal with the trauma of her experience. It just about broke his heart to see her so unhappy.

"Well, how about I come back tonight after work, grill us a few steaks, and teach you how to do a cannon ball off the side?"

Kayla's eyes lit up and she smiled, but then the smile disappeared as she again deferred to her mother.

"Would that be all right with you?" Kel asked Laura. He was afraid she'd say no to him, but he didn't think she'd deny her daughter anything right now, and he wanted to see this little girl smile again.

Laura looked down at her daughter who was bobbing her head up and down. She laughed at her daughter's antics and said, "Sure, why not? I have the grill but I didn't get any steaks at the store."

"I'll stop and pick a few up on my way back. You sure this is okay? I didn't mean to waggle an invite. I just thought she needed a distraction."

"It's fine. It should be fun. It's about time Kayla learned the cannon ball anyway," she said with a big grin.

"Okay, I'll see you around seven."

As Laura walked him to the door, she asked why he had come.

"I needed to know you two were safe."

They stood on the front steps of the beach house looking into each others faces, eyes locking, then traveling to lips that suddenly needed wetting as invisible magnets pulled at them.

Laura felt a tightening in her chest and a quickening in her blood, something warm pooled in her and made her feel lightheaded.

Kel felt desire spiraling out of control. The sound of a far off siren jolted him back to the present, and he ran his hand tenderly down her arm, lightly squeezing it at the wrist before racing down the steps.

On the way back to the station he asked himself how long had they stood with so much feeling flowing between them. He had no clue.

Chapter Thirteen

At the station he collected the faxed lab results from Kayla's clothing and the duct tape. The DNA testing on Laura's bra would take at least two weeks.

The duct tape yielded some prints, mostly Laura's. But there were two other adult prints. They had been run through the Automated Fingerprint Identification System, or AFIS, but no match was found. Unidentifiable, they were catalogued and entered as evidence before they were sent to the FBI to be checked against their system. The same prints, a thumb and a middle finger, were on the rubber edge of Kayla's shoes. The fingerprinting system didn't work very well if the culprit's fingerprints weren't on file anywhere. And apparently this madman's were not.

Kayla's urine-soaked, feces-covered, little pajama-styled overalls were covered with carpet fibers and tiny pieces of grass. These were being run through several computer matching programs, but the information garnered would only help to convict, not find the perpetrator. Unless the fibers came from specialized high-end carpeting, they would be impossible to trace; low-end carpets were run-of-the-mill and mass marketed to too many places to be tracked in most cases.

The scrapings from Kayla's nails, dirt brushed from

her hair, mucus taken from her nose—none of those, once analyzed, were of any help; there was nothing unique, nothing to trace. But like a hunter, Kel scanned the paragraph written about each thing that had been tested, hoping to find the one unusual thing he could use to catch this foul creature.

He went over the notes he had taken when he had first talked to Kayla after her return, and then the notes the child psychologist had sent him. Kayla knew very little about what had gone on. Mostly because she had been blindfolded the whole time, but also because she was young and scared. She didn't remember very much except that it was a man who had taken her and that he had not fed her, given her anything to drink, or allowed her to use a bathroom. She had heard a television on almost all the time and had recognized the sounds of the "Big Money Show," which Laura informed them was actually called "Wheel of Fortune." She also said she heard breathing, lots of loud breathing and women crying out, sometimes yelling "yes" over and over again. Kel could only surmise she had heard the soundtracks of porn movies.

She did not know if she had been riding in a car or a truck, but did remember that she had been lying down, rolling with each turn into something, "really smelly." When asked to describe the smell, she couldn't other than grimacing.

There did not appear to be anyone else involved, or if there was, they never made a sound that Kayla heard. She mentioned that she heard a fire engine siren and something that sounded like an air horn once, and that it had been very loud before it stopped. It had hurt her ears, and her hands hadn't been free to cover them.

She mostly remembered how badly she felt to have wet herself. And then she was cold because she was wet. When she had to eliminate solids, she said it burned her. The doctor saw evidence of that in the form of a diaper rash, and had speculated that her anxiety had caused stomach acid,

111

which in turn had led to diarrhea. She definitely had been miserable, and yet when Kel talked with her, she had her mother's sense of being above complaining. She was a nice, quiet, polite little girl, and this should not have happened to her. Kel hit his fist on his desk.

Piles of papers were faxed and dropped on his desk hourly, but nothing so far was workable. Nothing.

He met with his supervisor, the Chief of Police, and later the Mayor through a conference call. Everyone wanted to know about the progress his team was making and he was disheartened with each new report wafting down onto his desk.

At a quarter 'til six the electronic surveillance experts accompanied by the department's computer whiz, and Kel's best bud, Mark Twiller, marched into his office and closed the door behind them. Kel pushed back his chair, raised his eyebrows, and said simply, "Well?"

Mark spoke first. "Nada at the motel. The surveillance camera's been in place for at least six months. Doesn't look like anyone's been near it. It feeds directly to a web site. It's all digital, so it doesn't even need film to loop. It was set on auto-focus and had fairly good quality imaging within three to ten feet."

Kel winced at that, remembering the distances at which he and Laura had been videotaped.

"We dismantled the whole system, fingerprinted the camera, the TV, and all the connections. So far, the results are pretty pathetic. Outside, on the backing, we had the most prints. We're running them all down now. Inside, we got one thumb, one forefinger and a palm print."

"How about the manufacturer?"

"Cannon. Serial number indicates it was originally purchased from Circuit City in 2002. We contacted the original owner, he said he sold it to his neighbor when the new model came out. The neighbor sold it through the classifieds last summer when he was low on cash. The man who bought it paid cash and he doesn't remember what he looked like, only that he was middle-aged and scruffy-looking. He said he was glad the man paid in cash because he wouldn't have trusted him with a check. He saw what the man was driving, but only remembers that it was an old, dark blue Buick sedan, maybe a Century, he wasn't absolutely sure."

"How about the web site?" he asked turning to face Mark.

"Owned by a porn company in California. The dedicated link feeds automatically once the camera starts filming."

"What turns it on?"

"The power is on whenever the television is off, any movement in range triggers it to start recording. There's a lot of footage of housekeeping on the Green Door site. One particularly interesting one where one of the maids sits on the end of the bed and picks her nose for ten minutes, wiping her buggers on the bedspread."

Kel cringed. "Did any of the employees you questioned know about the camera?"

"They all said they didn't, but the manager started stuttering as soon as we showed him our badges and the warrant."

"Did you bring him in for questioning?" Kel asked.

"Charlie's with him now. I think they're planning on doing a polygraph if he doesn't come clean."

"That could be just the break we need."

"No way it's him, he's scared shitless. I wouldn't count on it." Mark was shaking his head dolefully. "And of course you know they don't keep any record of the people who use these rooms."

Kel acknowledged that with a slight nod. "Well

maybe he's being paid to grant access and to keep his mouth shut."

"Well hopefully he's not being paid enough to shield a murderer," one of the other cops injected.

"What should we do about the web site?" Mark asked.

"Is it legal?"

"From all appearances."

"Does the porn company have any information about the camera?"

"They're in California. They say they don't much care what's sent or how it's acquired, just so long as the monthly bills are paid."

"Who's paying them?"

"It was paid up front until 2007, by money order. No one knows, no one cares. When the money stops, the uplink is shut down. Until then anything sent is broadcasted."

"To whom?" Kel's eyes narrowed, hopeful there was some kind of clue here.

"Anyone who has the code. The digital network tracker sends signals from one computer to another, it monitors in real time. But most of these geeks have an evidence eliminator that erases all record of Internet contact before shutting down, so there's no way to follow it. The sender used an anonymous remailer, there is no way to trace it back."

"You mean this is not shared porn?"

"No, not at all. At least not in this case. It's a private deal. You pay the fee, set up the camera, hidden wherever, the dedicated line sends the feed to the web site. You log in using a password and a PIN number and then you select from a menu, set up chronologically I believe. You only get to watch your own stuff unless you pass around the code so others can watch."

"And pray tell, how is this profitable?" Kel asked.

"You'd be surprised. There are hundreds of clubs in this country alone dedicated to a very sophisticated version of the old mirror trick."

"Mirror trick?"

"You know, where you lace a mirror onto your shoe and then slide it under a girl's dress."

"That's high school stuff!"

"Not anymore. All over the world men hide small mini-cams in briefcases or shopping bags and videotape up the skirts of unsuspecting women. Men all over the world get off on that. And they share. You can go on line right now and find sites like Crotch Cam or Beaver Babes, where twenty-four hours a day, a camera is positioned and broadcasting back live for these sickos."

Kel let his head fall back against the headrest of his chair and he let out a long, hard sigh. Then he blew through his lips, sending the lock of hair on his forehead airborne.

"So, the show Laura had to put on for the kidnapper is only being viewed by our man," Kel stated.

"If you're lucky," the officer behind Mark said with a snicker.

"What do you mean if I'm lucky?"

"C'mon Kel, do you think we're stupid? We know you had a part in this." The same officer flashed a knowing, sideways grin, one Kel had seen often while playing cards with him, it wasn't amusing to Kel to see it right now.

"How could you know that?" Then in a panic, "You didn't see the tape did you?"

"No. But there's no other reason you would have stumbled across this hidden camera unless you were involved. We didn't get the ransom note from Mrs. Wyndham until after Kayla was returned, but you set up surveillance that afternoon."

Kel glared at Mark. "You told them, didn't you?"

Mark put his hands up in the air, palms forward. "Honest, Kel I didn't say a word to anyone. Not a soul. You told the brass, maybe one of them couldn't keep your secret."

"So, we were right," the other detective said, and nodded knowingly to the other two.

"This had better stay in this room or there will be some seriously messed up careers, not to mention faces," Kel said angrily.

"Kel, we're here to help you, buddy. We ain't got no beef about how you're getting the job done. Fact is, any one of us would have been happy to help Laura Wyndham out, and before you get all hot and bothered by that statement, I'm not saying that in a lecherous way."

"I'll just bet." Kel said as he crossed his arms and lowered his head to his chest.

"Really, Kel. Hey, there's a lot of off-color things that could be said here, and maybe sometime when this is not so damned serious, you'll hear a few, but right now, the only thing we care about is getting this creep. You do what you gotta do, we do what we gotta do."

"And that would be?"

"Well, for starters, can't we get a warrant for this company so we can access the link and trace it to the account that was set up?"

"I doubt it. But even if we could, it's not likely he used his real name and address now, is it?"

"With access, we could erase what's there, if you don't want something to be there . . . ."

"That would be ideal, but it might be better if we don't tip our hand. He has no idea that the man on the video was in on this . . . this . . . thing with Laura. And he certainly should have no inkling that the man is a cop. Unfortunately, unless we catch him soon, he may have use of that camera and TV again, and him having no idea it's been dismantled could have a disastrous effect on the next victim. Let's close up shop there and keep tabs on the room. Maury, you and Josh arrange for our own brand of surveillance, the twenty-four hour kind. Draw men from the squad room if you need to, I've already cleared it."

"Kel, you are going to get some sleep soon aren't you? You look bushed," Mark commented.

"Yeah, yeah. Maybe tonight. Right now I've got to get over to Wrightsville."

"What's going on over there?"

"Just a little barbecue, is all. I'll expect everyone to check in by ten A.M., we've got to get something going here before the mayor has a shit fit."

Chapter Fourteen

By the time Kel picked up the steaks and headed over the Wrightsville Beach Bridge, he was almost sorry he had agreed to this pool thing. He was bushed, and now he was beginning to really feel it.

He knocked on Laura's door and heard her call something back to Kayla before she opened the door for him. The full, beautiful smile she gave him erased some of his tiredness. Kayla running to the door to see him erased the rest.

"You're here! You're here! Momma said you might not come."

Kel stooped to Kayla's level and looked up at Laura. "Now why do you think she'd say that?"

Kayla innocently shrugged her shoulders, ran for the stairs, and imperiously called out behind her, "I have to go put my suit on!"

"A bit excited are we?" Kel said as he stood and looked into Laura's face.

"She's been talking about you and that cannonball ever since you left."

He gave her a sideways grin and followed her into the house, closing and locking the door behind him. "Why didn't you think I'd come?" he asked, curious what she

118

would come up with.

"I don't know, I just thought you were being nice before. And you must be tired."

"It's not nice to promise a child something and not follow through, and yes, I am a bit tired."

Laura was in the kitchen now, and she turned to lean back against the counter. "Kids are used to it these days. No one keeps their word anymore."

"I do," he said as he took the steaks out of a bag.

"Thank you," she whispered. Then she reached for the steaks and began unwrapping them.

"Is there a place I can use to change?" Kel asked.

"I didn't see you bring in a suit."

Kel reached into his coat pocket and pulled out a little scrap of material. "Got it right here."

Laura stared at the tiny Speedo that hardly covered his palm. Her throat went dry and she knew her eyes had betrayed her when he chuckled.

"It's bigger than it looks," he said, then realizing what it was that he had just said he corrected himself. "I mean it stretches." Realizing that that wasn't much better, he simply added, "I like the European-styled suits, more freedom of movement."

"Uh huh," she replied, tongue-in-cheek. "You can change in that powder room over there if you like. There's a hook on the back of the door where you can hang your things."

"I neglected to bring a towel."

"I have plenty. I'll take one out to the pool for you."

"Should we plan on eating now or later?"

"Later, if you don't mind. I already fed Kayla. She's not much for steak and since her bedtime is rather early, I don't think she wants to waste time watching us eat. We can eat after she goes to sleep if that's all right with you?"

"Sounds great. I'll just put this on," he waved his hand with the suit in it, "then I'll head out to the pool."

"We'll be right out. It won't take me but a minute to change."

Leaving his clothes on the countertop in the hall bathroom, Kel opened the door and listened. Hearing no one moving about, he stepped out of the bathroom and headed for the pool, his bare feet softly padding on the hardwood floors.

He unlocked the sliding glass doors and stepped out onto the patio. The pool looked inviting. His trained eye checked out the perimeter, scanning the nearby beach and zeroing in on the path beside the house that led beachgoers down to the water.

He was surprised. This was not the kind of place he would have thought a mother would retreat to after having had her child taken from her. It was far too open and accessible and he wondered if he should advise her to find a more secured place. Then his eagle eyes spotted the trip sensors and the tiny stanchions for infrared receivers. He started counting them and realized that when the alarms were set, this place was a virtual fortress, barring a power blackout.

He walked over to the pool, ignored the sign at the deep end about diving, and took a shallow dive that propelled him halfway across the pool. The water felt refreshing and his body became energized. He began swimming laps. Slowly, leisurely, he exercised his body, letting the tautness of his muscles play out. He was on his fifth set when he heard voices on a turn. He stopped and stood and tossed his head back to move the hair out of his eyes.

Laura and Kayla stood at the edge of the pool smiling down at him.

Laura smiled and he felt a little self-conscious. She

was wearing a cover-up over her suit and all he could see of her body was her legs, but they were gorgeous, long and shapely. She could hide her slim figure under terry cloth, but his memory had no trouble filling in the blanks.

"You swim beautifully," she said. "Like an athlete."

"I was on the swim team in school. I still enjoy doing laps whenever I can."

"Well, don't let us stop you."

"Oh, no. It's time for this one to learn the cannonball." He grabbed Kayla by the ankle and jerked her toward him. She screamed and laughed as she landed in the water in his arms.

"That wasn't a cannonball!" Kayla said.

"No, that was just to get you wet. Now we have to get your mother in."

They both looked expectantly over at Laura.

"I think I'm just going to take this time to relax in this lounger and watch you two have your fun."

"Party pooper," he taunted.

"I don't want to get my hair wet."

"That's probably something you shouldn't have told me. Too much of a challenge to put in front of me." He sat Kayla on the side of the pool and instructed her on the finer aspects of the cannonball, then he climbed out of the pool to show her.

Laura watched as water sluiced from his body as he lifted himself out of the pool. Dark hair, flattened into lines by the water filled his broad chest. Strong arms hoisted him effortlessly over the side, while muscled thighs pulled him out. When he was standing, dripping on the patio, she was so impressed with his physique that her hand went reflexively to the base of her throat. Not wanting to be betrayed by her reaction to his body, she fumbled with the collar of her short terry robe. In the motel room, she'd felt his large body moving on top of her, but she hadn't visualized him looking as good as this.

She watched him as he walked to the deep end of the pool, called to Kayla to watch carefully, and then lifted his body off the side. Up he went, arms straight, legs pulling forward until his arms clasped his knees and he tucked his head. When he hit the water, huge walls of water spewed up and then surged back, soaking Kayla in their wake. When he surfaced, she was laughing herself silly. "Do it again! Do it again!" He tousled her hair on his way back to the deep end and gave Laura a sheepish smile.

"I'm duly impressed," she called over to him.

He stopped in his tracks, eyeballed her, then the pool, then her again, before adjusting his point of entry. Before Laura could move, he ran into the pool, tucked his body and sent a flume of water cascading over her.

When he came up, she was wiping water from her cheek and pulling a wet strand of hair from her neck. Kayla was laughing so hard she didn't notice when he swam alongside, snaked over, and toppled Kayla in beside him.

They played until Laura said it was Kayla's bedtime and Kel was mildly shocked when Kayla didn't protest. She simply swam to the edge of the pool where Laura lifted her out and wrapped a towel around her. Kayla turned to look back at him as she was being led away. "Will you come back?" she asked.

"Certainly," Kel answered as he used the steps at the end and walked out.

Kel watched as Laura took Kayla's hand and led her into the house. He heard them talking softly as they went through the door and up the stairs. He grabbed a towel from a bistro table and started drying himself. When he finished, he wrapped the towel around his hips and finger-combed his hair. He listened as he heard birds rustling in the hedges, and watched as a sea breeze fanned the palmetto grass on the dunes. When he heard tiny clicking sounds, he turned to see the red infrared dots flicking on. Laura was setting the alarms on the outer perimeter, at least some of them. In another hour, the automatic lights would come on, too. When you lived on the beach, you couldn't have lights on all the time because it disconcerted and disoriented the wildlife, especially the turtles, so the alternative was sentry lights. Laura wouldn't be taking any chances, he knew she'd keep the sentry lights burning bright all night. What could the police possibly say if they came to her door to ask her to turn them out? Her reason for having them on was better than the turtles' for having them off.

He heard the door open, but not close. No, she wouldn't be closing that door either, not as long as Kayla was on the other side of it. He wondered how long it would take for Laura to relax her guard. From what he'd seen so far, Laura wasn't going to be beyond the area where the low hum of the child monitor could be heard for quite some time. He should mention to her that she should get some help. She could benefit from some counseling on how to recover from this.

He turned to see her walking toward him. She tossed her cover-up on a chair as she went by. God, she was beautiful. The flattering one-piece didn't need anything but classic, simple lines to show off her body. The high cutout legs showed off her slim hips and made her long legs impossibly longer. The plunging vee neck highlighted a deep line of cleavage. He doubted that he'd ever seen a woman so graceful and so sure of herself in a bathing suit.

She walked down the steps and into the pool, then disappeared into the dark, shadowed water. When she came up, she arched her back and tilted her head so she could slick her hair back.

"I thought you weren't going to get your hair wet?"

"Well, you took care of that now didn't you?" she said with a wry smile.

"Sorry."

"I'm not. This feels delightful. What a beautiful night," she murmured as she stared up at the stars. She walked to the edge of the pool where she crossed her arms on the cement before placing her head down. She stood there staring over at him, looking dreamy and content.

God, you're delightful, he thought to himself. Her expression told him that she was comfortable and pleased, captivated by the night and maybe a touch woozy from days without sleep. "If you're hungry, I can start the steaks now." He couldn't take her looking at him like that. She was sending him messages that he was sure he was misreading.

"That would be wonderful. I'm starved, how about you?"

"I could eat. I can't remember my last meal, so I suppose I'm due."

Lazily, she lifted her head, forced her body away from the edge, and slowly climbed the steps out of the pool. The way the water ran down her arms and legs in the faint light made her look ethereal, she glowed.

As she stood on the apron toweling her hair, the interior pool lights came on.

"Must be nine o'clock. Do you always eat this late?" she asked.

"No. It's been an unusual day."

"And I thank you for that. I know how hard you're working on this." She pulled on her wrap and tugged it close. He saw her shiver. But it wasn't because she was cold.

He uncovered the grill, adjusted the propane, and lit it. Then together they walked into the house where he worked on getting the steaks ready for grilling and she made

124

a garden salad.

"Is Kel your real name or is it short for something?"

"Kel? It was my grandmother's idea. She was French. Originally it was supposed to be Q-u-e-l, French for 'how.' Quel Vain. Get it? 'How Vain?' She thought I'd inherit my grandfather's dashing good looks and like him, I'd be vain about it."

"Interesting." She stood back like an artist, eyes squinting, assessing. "Yes I can see dashing good looks. Can't see vain though."

"Looks get you in the door, but they don't do the work for you."

"So you'd rather be known as brainy?"

He smiled over at her as he shook spices on the meat. "I am known as brainy."

"Oh. Sorry, I didn't mean to be insulting."

He laughed and took the steaks out to the grill.

As he tended to the steaks, she poured wine out of a crystal decanter into matching wine glasses then handed him one.

This was significant, he thought. She had planned ahead. The wine was nice and cold. It touched him that with everything going on with her, she had thought to chill some wine for them, unless of course she was the type who always had a bottle chilling.

"Tell me about your ex. I can't see you two together. He's not very nice."

"Oh, at one time, he was quite charming. I smack myself in the head everyday for not seeing his ambition."

"He hurt you?"

"Not physically. But I never knew how much it could hurt to be ignored. Then I found out it hurt a lot worse to be ignored because something better came along."

"Not something better. Just different, maybe."

"Thanks. It shouldn't have hurt as much as it did, it wasn't like my heart was broken. I guess it was a matter of pride more than anything else. I apparently hadn't learned the 'womanly arts' to his satisfaction. I was always an 'A' student in everything else. I thought I'd learned my lessons well. He thought not."

"I'm sure you learned your lessons just fine. Some men just can't be satisfied, unless it's with variety. And even that doesn't always satisfy some."

"Are you one of those men, Kel?"

Suddenly, an ear-piercing siren came from a speaker mounted inside the house. Laura spun around and dropped her wine glass. It broke into hundreds of shards against the concrete of the patio. Kel took off running for the house, Laura following right behind him.

As Kel ran past the bathroom, his hand snaked under his clothing on the countertop and he grabbed his gun. As he ran up the stairs, he released the safety. At the top of the stairs, he nearly bowled Kayla over. Unable to check his momentum, he grabbed her and tumbled with her.

When Laura reached the top of the stairs, he was sitting, legs splayed with Kayla in his arms, his gun in the air.

"I had to go to the bathroom. I forgot about the alarm," the little girl cried.

Laura bent and gathered her into her arms. Kel staggered to his feet and tried to figure out where his towel went, while asking where the control board for the alarm was.

Laura pointed back to the kitchen and he ran to shut it off.

"Does that relay?" he called up to her.

"Relay?"

"Call the alarm company, who in turn call the

police?"

"Oh, yes, it does. I need to call them!"

He climbed the stairs again and took Kayla from Laura's arms and whispered to her, "Still need to go?"

When she just nodded, he walked back into her bedroom and then into the bathroom. He checked the room and then waited outside the closed door until she was finished. Then he carried her downstairs to where her mother was talking on the phone. He set her on the counter in front of Laura and went into the bathroom to change into his clothes before going out to the garage to find a broom for the shattered wine glass.

By the time Laura had changed, tucked Kayla back in, and reset the alarm, Kel was using a hose to rinse the wine and whatever miniscule particles of glass that remained into the mulch under the bushes on the edge of the patio.

"Everything all right?" he asked.

"Mmmmhmp," she said tiredly. He couldn't help but notice she hadn't taken the time to put on a bra under her sweatshirt. Soft, full mounds moved freely as she heaved herself into a lounger. He wondered if she'd taken the time to put on any panties under her jeans.

"You stay there. I'll move the table away so there's no chance of anyone getting cut on a piece of glass, then I'll set the table for dinner."

"No, no, I couldn't possibly let you do that."

"Stay!" he ordered, brooking no argument. "I'll take care of it. You rest."

He moved the chairs, set the table, and retrieved the steaks he had barely rescued in time, along with the salad that was in the refrigerator. Then he walked over to the lounger, offered his hand, and pulled her up.

"C'mon and eat, then I'm going to go so you can get some rest."

While they ate, he asked how she thought Kayla was doing and if there was anything she had remembered since last night.

"She seems fine. She doesn't want to talk about it though. Sometimes I catch her staring into space, like she's in a daze, it worries me."

"That's normal, she needs time to adjust and to get back into her regular routine. I know how your meeting with your ex went, did your parents get in today?"

"Oh yeah. Did they ever. It was quite a reunion. They left half an hour before you arrived. Dad is furious that I didn't get help from the police. Little does he know," she said with a wicked chuckle. "And he practically insisted that I hire a bodyguard for Kayla, but I finally talked him out of it. And Mom, Mom just couldn't stop crying. Over and over again, 'My sweet little Kayla.' Stroking her head and crooning, 'Baby, baby, baby, oh you poor dear!' I thought it would never end. One was chastising me, and the other was crying and moaning, unable to move on. It was terrible. I was so glad when they finally left."

"And the repercussions?"

"Too soon to say, but they are mighty upset. When they start getting out around town, the Hilton thing is going to be the capper. I don't think my parents are going to be able to deal with that very well."

"And how about you?"

"It's probably time I back away from the social thing anyway. I want to do some volunteer work at the hospital and at the library. Let someone else do the fundraising while I help out in other ways. I can't see purposely putting myself through the repeated embarrassment being out in public would cause right now. Not that I'm afraid, mind you, I just don't need to deal with that right now. Maybe later, after everything settles down some."

He hated the thought that she was backing down and going into hiding. But he had to agree with her, there was nothing to gain right now by being out and about where she would undoubtedly be the main topic of conversation in the hushed circles of the ladies rooms, men's rooms, country clubs, and restaurants.

Kel helped Laura clear the dishes and lock down the pool area. Then Laura went inside to load the dishes in the dishwasher and he cleaned the grill tools. Both were yawning by the time she saw him to the door.

"Thank you for making Kayla's day. She'll remember her first cannonball and who taught it to her."

"I enjoyed spending time with her. She's a very sweet kid, you've done a good job with her."

"Thanks."

"Well, good night," he whispered.

"Good night, Kel."

They were both reluctant to end the evening without some promise of a future meeting, but neither said anything.

Balling it up, Kel tossed his damp suit in the air while slowly walking down the street to his car. When he turned to look back at the house, all the sentry lights were on. At least she remembered to turn them on, he thought with a smile.

Chapter Fifteen

*H*arold Francis Satterfield sat back in his recliner, clicked a button on the remote, and watched as the last scene of a homemade porn movie flashed off. It wasn't one of his, so it wasn't one of the better ones, he thought as he scratched his naked belly. Not one of his special ones, the ones with his sweet little mothers that he forced into making movies for him. His dirty fingernails dug into his greasy hair as he belched his SpaghettiOs. He was tired; it had been a stressful couple of days. That stupid kid had wet all over herself and had diarrhea, now he couldn't get the damn stain up off the carpet. There would be hell to pay when Gloria got back from her business trip. Last time he'd had a dickens of a time explaining away the scuff marks on the bedroom wall from that boy's shoes.

He scooted his butt into the hollowed-out depression he'd made in the chair over the years, and hitched the chair lever all the way back until he was almost prone. Then he closed his eyes and made himself have the dream again. It was his favorite; one that he often thought had spurred him to action. *Not So Private Photos,* the one that had created a fantasy so intense inside him that he finally had to find a way to live it or at least parts of it.

In his dream, he was handsome and thin; suave and

"de-bone-yar" as his old school buddies would say.

∂℘

They had just finished shooting. The head photographer waved his arm to signal to everyone on the set that this was a wrap, that they were done for the day. Dane Albrecht looked over at his wife who was standing against a fake waterfall backdrop in her transparent black mesh swimsuit. God, she was beautiful. Too beautiful for words. Her long blonde hair was tossed over her shoulders; a few stray strands had been allowed to fall over her chest, but strategically placed so as not to cover the hard nipple peeking through the taut mesh. Looking further down her slim torso, he could see the defining triangle of her partially-shaven blonde bush and it more than hinted at her femininity as it slightly shadowed her mound under the mesh. Stunning, there was no other word for the effect she had, erotic beyond most people's imaginations. Her bright blue eyes met his and she gave him one of her enchanting smiles. She was so young, and still incredibly naive.

He briskly walked onto the set, his suit jacket slung over one shoulder as he made his way over to where she stood. The costume and makeup women on the set all stopped what they were doing to admire him. He was tall and good-looking, as handsome as any male model they'd ever seen, only rugged in a way that said he'd never have the patience for this kind of frivolous activity. They all knew him; he was often there to pick up his wife after their work sessions. He owned a very successful architectural firm that was just around the corner from the studio. All of them envied the way he looked at his wife, like she was a lollipop he couldn't wait to eat. They watched him go over to her and tilt her chin to receive his kiss. Then they watched him chivalrously wrap his jacket around her shoulders, carefully pulling it around the front of her so that the long lapels covered her breasts.

Theirs was a strange relationship. It appeared for all the world that he worshipped and idolized her, yet he allowed her to pose practically naked. How could a man who seemed so possessive of his wife put up with her posing so provocatively and darned near nude, flaunting everything that was rightfully his and meant for his eyes alone?

The men on the set, the photographers and set directors, feared him and had often seen his spurts of anger, but it was never because of what they'd captured on film. In fact, if the truth were known, he seemed to almost encourage her to be more scantily clad. They just had to be extra careful not to upset her, or to overtax her. And who could blame him? If any one of them were married to her, they'd want to be sure she had plenty of energy left at the end of the workday.

His hand went between the jacket opening and he cupped a weighty breast, allowing his thumb to gently caress the nipple as he looked down at it. "Been showing my titties to the whole world again?" he asked with a sideways smile.

Her eyes met his and she smiled slightly, blushing at his intimate touch. "Uh huh, I have."

That she could still blush so naturally bespoke of her youthful innocence.

"Good, I like that. How about this?" he asked as his hand slid down her belly and he stroked her mound over the transparent mesh, "been showing off my pussy, too?"

"A little. They took two blurred close ups in this suit, plus a few distance shots."

"Good. Well how 'bout I take a few close ups that aren't blurry? C'mon, let's go to your dressing room. Or should I say your undressing room?" he said with a wide, sexy grin.

She smiled up at him and let her fingertips fan his

high cheekbones. You could see the love in her eyes. The love and absolute obedience of one who was being led by a cunning, devil-may-care Svengali who had long ago bought her, body and soul.

As soon as they were ensconced in her dressing room with the door locked, he instructed her to remove the suit and climb up onto the bed. It was a Hollywood-style bed, the whole headboard fully padded, quilted, and curved at the top. The bed coverings were a light cornflower blue silk, specially selected by him to compliment her fair skin tones.

"Ah, ah, ah. I think you might have forgotten to put something on," he lightly chided.

She gave him a questioning look and then it dawned on her what he was referring to. She jumped down and ran over to her jewelry case to get her rings. Her wedding rings. Her signature sapphire and emerald engagement ring with the gold diamond-studded band that fit into it and around it. When they had become engaged it had made headlines all over the world, and her rings had been photographed almost as much as her that month. Now, he never photographed her without them. She thought that was sweet.

For him, it was his way of saying, You can look at her, but she's mine. She belongs to me.

She slipped them on and hurried back to the bed. He unbuttoned his shirtsleeves and rolled them up before opening a dresser drawer and taking out a very expensive 35-mm. camera. He checked the settings and flipped a few levers, then he was ready to shoot.

"Sit up against the head board, sweetheart. Sit nice and tall with your back straight. Good, good. Now take your tits from the bottom and push them together for me. Yes, yes, that's right. Wait, let me lick them to make them bud more and to make them glisten a little." He walked over to the side of the bed, bent and took each peak into his mouth as she held them up for him. "Mmmm, nice." He gave each nipple a long hard lick and stood back to look at them through the viewfinder. "Beautiful," he murmured as he clicked the button. The shutter instantaneously opened and then closed, capturing the image of her—the image he was saving on film.

"Bring your hands up and over a little so I can see your rings better. There, that's good." He moved to the middle of the bottom of the bed. "Now, spread your legs for me baby, let's get a few good cunt shots. Wide ones now, okay. I want you to show it all to me. And I want to see the rings too, make sure the stones don't turn."

She did as he instructed. She opened her legs, parting them all the way as he continued snapping pictures, totally focused on the area between her thighs, the camera never moving from in front of his face.

"Okay, honey, now bring your knees up and spread them as wide as you can. This is the shot I've been thinking about all day," he added huskily.

"Are you sure there's no film in that camera?" she asked timidly.

He chuckled and smiled at her. "Now, sweetheart, you know this is just a fantasy of mine, to be the photographer you're posing for. Only I want to be the kind of photographer you bare it all to. All of it sweetheart, wider. Wider. There, that's good. Real good. You have such a beautiful, sweet cunt, baby." Click. Click. Click.

"Now use your fingers and pull your lips apart. Yes, yes. Now press against the lips so you flatten them out a little. I want you to show me your honey hole. That sweet place I'm going to stick my rock-hard prick into real soon. Scoot your ass out a little. Yes there, that's it." Click. "Now, the same shot, only this time I want you to lift your bottom up a little and fold your legs back so I can get a shot of your little asshole puckering along with your nice slick opening. Check your rings. That's a good girl. Your nails look nice today, just have them done?" Click.

"Yes, Tina did them today, we needed them pink for a shot."

"Well, let me tell you, they look real nice, that pink against the other pink." He gave her a wicked smile and her heart fluttered. God, she loved this man so much.

"Ready? This time you need to hold your back straight too, 'cause I want to get your tits in this shot also. A shot right between your legs, getting it all, your asshole, your cunt and those luscious globes thrusting out to me. Excellent. Just drop your knees a little more, I want you to show me everything you've got. Now pull up a little. There. Perfect." Click, Click. Click.

He placed the camera on the night stand and sat down on the edge of the bed. He put his hand on her and cupped her while he pushed his middle finger inside her. "Ah, this is so nice. You are so wet. Do you know how many men would love to have their hand where mine is now?"

"How many?" she teased.

"Hundreds, thousands, millions, probably even billions. But it's me who's holding you here, me stroking you, me licking you." He removed his hand from her and bent low to kiss her. Then he climbed up onto the bed and pressed his whole face into her snatch. With his face still buried in her, he blindly reached for a remote that was on the opposite night table and, finding it, he pressed a button. When he heard the low-pitched whirring sound letting him know he was recording, he relaxed his legs and pulled her down to lay flat on the bed. He positioned her legs so they were wide apart and then he stood to remove his clothes and to check to make sure the angle of the video camera on the tripod was aimed properly. Then he laid down beside her, urging her legs even wider for the camera by bending her knees out. As he fingered her and diddled her, he urged her to play with her flattened breasts, telling her to pull on her nipples so he could watch her play with herself and then, just as she was about to come, he bent over her and took one large nipple into his mouth. He suckled her as she climaxed against his fingers, spasming and contracting. Her sweet cunt muscles twitching and throbbing for the camera. He took her swollen clitoris between his thumb and forefinger and urged it out of its little hood, hoping that the camera was focused enough that it would pick up the image of that little quivering nub.

God, this was heady. He would never get enough of this. Sleazily photographing his beautiful supermodel wife in the most intimate ways. Doing everything he'd ever dreamed of doing to a woman and what's more, being allowed to capture it all on film. It hadn't initially been easy to talk her into it, but he'd been persistent and she'd finally agreed, secure in the knowledge that these were private moments captured only for them. She didn't know that he threw parties, parties where men paid him big bucks to view his wife, the famous celebrity Althea, in the most graphic positions, doing some of the most perverse things imaginable. Oh, the things he had shoved up inside her for the camera's pleasure. And his.

Soon, he was going to arrange to have a few videotapes from their private collection "stolen" so he could capitalize on the lucrative Internet market. She would most certainly be devastated when she learned the whole world was viewing her like this, but at least she would never know he'd orchestrated it. And not just for the money, which was certainly substantial, but because he wanted everyone, every man he had ever met in his whole life, to envy him.

He looked down into her beautiful, smiling face. She was a delight. A beautiful, innocent sex kitten and he loved showing her off. His tits, his cunt, his asshole. They belonged to him. She had agreed to all that the day he had married her and he had slipped those telltale rings on her fingers. The rings that proved she was who he said she was when he sold a picture of her. Her easily recognizable jewelry proved that the black market clips were not computer-enhanced images or pictures of another model whose face had been deleted and his wife's lovely face superimposed in its place. Her rings were her trademark in the triple X business. The business she was involved in that she had no idea about.

When he'd met her two years ago, she'd been a high-class lingerie model. She was known in the world of fashion for her beautifully shaped, full breasts that could stop a guy in his tracks from across the street. She'd posed in bras with the absolute lowest décolletage, but she'd never been photographed topless, she'd never allowed it, until he had married her and convinced her that she should. Her nipples he'd told her, it was her beautiful pink nipples that were the icing on the cake, the defining part of her breasts that she was denying the men who viewed her. He had told her that she was being selfish and vain and quite prudish to keep them under wraps. Then he'd accompanied her the first time she bared them completely for the photographers and the men on the lighting crews, and he had swelled with pride when he'd heard their gasps of surprise and pleasure. Their cameras had clicked frantically as they moved around trying to capture every nuance, every angle before she had been overcome with shame and changed her mind. She had pulled the straps of her bathing suit back up despite their woeful protests, and she hadn't posed completely topless again, knowingly at least.

But enough of those pictures had circulated and her career had really soared as European magazines and swimsuit manufacturers flocked to photograph her seminude. He had almost talked her into losing her bikini bottom for a few low-life photographers who had greased his palms pretty heavily, but he'd never been able to pull it off. But today, he thought as he smiled down at her, she had been photographed in a transparent mesh suit that, unbeknownst to her, hid nothing. He was proud that the whole world knew his wife was a true blonde with great big, homegrown tits.

All he had to do was make sure she never found out that their private sessions, and their most intimate lovemaking, was being viewed by an increasingly demanding and lecherous clientele.

He was hard and thick, hard as granite and so thick he could hear the pumping blood pounding in his ears. He rolled on top of her and eased himself between her silky thighs, careful to keep himself raised high in the air so the camera could see the penetration as he speared and entered her. He rode her high so his cock could be seen sliding in and out of her wet and sticky cunt. He plunged down deep, driving her into the mattress, then he reached under her and, gripping her buttocks, he pulled her up to meet his now frantic, rapid thrusts. He felt his body start its telltale trembling, then he felt his muscles tighten so tensely that it caused his teeth to clench. His jaw muscles bunched and he groaned, but not before pulling out and allowing his load to discharge itself into her soft, curly blonde thatch. Artfully, he laid his now limp member down between her swollen pussy lips and let the camera film the few glistening drops still oozing out into her gaping pink crevice.

Then he took all his weight on his shoulders and arms and like a man doing a push up, he levered himself off her. He landed on his feet by the bed and nonchalantly reached over and flicked the button on the camera that shut it off.

"I still don't understand why you won't come inside me, you know I'm on the pill."

"I don't want to take the chance. Your body is prime right now, having a baby would ruin it. As I've told you before, the pill is not one hundred percent effective, we need to take a little extra insurance." He couldn't possibly tell her that a successful X-rated video required that the man come in such a way that the audience had proof of his ultimate climactic pleasure. That's what it was all about to the men watching these videos. It was the ultimate release brought about by the ultimate fantasy. And how much better could a fantasy get than this? The ultimate cover girl innocently baring all, giving their eyes an exclusive feast of prime flesh. Most of the men knew he was filming her for them without her knowledge. It just didn't get any better than this.

❧

The door slammed and he jumped in his chair, the remote crashing to the floor.

A huge woman with hair bleached blonde so many times it tended toward orange, stomped into the room. Her double chin jiggled as she screamed, "Hey dick head! You were supposed to pick me up at the airport an hour ago!"

His fogged mind reeled as he went from ultimate fantasy to dreaded reality. His eyelids pulled back to his forehead as his eyes popped wide open. Oh Christ! He had forgotten. Shit! She was surely going to kill him now.

"Gloria! Oh dear Heaven, I completely forgot you were coming back tonight." His voice was low and contrite. He knew better than to stay remaining in the chair while she stood in the hallway with her suitcases in her hand. He quickly engaged the lever on the side of the chair and with a loud thump, the footrest closed and he was catapulted out.

"I am so sorry dear! Very, very sorry. Here, let me help you with those."

He got just close enough to reach for a case when she whacked him upside the head with her purse, sending the

139

contents flying. The metal frame caught his ear and it stung as flesh was ripped away.

"You worthless piece of shit! I travel all over the country doing everybody's dirty work, fixing their damned computers that they spilled coffee all over, and here you are on your lazy butt watching TV."

"I cleaned the house while you were gone. I got your dry cleaning. I even made a few casseroles for when you got back. I know how you hate to cook." He was almost whimpering as he held his smarting ear. Blood was wetting his palm.

She dropped her purse to the floor, scattering the rest of the contents. "Well clean up this shit, unpack my bags, and fix me something to eat. And you better not have missed taping any of my soaps. Where are they?"

Quickly he went to the VCR, ejected his tape, and inserted hers. Surreptitiously, he tucked his under the TV stand in the small space between the carpet and the first shelf. He pushed it as far back as he could with his fingers. "Here you are honey bun, I just put the first one in for you. You got four tapes. They're all in order stacked here. Just sit down and I'll press play."

"That's better," she said kicking his butt as he knelt on the floor in front of the entertainment system. "Now clean up this mess and get me a drink. Then you can fix my dinner."

"Yes, of course. It won't take me but a minute."

He scrambled out of her way and made his way to the kitchen. Experience had taught him that the drink was priority number one. Dinner could wait until he put all her things away. Then if he was lucky she'd be too tired or too drunk to berate or beat him anymore and just fall asleep watching her precious soaps. At least he got to finish his dream. His wonderful dream where he was powerful and handsome, and his wife was young and beautiful and he had the pleasure of showing her off.

Chapter Sixteen

Yes, Meggie I've got him. I have your Toby. Follow every instruction, to the letter, and I'll bring him back. Call the donut brigade, and I'll kill him.

First: It's a little known fact, but Topsail Island allows topless sunbathing. They can't kick you off the beach for it, all they can do is ask you to move to a more secluded area. Do that for me—go topless on the beach. From the moment you cross the beach access, I want to see you topless and wearing a thong. Yes, I'm going to be there along with hundreds of others. I can't wait. Tomorrow at eleven. Stay on the beach until noon, so I'll have ample time to ogle you. And don't forget to wear sunscreen.

Second: I love your new Sebring convertible. Put the top down and drive to Westfield Mall. Park in front of Sears tomorrow afternoon at three. Take off all your clothes then get out of the car and put them in the trunk. Get back in the car and drive up and down Oleander Avenue until you get pulled over by a cop. I guess if you want to get this part over with sooner, you could run a red light or break the speed limit to get their attention. I don't care whether they write you up or not, I just want them to see you—naked. Along

**with everyone else driving on the avenue, especially
the truckers. You never know, I might be one of them.
Third: Your ex is a piece of work, isn't he? Let's give
him a real reason to be jealous. Let's set up a nice
little betrayal. Have Dr. Rand Cheswick, his best friend
and tennis partner, bugger you on the first green of
Wilmington National Golf Course tomorrow night at
eight P.M. In case you don't know what buggering
means, it means he has to take you in your asshole.
Tell him to come in your crack right in front of the
swing check video camera, or it doesn't count. Now
for the betrayal—your ex has to catch the good doctor
fucking you in your ass. Set it up and see to it. Do
everything right and Toby will come home shortly
thereafter.**

So far she'd done everything right. With nervous,
sweaty palms she'd driven to Topsail. At the access, she'd
removed her cover up and dropped it into her beach bag,
then proceeded down to the beach. The first people to see
her were surfers coming off the beach and the shocked looks
on their faces as they had approached and then passed by,
shamed her to her toes. But she'd held her head high and
kept on walking, hoping that the beach wouldn't be crowded.
But it had been. And within a span of five minutes, she'd
known that over 300 men, women, and children had seen
her exposed breasts and buttocks as she'd made her way
through the sand to an out-of-the-way spot. The oversized
sunglasses had helped to hide her tears as she'd walked by
men openly leering and commenting. "Holy shit!" "Look
at that!" "Momma Mia that woman's topless!" "Shameful
hussy!" a woman had yelled. "Nice ass!" "Momma look
that lady has no shirt!" The final humiliation had been when
she'd seen several teenage boys with camera phones taking

142

pictures of her and presumably sending them off all to their friends.

A beach patrol officer on his trike had pulled up and rode along side her as she walked. Then he had cleared his throat and called over to her, "Ma'am, you'll have to move to a less populated part of the beach."

"I am officer!" she had yelled back. "I am!" He'd ridden beside her, his head turned to watch her, until she was at least the length of two football fields away from any other sunbathers. When she'd put her beach bag down and spread her towel out, he'd nodded, tilted his head as if he'd suddenly recognized her, then made a big turn in the sand. When he'd taken off down the beach in the opposite direction, he'd sprayed sand over her and her towel. She'd picked it up, shook it out, and then laid it out again. Kneeling, then stretching out on her stomach, she cried.

Over the course of an hour, no less than six trikes had come down to check her out, all with a different male on board. She hadn't given them the benefit of turning over. When the hour was up, she'd picked up her towel, shook it, and put it back in her beach bag to make the long, degrading trek back. "There she is again!" "Good God Almighty!" "Martha, would you look at that! She's showin' her ninnies!" "Fabulous, just fabulous," a middle-aged man in a Speedo had said, and then had practically followed her all the way to the access. She looked around trying to see if she could pinpoint the man who had her baby, but no one fit the sleazy image that she had of him in her mind. And actually, most of the men leering at her had that lusty, half-lidded glazed look, and no wonder!

By the time she got to the access, word had spread up and down the beach and people were walking fast to have their own look-see. She'd walked quickly down the access, and when she'd come to the end of it, she'd whipped her cover-up out of her beach bag and put it on. It was the most wonderful thing, to be able to cover herself and deny the curious eyes.

At three she'd pulled up in front of Sears, removed her clothes, got out of the car, and put them in the trunk. Several shoppers stopped in their tracks to ogle, but she hadn't given them the time of day. She'd quickly gotten back into her car, pulled out of the space, and had headed for the exit to Oleander Avenue. She'd had to wait at the light, and when a pickup truck pulled alongside, she'd cringed. The window had come down ominously slow and an old black man with white whiskers had whistled through an almost toothless mouth. "Honey Pot! You ain't got no clothes on! Mmmmm, mmmmm, mmmm!" The light changed and she'd peeled off to the right, cutting in front of him. From that moment, she'd tried everything she could to get noticed by a cop. But there didn't seem to be any cruisers around. She'd prayed that the light at South College would be green for her, because that was the longest light in the city. No such luck. When she'd seen it turn yellow a full block away, she had slowed and inched her way forward. A carload of teenagers had passed her. Then it had stopped, waiting for her to catch up. The whooping and hollering as the boys in the car had leaned out of the windows for a better look had drawn the attention of a family in an SUV. They had been cruising on her other side. The husband started craning his neck from the opposite side of the vehicle to get a better look. Her eyes had met the woman's, and she had seen the disdain in them. Lady, if you only knew, she had thought.

She'd had to drive almost to the end of Oleander Extended before she saw a cruiser come onto Oleander from a side street. She'd taken that opportunity to lay on the horn and then had flagrantly cut two cars off to get to the opposite curb lane. When she'd seen the blue light and heard the loud whelp coming from behind, it had been with both relief and dread. She had pulled over and waited for the cop to walk to her car. Then she'd simply sat there staring straight ahead as he'd taken inventory. "Ma'am you do know that's illegal, don't cha?"

"What? Cutting those cars off or driving naked?"

"Both. But let's just talk about one." He'd looked around the interior of the car. "Where are your clothes?"

"In the trunk."

"How about your license and registration?"

"Also in the trunk."

"Well, normally, I would ask you to get them for me, but how about you open the trunk for me and I'll get them."

"Sure." She'd hit the button on the dash and popped the trunk. He'd stepped back, shaken his head, and had spoken something into the microphone at his collar. She hadn't heard what he'd been saying as he'd walked to the back of her car, but she'd heard him chuckle a few times.

Traffic had slowed considerably as people rubbernecked to see what was going on. When they'd caught a glimpse of a naked woman behind the wheel, their eyes had flown wide and their heads had turned back as they'd crawled along. She'd wanted to hang her head, but she'd forced herself to look up at the sky instead.

He'd come back with a pile of clothes, which he'd dumped in her lap along with her purse.

"How about you dress first, then look for your license and registration."

"Happy to."

She'd taken the citation he'd written for unlawful lane changing and thanked him for stopping her. He'd quirked his eyebrow and bent his head to her. "How's that?" No one ever thanked him for pulling them over.

"I said, thank you for being there and pulling me

over. I appreciate it."

"Sure. Anytime," he'd quipped and had turned to go back to his cruiser. Then he had stopped and turned back. "Is this something you plan on doing again sometime?"

"No. This was the first and only time."

"Do you mind my asking . . .?"

She cut him off. "I lost a bet. Don't ask."

"Oh." He'd shaken his head and sauntered back to his car.

She'd dropped her head onto the steering wheel, waited for her heart to slow a bit, then driven to the hospital to find Dr. Cheswick.

❧

Dr. Cheswick was off duty so she had to have him paged. She waited for him to call the number she left for him, the number at the nurse's station on the surgical floor.

When it rang, she picked it up as she normally would have, "Nurse Ryan."

"This is Dr. Cheswick, someone there trying to reach me?"

"Yeah, me."

"Is this Meggie Ryan?"

"Yes."

"What can I do for you, Meggie."

"Can you spare a few minutes, I need to talk to you."

"Is this about a patient?"

"No, it isn't."

"Is it about Thomas?"

"No, not really. It's about my son."

"Sure, I can spare the time. When?"

"Now would be good. Can you meet me now?"

"I'm just coming off the golf course, I'd like to take

a shower. Where do you want to meet?"

"How about the bar at Eddie Romanelli's in half an hour?"

"Make it an hour."

"All right. I'll see you there."

She spent the hour building up courage and trying to figure out how to approach him about helping her with phase three of The Voyeur's ransom demands.

When she saw Rand Cheswick come into the restaurant bar area an hour later, she had to blink hard. The man was an Adonis, tall and broad shouldered with wavy light brown hair. He was wearing a white polo shirt that stretched across his broad chest. The Izod shirt was tucked into tan Dockers. On his feet were brown loafers, worn without socks. He looked some kind of sexy. How was it she had never noticed how handsome this man was? Could it be that the only other times she'd seen him he'd been wearing a surgical cap and mask? She waved to get his attention and he gave her a broad smile. What a perfect mouth! Straight white teeth and full sensual lips! *Good God Almighty!* she thought as he walked over to where she was sitting at the end of the bar. His being so attractive made her even more nervous.

"Hi!" he said as he took the empty seat next to her.

"Hi!' she said sticking her hand out. "I feel like we should introduce ourselves as I've only seen you over an operating room table."

He chuckled, took her hand in his and gave it a firm shake.

"Would you mind if we got a booth? What I have to talk to you about is very private."

"I don't mind at all." He stood and waited for her to slide off her stool, then he led her to the hostess station where he asked for a booth in a corner.

When they were seated he asked her what she wanted

to drink. "Just a Coke, please." When the waitress came to their table he ordered her a Coke and a vodka tonic for himself.

"So what's on your mind?" he asked.

Even with the extra hour, she hadn't figured out how to broach this with him, so she just took the note out of her purse and handed it to him. "I got this yesterday."

He unfolded it and read it while she waited, while she watched his expression change from idle curiosity to outright horror.

"Jesus!"

"Yeah."

"Oh my God. Meggie, I am so sorry." He shook his head more than a few times and then he read it again. When he finished, he folded it and handed it back to her. "So, am I to believe you've already done the first two?"

The tears that had been pouring down her face had been confirmation enough. He slid off of his bench and moved around to slide onto hers. He wrapped her in his arms and he held her face to his chest while she cried. "Oh, Meggie. Jesus Christ," he whispered.

He continued to hold her, stroking her hair and her back, and even though she was trying to be quiet, her sobs attracted the attention of nearby diners. When the waitress left their drinks on the table, she gave him a questioning look, but he just waved her away. Everybody probably assumed that he was breaking up with her and he felt like a cad.

When she finally cried herself out, soaking the front of his shirt in the process, she pulled away from him. "I'm sorry. I just couldn't take it anymore. I've been strong all day, but I just can't believe all that's happening! It's been awful. I have never been so humiliated in my life."

"I can imagine." His eyes dropped to her chest and he thought about the full swells that were under her light summer sweater. Quickly he looked back to her face, but not before she had noticed where his eyes had been.

"Sorry." What else could he say?

A moment of silence ensued before he asked, "How is it that he knows you so well?"

"I have racked my brain for hours trying to figure that out, but no one comes to mind, no one at all."

Again there was silence for a few moments, then he asked another question, "Have you ever done this before?"

"What? Paraded around naked?"

"No, anal intercourse."

Silence again. "Well, not intentionally. Thomas was really drunk one night and forced himself in the wrong place. But he'd liked it so much that I couldn't get him out. It was awful."

"It's going to be awful this time too, then."

"You're up for it?"

"Well now that's an interesting choice of words."

She blushed so quickly and so completely that he had to laugh.

"Well the way I figure it, Thomas will kill me if I do, and he'll kill me if I don't. But there's no choice here Meggie, for either of us. Thomas and I have been good friends for many years, I knew him before he started drinking. I remember when he fell in love with you. And knowing how he still feels about you, this smacks of betrayal, big time. But we have to think of Toby and what's best for him. I just hope Thomas realizes that."

"Thank you," she whispered.

He reached over, picked up her hand and gave it a squeeze. Then he looked at his watch.

"I have to make a phone call, I'll be right back."

"You're not calling the police are you?" she asked, her eyes accusing him of betrayal before his confirmation or denial.

"No, I'm canceling a date."

"Oh."

She watched as he walked outside to use his cell phone.

Oh yeah, cancel your date, by all means. You have a sure thing with me tonight. She was pleased to find that she still had her warped sense of humor.

And so it began. She called Thomas and told him to meet her on the first hole of the golf course at eight.

Chapter Seventeen

As they walked up the emerald green mound of grass, one phrase kept repeating itself over and over in their fogged minds: *He has to take you in your asshole. Tell him to come in your crack right in front of the swing check video camera, or it doesn't count.* His first thought following, was how awful this was going to be for her, hers was how grateful she was that he had agreed to do this despicable thing.

Upon reaching the designated tee box, the single flood lamp triggered by the motion sensor clicked on, and a stark, white light that illuminated the area instantly blinded them. They both knew the camera had started filming.

"Should have figured he'd have the lighting taken care of," he muttered.

Rand turned to her and whispered, "Well, this is it. I don't see anyone around," he checked his wristwatch. "But he should be here any minute now. What do you think, should we wait until we hear him coming?"

"I don't know. How long will it take?"

"Not very long, I don't imagine, but I honestly don't know. There are some extenuating circumstances here," he said with an ironic smile.

"Well, how do you suggest we get started?"

He pulled on the crease of his trousers and bunched

151

them at the top of each thigh and knelt, his knees slightly parted. Then he inched around, making sure he was in front of and parallel to the camera. "Come over here and kneel in front of me."

She slowly walked in front of him and then gingerly knelt with her back to him. With an encouraging hand on her lower back, he pushed her forward until she was on her hands and knees. Then with sure hands he skimmed up the outside of her thighs until her skirt rose above her hips. Before either of them could react, he deftly hooked the fingers of both hands into the elastic of her panties and drew them down to her knees.

A small gasp couldn't be helped as she sucked in as much of her breath as she could. She closed her eyes tightly and trembled as the heat of her embarrassment flooded through her.

Her smooth, pale cheeks glimmered in the bright light and he was tempted to run his hands over them. Instead, he blinked his eyes hard and called on his professional demeanor to get him through this. Clinical, he told himself, just keep thinking clinical. He drew a tiny white tube out of his jacket pocket and squeezed two inches of a clear substance onto the middle finger of his right hand. Then using the fingers of both hands, he spread her cheeks and lavishly spread the cream around her anal opening.

Her humiliation was complete; she knew his eyes were following his fingers as they readied her for him.

With his left hand, he unbuckled his belt, drew down his zipper, and reached inside the opening of his boxers. He wasn't surprised to find that he was rock hard, he'd expected it in fact. And that was a blessing, because this just wouldn't work unless he was, and there was a little boy's life at stake here.

He smoothed nature's own lubricant, the creamy

substance that had oozed out of the tip of his penis over the angry-looking swollen head and placed it centered at her opening. "Meggie, I'm sorry," he whispered as he slowly attempted to insert the thick length of him inside her.

Her muffled moans tore through him as he fought his way inside. She was tight, very tight. He rubbed his thumbs around her opening while he thrust his hips forward, trying to stretch her, trying to make her accommodate not just his ample length, but his sizable thickness. He pulled the skin of his penis back toward his body, trying to squeeze it past the barrier of her tight rim. Her puckered opening was no longer visible as he slowly sank his manhood into her. Muffled sobs racked through her as she lowered herself to her elbows and bit the fleshy pad of her thumb. All he could say to ease her suffering was, "Go ahead and cry baby, it's okay. Don't hold back, I know it hurts."

His own tears were forming and pooling, threatening to overflow as he finally seated himself. And damn, this was not even the worst part. The hard part would be doing this over and over, however many times it took before he could bring himself to climax.

He leaned over her and shhhed her and crooned softly into her ear as he forced himself to retreat and plunge in short, irregular strokes. Soon, he could feel the sensual heat overtaking him and then that delightful throbbing that urged him on. He was afraid of being rough with her, yet without the friction it just wasn't going to happen. He knew that he could think about sodomizing a woman from now until doomsday and not feel the gratifying fullness or the gut-wrenching tightness needed for his release. It wasn't in his repertoire of favored sexual positions.

He heard a car door slam and realized it was now or never. He reached under her sweater, found her bra cup, and pushed it aside. Then he cupped her breast in his hand

and rubbed his thumb over her nipple. It grew for him and that was all it took. Abruptly, he straightened, and with one hand he spread her cheeks, while with the other he forcefully withdrew and quickly slapped himself against her furrow. Within seconds he spurted his seed between the two white globes of Meggie's bottom. He watched with a strange fascination as it ran down between the crack of her ass to the grass below. He heard the echo of his labored grunts and the wretched howling groan that had been his, ringing in his ears, reverberating in his skull, and he realized that he sounded like a goddamn animal. A fucking rutting beast! A caveman who had just plowed a helpless unwilling victim! And it made him sick. But he didn't have time for that right now. Thomas was coming over the rise and his eyes were wide with disbelief.

"What the hell?"

"Thomas, let me explain—" Rand said as he stood and pulled up his trousers.

"Hell, I don't need an explanation! You were fucking my wife, you bastard! On my own goddamned golf course!"

"First, I was not fucking your wife, she's not your wife anymore, and second, it's not your goddamned golf course, you just work here! Now if you don't want to listen—" That's all he got out before Thomas lunged at him. Rand sidestepped him and Thomas ended up sprawled on the grass, the momentum bouncing him on his head. Rand quickly helped Meggie, who was putting herself back together, to her feet and grabbed her hand. He ran with her to his car, calling back to a dazed Thomas. "Trust me, what I did was necessary!"

"Necessary? Necessary!" Thomas hollered, just managing to get to his knees. "Since when is buggering necessary, you pervert! Get out of my sight! Meggie, Meggie,

I can't believe you'd even let him do that to you. And here, where I work! Both of you get out of my sight!"

"Thomas . . . Toby—"

"No, Meggie. Not right now." Rand said harshly, gripping her hand tight. "It won't help. He's not in any mood to listen. C'mon, let's go."

❧

After dropping Meggie off at her house, Rand drove to the police station. He said he had information about the serial kidnappings and was sent to the officer in charge of the investigation, Detective Kel Vain.

After introductions in Kel's office, Rand walked over to the tiny window that looked out on the old city. "I just thought you should know that there could be a child turning up soon."

"What do you mean?" Kel's eyes were sharp. He didn't miss a thing. The man's clothing was first-rate, but he was rumpled, seriously rumpled.

"She'll probably kill me for coming here and telling you this, but this woman I know, her child was kidnapped . . ."

"And . . .?"

"And I just helped her complete the third thing she had to do to get him back."

"Oh, Jesus."

"Yeah."

"Is she okay?"

"She will be."

"Was it bad?"

"Bad enough."

"Where is she now?"

"At home waiting. But I don't think he'll bring the boy back there. It's an apartment in a huge complex. I don't know how he got him out of there in the first place, but I

155

doubt he'll chance bringing him back."

"I need to get your statement."

"Later. After he's back. I've got to go back and be with her now. I just thought you should know to look for her little boy. His name is Toby."

"What's her name?"

"Meggie. We'll tell you everything once the boy's home. My name is Rand Cheswick; I'm a surgeon at New Hanover. I'll give you my cell number. Call if you find him, I'll call you if he shows up first."

"How long ago did you . . ." Kel waved his hand vaguely, "pay the ransom, so to speak?"

"About an hour ago."

"On camera?"

"Yeah."

"Do you think it was linked on line?"

"No, it was just a portable video recorder."

"You aren't going to tell me where it is, are you?"

"Not yet."

"I could keep you here."

"What good would that do anybody?"

"None, I guess. Here," Kel said as he handed him a pad. "Write your name and number on this for me."

Rand took the pad and sat in the detective's chair behind the desk. He crossed one ankle over a knee and started writing. Then as he handed back the pad and put his foot on the floor, grass cuttings from his cuff littered the floor. "Gosh, I'm sorry," Rand said as he stooped to pick them up. "Didn't even get to play golf and I still manage to take away some of the turf."

Kel looked at the grass stains on the otherwise pristine, albeit wrinkled trousers. And suddenly, it clicked. "A golf bag!"

"What?"

"That's what he uses to get the kids in and out! The grass . . . give me some of the grass from your cuffs. Do you know what kind of grass it is by any chance?"

"Yeah, I do. I know the man who manages the course. They overseed with rye during the winter. This time of the year they've got a new crop of Bermuda coming in. Why?"

"Because it's the same kind of grass we found on one of the kid's clothes. What course is it?"

"I'd rather wait . . ."

"I'll find out with just a few phone calls. It's probably your club, right? I'd hate to have to keep you here when I'm sure she really could use you right now."

"Wilmington National. There's a camera on the first tee box. But for God's sake, let him get there and get the tape first. If anything happens before Toby—"

"I promise, nothing will happen. If he's true to pattern, Toby's probably already been released. I'd better get the word out to the men, he could be wandering around the mall at this very minute."

"We could only be so lucky."

As Rand left, Kel picked up the phone and called the lab. "I need the report on the grass we found on Kayla Wyndham's overalls as soon as you can get it to me. I need to know what kind of grass it is." He wondered if the smell of dirt and grass could be the "really smelly" odor Kayla had talked about. Those two combined with fertilizers could create a memorable stench.

৯৬

When Rand pulled up in front of Meggie's apartment building, he found her huddled on the stoop, her portable phone clutched in her hand. She stood as he approached.

"What are you doing out here?" he asked as he gathered her up into his arms.

157

Tears had dried on her face and new ones threatened. "I just couldn't stay in there anymore. I thought if I just got out of the way, he might bring him back."

"Meggie, that's crazy. He wouldn't chance it, and besides this is the only way in."

"I left his window open and the back slider on the balcony."

"You're on the second floor!"

"He got in before!"

"You're not being rational. Let's go upstairs. I need to talk to you."

Her eyes widened with fear.

"No! It's not that. I don't know anything new. His arm went around her shoulders and he led her inside and up the stairs. "It's just that . . . . Well, I went to the police."

"You what?" she screamed.

"Don't worry, it's okay. They don't know anything about you, or even who Toby is for that matter. I only wanted them to be on the lookout for a lost little boy. You know as well as I do that it's more likely he'll be dropped somewhere. They needed to know how to get in touch with us."

She thought for a moment, then slowly nodded her head. "Yeah, I guess you're right. They need to know who to call. I'm sorry, I wasn't thinking straight. This waiting is killing me."

"I know. C'mon, I'll fix us some coffee. It could be a long night." He opened the door to her apartment and ushered her inside. Then just to humor her, he left the front door unlocked and didn't bother to shut the slider leading out to the balcony. A steady wave of heat met the cool air conditioning at the kitchen archway, and a few mosquitoes were making themselves welcome, but he didn't dare shut it.

They sat on the couch sipping coffee and tensing at

every sound in the stairwell. At eleven a slightly inebriated Thomas showed up at the door, banging to be let in.

"I want to know just how long you've been fucking my best friend," he said belligerently as he pushed his way past the door. He stopped dead in his tracks when he saw Rand sitting on the couch.

"Speak of the devil . . . ."

"Thomas," she pleaded, holding him back by gripping a section of his shirt.

"I'm going to kill him," he growled.

"Thomas, Toby was kidnapped."

Thomas spun and faced her. His eyebrows shot to his forehead as he dealt with the shock, and his mind began putting everything together. His expression changed and the harsh planes of his face softened the instant he had puzzled it through. "Oh, Jesus! Oh, Meggie. Shit, I'm so sorry. Oh, sweet Jesus. Rand, Rand . . . . Damn, I'm sorry!" He spun back to his friend and roughly jammed his palm to his forehead as if holding back a tremendous headache. "Oh, jeez, now it all makes sense. Baby, baby," he said as he reached for Meggie and took her into the shelter of his arms. But she didn't want the comfort of his arms; she wanted the comfort and security of Rand's.

Rand sat quietly on the couch watching his best friend hold the woman he had recently been so intimate with, and he wanted to run. Run and find someplace where he could be alone. Alone to jab his fists into the wall, alone to curse and decry the absurdity of the torrent of feelings he was experiencing. Then his cell phone rang.

Everyone stilled as he shoved over to his opposite hip in order to extract the phone from his pocket. "Don't get your hopes up, it could just be the hospital." But glancing at the caller I.D. screen he didn't recognize the number.

"Dr. Cheswick."

"We have him. Dorothy Hodder, the head librarian at the regional library on Chestnut was locking up. She found him in the women's bathroom. He's fine."

"We'll be right there."

"Prepare her. We had to cut off a lot of his hair to get the tape off. And make sure she knows we're going to have to interview her and her son and do a complete crime scene workup before she'll be allowed to take him home. And it would be a good idea if she brought some clothes for him."

"Will do. We're on our way." He clicked his phone closed.

"They found him. He's at the New Hanover Library on Chestnut Street. He's okay." His eyes met Meggie's. "I'm sure he wants his momma more than anything in the world. C'mon, I'll drive you." He playfully slapped Thomas on both cheeks. "You're certainly in no condition to drive. And you'd better hurry and sober up, the police may not be too thrilled to have to deal with a drunk."

"I'm not a drunk!" He faced Meggie and gripped her forearms tightly. "What else did you have to do? What other demands did this pervert have? There's always three isn't there?" When she just stared at him, he shook her, "Tell me, dammit!"

Rand rushed to Meggie's side and pried Thomas' hands from her. "I'd hate to have to cold cock you, but I sure as hell will. This is not the time to deal with this. Now leave her alone!" He wrenched Meggie from him and tucked her under his arm. "C'mon, grab some clothes and let's get going." He followed her into Toby's room and closed the window while she rummaged through drawers. When he sensed Thomas looming in the doorway, he turned to face him. The scowl on his friend's face told him that this was not over, not by a long shot. Thomas' feelings for Meggie and his blind jealousy were overriding his good sense.

"I want to know what else you had to do!" he screamed at Meggie, his fists balled tightly at his sides. "Tell me what this bastard did to you!" And he was pointing directly at Rand.

Well, that was it. Rand wasn't going to put up with this. He walked over to Thomas and growled, "She doesn't need this from you right now! In fact, she doesn't need you at all!" He pulled back his fist and connected with Thomas' jaw, sending him in a heap to the floor.

"Rand!" she screamed running over and restraining him by the shoulders. Rand shrugged her off and bent to grip Thomas by the shirt collar. He dragged him down the hallway to the bathroom, threw him into the tub, and drew the curtain. Then he turned the cold tap on full and pulled the shower lever out.

"He'll be fine. C'mon let's go," he said as he grabbed her arm and ran with her out the door and down the steps.

On the way over to Wilmington's downtown area, he reached over and patted her on the knee. "I don't recommend you tell him about the ransom requirements. I don't think he can handle it."

"He never was a strong man."

"You'd think that someone so blindly jealous of you would have been faithful to you. He sure as hell expected it of you."

"Men are an enigma," she whispered.

"We think the same thing about women." Then he let out a long sigh and said, "You know you're going to have to tell the detective everything."

"I know."

"Are you going to need me to be with you?"

"You've done enough, Rand. You helped me get him back. I can never thank you enough."

"Don't be stupid," he bit out.

161

"What you had to do . . . ."

"Was nothing compared with what you had to do."

There was silence in the car as a soft rain began to fall. Rand turned on the wipers and they listened to the soft squeak of the blades as they made a dry wipe between each wet one.

"You know, I'm very proud of you. You've shown great courage and a fierce loyalty. I want you always to remember that. Whenever you have bad thoughts about what you had to do, please remember that. It's not something any man worth his salt should have a problem with."

"Thank you, Rand."

They pulled up in front of the library. The whole block was alight with flashing blue-and-white lights and an ambulance was waiting at the curb, its back doors open. They could see two medics inside bending over a gurney.

"Go see your boy. I'll park and join you."

୬୪

For the next few hours Meggie felt like she was slogging through a deep fog: answering a myriad of questions, refusing Rand's offers of food and coffee, and keeping a desperate hold on her son's hands when she wasn't holding him on her lap. Twice, Toby had been taken aside as she answered intimate questions for Detective Vain. Rand went with Toby, partly to ease her mind that her son was in good hands, not just with strangers, and partly because he couldn't stand to hear her going over the details of her ransom assignments with the seemingly stern, unconcerned detective. He kept his eyes on her as she wiped at her teary face and alternated between nodding and shaking her head as the detective posed question after question. Finally, the doctor and the crime scene people were finished with Toby, and the detective was finished with Meggie. Detective Kel

Vain had added another ransom note to his collection.

They were all on their way to Meggie's apartment now, where Thomas would no doubt confront Rand, and the police would look for evidence of the kidnapping.

God, he was tired, he thought as he looked in the rearview mirror and smiled. Meggie was in the back seat with Toby. Both of them were belted in as she rocked him back and forth, his head cradled against her breast. Her smooth, plump, heavy breast. He remembered it from when he had reached for it as a way of sending his body over the edge for her. And he knew that if he had been pleasuring her instead of hurting her, that he would have had no trouble unleashing his passion. He suddenly wanted this woman as he'd never wanted any other. This quiet, strong woman who did whatever it took to protect what she loved. He thought about her laying under him reveling in his gentle touches, and then becoming frantic with desire as he touched all the right places. And he didn't know if it could ever be like that.

He didn't know what he'd be facing when he saw Thomas, but he knew one thing for certain: this woman was worth fighting for, and he was going to be the victor. Even if it cost him a ten-year friendship and a hell of a good tennis partner.

Chapter Eighteen

Kel and his crew finished up at Meggie Ryan's apartment around two in the morning, too late to call Laura and fill her in. As he drove back to the station and then home, he tried to decide when would be a good time to call her, a time when he wouldn't wake her, but before she had the chance to hear all about this latest kidnapping on the news. It had been three days since he'd taught Kayla the cannonball and had dinner with Laura on her patio. But it hadn't been three days since he'd thought about her. He thought about her constantly.

He decided to sleep until six, then shower and dress and get over to her place by seven. That should be enough time to refresh his body and his brain, if he managed to get any sleep at all. He thought about Meggie Ryan and how hard it had been for her to relate to him the atrocities she had been forced to perform. But he had noticed that when she had described the third demand, she hadn't seemed as disgusted, as devastated by it. Cheswick must have handled things better than most would.

His mind recalled the hard planes of Dr. Cheswick's face and he tried to fill in the blanks of what that act must have looked like between the two of them. It hardly seemed like something either might have considered doing before, but you never knew about people and their sexuality. He knew anal intercourse could be sensual, if done properly; he had tried it a few times himself. No, it probably wasn't their speed, he decided. Still, there was definitely something between them, something unspoken, a bond of some sort. Could it possibly be similar to the kind of bridge he and Laura had experienced? Distaste for a dreadful act that culminated somehow in respect and admiration? It was an intimacy they had shared after all, even if it wasn't done in the conventional way under the most ideal conditions. They had still shared a part of themselves, along with their bodies, in a mutual, consenting way just as he and Laura had. He smiled to himself as he pulled into his driveway. He wondered where this would all lead between the good doctor and the nervy mother. He had seen the look of protection on Rand Cheswick's face several times, and a steely, determined resolve had set into his jaw when he'd dealt with her tipsy ex-husband who'd been waiting in the apartment when they'd all gotten there.

Kel opened the front door to his house and made his way to the bedroom. He dropped his badge case and gun on the night stand, along with the notebook filled with the copious notes he had taken during his interview. Thoughts of the case swirled around his head as he stripped and slid between the sheets. He had to get over to that golf course tomorrow. The grass taken from Dr. Cheswick's cuffs matched the grass found on Kayla's pajamas. With any luck, they'd find the common denominator. Then, as he turned his head and snuggled into the pillow, he thought about Laura. How nice it would be to come home after a stressful day and find her here in his bed waiting for him. Her willing, sleek body inviting him inside. He fell asleep with thoughts of her lying beneath him, writhing in their shared passion, and sending each other into sacred oblivion.

Chapter Nineteen

*E*arly the next morning, Kel was on Laura's front porch knocking on her door, listening to the sounds coming from within, trying to determine if it was indeed, too early to come calling.

Laura answered the door with tumbled locks falling over her eyes, as her fingers plowed through her thick tresses. She was beautiful. All of his senses went on alert as he observed her tousled and sensual appeal.

"Oh, I'm sorry I woke you," Kel said and Laura smiled at his sincerity.

"You didn't wake me. I just didn't sleep very well. Kayla was restless."

"Is she sleeping in your bed?"

"Yeah, I can't make her sleep in her own bed yet. I'm not ready."

"The longer you wait, the harder the transition will be."

"I know, I just can't yet."

"So when she has a bad night, you have a bad night."

"Something like that. Come on in," she gestured, standing off to the side. Her robe parted just above her knees and he had a glimpse of a soft lavender nightgown. It appeared to be silk, and it thrilled him to see it move between her thighs as she turned. And he could smell her. She smelled of citrus and baby powder and something spicy. It kicked his libido into high gear.

"Why the visit at the crack of dawn? Not that I'm not delighted to see you, but I can see you have a reason for being here."

"Boy, getting intimate with someone opens your soul to them," he murmured with chagrin.

She blushed, smiled over at him, and turned to pull the coffee pot from the warming burner.

"I do have something I need to tell you."

"I thought so."

"You might want to sit down. It's not all good news."

"There's been another kidnapping."

"Boy, you are astute."

"Figured it had to happened. And it will probably keep happening until you catch him."

He liked the confidence she had in him, it puffed him up and made him unaccountably proud.

"A little boy this time, named Toby. He was returned last night."

"By being returned, you mean she did his bidding?"

"You do zero in, don't you?"

"It's the only point you're concerned with, right now. You were afraid to have me find out on the news."

"I've gotta tell you, you get an 'A' for effort."

"How's the mother doing?"

"Last night was a bit rough," in more ways than one, he thought, "but I think she's going to come through it all right."

"Would it be okay if I called her?"

He smiled widely and endearingly shook his head.

"You amaze me. Here you are just beginning to deal with your own crisis and all you can think about is someone else's pain. I am absolutely floored by you."

"It only stands to reason that I can commiserate with her better than most."

"I'm sure she would love for you to call. I'll leave her number. Other than not sleeping well, how's Kayla doing?"

"She sees the doctor again today. My mother and father are going to meet me there. The psychiatrist seems to think we all need to know what she's dealing with now and what's in store for her later as it keeps coming back to her over the years."

"That's excellent. I'm glad you're doing this. A lot of people don't know how important getting the right kind of help is. And you, are you going to start seeing someone?"

"I don't think I'm ready to date yet."

"I didn't mean that! I meant professionally. A shrink."

"Oh. I'll think about it. Kayla's my main concern for right now. If she's fine, I'll be fine. Coffee?"

He took the cup she offered and sat on a stool at the counter.

"Kayla may be your main concern for now, but if you don't deal with this problem soon, it'll come back to haunt you and will be harder to deal with later. You don't know how this will affect you down the road, Laura. Get some help."

"Maybe I will, just not now. I'm not ready for all that entails." She sipped her coffee and looked over at him. "I appreciate you coming here to warn me."

"It'll be all over the news this morning."

"Does the press know who she is?"

"Not yet, but I'm sure by noon they'll get a line on her."

"How old is her son?"

"Five. Do you know a Dr. Cheswick?"

"Yes. He works at New Hanover. Neurosurgeon, I believe. I didn't think he had a son. I didn't even know he was married."

"It's not his son, but he's the one Meggie, that's her name, uh . . . recruited, if you get my gist. But that's confidential."

"You mean like I recruited you?"

"Yeah, sort of."

"So she fits the profile. She's a single mother, too?"

"Yeah, divorced for two years. Only from what I can tell, her ex-husband was a class A fool and now he wants her back."

"Well, sometimes an experience like this can draw people back together."

"Will that happen with you?" He thought for sure he knew the answer to that question, but he needed to hear her say it.

She laughed and the sound was musical. She even had a cultured laugh, he thought, a sweet, tinkling one, not a brassy guffaw like some women he knew.

"Not a chance. I might be able to forgive a man some indiscretions, but I could never forgive him if he abandoned us, the way Ryan did. Especially the way he just walked away from Kayla. Although, now, I must say I'm rather happy about that. His influence on Kayla would not have been a good one. I wish I'd seen that at the time. I practically begged him to keep in touch with her when we split, it's good that he hasn't."

As if on cue, they heard a loud wail and both of them bolted to the stairs. Taking them two at a time, Kel beat Laura to the top. He drew his gun and spun around the doorway into Kayla's room.

She was tossing on the bed, moaning in the throes of a nightmare. Kel shouldered his gun and pulled Laura into the room. "Looks like she's having a nightmare."

Laura rushed to Kayla's side and gently shook her. "Kayla, wake up baby. It's just a bad dream. C'mon, baby, open your eyes."

Kel sat on the opposite side of the bed watching as Laura gently tried to prod Kayla awake. Kayla let out a loud wail and flailed her arms out before flipping to the other side of the bed. She would have fallen out if Kel hadn't caught her.

"Kayla!" he called more firmly. He shook her and lightly slapped her cheeks. Then he pinched her hard on the thigh. "Wake up, Kayla! Wake up!"

Big bright blues eyes opened and she sniffled. " 'Tective Vain?" she whispered.

"Yes, sweetheart, it's Kel. You were having a nightmare."

"It was a very bad dream," she moaned as she pulled herself up and crawled into his lap. "Bad, bad noises. Bad, bad man. Sirens. Loud sirens. Right there."

"Right where, honey?"

"Right there. I couldn't see. But it was loud. My ears hurt. I'm afraid."

Kel gathered her close and gently rocked her as he stroked her long hair. "You don't need to be afraid anymore, sweetheart. Your mommy's here, and so am I. We won't let anything bad happen to you anymore. Trust me," he whispered. "The bad man's not going to get you again."

He softly crooned to her until she settled down and her sobbing quieted. He used his thumb to wipe the dampness from her cheeks and he looked over at Laura who had a hopeless, quiet fear in her eyes.

"It's going to be okay, Laura. She's going to be fine.

As long as she keeps expressing her fears and being open, she's going to be just fine. Don't worry about her, honey," he whispered, and he reached over to wipe the tears from Laura's pale face.

After a moment, he chuckled. "What am I going to do with you two, all somber and teary-eyed? You need to get up, get your suits on and get down to the beach. It's going to be a perfect beach day. A great day to build a castle in the sand."

Kayla opened one eye and looked up at him. "Can you come, too?"

"No, honey, I can't. Not today. I have work to do. But you and your mom . . . ."

"Can go later this afternoon, Missy," she said as she took Kayla from him. "Right now we have to get ready to meet Grandma and Grandpa, and if you're good, maybe I'll take you to Toys 'R Us and see if we can find a new game."

Kel stood, then bent low to kiss Kayla's cheek. "I like dominos," he whispered. He straightened, winked at Laura, and walked to the door. "I'll leave that number."

"I'll walk you out." She set Kayla on the carpet and told her to go use the bathroom, that she'd be right back to help her dress.

"Thanks," she whispered as she followed him to the kitchen counter where he scrawled a name and a number, then to the front door. "You're really good with her."

"She's a great kid."

At the door, he turned to her. "Are you sure about that dating thing? You think it's too soon?"

"Who wants to know?"

He bent, took her by the arms, and pulled her to him. He looked into her face and met her eyes with his. "Me," he said just before taking her lips with his. It was a sweet kiss, tender, but without passion, it spoke of promise and friendship. "Me," he repeated as he let her go.

Then he slapped his forehead with his broad palm and shouted. "The siren! Damn! Why didn't I connect that before?" Then he was out the door and running down the steps before he heard her answer.

"No, I'm not sure. I'm not sure at all," she mumbled to the back of the door. Then she smiled and turned to go back upstairs.

Chapter Twenty

Kel was busy for days as he followed one lead after the other. The siren thing had stirred up his juices. Kayla had told him about the siren before. She had told him that it was loud and that then it had stopped. That's what should have hit him at the time. It could only have stopped because it had reached its destination or arrived back at the firehouse. If Kayla had been kept anywhere near the firehouse, she would have heard the sirens all the time. But since it was only the one isolated instance, there must have been a fire or an accident near the place where she had been held.

He spent an hour at the firehouse writing down all the places the engines had gone from the time Kayla was taken to the time she was returned. Then he drove to each place, five in all, and scoped them out. All were in the old section of town; two were in residential areas. But there were still hundreds of places she could have been and heard the sirens equally loudly. If only she hadn't been blindfolded and he could have known whether or not she had seen the lights bouncing off the walls.

After a morning of free association list writing, trying to let his subconscious take over and sort clues, he came to the conclusion that his inherent sixth sense was failing him. The only thing that had occurred to him was that whoever was doing this had to have access to secured areas. The security office in the building and the elevator where one of the first mothers victimized had had to go down on a man, for one. And the quick mart where they'd discovered the monitor tape missing mere minutes after the robbery had been reported where the distraught mother had to flash her boobs. After mulling it over for a few minutes, it occurred to him that cleaning companies had unrestricted access.

He set up a team to research all the cleaning services that were used by all the locations where "ransom" activity had occurred. And unbelievably, that afternoon they came up with just one company.

The owner of the cleaning company had only one employee that she'd hired without proper references, a female crew member who had been with the company less than a year. But so far she'd had no complaints; none whatsoever, she had added with concern—except that the employee had just stopped showing up for work about two weeks ago.

When the owner went to find the file, it was missing, along with what Kel supposed had been a bogus copy of a social security card and a driver's license complete with picture. The copy of the application for bond insurance was also missing. The owner of the company said they knew the crew member only as Frances or Frankie and they had no idea where she lived or how to get in touch with her. She had always shown up on time and had been an ideal employee until she had just stopped coming in.

After Kel left their office, he thought hard about calling the Employment Commission and suggesting they investigate the company. Employers were supposed to have much better records than that. And it ticked him off royally that because they didn't, he'd hit the wall on the best lead they'd had so far. Except that the employee turned out to be

174

the wrong gender. After stewing about it for a few minutes, he thought better of reporting the company; if this had actually turned out to be their man, then it probably wouldn't have been the cleaning company's fault. The Voyeur was cunning and far too clever to leave those kinds of documents behind.

When the final report on the grass cuttings came in, Kel went to visit Thomas Ryan at the golf course where he worked. The report said the cuttings were uniform and came from a mower capable of cutting infinitesimally short pieces. And they were mostly rye with young Bermuda mixed in. He looked at several of the oversized golf bags in the pro shop—the tour bags, the ones that could accommodate a small, bound child.

Mr. Ryan was working at the counter and he looked far better than he had looked the night they had taken Toby home. Kel found himself feeling sorry for him. Thomas wasn't strong enough for Meggie and he suspected that he was having to deal with that. He had tried to find out Meggie's list of demands from the police since she wouldn't tell him herself. But they had refused to tell him anything. He didn't need to know, and now that Kel had had a chance to talk to the man when he was stone sober, he knew that Thomas was not the kind of man who could deal with knowing. He was the kind of man who would never forgive her for what she had done, regardless of motive. He'd never be able to put it aside. And Kel sensed a hollowness in Thomas as the man dealt with his futile chase for his ex-wife's affections.

"How many of this type of bag have you sold lately?"

"Lately? Meaning?" He was belligerent and it didn't appear that he cared to hide it. Nothing was going to make this man happy, and Kel found that he was no longer feeling sorry for him. He certainly came off as a self-serving jerk.

"The last six months."

"Probably one. We're off season now, that's more of a winter item."

"Who bought the one you sold?"

"A guy from New Hampshire. His clubs were lost on his flight down. They think they were stolen at the airport up north before they were loaded. The airline paid to replace everything. We even personalized the bag for him."

"You know for a fact that it went to New Hampshire?"

"Yeah, the airline came and picked it up when it was ready."

"No others sold that you know of?"

"Well none sold, but we did have a display model that we replaced. The one we had was getting a bit ratty looking. We rented it a few times and then took it off the floor."

"What happened to it?"

"If memory serves, I think the man who does our custodial work asked if he could take it."

Kel threw back his head and closed his eyes. He allowed himself the satisfaction of saying *bingo,* before plodding on.

"And who might that be?"

"I don't know his name. He comes here once a week, vacuums, dusts, and squeegees the windows."

"What's the name of the company?"

"Clean-All Cleaning. We've used them for years."

"Would his name be Francis or Frankie?"

"Yeah, I think so. Frankie, I think he goes by that."

Well, well, well. So much for the gender. So, was Frankie male or female? Was his madman actually a madwoman? Or was his madman masquerading as a woman? He was getting closer and he could feel his adrenaline kick in.

176

He drove back to old town and to the neighborhoods that had recently had a fire, and spent his lunch hour walking around looking for anything unusual, looking in the cars and trucks for a tour-sized golf bag. It was the break he needed. Unfortunately, it was not the break he got.

Chapter Twenty-one

*H*arold Francis Satterfield let the Penthouse fall from his fingers to the carpet and pushed against the back of the recliner. He slid into the comfortable position he often used when he pleasured himself. But first, he thought, closing his eyes, he had to slip into his fantasy world.

He never had sex with Gloria anymore. Not that he would. But she wouldn't let him anyway. Said she couldn't stand his slobbering kisses, his heavy body on top of her, and most of all, she couldn't abide his evil, devil-inspired lust. After what he'd done to her, she wanted nothing to do with him in a physical sense. And she certainly wouldn't tolerate his penchant for porn. Not the magazines, not the books, but most especially, not the videos. When she found one, she used to just toss it out; now she broke them, then pulled the tape out and burned them in the sink.

But it didn't matter. He didn't want Gloria anymore either. When they were dating she'd had what was referred to as a Rubinesque figure: full and lush, with large fleshy tits, meaty thighs, and a slightly rounded tummy. But it had all been tight then. Now everything sagged, was loose and floppy. She had no tone, even her earlobes were like mush, he thought with disdain. The woman had truly let herself go. Well, that was always the way when they got what they

178

wanted. He should never have put a ring on her finger, it was just like giving permission to a woman to let herself go.

Gloria had gained so much weight that even after showering he could still see dirt in the crease of her folds. The woman would never be clean again. The things she had done years ago to trap him she refused to do now — not that he blamed her, he had changed physically, too. He had a paunch and his hairline was starting to recede, but he didn't have jowls, not like Gloria. He would never consider ever going down on her again, or doing anything other than fucking her tits. She did have the biggest nipples he'd ever seen, he thought fondly. They reminded him more of a nipple on a baby bottle than any nipple he'd seen on any tit in all the hundreds of magazines he'd purchased.

He remembered one of the first women he had ever conjured up, a woman taken from a secret book of sex stories. A daydream of a woman with nubile, big tits, and her sex partner, who of course was himself, as the all-powerful and domineering boss. *A Man and His Sexretary,* he thought and nodded with a devilish smile spreading over his face. He hadn't read that story in quite some time. It used to be his favorite. It was in one of his first dirty story books, the ones where the meet and greet and the act of plowing the woman all happened within ten smut-filled pages. The pages of the book were dog-eared and soft from use. He put his hand behind him and dug around in the inner mechanism of the recliner until he found the soft, worn paperback. It was losing its pages and the cover was torn in two places. It had a big grape jelly stain on the cover page, a stain it had acquired from the trash can he'd had to fish it out of when Gloria had found it, thumbed through it, and thrown it away in disgust.

A wicked grin spread across his grizzled face as his hand went to his zipper. He settled into his seat to read his favorite story: *A Man and His Sexretary.*

179

ॐ

"Mrs. Rowe, I've interviewed over thirty women for this position, but none have come close to pleasing me as you have."

"So, I have the job?" she asked, unable to hide her smile.

"You have the job. That is if you want it."

"Oh, I want it!" she crooned.

"You don't even know what it is yet."

"It's the job of your secretary. That's what was advertised."

"Yes, it is indeed the job of my secretary. But the duties I require aren't typical."

"It's a generous salary so I assumed there was a bit more to it, some traveling perhaps?"

"Oh, there's definitely a bit more to it and some travel will be involved from time to time, but that will be later. The office duties I am referring to are exceptional."

"I assure you, Mr. Coxworthy, I am quite capable. I have been very well trained as an executive secretary. I am qualified for anything you need me to do."

His eyes dropped from her pretty young face to her full breasts, jutting out so far that they created a ledge for the lacy jabot of her silk blouse to rest on. "You are indeed qualified. But let me fully outline your duties before you accept the position."

"I don't understand."

"You will. I need a secretary, one who has the normal, usual office skills: typing; taking dictation; some filing; greeting clients; answering phone calls and taking messages; arranging meetings; scheduling trips and the like."

"No problem."

"Well there is a slight problem. I need a few other services, ones I'm willing to pay quite handsomely for."

"The paper said $35,000 a year, that's a salary commensurate with my skills."

"The paper was wrong. The position pays $70,000 a year."

She gasped and her hand went to her throat as she croaked out, "What?"

"As I told you, I need other duties from you. I find I am most creative and able to work more efficiently if I have a topless and sometimes bottomless woman in front of me."

"Pardon?" she asked unable to believe her ears.

"I like to see titties while I work. Nice, big, plump ones. You seem to have those."

She blushed full red and blinked her eyes. Then swallowed. Surely she wasn't hearing right, this must be some kind of joke. "I'm married Mr. Coxworthy, it says so on my application."

"I know that. And so am I. This is not about having sex. I have no need of sexual favors from you other than you exposing yourself to me, at anytime I desire, in any position I propose, for whatever whim I'm having at the moment. I want to be able to view you partially or completely unclothed here in my office anytime I wish, for as long as I wish it. For that I am willing to pay you double. Your husband does not need to know this. Believe me, I don't tell my wife."

"I'm sorry Mr. Coxworthy, I can't take the position," she said, trying to keep the tremble out of her voice. "That would be like having sex. I can only permit my husband to see me naked."

"It's not like having sex. Nude models in magazines let pictures be taken of them all the time and they aren't having sex are they? They're just letting others appreciate their charms, and many of them are married—in fact, a lot of them are photographed by their husbands. Remember Bo Derek and her husband John Derek? His pictures of her when she was only eighteen made her famous. You'll still be faithful to your husband. I am not asking you for sex, although there may be times that I ask if I can touch you in certain places. But I won't if you say not to. And I will never hurt you or ask you to do anything you don't want to do. Are you certain about this? This is a lot of money you're passing up. Seventy thousand a year is a formidable salary. It would take you at least fifteen years to work yourself into that kind of salary in the conventional manner."

He had a point there. It was an incredible amount of money. She and Robert would be able to afford to buy a house this year and a baby could come next. They would actually be able to put money away!

"I would be too embarrassed."

"You would at first. But then you'd get used to it. I assure you that after a while it would be old hat. Not much to it."

"I don't think so. I think I would always be nervous and uncomfortable with it. Heck, I still dress in the bathroom and I've been married for three years."

"That's your husband's fault. He hasn't made you comfortable in your body. You have a luscious body. You deserve to show it off. And I am willing to pay for the privilege of seeing it."

"If you don't mind my asking, what happened to your last secretary? And did she . . . you know, did she . . . "

"She left to go on maternity leave. She was with me for over a year, and yes, she did disrobe for me. Often, one might say. Daily even, except that we only work a four day work week." He didn't bother to mention that the child she was carrying was his.

"Only four days?"

He grinned at her. He knew he had her now. "Off Friday, Saturday, and Sunday, and of course, holidays. And we have great benefits also, health, dental, a 401—all included."

"All included?"

"Yes. Even the 401. I contribute $500 a pay period after you've been with me for three months." *And I mean with me*, he thought to himself. Sure, he always said they didn't have to have sex with him, but after a while, they always wanted to.

"I'll have to think about it."

"I can't afford you the luxury. I have other women vying for the job, I have to hire someone. Today's the day I set aside to do that. Now, do you want the job or not?"

Jeez Louise! What a spot. A dream job was just dumped in her lap. Except for that one little thing. What would Robert say if she were to ask him? Oh hell, she couldn't ask him! But maybe he would say yes, if she were able to. That was a hell of a lot of money. And how bad could it be? She looked around the very large office, taking in the two luxurious seating groupings—a contemporary leather sofa and love seat on one side, cozy barrel chairs and another sofa on the other, the conference area with its long, shiny teak table, and the kitchenette area with the adjoining bathroom. It truly was private.

He read her mind. "I can always close the drapes unless you'd prefer I left them open."

The huge panes of glass looked out at the city skyline. The expanse of blue sky filled most of the area as the closest office building was a block away. Still, she probably would feel better with the drapes closed. What was she thinking? She wasn't going to do this!

As if sensing her mood, he pushed a button on his desk and the drapes that had been tucked to the sides of the wall began to move in toward the center of the room. With his other finger he flicked a series of switches, and lights came on all over the room, softly illuminating the different areas and compensating for the lost light.

"It'll be cozy. Just the two of us." Another finger pressed a button and she heard the lock click in the office door behind her. "Private. No one will ever bother us. I don't allow it. It's my company and everybody knows my rules."

"If I were to take the job, when would I begin?" she asked timidly.

"Now. I would like you to take the job right now. He nodded to a pad at the corner of the desk and handed her a pen. "I have some dictation we can work on right this very minute."

"Naked?"

"Well yes, one of us anyway. I don't get naked, unless of course you insist on it. And actually I don't need you naked today, just topless. Strip from the waist up and we can get to work."

"You're serious aren't you?"

"Of course I'm serious. Now either accept the position and take off your blouse and your bra, or decline so I can continue the interviewing process." He was getting impatient and it showed.

She dropped her head and stared into her lap, wondering if she could even do this. Then she thought about the previous secretary and how she was on maternity leave to have her baby. She'd wanted a baby for three years now, but Robert kept saying they didn't have the money for a baby yet. She lifted her head and pushed her shoulders back. "Okay, I'll do it. I'll take the job."

"Good. You're welcome to disrobe in the bathroom or I'd love watching you strip right there."

She met his hot eyes with hers and wanted to cringe. He was not a bad looking man, in fact, some would consider him handsome. But she didn't feel anything for him, no attraction, no lust, and certainly no love. How was she going to do this? She opted for removing her clothes in the bathroom, but then realized that meant she'd have to leave them in there. And in case she had second thoughts about this, it would be better to have them close at hand. She put her purse on the floor, took the pad from the corner of the desk, and reached for the pen he was handing her.

"Welcome aboard, Mrs. Rowe. Now show me your titties."

She did cringe then, and he laughed. "Sorry, the vulgar talk goes along with the job. You'll get used to it."

She sat there and just stared at him until he had to prompt her. "Uh, unbutton Mrs. Rowe, if you please. I'd like to get started."

Slowly her hand inched its way to the lacy jabot at her throat. She undid the button holding it on and let it fall into her lap. Then keeping her eyes on the green floor-length drapes behind her new boss' desk, she undid each button. When they were all undone, she spread the plackets wide and let him view her in her plunging bra.

"Lovely," he murmured. "Absolutely lovely. If any cleavage should boast diamonds, it certainly should be yours." He was referring to the small mustard seed encased in a glass bead that dangled between her breasts. "I hope your husband rectifies that one day. If not, in time, I surely will," he whispered.

He was so reverent about her breasts that it humbled her. Here was a man who deserved to see her breasts, a man who could appreciate them. Robert didn't often seem to, and lately he referred to them as her "jugs." Now what woman would like that?

"I can't wait to see them in all their glory," he said, hinting that he was ready for her to carry on.

She smiled over at him as she tried to build the courage to bare her breasts completely.

She removed her blouse, reached both hands behind her back, and unhooked the clasp of her bra. She felt the elastic of the bra go loose and sighed before crossing her arms over each other and covering her breasts. Then she pulled the straps off her shoulders before letting the bra fall to her wrists. She hung her head in shame.

"Move your hands," he said, and the huskiness of his voice caused her to look back up at him.

As she moved her hands to her lap, she watched his hungry eyes feasting on her.

"Luscious. You are simply luscious. Great tits, Mrs. Rowe."

He sat there for many minutes just staring, taking her in, and she could feel her nipples tightening, puckering into tight little buds. And it wasn't because she was cold. Somehow, this was what . . .? Erotic? Yes, that was it exactly. She felt wanton, but beautiful. By his reaction, he was making her feel more beautiful then she'd ever felt in her life.

"Pick up the pad and pen. It's time to get to work."

She did as he asked, then was amazed as the words flowed out of him. He dictated a letter that was amazing in its clarity, succinct in its message, and compelling in its closing. Good God, the man had an exceptional way of putting words together. The fact that he said he needed her for the stimulation required to write it made it all the more thrilling.

They worked for an hour. She wrote his thoughts on her pad using shorthand and he mulled over his ideas, never once taking his eyes from her bared breasts. Once, he paused between sentences to ask, "Are you cold, or just excited?" and he tilted her a smile as he lifted an eyebrow in her direction before going on.

After the fourth letter, he said, "Let's take a break. Would you mind getting me a cup of coffee? There should still be some on the warmer plate. I take it black."

She bent to retrieve her blouse from the carpet.

"Oh no. Serve me topless and let me watch those beauties jiggle. I couldn't stand it if you were to cover them now."

She slowly stood and made her way over to the coffee maker, found the cups, and poured them each some coffee. She was conscious of his eyes on her and even though he had been looking at her for over an hour this way, she blushed. She looked down at the cups as she walked back and saw her big breasts swaying with her movements. This was vulgar, she thought. And wicked as sin. She took the mugs over to the work area and walked around his desk to hand him his. He remained sitting, although he did swivel his seat to get a better look at her breasts close up. While it unnerved her, it also excited her. She could feel her nipples reaching out for something. A touch, a lick, anything. She was becoming aroused and it scared her.

He took the cup from her hand, careful to stroke her fingers as the cup was passed to him. It sent a shiver though her.

"Sit, we'll sip our coffee for a few minutes, then get back to work." He was motioning to the edge of his desk, patting it to indicate where he meant for her to sit. Much closer than she had been in the chair on the other side of his desk.

She backed herself up to the desk and lifted her bottom until she sat squarely on the desk in front of him. She was wearing a short skirt and it became much shorter as she slid back onto the desktop.

"Spread your legs and let me see your underwear," he whispered over the top of his coffee cup. She watched him take a sip and noticed his full, ripe lips. He sure was sensual, she thought as she complied, and spread her thighs just the barest amount. He backed his chair up and angled it in again so she was now directly in front of him, her lap right in his line of vision.

"Wider."

She moved her thighs further apart. Her knees were now almost pointing at the opposite walls.

"Pink. Pretty pink. With lace. Nice."

She shivered and to cover up, she took a sip of her coffee.

"One day soon, you're going to show me your pink, the pink inside your sweet nether lips."

She choked on the coffee.

"What are you thinking right now?" he asked.

She sucked in a deep breath. "I'm thinking that this morning when I dressed for this interview, I should have paid more attention to my lingerie than to my resume."

Her crooked smile told him she was teasing, almost flirting. It was working, he thought, it always did.

"Never occurred to you to wear your finest?"

"These are my finest. They match at least."

"Write down your sizes, I'm going to have to buy you some really nice stuff."

"And how will I explain that to my husband?"

"The fact that another man is buying you sexy lingerie or that you're wearing it?"

"Both. Though I doubt he'd even notice if I paraded around in front of him in it."

"What a shame, a waste in fact. You have gorgeous tits and I'm betting your pussy is superb, too. But let's get back to work, I'm on a roll." He put his coffee cup down and his fingertips brushed along the outer edge of her exposed thigh. She thought she was going to melt and slink off the desk onto the floor.

Then she looked down into his face, and the heated look in his eyes mesmerized her.

"Why don't you take your panties off, but leave your skirt on? I'll ask you to pull your skirt up in a few minutes, but for now it'll be enough just knowing you're not wearing any panties under it.

He helped her off the desk, then held her by the waist to balance her while she ran her hand up her hip and snagged the elastic, then slowly wiggled out of her panties. She noticed his eyes dancing as her breasts jiggled and she so wanted him to lean in and clamp his lips on one. Or both. His breath fanned them as she bent to pick up her panties and she thought she was going to die from the sensation as heat coursed through her, flushing her face.

"Don't be embarrassed. You're beautiful. You're in the wrong profession, Mrs. Rowe. You should have been a stripper. You would have made history. You put Pamela Anderson to shame."

God, the things he said! And even though she was topless and going commando under a short skirt in his office, she was suddenly jealous of his wife. Her eyes flicked over to a picture on the credenza behind his desk. A stunningly beautiful woman smiled back at her from a polished silver frame. What must she be like, she wondered. What must their sex life be like?

She was starting to feel guilty for her thoughts when he said, "She thinks I'm insatiable, and maybe I am. I can't get enough of looking at beautiful women. Some men need more than one woman. I guess I'm one of them." He indicated for her to take the seat opposite him, the one that didn't have the desk as a barrier. Then he started dictating another letter, another wonderfully composed letter that astounded her. Halfway through, he switched gears and she didn't notice his mind wasn't on his work anymore until she realized she had written, "spread your legs wide for me," on her steno pad.

She looked over at him and saw that he had a look that said, "Don't mess with me, just do as I say." It was a hard look, unyielding as he commanded her to do his bidding, and it was sexier than all get out. She let her knees fall wide as she sat in the armchair not four feet from where he sat, watching her.

"I can't see what I need to see. Scoot your bottom to the end of the chair."

Very self-conscious now, she hesitated.

"Do it and do it now!"

Instantly, she moved forward, so much forward that it caused her to slump in the chair, showing him oh so much more than she had intended.

"Excellent, excellent." His eyes burned into her as he lasered them into the area between her spread thighs. "A nice fair blonde color. I like that, less hair to diminish the view."

She closed her eyes tightly and mentally took in her position. Here she was, her breasts no longer squarely in the center of her chest as they fell off to the side. And just what was her position? She was practically on her back, knees bent and splayed wide giving him an unadorned view of her womanhood. He'd noticed that she was a true blonde, from this range it would be hard not to. She cringed as she realized he was seeing much more of her than she wanted him to. Yet, she didn't close her legs one iota.

His eyes burned into her, she could feel the heat of them on her, there, between her legs. Then he started dictating again. For the next fifteen minutes he dictated nonstop while she wrote the rapidly flowing words in shorthand on the pad poised in the air above her face. Then he ended the letter, stood, and walked over to where she half sat, half slid out of the chair. Before she knew what was happening, he had knelt on one knee in front of her and was examining her up close, so intimately she could feel his breath on her thighs.

She didn't move, didn't want to upset him. He was doing something to her, something mental, and somehow the gradual . . . what was it? Was it foreplay of some kind? And what was with that incredible genius that spewed forth while he viewed her? He examined her minutely as if he had taken her prisoner and thereby was entitled to this graphic sight. She didn't know why, but suddenly she wanted desperately to please him. She needed to hear his words of praise.

"Let's pull that skirt up and out of the way, shall we?" Never taking his eyes from her.

She should object. She should refuse. But she couldn't. She simply reached down and with both hands inched it up over her hips until it was bunched at her waist. And now she was topless and bottomless, showing him her pussy, blatantly wide open.

"Wider. I need to see more of you. Put your feet on the arms of the chair. Come, I'll help you."

And before she could protest, he had slipped off her clunky, high-heeled sandals, cradled each soft foot in a warm hand and lifted them to the arms of the side chair she sat in. And now she was exactly as she would be for her obstetrician. Splayed open as far a woman could possibly be. Showing him everything she had.

"Yes, I knew you'd be lovely here, too. I didn't know you'd be so moist though, that's a pleasant surprise."

He was mocking her and she knew it. He knew the effect he was having on her. How could he not?

She looked down, trying to see his face, to register his reaction, but the sight of her open legs, her spread thighs and his face staring between them, caused a rush of sensations. She felt herself flooding down there, and he chuckled.

"Show your pink, Mrs. Rowe. Take your fingers, put them between your legs and spread your slick lips. Show me the pink of your love tunnel."

191

"Mr. Coxworthy, really! This is going too far!"

"No, I don't think so," he whispered, as his hands went to cup her knees to hold them open. "Don't take this pleasure from me. I am in a visual heaven. Your cunt is incomparable. I've never seen one quite so lovely. Or so denuded. Your blonde tufts hide nothing. Everything you have, everything you possess is within my view and it is quite perfect. Please, spread your cunt lips for me and show me your pink. Please."

His plea was so soft and so mewling that she was humbled by it. He truly seemed to be worshipping her. And she loved it. She reached her hands down and deftly spread her nether lips for him.

"Wider," he breathed and she felt the warm moistness of it caress her.

"Is that the only word you know?"

"It's the only word that matters right now. Wider."

She used two fingers on each hand and pressed her protruding lips even further apart.

"Ahhh. There it is. Nirvana. Your sweet cunty hole. It is exquisite. More lovely than I could ever have imagined."

She dropped her head back, as she was almost completely horizontal, and looked up at the ornate ceiling. She couldn't believe it. Here she was, buck naked on a chair, with her feet on the arms of it, her knees as wide as they could possibly be, and her fingers were holding the most intimate part of herself open for a man who was a virtual stranger—her new boss, a man she'd known less than a few hours!

She closed her eyes and a tear slipped out. Yet, she didn't want him to stop looking at her or praising her.

"Slide forward now and lift your bottom up, I want to see your bum hole, too."

"Good God No!"

"Good God Yes! He's made a Venus here, and I want to see every inch of her."

Helpless against his words, she lifted her bottom up and slid forward until he had guided her to the edge of the chair. His hands on her hips, then on her bottom, were warm and smooth and she reveled in his touch.

This was the ultimate. Her breasts, their nipples hard and engorged were his for the viewing; so was everything she owned, her pussy, her asshole. They were all his now. He was seeing all of her, and she felt like she belonged to him.

"I need a picture of this," he whispered.

"No, no, no," she whimpered.

"Yes. You must allow me one picture."

"Please, no."

He bent forward and touched his lips to her. She sobbed her pleasure as his lips touched the nubbin at the top of her slit. She cried out and convulsed when he sucked her clit between his lips and made her come.

When the aftershocks had worn off, he moved back and clicked off a few pictures with the small digital camera he'd had in his pocket.

"Lovely, just lovely," he whispered as he took more close-ups. She whimpered and cried softly but didn't dare stop him. Didn't dare move her fingers from showing him all of her, opening herself for his hot gaze.

"Tomorrow, we're entertaining a small delegation from Japan. I'll give you a bonus of ten thousand dollars if you greet them topless and then let me show them your cunt before they leave. They don't speak English, but this, these tits of yours and this pussy, it speaks a universal language. Wider, use your fingers to spread your lips again, I need one more shot. I need a shot of your pink. Show me your sweet pink again, my beautiful, sexy secretary."

She was crying uncontrollably now, yet she was

doing as he asked.

He knew he owned her, body and soul. He could do whatever he wanted to her and she'd be helpless to his demands. Women wanted to be viewed and told they were lovely. They were so predictable, he thought with scorn. It was so easy to get their clothes off. They were so vain. He left her gaping open for him and walked over to his desk. He hit a control button and the drapes separated in the center and began moving to the opposite sides of the room.

"Let's get a little more light on the matter, shall we?" He sauntered back, cocked his head, and stood looking at her with hot eyes before repositioning her chair, pulling her forward, and facing her toward the window. "Yes, you're definitely going to make a lot of bonus money this year." *And maybe my colleagues with their high-powered telescopes in the office building across the way will enjoy the new view on this side of the street. As long as he praised her and told her how beautiful she was, she would display herself for him. And for others, many, many others.*

⚬⚬

There in the ratty old recliner, he finally managed to come. His meager load spurted out of him into his waiting hand and he cried out. It was not the orgasm he had wanted, it never was anymore, but it would suffice. Yes, it would do. He dropped the booklet to the carpet and sighed. He did better with the visual. The visual of "his women," doing his bidding, the women he made bare it all, for him. Damn Internet. It was always going down just when he needed it most. He missed his girls. But now it was time for a new one.

Chapter Twenty-two

Caison was sitting behind his desk, studying his sermon notes when she came in. A woman who looked familiar knocked timidly on the door, walked inside, and slowly shut the door behind her. "Reverend, do you have a minute? I just have to talk to somebody."

He put aside his book as he looked over at her. The sun from the window behind him lit her face and he thought to himself, *Now I recognize her.* She attended the ten-thirty service on Sundays, sat in one of the last rows and was always alone, always regal, and always the first to leave. It was rare that he was able to get to the back of the church in time to shake her hand and wish her a good morning.

Now that she was close, he could see that she had been crying. Her beautiful, pale, porcelain face was a stark contrast to the vivid green eyes that were framed by dark, feathered lashes and her coral-colored lips. *Natural,* he thought. He couldn't detect any signs of makeup. She was angelic in her perfection, in her petiteness.

"Please have a seat. It's Mrs. Lawson isn't it?"

"Yes, Paige Lawson." She took the seat he indicated and pulled it closer to the desk. She propped her elbows on the edge of his desk, framed her fingers so that they pressed in at her temples while her thumbs held up her jaw.

"Mrs. Lawson? Are you okay?"

"No, Reverend, I am not. Nor will I ever be again, I fear. It's my son, Joshua. He's missing, he's been taken."

"Missing? Taken?" He didn't even know she had a son, she had always been alone in the service. "Do I know your son?"

"He's in the nursery when I'm in the service, so you wouldn't remember him. He's four, he's autistic and he's gone! He must be so scared!" she sobbed and her hands closed in over her face.

He stood abruptly and came around to where she sat. Unsure of what to do, he sat in the chair next to her and pulled on her shoulders until she came into his arms.

"There, there. Why don't you tell me what this is all about. I'm sure I can help." He was also sure that this was just another domestic situation, another hotheaded, estranged husband with an ax to grind—using the kid as ammo.

"Oh, Pastor Cayce, I hope so! I don't know who else I can go to."

He handed her a tissue from the box on his desk and instructed her to blow. Then he reached behind him to the water cooler and filled a tiny cup for her. "Here, drink this and breathe slowly. Full breaths, that's it. Now tell me about your son. Who took him, his father?"

She shook her head violently then told him about Joshua and how he'd been taken from his bedroom that morning while she was in the shower getting ready for work. How she'd found the ransom note propped on his night stand. She told him she had no place else to turn. Her husband had been killed in Iraq four years ago and her family and friends were all on the west coast. She had just relocated to the area for her job and knew practically no one. And she asked him to pray for her son and for her, and for what she was about to do.

196

Cayce closed his eyes tightly, for now, he knew without a doubt who had her son; the kidnappings were all over the television news and in every newspaper.

"Let me see the note."

"He says he'll kill Josh if I involve the police."

"I'm not the police," he said succinctly as he stood and went behind his desk to the credenza. He grabbed his reading glasses and went back to stand over her. He was holding out his hand and it was clear that he wasn't going to let her leave until she gave it to him. "I can't help if I don't know everything."

"It has awful things in it!"

"Awful things you have to do?" he asked softly.

"Yes," she moaned and her hands wrapped around her waist as she doubled over and sobbed.

"Give me the note. Let's see what has to be done," he said as he put the studious-looking glasses low on the bridge of his nose. His voice was so tender and so soft that she thought for a minute that he could actually, possibly help. And he looked so smart, like he knew positively everything.

She dug in her purse for the crumpled letter and handed it to him, then dropped her head while he unfolded it and silently read.

He read for a minute, his brow furrowed, then he dropped heavily into the seat beside her.

When she looked up, he was staring at her with a tender expression and quiet, patient eyes. They were light brown and she wanted to swim into them and leave everything else behind.

He took her hand between his and rubbed it gently. "We don't have a lot of time. We have to get the equipment we'll need at Circuit City, take care of the pictures, and then get over to the beach before sunrise. We'd better get started." He dropped her hand and went back to the other side of his desk.

She looked up at him in confusion. He was fishing in his drawer for something, after a few seconds, he pulled out car keys.

"Oh," she said as she realized the help he was offering. "I couldn't . . . I just wanted prayers. I couldn't . . . we couldn't . . . ."

"Yes, we can. Yes, you will. You have no choice, Paige. You have no choice. But I'll help you. Together we'll do this, we'll get Joshua back."

She started sobbing again, mortified by what they were talking about doing.

He tried to change the subject. "I don't suppose you have any of the equipment we'll need, a computer, printer, DSL, digital camera?"

"No," she whispered. "I don't even know how to use any of those."

He fished in a different drawer and brought out a checkbook.

"We should take both cars. I'll meet you there."

He lifted his head and looked over at her. She had a stunned expression on her face, her eyes were wide and her jaw open.

"You did come here for help, did you not?"

"Well, yes . . . but I didn't think . . . ."

"That I would help you?"

"Well, not in this way . . . ."

"What other choices do you have? For that matter what other choice do I have?"

She blinked, closed her mouth and stood. "I . . . I . . . don't know. None I guess."

"Then let's just do what has to be done and get it over with. God will help us. He's already helped you, by bringing you to me. You can trust Him to be there for both of us, and you can trust me to do what has to be done to get your son back."

Pastor Cayce was legendary within his church family for going all-out to help his parishioners. He was devoted to his flock and had once even flown to Alaska to bring a runaway teenager home. It was a pledge he had made long ago, to make himself available to anyone who needed him. He was a shepherd in the truest sense. This was his calling, his ministry, to be there during a crisis in whatever capacity he was needed.

He pressed a series of numbers on the phone and picked up the receiver. When the person on the other line answered, he calmly informed the church secretary that he would be out of the office for the rest of the day. He told her something had just come up and he needed to handle it right away, and that if he was needed, they should track down the assistant pastor.

He took Paige by the elbow and led her out of the building and to her car. "Follow me, but in case I lose you meet me at the Circuit City on the north end of Market Street. Do you know where that is? It's close to the IHOP."

When she nodded, he reminded her to buckle up and then he shut the door. He sprinted to his SUV that was parked on the opposite side of the lot. He looked like he could run forever and never tire.

As he got into his truck and started it, he reflected on Paige. She looked like she was in shock, and he wondered if he should have sought medical treatment for her. But it couldn't be helped, she probably was in shock; but it was probably the inaction and the worry more than anything that was making her look so fragile. He thought about her as he drove, trying to keep her in sight in his rearview mirror. Hell of a time to travel the length of Market, he thought as he glanced at his watch. Three-thirty. They really didn't have a lot of time. What the hell had she been doing all day? He took out the note he had stuffed into his sport coat pocket and unfolded it. At the stoplights he reread it.

Paige Lawson: I have Joshua. If you want him back, don't go to the cops, they're as useless as tits on a bull anyway. By now you should know the drill. Do what I ask—you'll get your son back. Don't and you won't.
First: Send me five digital pictures of you naked in jpeg attachments to: randymanseesu@hotmail.com The poses you send must be as follows: 1. Full frontal, with your hands folded behind your head making your titties stick out like a pinup girl. 2. Back view with your hair up and wearing high heels a la Betty Grable, don't forget to look over your shoulder and put one hand on your hip and smile. 3. Sit at the edge of a chair and spread your knees as wide as you can get them, then put your arms behind your head, elbows as far back as you can get them, and arch your back so your titties are high on your chest. 4. Same as three but slide forward until your butt's almost off the chair, I want to see both of your sweet little holes in this one. 5. Lay on a table, bring your knees up to your chest, then spread them as wide as possible. Use your fingers to spread your cunt lips. Make this one a close up. I want to see into your little rosy hole.
Second: Bring a man to Wrightsville Beach Saturday at 6:00 A.M. Use the access closest to the pier. Find an orange marker staked at the dune line on the northern side, attached will be a string. Walk it down to the water and where the string ends, go down on him. Have him face northeast. Surprise! You'll be in the path of the Weather Cam. I know you don't know any men locally, so whomever you manage to find will

certainly be a stranger. Let's make this fun. As I know you're quite shy, kiss him first to break the ice before you suck him dry and swallow his cum.

Third: Print a hundred copies of picture number five mentioned above. Put them under the windshields of the cars in your church parking lot this Sunday morning during the late service. Print your name across the top so everyone will know whose pussy they're looking at when they come out.

Do all three and your boy will be home in time for Sunday dinner.

Forget something? Forget him!

The Voyeur

Cayce shook his head and wondered about the evilness of this man. How could anyone have a heart so black and a mind so wicked? In rereading the demands, he picked up on the fact that the man was quite educated. The words were all spelled correctly, the punctuation proper, the wording almost impeccable. How many people knew how to use whomever in a sentence? And he bet even fewer knew how to abbreviate ante meridiem properly, that is was considered proper to capitalize the A and the M? He envisioned a sleazy academic or a well-rounded businessman. That was the trouble with porn, it pervaded through to every segment of the population. Rich, poor, young, old. If you could pay for the book, you could lower yourself and degrade women at the same time.

He folded the note, replaced it in his pocket, and took a moment to say a prayer for both him and Paige. The next few hours were going to be awful for both of them and he hoped and prayed that Paige could get through them without falling apart.

He tried to think from a woman's perspective for

a moment and couldn't imagine anything much worse, other than possibly the loss of her child. Or her husband. And she had already experienced that one. He prayed hard that in the end, she wouldn't be experiencing all three—the denigration of her body, the passing of her husband, and her son's murder. She was going to have to at least deal with two of those scenarios, and he hoped fervently that she was a strong woman. Though from what he'd seen so far, he had his doubts. The Voyeur knew she was shy, how did he know that? And how did he know she knew no one locally, at least no man well enough to perform oral sex on him?

He put his turn signal on and pulled into the parking lot for Circuit City. Then he sat and pondered the logistics for a minute. He had a computer hooked to DSL, a printer, and he also had a digital camera. If they went to his townhouse instead of to her place, what exactly would they need? She pulled up alongside him and he managed to smile over at her. Then he picked up his checkbook from the seat, got out of his truck, and went to open her door.

"Let's take a minute to regroup," he said and leaned back against her vehicle. "If we go to my place," he looked up just in time to see her cringe, "we can save some money and some time. Plus I'm pretty sure we couldn't get a DSL up and running fast enough. By the way, what have you been doing all day? When did you find out Joshua had been taken?"

"I was getting ready for work. I was going in late today. It was my turn to work the ten to seven shift. When I read the note, I just fell apart. I tried to remember every person I've met since coming to Wilmington. I thought since he knew so much about me, that surely I must know him."

"I gather that didn't do any good?"

"No, I can't think of who it could possibly be, but I know I wasted a lot of time trying to figure it out."

"You thought someone you'd met was capable of this?" he gestured to the note.

"I don't know. I just didn't know what to do. At first, I decided to go to the police. It would have been so much easier to just let them find him."

"What changed your mind?"

"He's all I've got. I just couldn't take the chance."

He unfolded the note and scanned it quickly. He explained what would be needed using computer language she didn't understand. But every time he mentioned putting pictures on smart cards, downloading pictures to his computer, sending jpeg attachments of pictures, and photocopying pictures, she not only cringed, she reddened. He was talking about pictures of her. Naked pictures of her.

It was dawning on them how they were going to spend the evening and it wasn't a comfortable feeling for either of them.

They would need a smart reader card and a reader to connect and convey the images to his computer, some ink, and possibly a tripod. He already had lots of paper. Not photo quality paper, but then they didn't want clear, sharp images now, did they?

"Paige," he said as he grabbed both her forearms and forced her to look into his eyes. God, she was so beautiful, so . . . pure looking. His mind instantly flitted and he saw her in some of the prescribed poses. He shook his head to force out the images that were beginning to crowd in. "Paige, with my camera, I believe there is a way I can set it up for you on a timer and you can be in the room alone for each shot. It'll require a tripod. Is that what you want? Would that make it better for you?"

She closed her eyes and simply nodded.

"Okay. Let's see if we can find one here. If not we'll go to a camera store." He wiped tears from her cheek with the back of his hand, then he took her hand in his and led her into the store. "Do you have any high heels like he described?"

When with a worried frown, she shook her head, he said, "Not to worry. We'll pass several consignment shops on the way to my house. One will have some vintage high heels, I'm sure of it. It won't matter if they fit or not."

At the register, she offered to pay, but he could see she was counting her cash very carefully, so he forced her to take the bills back. "Except for the tripod, I've been meaning to get this stuff anyway." He wrote a check and she noted that it was on his personal account.

As Paige watched him write the check out, she had the worst sensation in the pit of her stomach. He was treating her, almost like a man buying dinner before taking his date home, to his place, for the entertainment part of the evening. It sickened her to be thinking this way about Pastor Cayce. He was only being thoughtful, chivalrous in a very weird way. Her eyes followed his hand as he wrote out the check and she noticed the light sprinkling of hairs on his knuckles, the back of his hand, and his wrists. His skin was dark against the crisp white of the shirtsleeve that peeked out from his camel-colored sport coat. He was fair skinned, but tanned. He was tall and had an athletic build, and she wondered what he did to stay in shape.

She had noticed a wet suit in the back of his SUV and wondered if he surfed. She'd heard that surfing was a really popular sport here at the beach. It would certainly account for the flat stomach and the sun-bronzed color of his skin. Her eyes swept up to his face and she couldn't help but smile at his grim expression. His full lips were stretched thin and his firm jaw was set. While the cashier approved his check, he ran his long fingers through his sandy blonde hair. It was a bit long, renegade long, as though it were a statement. He wasn't your typical pastor, and maybe that was why she liked going to his services. Maybe that was why he had come to mind when she was at her wit's end. He was the only person she had been able to think of who might be able to help her, and now, she was glad she'd decided to go to him for help.

They left the store, stopped at two thrift shops, then she followed him to his townhouse off of South College. It was everything she thought a bachelor's place should be, and nothing like she thought a bachelor's place would be. The furnishings were exquisite, top of the line and formal, not contemporary, as she would have thought. Heavy, dark woods with thick bolsters and cushions, designed for comfort, not typical of what was normally found in a beach town. The decorator touches were everywhere, and she suddenly wondered about her pastor. What did they pay pastors in this town?

He saw her looking around and smiled. "My mother's touch. She has a hand in everything I do. We had some powerful arguments about some of the pieces, but in the interest of family harmony, I acquiesced. But I did finally manage to take her key away and send her back home to Asheville. When she showed up here with a crystal chandelier, I knew it was time to cut the apron strings." He smiled broadly and she was touched by the warm thoughts he was apparently thinking about his mother. Her own mother had died the year after her husband had, and her father was making the rounds working in the stockyards of Kansas.

Cayce placed his keys on the counter and walked into the kitchen. It was an open floor plan, every room on this level was visible except the master bedroom, the laundry room, the powder room, and the study. She'd looked at renting something similar to this, but it wasn't in her price range.

"Would you like something to drink, maybe even

something to eat?"

"Some water please, if you don't mind. I don't think I can eat. I just want to get this over. I want Josh back," she said on a sob.

He took her hand, walked her over to the massive sofa, and sat her down. Then he sat beside her and held her close to his side while she cried. Then she slept.

Ten minutes later, he gently eased her off him, laid her on the cushions, and went into his study to get everything ready.

Paige woke with a start and tried to remember where she was. The rich texture of the fabric on the sofa against her cheek wasn't familiar. The soft light coming from an elegant, tall, sculpted torchiere was somehow regal, yet inviting. She pushed herself up on her arms and stared around the room, and then she remembered where she was and why. A small sob escaped her. Instantly, Cayce appeared in the doorway, concern and caring on his face. He had taken off his sport coat and was in a white dress shirt, the sleeves rolled up to his elbows. The soft, pleated chinos he was wearing, as well as his tasseled loafers, made him look preppy and younger than she knew him to be.

"Hi," he said with a tiny smile. "You were sleeping so soundly, and I knew you needed it, so I didn't have the heart to disturb you."

She ran her fingers through her long, tousled curls and looked over at him. The worry in her eyes was evident and alarming. "What time is it?"

"Only seven. We have plenty of time. I have everything all set up. Would you like something to drink?"

"Could I have another glass of water?" she asked

"How about a glass of wine instead? You could use a little mellowing out before we begin, don't you think?"

"I rarely drink."

"Better yet," he said as he moved away from the doorway.

He walked over to a large, ornate piece of furniture. It looked like a Bombay chest of sorts, only much larger. He pulled a knob on the front, a shelf dropped down, and she saw a bar. Below, he opened a cabinet and she saw fully stocked wine racks.

"A Shiraz I think, soothing and mellow and good for the heart," he pronounced.

She watched him expertly uncork the bottle and pour some of the deep, rich burgundy colored liquid into two etched wine glasses. They had a medieval flair to them, oversized heavy crystal goblets with long ornate stems. Then he walked over to where she sat and handed her one.

Her fingers stroked the beveled glass and he smiled. "Another of my mother's contributions. She has impeccable taste don't you think? She would have loved living during the Baroque period."

"They're very nice, quite beautiful." Oh, to have only this on her mind, she thought. Admiring beautiful stemware, sipping vintage wine and being with a man she could talk to.

He took a moment to study her while sipping his wine. Speaking of beautiful, she was that. She still had the flush of sleep about her, but her eyes were bright and alert. She had the most incredible green eyes, flecked with brown and fringed with sable lashes that the soft lighting turned to burnished gold. Her lips, plump in all the right places, were a pale peach, and the natural color of her skin was fresh and smooth, devoid of makeup. He could see that at one time she'd had some hair spray or mousse in her hair as it spiked and defied gravity in a few places. Lovely hair, thick and lustrous. A coppery brown in this light, it had held more honeyed tones earlier in the day.

He wished he knew more about her. He wished he'd asked her out when he'd first noticed her, and he wished they didn't have to do this.

"Tell me about Joshua. How severe is his autism?"

She blinked and focused on her wine glass. He saw her eyes cloud over momentarily, then brighten with love. "He's so sweet. A wonderful little boy. Full of energy at times and then quiet at others. He doesn't talk as much as kids his age, but he has a great vocabulary. He's learning to read a little and he loves every kind of furry animal, especially raccoons for some reason." She smiled at the memory of him sleeping in his own bed with Cuddles, his raccoon, tucked up under his chin.

"He's good with numbers, and showing some signs of being creative, but he's not very good with people yet. Kids his age take a lot longer to warm up to him than they should because he gives out the wrong signals at first. He went through a biting spell at his last daycare. But we nipped that in the bud," she said and then chuckled at her pun. "He's responding wonderfully to chelation therapy and since we caught it early, his doctor thinks he could be very close to normal in just a few years."

"Chelation therapy?"

"It's when metals are removed from the diet. Joshua's blood, urine, and hair tests show he has toxic levels of mercury, arsenic, and aluminum. But he's deficient in zinc, calcium, and vitamin C. He won't get his pills now!" she sobbed.

He reached over and gripped her forearm. "Was he close to his father?"

"He only saw his father three times. And those times, I'm afraid, were too full of family and friends for them to get close. And he was too young. I guess now, it's probably better off that way. But he does seem to like men better than women. Women tend to be bossy with him, men seem to take him more in stride."

"So how do you think he's fairing right now?"

"I don't know. He scares easily and I'm sure he has no idea what's going on."

"Does he have any other health problems?"

"No. Sometimes he sleepwalks, but I've read that this . . . this Voyeur keeps his hostages bound." She whimpered and he moved the glass closer to her lips.

"Drink. We're not going to start until I can get you at least a little bit snookered."

"In case I'm in no condition to remember later, thank you," she whispered.

"You're welcome. It's my job though, to help people in need."

"Why did he let this happen?"

"Who, God?"

"Yes. Things were hard enough on us as it was."

"This is the devil's hand, Paige, not God's. God is with you now, He bears your pain and suffering. We don't know how this will end, but you have to know that He loves you, and that for all eternity, you and Joshua are His. He is fighting for you, just as you will fight to get Joshua back. He is a father Himself and He knows how much you are hurting right now. And so do I. Somehow He's brought us together to handle this and we can't let Him or Joshua down."

"I don't know how I'm going to get through this."

"It's just flesh you know. A part of you that won't follow you into eternity. Your spirit will remain, but you'll get a whole new body, a perfect body that there's no shame in. There will be no reason for anyone to covet it or to abuse it."

"Or to want to leer at it," she said with contempt.

"I know that this will be very hard for you to accept.

And even in years to come, it will always haunt you. But the guilt of doing nothing and letting Joshua die would be far worse for you to live with. This, you can overcome."

"You say that. But it's not you."

"It will be tomorrow at sunrise."

Her face burned crimson. She had forgotten all about that.

"Oh, my God."

"Seems we all have a role to play. I can only hope none of my parishioners go on line to check the weather on the beach."

"Oh, Jesus!" she said as her hands covered her face. "Is that what could happen? Could we really be on the air? On TV?"

He reached over and, using gentle fingers, removed one of the hands that covered her face. Then he bent to look at her. "Probably not. They have a delay on those things and I would imagine that somebody's monitoring it all the time."

"Do you think that could be him?"

"It could be."

"Are we making a mistake by not involving the police?"

"I don't think so."

"We have his e-mail address. They could probably find him with that."

"He knows that. He's probably planned for that contingency."

"I guess you're right. I'm not going to get out of this am I?"

"No," he said as he pushed a lock of hair from her face. "As hard as this is going to be, it'll be a lot easier than saying good-bye to your son for the rest of your life. This man has already killed a few children."

"I know."

"I'll get you a robe so you can undress, then I'll show you how to use the camera and how to check each shot to make sure you've complied with this bastard's sick demands before going on to the next one."

"Thanks."

He left her for a minute, admonishing her to finish her wine before disappearing into the master bedroom and coming back with a soft plaid robe. She took it and brought it to her chest, then looked up into his face. She was like a little angel, getting ready to fall from grace, and it sickened him to watch what she was going through.

"You know, I was thinking. We could disguise your face a little, maybe even enough to make you unrecognizable to the average person who might somehow end up looking at these."

She cringed and shuddered. "You think people other than him will see these?"

"I'd count on it if I were you, and you know for a fact that one of these pictures has to be put under the windshields at church, so that one will be seen by many people. We definitely should make some attempt to disguise you."

"They have to have my name on them, remember?"

"Oh yeah, I forgot all about that."

She gave a big sigh. "I'll just go put this on." Now she was the one resigned to her fate.

When she came back a few minutes later, he noticed her fair skin had paled even further. He wished there was some way he could spare her this aguish.

"C'mere. Let's try something." He walked her into the master bathroom. While she watched, he opened drawers and cabinets and took out some eye pencils, shadows, and cans of hair-coloring mousse. It was quite a collection of makeup and hair dyes.

"Why do you have all this?" she asked, then quickly

covered her mouth with her hand. "I'm sorry, I shouldn't have asked that, it's none of my business."

"No, no. I would have been surprised if you hadn't. I suppose I could say they're my sister's, but I don't have one. So I guess I'd better not compound my sins with a lie." He turned and looked her in the face.

"I had an affair a few years back. I'm not proud of it, it wasn't something I'd ever done before. But hey, I'm human. I was tempted and I didn't fight it. It ended badly. She had lied about not being married. I could've lost my job, she could have lost her husband. We both lost each other because there was no trust. I thought it was love at first, but it turned out it was lust. I was actually relieved when she went back to her husband."

"She lived here?"

"For two months we set up housekeeping. When her husband found her here it was ugly. We beat each other up and afterward we sat down and had a few beers together. She grabbed her things and cut out while we were knocking the stuffing out of each other. He said he didn't want her anymore. I knew he was lying. I told him I didn't want her either and he smiled. For his silence, I agreed never to see her again. We shook hands and that was that. I never got rid of her stuff, though. Don't know why. Just never took the time, I guess."

"You didn't need to tell me all that."

"Yeah, I did. I've needed to tell someone for a long time. Forgive me?"

"It's not up to me."

"I know. God forgave me a long time ago, but I wanted to hear you say it doesn't matter to you."

"It was a long time ago, Pastor. It doesn't matter to me. Why would it?"

"Call me Cayce. And I guess it shouldn't matter to

anyone. I wasn't being unfaithful, just foolish. It was a long time ago. Here sit on this stool, let me take a look at your face and see what tricks we can use to make you look less like yourself."

He looked at her straight on and then turned her head from side to side, studying the fine-chiseled angles and the soft, high-plains of her cheeks.

"I've heard that changing the shape of the eyebrows can alter the whole effect of a face," she offered. He picked up an eye pencil and handed it to her.

"Okay, let's try that."

She looked down at the pencil, then exchanged it for a darker one on the counter. "If we're going to alter, might as well change the color, too," she said as she started penciling in her brows, making them longer and more exotic.

He appraised her work and nodded. "Good, try this."

He handed her a kohl eyeliner pencil and then smudge pots of eye shadows.

Fifteen minutes later, when they were done, she was a dark brunette, with vivid coloring, pretty in a different, but harder way. Not at all like herself, so strangers wouldn't be clued in to who she was, but still close enough for the Voyeur to know that it was her.

Cayce was clearing the counter and putting away the cosmetics when she heard him clear his throat and say, "I found some body makeup in this basket. Do you have any, uh . . . birthmarks on your body that someone . . . how can I say this gently? That someone who's familiar with your charms might identify you by?"

She smiled at him, grabbed the tube from his hand, and put it back in the basket. "No, the only birthmark I have is a strawberry mark behind my right ear. As for the other, the only man familiar with my 'charms' is no longer able to care."

He nodded then whispered, "I'm sorry."

"No problem, I know you're only trying to protect me."

Cayce took her hand and led her into his study. He showed her how to set the timer on the camera, which was now mounted on a tripod. He also showed her how to review the shots to make sure they were framed properly and to check if they showed her exactly as instructed. "I'll come back in and we'll get each shot set up. Then I'll leave the room. You disrobe, set the timer, get back in position and pose for the shot. After the picture's taken, you'll switch this dial to view, check the shot, then put it back to the original position so I won't see it when I come back in to set up again. Then put the robe back on, call me, and we'll see to the next one. Got it?"

"I appreciate you going to all this trouble. I originally thought you were going to be taking the pictures."

"I thought this way would be better for you." *Certainly better for me, he thought. I don't think I would have been any help if I had to be in the same room with you while you were naked.*

"Okay, let's set up the first shot," he said. He took out the note, read the pertinent part, refolded it, and jammed it into his pants' pocket. "Go stand where I put the tape on the carpet."

She turned and walked a few yards, then placed her toes on the tape. He noticed that she had nice feet before stepping behind the camera. He bent and looked through the viewfinder. "Raise your arms." She raised her arms. The robe gaped open and he just about fell to the floor. Instantly, she clutched at it and held it closed. He blinked hard, shook his head, and bent to look through the lens again. Then he stood, looked at her, and walked over and repositioned her.

"I think this is what he means," he said, mentally envisioning her without the robe. *Whoa! He had to stop that. Especially now that he'd had a pretty clear image of an ample part of her breasts.* He walked back to the camera, bent again, and rechecked the shot.

"Okay. I'll go into the living room now. Call me when you're done."

He gave her a last look, then spun on his heel and left the room, shutting the door firmly behind him.

On the other side of the door, he could her moving around for a minute then silence. Then a sob of anguish, then a loud "Shit! I can't do this!"

He waited a few seconds, wondering if he should knock and then go back in. Instead he was surprised and had to jump back when she opened the door right in front of where he'd been pacing.

"Uh, how'd it go?" he mumbled.

"Swimmingly," she retorted, "just swimmingly. Why couldn't the man just ask for money!" she screamed.

"Would that have been better? Do you have lots of money?"

"No! But at least I could have called his grandparents and asked for their help! How the hell can they help with this?" She waved her hand down the front of the robe and he noted that the belt wasn't secured very tightly. He could see her cleavage and the swell of her breasts where it parted.

Tears were streaming down her face, and he wished he could pull her into his arms and comfort her, but knowing she was naked under his robe, he didn't trust himself. She was experiencing anguish, while he was experiencing anguish of a whole other sort. She was doing something to him. Her innocence was warming his heart and other places, too. He could not believe that in the midst of her vile degradation and utter humiliation that he was lusting for her.

215

That when the robe parted and fell to the floor he wanted to be inside of her.

He reached into his pocket and took out a handkerchief and dabbed at her wet cheeks. "Just a few more, honey. Just a few more." He walked her back into the room and back to the tapeline.

"This one won't be too bad." He positioned her with her back to the camera then watched as she piled her hair on top of her head and secured it with a clip. The robe fell off her shoulders and he saw her creamy, smooth shoulders. She had the kind of body that accentuated the sleek, sexy curve of her back. And for a moment, he actually tried to stare through the robe, wondering if she had those cute dimples above her ass that men loved to search out with their fingertips.

He walked over to her and ran his finger up the back of her neck until it rested on the small strawberry mark he found by her ear. She trembled at his sudden touch and he had the most profound desire to lick her there, then nip her ear lobe. But he checked himself. She sure didn't need him coming on to her on top of everything else. To cover his faux pas, he murmured, "This the birthmark you mentioned earlier?"

"Yes," she whispered. Her voice was more of a sigh than anything else.

His hands fell to her waist, securing her in position, then he pulled her arm around and propped it on her hip. "Hold it like this, with your fingers splayed," he said. Then with his other hand he tilted her head and turned it so she was looking over her shoulder at him. Their eyes met and held, and he swore. After staring into the depths of her wide green eyes, he knelt behind her and eased her bare feet into the high heels they'd bought at the thrift shop on the way to his house.

He told her to bend her left leg at the knee, then went

back to check the shot. He couldn't get her feet into the shot, so he moved the tripod back and checked it again.

"Okay, you're set. Make sure you're right in the middle of the tape mark or you won't be centered. And this time, you're going to have to toss the robe out of the way, otherwise it will hide the shoes. And I know this is going to be really hard for you, but you have to smile when you're looking over your shoulder. Try not to think of this picture as lewd, try to be flirty, like you know how beautiful you are and aren't ashamed to flaunt it. I know that's not like you, but see if you can slip into a little fantasy here. Who knows, it might make it easier.

"If you think you're all set, I can set the timer and get out of here before you toss the robe. You'll have forty-five seconds. That way you won't have to run back and forth. That okay with you?"

"Yes," she whispered. Her voice was very tiny.

"Good, I'll slam the door so you'll know I'm out." He walked over to the camera, set the dial, and quickly left the room, closing the door with a pronounced bang.

Two minutes later, the door opened and she called him to come back in. She didn't seem as shook up this time. *Maybe she was getting used to this,* he thought.

He took out the note and silently read the third pose. This one was going to be hard, so was the next. If she was sane for the last one, she might be inured.

"Time for a break," he said as he walked over to a decanter set on a bookshelf. "And some brandy."

"No, no brandy."

"Yes, you're going to need something to brace you for the next one." Ignoring her pleas, he poured her a half snifter full and walked over to where she stood looking at a painting. He wrapped her fingers around the glass and placed his over hers, then he led it to her mouth. "Nice big sip, c'mon."

"I can't be drunk for this."

"Why the hell not?" he asked.

She shook her head and took a big swallow. It was smooth and only mildly flavorful until it went all the way down, then she felt the warmth and the burn. And remarkably, she did feel better. She took another sip and he laughed.

"Who did this painting? It's wonderful."

"My father. He likes to dabble now and again. He likes to think he's an undiscovered Kincaid." His tender smile told her that he thought the world of his father.

"It's as good as any I've seen."

"I'll be sure to tell him that next time I see him." He laughed out loud just then, and she blinked up at him with a curious look on her face. One finely sculptured eyebrow shot to her forehead demanding explanation.

"Oh no! I can't tell you what I was thinking."

"Sure you can. We should be able to tell each other anything after this. Look what we're doing together for Crissakes."

He was honored she had said that and so felt compelled to share his thoughts.

"Just thinking how I would broach the subject. 'I was entertaining a young woman here in my study, a beautiful young woman who at the time was wearing my bathrobe. While we were taking naked pictures of her, she commented on your painting.' "

He watched her face freeze, then break into a wide grin. She laughed and he laughed along with her.

She finished her brandy and walked over to place the glass back on the tray. He noticed that her gait was a bit loose and when she replaced the glass, it clunked harder on the tray than she had probably meant it to.

"Time to finish," she whispered. It was as if she knew

the gallows were waiting for her and she had no choice but to walk her last steps to it.

Cayce went back to the camera, made a few adjustments, moved the tripod so it was focused lower, and placed a chair a few feet in front of the camera.

Slowly she sauntered over and sat lightly on the chair. She watched as he looked through the viewfinder, centering her.

"Okay, this one's going to be tough. You have to remember the placement of your arms as well as your legs. Make sure you're in the center and that you don't move the chair and it'll be over with. Check it, then go back for the fourth one. It'll be the same pose, just scoot forward a little, being careful not to move the chair when you shift your body. Okay?"

She closed her eyes and shook her head, "No, it's not okay. This is so sick!"

He walked over to where she sat and bent down to caress her cheek. "I know it is. Just focus on getting the shots right. You can take the time to dwell on everything else later. There will be plenty of time to deal with the horror after we're through. We have a timetable we have to stick to and roles both of us have to play before you can hold Joshua in your arms again. This is not a time to think of yourself. Others have made far greater sacrifices for the ones they love. Through the ages, men and women have had to die for lesser causes. This won't matter a hoot or a holler in Heaven. Once you get there, the memory of this will be erased for all eternity, but the deed will be recorded and your place assured, trust me on this."

He walked back to the camera, checked the viewfinder, and asked if she was ready for him to set the timer.

Her hands were on the collar of his robe, as if she were ready to spread it wide. And he was momentarily surprised that at that moment he wanted her to—but for him, only for him. Her large green eyes appealed to him and he wished there was some way he could protect her, shield her from the eyes of the evil demon who lusted for her body.

He set the timer, and as it made its low whirring sound, he again left the room.

After a minute he heard her moving around, then silence. Then she was up again, then silence again. Then a long anguished sob before he heard something crash into the wall. He ran to the door and knocked quickly, then hearing no reply, he carefully opened the door and called softly, "Paige?"

He heard a soft whimper and saw her in a disheveled heap on the floor, her head on her arms, sobbing into the seat cushion. A quick look around satisfied his curiosity about what she'd found to throw. On the wall opposite his desk, was the slow trickle of many connecting lines of water. At the floorboard was a shattered crystal vase and the flowers it had contained. It had been Waterford, something his mother had given him, but as he heard Paige's heart breaking, he wished he had a hundred of them for her to throw up against the wall. He would have done anything to drown out the sound of her tears.

He went over to her and knelt, then he put his arm around her shoulder and pulled her into his chest. She hadn't bothered to close the robe and he was shocked to find her bare breasts pressing against his shirt. He held her close and listened to her cry until her sobbing became softer, and then he realized that she was trying to tell him something.

"I can't get the picture right. I tried five times! I can't do it!"

He massaged her shoulders then gently lifted her into his lap on the chair. He pulled the lapels of the robe together and tucked her under his arm as he rocked her. The robe was lying open over her legs, barely covering her upper thighs. He felt desire, hot and intense, shoot through him and settle in his groin. He knew his body and he knew that within seconds he would be hard and heavy and jutting against her bottom unless he moved her.

He lifted her in his arms and carried her to the love seat on the opposite side of the room.

"I'm sorry about your vase," she sobbed.

"It wasn't a favorite," he lied.

"And the beautiful flowers."

"It was time to replace them."

He held her close and with his lips touching the hair at her temple, he half hummed, half crooned Schubert's version of "Ave Maria." It always had a calming effect on him. He could only hope it would calm her also.

After she stopped crying and had wiped her tears on the sleeve of his robe several times, he tilted her chin so he could look into her face. He took in her red eyes, now outlined with blotchy mascara, her smooth, pale cheeks and her soft, full lips. Lips that were no longer colored with lipstick but pink-tinged naturally. She looked so vulnerable, yet so beautiful at the same time. He couldn't resist, yet he had to. It was everything he could do to keep from bending his head and putting his lips to hers. His breathing stilled as he stared at her soft lips and imagined what it would feel like to kiss her. He thought he actually heard the mantle clock stop ticking for the brief seconds he contemplated taking her lips with his. He closed his eyes tightly to deny the temptation that was only inches away.

While drawing away from her, he forced his eyes open and they grew wide with wonder. She was looking back at him, confused and unfocused as if in a trance.

Her fingers uncurled from where they sat resting in her lap and she brought them up to touch her lips. "I thought you were going to kiss me," she whispered.

"I thought so, too. I'm sorry."

"Please don't be sorry. I wanted you to," she whispered.

"I'd like to kiss you, sometime when you can think about kissing me back."

"Okay," she answered, drawing out the word.

"Right now," he sighed heavily, "we'd better get back to those damned pictures."

"I can't do it. Could you?" she asked timidly.

"Could I take them?" he choked.

"Yes, could you, please? I just can't."

"Won't that be worse?"

"Will you make it worse?" she asked and her voice was so tiny and so scared that he felt a physical pain in his chest.

He hugged her close and put his face into the terry cloth at her neck.

"No, sweetheart, no," he groaned, "I'll try not to make it worse. I'll try."

"I'll close my eyes. I think I can get through it that way."

She heard him start to pray. She could make out phrases where he asked for guidance, for strength, and then finally to be saved from temptation. Then he lifted his head and simply nodded.

She wiped the tears from her face using the back of both hands then stood to get a tissue so she could blow her nose. She used a corner of the tissue to repair her eye makeup then turned from the mirror and gave him a tremulous smile. "Ready," she proclaimed.

He walked over to the camera and she went over to the chair. Before sitting, she let the robe fall from her shoulders to the floor. And there she stood, naked before him. Naked, and as lovely a creature as God had ever created, he thought. He forced himself to look away from her standing there, just a few feet away, and bent to look at her through the lens of the camera. This was worse. It brought her even closer and more clearly into focus. Her breasts were lovely, high and small on her chest. They were stunning little globes of perfection, alabaster white, tinged with the blossoming pink growing from her shame. His eyes lowered and fell on the sable triangle guarding her womanhood. The soft tufts looked like the down on a baby's head and he wanted to run his fingers through it so badly that he had to stuff his hands into his pockets to keep them from reaching for her.

As he looked through the viewfinder, she suddenly sat down in the chair, and before he could blink, she spread her knees wide and raised her hands behind her head.

Sweet Jesus! It was all he could do not to drop to his knees from the sight of her sitting there baring everything.

"Take the picture!" she barked.

His finger, unconscious on the button, pushed it down.

When she heard the click, she quickly slid forward, spread her knees as wide as they would go, and screamed, "Take the picture!"

Again, his mindless body performed, and he took the picture.

Jumping up, Paige grabbed for the robe. Cayce had turned to face the wall.

After a long silence Cayce whispered, "Don't ever forget that your body was made to give and receive pleasure with the one you love, not for viewing by this sick bastard!"

She shivered as she stepped into the robe. He made her feel lovely, not tawdry and lewd as she had been feeling.

"More brandy," he whispered. "This time I think I

223

need it more than you," he said as he let out a long breath.

They walked together over to the decanter and he reached up to rub the back of her neck. "You're doing great."

"One more."

"One more," he repeated before downing his glass in one quick swallow.

He left the study and walked into the dining area. He raked his fingers through his hair, mussing it and unknowingly making himself rakishly attractive in the process. His mind was in overdrive as he walked around closing all the blinds. She was going to be naked on his table, spread wide and making him take the picture!

The prayers he called forth to fill his head as he removed the candlesticks and the centerpiece weren't helping. *Lord, protect us. Me, from carnal thoughts, her from me.*

She had followed him and now watched as he rearranged chairs and removed the tablecloth. His lips were moving, but she couldn't quite catch what he was saying. She knew he was praying and wondered exactly what he was praying for.

He walked past, not even acknowledging her as he went back to his study for the camera. When he returned and had it set up, he unceremoniously dragged her over to the table and picked her up by the waist and plunked her on the end. Then he went back to the camera and focused it before looking up at her. He removed the tattered note from his pocket and handed it to her. He wasn't about to read it out loud.

And she was grateful.

5. Lay on a table, bring your knees up to your chest, then spread them as wide as possible. Use your

fingers to spread your cunt lips. Make this one a close up.

Her nerves were shot. She could feel how frayed they were. The brandy helped, she was even a little high, but not high enough to forget that the next pose would remove any shred of dignity she had ever had, forever. When this picture was circulated, which was exactly what was supposed to happen this Sunday morning, she knew she would never be able to look anyone in the eye ever again, certainly no one in her church.

Cayce, watching the expression on her face, knew what she was thinking. He wanted desperately to be able to save her from this. "Even though you have to be naked, because of the close-up I can frame this so the rest of you is not in the shot." That meant her breasts and her face would not be visible. The only part of her that would be, was her womanhood. *What kind of comfort is that,* he thought, shaking his head.

"At least you'll be anonymous in the picture," he muttered. But he knew it meant nothing.

"Yeah, but he's taken care of that, too, hasn't he?" she replied bitterly. "I have to print my name across the top. Everyone will know exactly whose . . . whose . . . vagina they're looking at. Everyone," she said ending with a broken sob.

He walked over to where she sat at the end of his dining room table and with his finger he traced the path of a tear down her cheek. Then his head tilted and he smiled. "What's your full name?"

"Natalie Paige Lawson."

"And your maiden name?"

"Porter."

"Well, how about using your maiden name, your first

name and just your middle initial? Natalie P. Porter. No one will know you by Natalie will they?"

"No," she said thoughtfully, "I haven't gone by Natalie since grade school."

"It's perfectly acceptable for a widow to revert back to her maiden name."

"Yeah, but he doesn't know Porter's my maiden name or that Natalie's actually my first name. I'm afraid if I do that, he'll see it as defaulting and not return Joshua. It's a good idea, but I can't risk it. The idea that I could do all this," her hand waved up and down in front of the robe, "and still lose Josh, is more than I can bear to think about. We have to do it his way." She shivered with revulsion. "We have to," she whispered. And then without another word she slipped off the robe, letting it fall to the polished wood floor, scooted back from the edge of the table, and placed her feet on the opposite corners. Her hands went between her spread thighs and using her fingers, she parted her labial lips. "Take the picture," she sighed resignedly. "Just take the damned picture."

Not a foot away, he followed her movements. He knew that his eyes had gone wide and his jaw had dropped. But for the life of him, he couldn't move. The sight of her displayed like that caved him in viscerally. Desire, hot and searing, raced through him. Blood pulsed, making his muscles tense, and flushed through his veins so quickly that it made him dizzy. He was instantly lightheaded and was momentarily afraid he was going to fall to his knees, in front of her, right there. Where he could simply lean in and kiss her, wrap his tongue around the dainty fingertips that were showing him the way into her body.

"Arrgh!" he groaned before blinking hard and stepping behind the camera.

He opened one eye to look through the lens, willed

his forefinger to push the button down so he could capture the shot, and quickly spun around so he was facing the living room wall.

He heard her moving on the table and then heard her feet hit the floor. He listened for the rustle of the robe being donned before turning back.

She was crying again. Only this time, so was he.

Without saying a word, she walked into the kitchen, found some furniture polish under the sink, and grabbed a few paper towels. She was polishing the table when he forced himself to look over at her.

"You don't have to do that. I'll take care of it," he bit out.

"No. You've done enough. I'll put this room back to rights, then clean up your study. After you've sent the pictures over the e-mail, I want to go home."

"No," he whispered harshly. "There's no sense in that. Stay here. We have to leave by three to get over to the beach for the next part."

"I need to shower."

"I have a shower," he barked.

"I have to go home!" she screamed.

And he knew why. She couldn't be around him right now. She couldn't look at him, couldn't stand for him to look at her.

⁂

He insisted on following her to her apartment and walking through it before agreeing to pick her up at three in the morning. He let himself out while she was checking her phone messages. He didn't know what to say to her. What did one say to a woman who was a stranger, yet not. Soon to be a lover, yet not. He blinked his eyes and shook his head as he closed the door behind him. He had to remember first and foremost that he was her pastor. He was supposed to be her spiritual helm through this nightmare.

He drove back to his townhouse with visions of her swimming in front of his face. Visions of her crying and wiping her tears on the sleeve of his robe, visions of her laughing while drinking brandy and admiring his taste in art, visions of her exposed, her flesh as white as porcelain, her nipples dusky and pert. An image of her posing for the final degrading picture flashed in front of his eyes and he moaned. God, forgive him, but he wanted to touch her with his lips where the camera lens had been centered. She had been moist and dewy, opening like a flower, and he had wanted to put his face between her thighs and caress her with his tongue in the worst way.

That in itself was an amazing shock to him. He'd performed the gratuitous deed before on several occasions, but he'd never wanted to. The idea of delving into that particular arena had never been his. He had never initiated that type of overture and was never truly into lapping a woman's nether lips to appease her passion.

But now, now he was biting his lips to keep from moaning at the thought of his lips and his tongue nestling there and foraging into her center.

At the next red light, he closed his eyes and rolled his head in a circle as he stretched his neck and tried to work out the tension he was feeling. He dropped his head to his chest and moved his head from side to side, then he reached up and with his thumb and forefinger, stroked the bridge of his nose. How the hell was he ever going to get through the next twenty-four hours? How was she? And was what he was doing, the right thing to be doing? He had an obligation to his church, to his parishioners. This surely wouldn't sit right with them. Where should he be drawing the line at helping one of the flock? A horn sounded behind him and he jerked his head up. As he made his way through the intersection a thought occurred to him, like a divine inspiration, and as it grew inside his head, he smiled. He'd just figured out how Paige could follow the third missive to the letter, and how he could use his God-given gift of oratory and persuasion to protect her innocence. All while keeping his congregation blameless and in the dark about her dire predicament.

Now, all he had to do was figure out how he could be a man of God, a man devoted to his calling, while kneeling in the sand with his cock in Paige's mouth. The thought sent carnal thrills through him at the same time his mind reeled from the ramifications for them both. She'd never be able to face him again, she almost wasn't able to now. And he, he couldn't stand at the pulpit looking down at her in one of the pews and forget what she'd been forced to do. As a man, he was enthralled by her and not just a tiny bit excited by the prospect of her mouth being wrapped around his member. As a man of the cloth, he faced doubts about his ability to maintain control of his emotions, and guilt about the sin they would be committing. It would be a twofold sin for him: premarital sex, and spilling his seed, as biblically phrased, "upon the ground." For her, it was prostituting herself— giving up sexual favors for personal gain. The reason they had to do this vile thing, the purpose they had for committing such a grievous sin, didn't whitewash the act. He knew this. Just as one right didn't justify a wrong, one wrong certainly didn't justify another wrong. This monster's sin was his to bear, and his alone. But they were compounding it, accepting it, and making it their own by going along with it. They were all sinning. He understood that. He only hoped God would forgive it. But for the life of him he didn't see how it would be granted, knowing up front that he'd be asking for forgiveness going into the deed, yet still going along with it anyway. It was selfish he knew, but the man in him, the part of him that was now making his dick hard as pig-iron, didn't care how humbled Paige would be, how uncomfortable she would be with him in her mouth. He wanted desperately to feel her lips around him and to revel in the sensations her tongue would create as she brought him to climax and swallowed his seed.

The dichotomy of who he was, and the inner war he was having with himself as a human versus the God-fearing disciple of Christ, was wearing him out. The dilemma of what to do, how not to enjoy it so much, how to be supportive, but not encouraging, was dragging him down and by the time he pulled back into his townhouse, he realized he needed a nap, too. Maybe if he prayed and gave God His hand in all this, it would somehow all work out. He went into his house, set his alarm clock, and fell exhausted onto his bed. The Lord works in mysterious ways. This is His plan. He's got His hand in this. All things work for His glory and for the good of His people. I will not leave you. I am with you always.

He awoke without benefit of the alarm just two hours later. He was remarkably refreshed in body, but his mind still churned with thoughts of wrongdoing. He always sinned, who didn't? But after, he was truly sorry and repented passionately. After the affair he'd had, he'd gotten down on his knees every morning and begged forgiveness from his Holy Father. But the affair had irrevocably changed things. He had an eye for the ladies, always had, but now, he knew he didn't control it as well as he had thought. It was his Achilles heel, the admiration of soft curves under a sweatshirt, smooth lines under a tight skirt, legs that went on forever . . . . As a pastor, he could easily fall in love and marry, in fact as far as the church was concerned, it was preferable. But he couldn't, shouldn't, be thinking these types of thoughts . . . about Paige.

But he was. He was damned interested in a woman

again. That woman. The woman who had come to him for help. Shit!

For as long as he could remember, sin had always overcome him. He had never gone looking for it, had never planned for it, but somehow temptation always found him. Now it seemed his mind couldn't wrap around the idea of not having Paige in the most carnal way.

As he stripped his clothes off preparing to shower, his mind reverted to the instructions he and Paige were to follow when they arrived at the beach.

Bring a man to Wrightsville Beach Saturday at 6:00 A.M. Use the access closest to the pier. Find an orange marker staked at the dune line on the northern side, attached will be a string. Walk it down to the water and where the string ends, go down on him. Have him face northeast. Surprise! You'll be in the path of the Weather Cam. I know you don't know any men locally, so whomever you manage to find will certainly be a stranger. Let's make this fun. As I know you're quite shy, kiss him first to break the ice before you suck him dry and swallow his cum.

He knew a little bit about the weather cam. It was mounted to provide a view of the beach and the pier. The news shows tapped into it to let the setting say in a picture what it would take hundreds of words to say. He'd seen scenes before and during hurricanes captured and relayed, beautiful sunsets and foggy sunrises. But he never really remembered seeing many people in the shots. He knew the news stations wouldn't be broadcasting what he and Paige would be doing against the backdrop of a sunrise. They had many fail safes in place for this type of thing, but he also knew that the cam was live all the time on the website and that the people who would be awake and tuned in early this morning would get to see a sight they wouldn't soon forget.

The thought had him almost dropping to his knees. He could envision her kneeling at his feet, and while his body reveled and rose to the call, his mind sickened with the sudden flash of fear and humiliation he saw on her lovely face.

This was not how people were supposed to get to know each other, he said to himself as he stepped into the shower. There was an order to things if you were attracted to a person. He was now very attracted to Paige, but this heinous man had moved the timetable up to an intolerable speed. After this was all over, would they be able to salvage anything? Would she ever want to see him again or would she just take her son and run away from these horrible memories?

As he washed his body, paying careful attention to his privates, a strange thought occurred to him and he gave a loud hoot of laughter that echoed off the steaming tiles. What would his mother have to say about all this if she ever found out? A scenario played out in his head of a society friend confronting her with the news.

"Meredith, it was awful. He was right there on the screen, stroking her hair while she was, well, she was . . . down there."

"I don't believe you. Surely it was someone else, not my son."

"Meredith, it was Cayce, I recognized him immediately. He's rather well-endowed, unusually so, if I might add."

Meredith groaned and knew the woman had indeed seen Cayce.

"Family trait, I'm afraid."

Cayce grinned as he cupped his swaying sacs. He was rather large in all aspects, but in one, remarkably so. His balls were huge. A woman couldn't cup them in one hand. They hung full and heavy, quite obviously an anomaly and an inherited genetic "enhancement" as his father used to say. So much so, that he had to wear jockey boxers snug against his body to hold his parts high against his groin so he could walk and sit comfortably. And when he was aroused, they became even heavier, and while they lost some of the wrinkling from being distended, the stretched skin purpled as his sacs threatened to burst. Some women were fascinated by his size; a few had been more than intimidated. Paige, he was sure was going to wish she had opted for another man.

He exited the shower, shaved, and then knelt to pray for Joshua and then for both himself and Paige. When he was dressed he walked into the dining room and stared at the camera that was still set up, aimed at the end of the table. He blinked his eyes hard to ward off the tears he felt coming, picked it up by the tripod base, and carried it into his study. Images of Paige surrounded him as he tidied up and put things to right. Then suddenly overcome, he collapsed to the leather love seat and cried.

Why had God allowed something like this to happen to someone like Paige? Why hadn't He stopped this man? Why? He knew he sounded like one of his parishioners, wondering why they hadn't been spared some of life's hard lessons. And instantly he knew that his Lord wasn't finished with him in this. This wouldn't end badly. It couldn't. He would do what he had to and then, if there was anything that could be salvaged, he would make every effort to do so. Whether it was his career, his reputation, or his relationship with Paige. God just didn't allow these things to happen for no reason. Hard as this was now, especially for her, He would make it up to them. Suddenly Cayce just knew it. Knew it

233

more than he knew his name. His God worked for good. He had to remember that.

He went back into his bathroom, washed his face and brushed his teeth, then grabbed his car keys and a can of soda from the refrigerator.

All the way back to Paige's he prayed and asked God to use him as He willed and he begged Him to try to make things easier for her.

❧

Paige was waiting when he knocked on her door. It was the eerie time of night when there was hardly any traffic, hardly any noise and very little light.

"Ready?" he asked simply.

She nodded and pushed the button in on the back of the doorknob, then shut the door behind her. She had only taken two steps when she thought better about locking the door and used her key to unlock it. She wasn't going to bar the way for this madman; he was more than welcome to come through her front door if he was bringing Joshua back to her.

Cayce took her by the elbow and walked her to his car. They didn't speak at all the whole time they were driving through the city. Each was lost in their own thoughts. Hers about Joshua. His about her and how lovely she looked. Twice he had focused on her lips and felt a jolt to his groin.

It was monstrous that he was looking forward to their opening act and the kiss before her ministrations. And somehow he knew she would be delicate, perhaps too delicate. Suddenly it occurred to him that he could have a problem with this. Up until now, the idea hadn't crossed his mind that he wouldn't be able to perform. Now he was scared to death that that just might happen.

Crossing the bridge to the ocean, he broached the

topic. "Uh, Paige. Have you, uh, ever done this before?"

"What? Gone down on a man?"

"Well yeah, that's what I'm referring to all right."

"Yes. My husband tended to enjoy it."

"Most men do," he said with a sideways smile, trying to make light of the situation.

"Why do you ask?"

"I, uh . . . . Well, I uh, might require a firmer hand than you're used to using."

"You mean I may need to use my hand as well as my mouth?"

Liquid fire shot through him at her blunt words.

"Well, yes, maybe. I don't know. But I don't think we want to prolong this any longer than we have to. I might suggest using your tongue as well as your lips at the tip."

She turned her head and looked over at him with dull eyes. "Anything else?"

"Um, my sacs, they're quite sensitive. Whatever you can do in that area will certainly help. And, uh, don't be surprised by the uh, size. It's not something to worry about."

She nodded then shrugged her shoulders. The man was letting her know he wasn't abundant. Poor guy, now lots of people would know. She hadn't thought about this much from his point of view. He was actually being pretty wonderful about all this. She reached over and took his hand from the wheel and squeezed it. "We're going to be fine. It's what you do with it remember?" she said with a tiny smile and he instantly knew she had taken things the wrong way.

"No, I mean . . . ."

"It's okay." She squeezed his hand again. "It's easier to do this when it's smaller. My husband was adequate; at times like this, I was often thankful he wasn't larger."

He started to say something again, but clamped his

lips shut. She'd find out soon enough. He really didn't want to talk about this anymore. And he certainly didn't want to be compared to her dead husband in this way.

They drove down the quiet road in front of the beach. Then he parked, leaned over, and kissed her cheek and asked if she was ready.

"Yes. I am. I want my boy back."

He helped her out of the car and together they walked across the street to the beach access and then down to the sand.

The lights of the pier greeted them as they came over the rise of the beach access and now, as they neared the pier, they could see the faint glow of the sun attempting to rise.

Cayce took out the note, read over the instructions again, then began looking for the orange marker. Once he spotted it, he walked over and bent down to bring up a sand-encrusted string. Pulling it up, he walked backward with it to the prescribed spot. Then he faced the direction the note specified. He didn't know exactly where the camera was mounted, but he knew without a doubt that it was capturing his every movement.

"Show time," he muttered as he dropped the string and motioned for Paige to come toward him.

"Is it time?" she asked, a bit of panic appearing in her eyes.

He pulled up his sleeve and looked down at his watch and said, "Yes, honey. It's time. And before we go any further, let me just say that I'm so sorry you have to do this. I really will try to make it as easy on you as I can."

She simply nodded with resignation in her eyes, her beautiful sad eyes.

He took her in his arms then and whispered, "You have to kiss me now."

Her hands went to his shoulders. He was wearing a

thick fleece jacket and her hands fisted in the material as she stood on tiptoe to kiss him.

He took the lips she offered and softened them with his own as he forced her to linger and live for this kiss. Even if they had others, it would be the one they would both always remember and he wanted it to work.

His hands came up to cup her cheeks as she drew him down and he hungrily took all she was offering. Their tongues mated, hers tentative, his demanding and possessive. Then she broke away, buried her face in his chest, and heaved out one heart-wrenching sob before sliding down his chest to his waist. Her slide down the length of his body ended with her on her knees, her hands on his belt.

He looked to the rising sun to be assured of their positioning while she worked at undoing his belt and zipper. When his pants fell to his thighs she saw that he hadn't bothered with underwear. She also saw what he had been alluding to earlier and she felt herself blush.

Tenderly he put his hand on her head to encourage her and she leaned in and took him into her mouth. The shock of her lips touching him reverberated through his system and for a moment, he wasn't sure his knees would hold him upright. He steadied himself by placing a hand on each of her shoulders.

She closed her lips and slid her tongue up and down the length of him, then she brought her hand up and enclosed him in it. His sudden gasp startled but didn't deter her. With a single-mindedness that surprised him, she took to her task with abandon, licking, stroking, and sucking on the tip until he was whimpering. He tried to let go, to go against years of conditioning and let himself selfishly care only for his gratification. His mind knew it would help her if he could get this over quickly, but his body was savoring her touches, her lips on his manhood. When she reached down and gently cupped his heavy, full sac he was instantly lost. He locked his knees to keep from collapsing, threw back his head, and roared as the jet of hot passion poured out of him and into her waiting mouth.

He was hardly cognizant of the difficulty she had swallowing as he was careening outside of the universe at a dizzying, dazzling speed. But as he slowly came back into himself, he watched her struggle for composure. Instantly he reached into his deep pocket, pulled out a can of soda and popped the top. He knelt beside her and put it to her lips and she drank greedily, gulping the cool liquid down as fast as she could. Then she pushed the can away, whispered, "Thanks," and crumpled into a heap.

Cayce took a swig from the can himself, then dropped it to the sand before reaching down and pulling up his pants and zipper. He worked on threading his belt back through the belt loops as he watched Paige cry into her hands. Then he stood, pulled her up with him, and bent to put his arm under her knees. He lifted the quietly sobbing woman high into his arms and carried her over the dunes.

She was touched. It had been very thoughtful of him to bring a can of Coke in his pocket for her. And now, he was holding her against his chest and carrying her away from camera range.

She wished she could stop crying, she must be making him feel awful. But she just couldn't seem to stop, and now she had added hiccups to the cacophony.

"Shush, shush, it's all right. It's over now. Please stop crying Paige, you're tearing me up here."

"I can't. I just can't."

He had picked a secluded section of dunes to hide behind. Propped against the wall of sand, he held her against him as he patted her head and held her tightly to his chest. He let his head loll back against the dune, heedless of the sand getting in his hair, as he tried to catch his breath and steady his heart.

He had settled Paige against him and as he continued to stroke her hair and settle her, he turned her head slightly to kiss her wet cheeks.

"Imagine how I'm going to feel, how hard it's going to be for me to look over and see you sitting a few aisles down from the pulpit?" he teased, trying to get her to laugh, to do anything but cry.

"And it will be hard, I guarantee." He waited a few seconds and laughed himself. "No pun intended there."

She looked up at him then and blinked. "You're the biggest man I've ever seen there."

He gave her a wry grin, "So you noticed, huh?"

"Hard not to with my face right there. Did I hurt you? You yelled awfully loud."

He chuckled. "No, you didn't hurt me. Far from it."

"I feel so dirty."

"I'm sorry."

"I mean . . . I didn't mean—"

"I know what you meant Paige. You feel used. Like a tramp."

"Yeah."

"But you're not you know."

"I know," she whispered. "I know."

"C'mon, let me take you home. We've only got a few hours before it's time for church. And I for one, have a new sermon that needs polishing."

"Ohhh," she said with dread. She had just remembered the final degrading test.

"I didn't want to tell you before, in case I couldn't pull it off, but I think I may just be able to keep those pictures private. God willing."

He managed to get to a standing position in the soft

sand. Using his hand he brushed the sand out of his hair and off his clothes. Then he took her hand and pulled her to her feet.

"Besides, if the police don't arrest us for public lewdness, I'd sure hate to give them a second chance by having them spot us in the dunes. Then of course, there was the littering thing back there, too."

She gave an ironic chuckle then. "That would be just great. After having followed all the other things to the letter, we end up in jail just when we need to finish this damned thing to get my boy back."

"We're going to get him back Paige. I promise you that."

When they came off the sand much further up the street, he took her hand in his and told her what his plan was.

"So, you've heard me preach, think I can pull it off? Am I charismatic enough?"

She stopped walking and looked up at him. She really, really looked at him. He was very handsome in a collegiate way with soft light brown hair now mussed by the light breezes coming off the ocean. But even rumpled he was gorgeous, a quiet gentleman with a mischievous smile if there ever was one.

"I've always been impressed with your sermons. You do manage to mesmerize. But how are you going to convince almost a hundred people to ignore human nature, go against their baser curiosity and defy convention?"

He took her hand in his and continued walking with her back to his car. "I'm not. God is. I'll just do my part. He'll have to see to the rest. And you'll have to trust that He will. Can you do that?"

She looked into his sincere face, focusing on his concerned but intelligent eyes.

"Yes, if you tell me to, I will. Because I trust you and I know how devoted you are. God will work through you much more than through me."

"Why do you say that?" he asked with surprise.

"You're so good, so uncompromisingly good. I've never known a man who believed as much as you. You live the life you talk about."

He groaned, stopped walking, and let his head fall back. His squeezed his eyes shut and wanted to scream at her. *I'm not good! I'm terrible! I've loved every degrading moment you've had to be with me, and if we didn't have a rather tight schedule right now, I'd like nothing more than to take you to my bed and make love to you until you begged for mercy. I loved feeling your lips and tongue and hands on me, and I know that deep down in my black, black heart that I am going to do everything in my power to feel them there again!*

He shuddered from the act of suppressing those awful words, but he knew he had to face them. And her.

"I don't live the life I talk about all the time. I slip. I fall out of grace just like anyone else, maybe even more than anyone else. And to be perfectly blunt with you, I've thought and had to suppress more perverted, dark, carnal thoughts in the last few hours than I've had in the last ten years. Paige you make my blood boil and it scares me how much I want you. So please don't tell me how good I am, how worthy I am. Right now I feel like I'm the biggest hypocrite in the world."

The look of shock on her face humbled him. She truly hadn't known.

"I'm sorry. I'm just human. And you are so lovely. And I've had to see you in very sensual positions, provocative to say the least. Must be why those magazines sell so well," he said with a sheepish smile. They had reached his car. He unlocked the door and held it for her. Then he went to the driver's side, slid in, and turned to face her.

He looked over at her and noticed her dark fringed lashes were shadowing her cheeks. Her eyes were closed as if she was lost in thought.

"I had no idea you wanted me. Or that you still do. How can that be after all that I've done?" Tears were slowly seeping out of her eyes and running freely down her cheeks.

"Oh, Paige," he said as he drew her to him. "You haven't done anything wrong! Please don't allow yourself to be shamed over this. You did what you had to. No man can fault you for this."

"Even you?"

"Especially me."

"And will you still want me after pictures of me are everywhere, and everyone is talking about them and snickering?"

"Yes. I will still want you, even then. I may be jealous that others are viewing what I would like to consider to be mine alone, but that won't make me want you any less. I think I'm falling in love with you Paige and I'm not sure how to handle this. But for now, let's just say I'm possessive about you, and that I'm going to pray that I give the best sermon of my career so I can keep you all to myself."

"You think you're falling in love with me?"

"It's a distinct possibility," he said with a smile and a kiss for her nose. "Can't say for sure though. We're not exactly having your typical first date experiences. But I would like to. When we get Joshua back, I'd like to meet him and take you both out to dinner and to the movies, picnics in the park and birthday parties at pizza parlors."

"You've already met Joshua. He talks about you all the time."

"Really? I visit the nursery all the time, but I can't place him. What's he look like?"

She took a picture out of her pants pocket and showed it to him. He instantly recognized the little boy that had stolen his heart months ago. "That's Joshua? I've talked with him, he's talked with me, but I don't think I ever knew his name."

"He tells me that you talk to him. You're one of the few people he talks to. He says you walk with God and that you talk with God. It's why I knew I could come to you for help."

"Oh, Paige. I taught him that song, that's all. And he walks with me and he talks with me and he tells me I am his own . . . ." he sang in a clear strong voice.

Tears came to both of their eyes. "We're going to get him back, Babe," he whispered. Then he kissed her softly on the lips before turning back and starting the car.

Chapter Twenty-three

As he drove into her parking lot and pulled in front of her building, he reached behind the seat and brought out a large envelope.

"To save time, I took the liberty of printing out the picture you have to put on the windshields in the church parking lot. I copied it on the copier in my study. The computer print out was in color, but the copies are black and white. There are a hundred copies here along with the original. I deadened the image somewhat by fogging the glass on my copier with hairspray. If it weren't for the name you have to put on each one, I'm sure no one would know it was you. All you have to do now is print whatever name you choose to use on each one, and then while I'm giving the sermon, put one under the wiper on each windshield. If all goes well, when church lets out, it won't matter what's on each sheet."

She looked over at him and blushed scarlet. She wondered if he had looked at them. Seen her in that horrible, submissive pose again.

He knew what she was thinking, and was angry with himself that he couldn't reassure her. He'd not only looked at the print out and the copies, but he had studied them more carefully than he cared to admit, even to himself.

"Do you really think this is going to work?"

"We have to try, don't we?"

She nodded and took the oversized envelope he was handing her.

"I can't do any more, Paige. After the sermon, you and I will have done everything possible to get Joshua back. Whatever happens after that, we'll just have to deal with it."

"We could both lose our jobs."

"We could."

"I might have to leave the state, maybe even the country."

"If you do, I'll go with you."

"How can you be so sure of this, Cayce?"

"God has His reasons for things, Paige. He wouldn't have brought you into my life like this, just to yank you right out of it. He's the ultimate matchmaker. If such a bad thing had to happen, at least He did this for us. That's something. Do you have any feelings for me, Paige?" he asked and the hope in his eyes floored her.

She thought for a moment, unable to take her eyes from his. "I don't know. I just don't know right now. I know I trust you, and I know I want you to kiss me and hold me again when I can concentrate on you and the feel of you. But I'm very worried."

"About Josh?"

"Yes. And us. How can we possibly start a relationship after everything that's gone on between us is known. How can we go on when we've both lost our jobs and we're scandalized in the community?"

"Let God worry about all that. And me, let me worry some. And like I said, we'll deal with whatever we have to. As long as we get Josh back, we'll deal with all the rest. Now kiss me and go get ready for church."

She tilted her head while he bent his to hers and their

lips met softly, almost reverently. Feather-light, he brushed his lips along hers, molding them gently to his. Then he lifted his head, ran his tongue along his bottom lip, and closed his eyes. Yeah, he was definitely in love. No doubt about it. Not a one.

Chapter Twenty-four

"And so I ask, how can any one of you know God's will in your life? How can you know for sure what it is He expects of you? I'll tell you how you can know, and know for sure, beyond any doubt. If you show Him an obedient heart, if you let Him know that you are truly only concerned with His will and not yours, then you can overcome. Things will be set right, even the things that Satan has had a hand in. So my brothers and sisters, today, he has a test for you. A test of wills—yours, fueled by the devil's wishes and curiosities, against His. His righteousness, His all-knowing truth. So don't ask why, or how, or who, just accept that He has faith in you to do the right thing, and the right thing is to honor Him with your obedience. For you to revere His decision and turn away from sin. For sin is surely what you are being led to. Let us show our solidarity, our blind faith and devotion to the one who loves us unconditionally. Our love for the God who sent His son to guide us, and then allowed Him to die on the cross for us, must be strong. As His love for us knows no bounds, let us revel in that love and allow Him to redeem us. It sets us apart from sin, and from the desires of the flesh that keep us from being one with Him. Let us all be an example to the next man. Let's pass this test of faith and let Him see us strong and Christ-like instead of weak and easily led by evil. Remember, what you do, you are doing for one of us, one of Jesus' beloved. In Christ's name, we commit out hearts and our minds to His service. Amen.

"Your test is in front of you. You will all find a small card stuck in the crease of the last page of the hymnal. It says simply, that when you go out to the church parking lot, you will find a folded piece of paper tucked under your windshield wiper. If you want to pass this test and honor the Lord, your God, you are commanded to take that piece of paper, without unfolding it, for it is the work of the devil, and place it in one of the trash cans that have been placed at the curbs. Triumphantly, we as the united body of Christ, will stuff Satan's evil in the ashes. His evil deeds will burn as every sinner will burn in hell, but we, we will be victorious over sin. It will not touch us. We will dispose of it before it can eat into our minds, our hearts, and our bodies. Take your cards now, read them and do God's bidding. Let us rejoice in singing as we all march to be obedient."

Everyone stood as one, with card in hand, and as Cayce led them in song, he also led them out to the parking lot where Paige had interspersed every trash can the church owned between the cars. The contents of each wire cage had been set afire and there were flames licking the rims. On each vehicle there was a folded white sheet of paper.

Cayce, in great voice was still singing. "For He is Lord, He has risen from the dead and He is Lord, every knee shall bend, every heart confess, that Jesus Christ is Lord." Dramatically he tore the paper from under the wiper of his own car, marched purposefully to the nearest burning waste basket and dropped it into the flames. One, by one, they all followed suit. Until finally all the papers had been burned and accounted for. All except one. Deacons, stationed in each row, had been instructed to count how many papers had been fed into the cans. Paige had put out eighty-nine, eighty-eight had been burned.

Cayce led everyone in thunderous applause as the last person marched up to a can and dropped the folded white paper into it. Peer pressure being what it was, and with everyone watching to see if anyone was going to go against God's wishes and disobey, it was really no problem destroying all the evidence of Paige's desperation. Yet, when Paige and Cayce conversed, they had to acknowledge that someone had managed to slip one into their pocket, and without saying, they both knew exactly who that someone had to have been. The monster had her picture, her dirty, vile, nasty, pornographic picture. He had what he wanted, now all they had to do was wait for Joshua to be returned. Behind the closed door of Cayce's office in the now-empty church, in the shelter of Cayce's arms, Paige wept. For fifteen minutes, she cried her heart out while he held her. Then together they walked through the fellowship hall to the church. Silently, they both knelt at the altar and they prayed.

Then Cayce lifted Paige by her elbow and turned her to him.

"I'll stay here, you go home and we'll wait. He'll probably drop him off someplace innocuous. I'll call the police and alert them to be on the lookout for him."

"Should we do that now?"

"It's safe now. Josh has probably already been set free, it's been well over an hour since you met his last demand. He may even be home when you get there. Call me." He bent and kissed her by her ear. "I love you Paige," he whispered into her hair. "I won't ask you to reciprocate my feelings right now, because I know you have other things on your mind, but someday, I will ask you to love me Paige, someday soon."

He turned her toward the door leading to the parking lot and squeezed her shoulder. "Call me when you get home.

I'll be waiting here for your call."

"What about the police?" she asked over her shoulder when she had reached the door.

"I'll call them from here. Just go. I'll take care of it."

He watched her go out the door, and as it slowly closed behind her, Cayce asked himself if he'd just seen her for the last time. When all this became public in a few short hours, would she forget all about him and go hide? Would she need to put this so far from her mind that she'd force herself to forget him, too? He rubbed the back of his neck while he walked back to his office. He stared at his desk and the seat she had taken just a day ago when she'd come to ask for his help. Had it really been less than twenty-four hours ago since he first looked into her face and saw an angel? An angel in distress. His angel, his beautiful, brave, lonely angel.

Chapter Twenty-five

*D*etective Kel Vain could not believe that yet another man had stepped in to be a gallant knight to a damsel in distress. And this one, no less, was a pastor!

As he read the ransom note over again, he looked over at Caison Braxton, Pastor of New Assemblies of Christ.

He was standing in the hallway outside one of the examining rooms at New Hanover Hospital. They were waiting for the crime scene officers to finish with Joshua Lawson. The door was open and he could see the doctor and two technicians trying to hold the boy still while his mother paced at the foot of the table. They were trying to remove the tape and had been for quite some time.

Kel looked up from reading the note a fourth time and focused on both the pastor and the mother. He was trying to read the signals he felt arcing between the two of them. If they'd followed the directions in the note, then they had just recently been through a helluva lot together, and he was curious how they had been affected by it all.

When Kel turned from watching Paige cringe at each shriek from her child, he met Cayce's ardent gaze. With unflinching piercing eyes he dared Kel to further upset Paige, so he could prove his protective stance. She was oblivious to the fierce looks Cayce was shooting him as she moved to cuddle and coo her simpering child.

Kel motioned for Cayce to follow him into the hallway. "How's she handling knowing this picture's circulating?" he was pointing down to the third section of the note. This was a worse demand than Laura had been subjected to. And his stomach clenched from the thought that if things had gone differently that men, lots of men would be looking at Laura in her most intimate places, leering at blown up photos and jacking off while they stared at her. The Voyeur was escalating his demands, exacting a more onerous toll from his victims—his lust was getting worse, and probably harder to satisfy. The man standing in front of him now had this horrible nightmare to deal with. He didn't know how any man with feelings for a woman would deal with this kind of thing.

"It isn't circulating. I managed to convince my congregation to return all the pictures without looking at them. We got all but one back. We think he has that one. It was just a short time later that I found Joshua in the nursery playground at the bottom of the slide. As far as I know, all the pictures have been burned, all but that one." He didn't bother to tell Kel that there'd almost been two. But he wasn't going to tell this defender of the law that he'd thought about keeping one for himself. It sickened him to think about it now, how he'd been sorely tempted for a moment to possess her image this way. He had wanted to look at her one more time, in the privacy of his bedroom. He hated himself and the dark, sensual side of man. More so since Paige had told him she trusted him. But he hadn't kept one, he had seen they had all been destroyed.

After asking a few more questions, Kel left to go to his friend, Mark Twiller's house. It was late on a Sunday afternoon, but he needed the expertise of a computer wizard right away if they were going to have any chance of checking out the e-mail address on the latest ransom note.

He was amazed when he saw it and even exclaimed in triumph that that was "a really stupid screw up!" But it turned out that it really wasn't. The address was no longer viable; it led to a computer in a coffee house on 17th Street. The manager of the shop said that no less than fifty people a day had used the computer since the time the pictures were downloaded.

Kel held the handwritten note that had been pinned to Joshua's shirt when he'd been found in the playground.

Paige, you are a worthy mother. I enjoyed your pictures very much. Your pastor is smart and you were crafty to choose him. He certainly earned his blowjob with that sermon. And you've earned your son back.

The other notes had always been computer-generated. Kel smiled. Paige and Cayce must have taken him by surprise and The Voyeur had felt that he had to acknowledge that. The note was written on the back of a prayer card. According to Cayce they were only available in the pews. The Voyeur had attended church today.

Chapter Twenty-six

*H*arold Satterfield sat in a back corner of the booth at the McDonald's at Longleaf Mall. With his hands carefully shielding the picture against any prying eyes coming from the restrooms, he stared at his lovely Paige.

Paige as he had wanted to view her for months, Paige more lovely than he could have imagined. Even without benefit of his blue pills, he was getting hard. This was how a woman should display herself to the man she loved, how she should welcome him to view and explore her body. And Paige had done this for him. She had posed for him this way, knowing he would soon be feasting his eyes on her naked body. He wished the quality of the print had been better, he should have specified picture-quality photos, and larger. Yes, full page would have been very nice.

When he had been just fourteen, his friend's sister, Cindy, had entertained a group of boys every afternoon after school in their basement before their parents came home from work. For fifty cents each boy got to see her tits, for a dollar she raised her skirt and dropped her panties, for five dollars, she sat on a chair and spread her thighs wide. Cindy never charged him and she had always given him the full show, sometimes in private. He had always believed that she was compelled to show him her charms for free because he was not only very appreciative, but girls just found him to be very deserving. It was as if they read his mind and he managed to convey to them that he was entitled to see them. When he said, "Show me your pussy," invariably they did. They loved showing off to him because they loved his praise, and they loved to be adored by him. And he loved adoring them, worshipping the area between their thighs for as long as they would let him drink in the view. One night at the local drive in, his date had sat topless and bottomless with her back against the passenger door, spread wide for all the world to see for over an hour. He had just sat back, smoked cigarettes and guzzled beer as he ogled her. Then he called a few friends over from the next car to share the cock-stiffening sight. Of course, that girl had been a bit drunk at the time, and was really out of it. She hadn't even flinched when he'd switched on the glaring overhead light. Funny, he could recall every curve of her body, but not her name. He had always wondered what became of Cindy and the brother who loved to show her off and pimp for her. He wondered if she had ever married. One thing was for sure, if he had married her, she would never have been allowed to cover those gorgeous, huge tits.

Looking at Paige brought back wonderful memories of his teen years, he had been miserable at home, but the girls of New Park Haven High had kept him quite entertained until he had gone on to state college and met Gloria. Ah Gloria, if only things had stayed the same for them. If only she hadn't found out about his hobby.

He carefully folded the paper and tucked it into his shirt pocket, then he let his head fall back and he smiled. He was remembering Gloria and all the times he had photographed her and all the times he had climbed on top of her and found her willing and ready for him. Paige was ready for him now, so was Laura, Meggie, too. But he didn't want Meggie the way he wanted the others. Oh, he had loved looking at her on the beach, and watching her leave the Sears parking lot in her birthday suit, but Meggie had never really appealed to him like the others had, she was too bold, too brassy, too sure of herself. He liked his women to have more of an innocent appeal, always had. Meggie had been a means to an end, a way to put her cocky, arrogant, stupid ass of an ex-husband in his place. Every time he'd gone to the country club to clean, Thomas Ryan had looked down his nose at him. Thought he was God's gift. Man, he wished he'd known that the swing camera was broken, he had really wanted to see that jerk when he discovered his tennis bud pokin' his little doll baby of a wife. Wasn't to be though, but it was enough just knowing he had made that stupid prick miserable with jealousy.

Paige and Laura were his favorites. They had done what he had asked, blatantly displayed themselves and allowed him to feast his eyes on their sex, smiling like they were welcoming him. He wanted one of them. He wanted to possess one of his girls, to enter her body and take her, to show her the man he was. He wanted total submission and he knew that either one would be happy to have him between their thighs, once he showed them how masterful he could be. How proficient he was once he was in the saddle. He imagined himself thrusting, and holding, thrusting and holding, then exploding with his climax. But coming into which one? Which cunt would it be that he graced with his rock-hard cock? Laura, yes, Laura, it had to be Laura. She was so beautiful, so sweet, she would want him to pleasure her. His audible groan jerked him out of his dream world. He opened his eyes and saw that he had drawn the eyes of several diners. He slid awkwardly off the bench and made his way to the men's room.

Chapter Twenty-seven

It figured that it would be raining. There was no way to make pulling a child's body out of the murky waters under the Snow's Cut Bridge any worse than this—except by adding dismal weather to the event. It was raining in solid sheets, so heavy that you couldn't keep your eyes open against it. There was a heavy wind churning the water and making the current run fast. To the divers it was a relief to go underwater.

Before the storm, a boater had seen the body drifting, but before he could get to it, it had been swept away. So the Coast Guard had been called as well as the local fire department. The Carolina Beach Fire Department consisted of men who doubled as police officers, so it wasn't long before word got to Kel, and now he was standing along with thirty others waiting for the body to be brought ashore. They had just been notified that the divers had brought it up.

Ten minutes later, when the boat docked at the marina and the body was lifted out of the boat, Kel's heart sank. The girl child had duct tape over her mouth and eyes, as well as around her wrists and ankles. She had curly red hair and wore red shorts and a blue T-shirt. He couldn't stand to look at her. He closed his eyes hard, tilted his head back, and let the rain beat on his eyelids. It was painful, but he felt as if he deserved it.

An hour later he sat in his office and stared at the meager first reports. They hadn't made an identification yet. The body was with the coroner. He slumped dejectedly in his chair letting his head fall onto his chest then let out one of the biggest sighs of his life. He felt like a failure, as useless as a derelict. The City of Wilmington was paying a perfectly good salary for nothing. This sucked! He grabbed his raincoat and headed for his personal car that he often kept in the station parking garage, a vintage 1970 Oldsmobile 442. The rain would do it good—it was awfully dusty. He didn't know where he was going, but he needed a long drive and some time away from everything that involved death.

It should have surprised him, but it didn't when he pulled into the driveway of his old house. The one he had grown up in, in Benton. It was raining here too, but not quite as hard. A steady drizzle pinged off the roof of his car making it sound tinny. The dampness had intensified the musty, moldy smell of the old interior and he wondered why he kept the damn thing. God, what a mood he was in!

He sat in the car and looked at the old house. He had painted those shutters gray at least six times. And that porch railing every summer for as long as he could remember. He'd learned how to rake leaves when he was five and mow the lawn when he was eight. And they had both seemed like never-ending chores at the time. He had some fond memories of the house inside, but not so many of the outside. He fished in the console for his mother's old keys and opened the car door to a big gust of wind. He had to finish going through her things and make some decisions about the house. Now was as good a time as any as he was already depressed, and he figured, why waste a sunny day?

The box of photo albums he had left on the hearth

was exactly where he'd left it, dusty and collapsing from the weight of sixty-odd years of pictures. He went into the kitchen thinking he would start a pot of coffee before remembering that he'd had the power shut off months ago. He'd have to be out of here by dark, although it already was dark and gloomy throughout the house. He sat cross-legged on the living room carpet because he had already donated all the furniture he'd had no use for in his own house.

There was a slight chill even though it was late spring. Yesterday it had been in the mid seventies, but today it probably wasn't more than sixty.

He sorted through the photo albums and loose photos working his way to the bottom of the box, anxious to get this over with while bemoaning what he was going to do with this pile of junk and memorabilia. In one scrapbook there was an odd collection of postcards from all over the country, most from the fifties and sixties. Flipping some over, he saw that they were cards sent from his aunts and uncles over the years. It seemed that back then, no one went away on vacation without sending postcards back home. There were cards from the Grand Canyon, Carlsbad Caverns, Las Vegas, and Yellowstone Park, and apparently a very popular one back then was a man standing in a tunnel hollowed out from the trunk of a giant redwood. There were three of the same card, all sent by different people. He wondered idly if the man in the photo had given his permission for his image to be sent into strangers' houses all over the country. But people didn't think that way back then, he mused. Now, it was almost a given that the man would sue if he hadn't signed a release.

An hour into the box, he finally made his way to the bottom where he found a handmade journal. It looked like his mother had taken a composition book and wrapped the cover with contact paper. Centered and written in her perfect penmanship it was titled: Catherine's Musings. He opened it and started reading her entries.

It was getting too dark to read when he came to the last entry, written only a few months ago. He remembered that she'd always kept a flashlight in the laundry room, so taking the book with him he went to find it. Sitting on the dryer he read the final words she had written. A letter to her husband, his father, the low-life bastard.

I just can't do it anymore. I've tried. They're all smarmy. They pick their teeth at the table, pluck food from my plate as if it's community property, and they snicker and wink when one of their friends stops at our table, as if I'm a sure thing since I'm a widow. It's not that I enjoy living alone, but I'd much rather be home alone with my memories of you and our wonderful life together. I love to relive our beautiful moments, I treasure each event like a brilliant jewel. I close my eyes and I take them out one by one and watch them shine all over again in my mind. How can another man possibly compete with that? We had the best there could be between a man and a woman, how could I ever hope to recreate that? I understand this, I only wish that Kel could. Anyway, it's too much work getting up for these so-called dates. Tonight was my last one. I get nothing out of them but indigestion. I was only doing it for Kel. But I have decided not to waste my time or give him hope anymore. It is only you that I want and if I can't have you, I am quite content to live with just our memories. We had twenty-six wonderful years together and I wouldn't give up one day for anything this world has to offer. I wish with all my heart that Kel could stop worrying about me and see that I am not living with the pain of losing you when he sees me so quiet and thoughtful, but that I am reveling in the love that we share, even now though we are apart. Had I known that I would spend the last decade of my life without you, I wouldn't have changed a thing. Well, maybe I would have gone to fewer women's club meetings and spent those evenings going bowling with you instead.

She had never mentioned his infidelity, never written anything about his father's last year. Never said anything about the other woman who had ruined everything, including Kel's views on marriage. That's because in her last years she'd lost all her short-term memory. The only things she remembered were the memories from long ago. A blessing in disguise, he thought. But he remembered! He was sure that he'd never forget.

He closed the book with a snap, hopped down off the dryer, and flashed the light around. Then he went from room to room remembering: in the kitchen he remembered the times he and his mother had made cookies together; in his bedroom, he remembered all the stories she'd read to him; in the main bathroom he remembered the time the two of them made their first and last attempt at wallpapering. He knew that he was purposely blocking out the memories he had of his dad, because he was still fighting mad at him for what he'd done to his mother.

Walking into the master bedroom, he gave a heartfelt

sigh. He peeked into the bathroom and the beam from the flashlight ran over the walls of the huge fiberglass Jacuzzi. They'd had a bad leak in the wall one year and had to redo the whole bathroom. For a Christmas gift, Kel had bought them the tub, hoping it would help his mother's occasional lower back pains and his dad's sore muscles since he was no longer around to help him with the yard work. He clicked the button and shut down the beam. He didn't want to see the thing that had caused all the problems.

Feeling his way back down the hall, he tossed the journal on top of the box and then gathered the box under his arm. This was all he needed to get out of the house. Now he could sell it. He'd made his good-byes, if not his peace with the past.

He took the box out to the car then came back to make sure the house was secure. He mentally reminded himself to mail the realtor a key. He wasn't coming back.

On the way back to Wilmington, his cell phone rang. It was one of the officers on his team. "I just thought you'd like to know that the preliminary autopsy came back on that kid's body. She was beaten and raped. She was dead before she was wrapped up with the tape. This wasn't our man. They think it was her stepfather doing a copycat to cover up her death."

It wasn't their man. The words rang over and over in his head. It wasn't The Voyeur who had taken this girl and killed her. It wasn't his fault. It wasn't because he hadn't stopped him that another child had died. It wasn't because he was so distracted by Laura that he couldn't think straight. The relief was staggering and he had to pull off the road to come to grips with it. He asked the officer a few questions, then clicked the phone shut. He sat behind the wheel watching cars go by doing well over the speed limit. After a few minutes he turned his head and stared through the spotted windshield. He had more time. It wasn't over.

He drove straight to Wrightsville Beach and to TIDES AWASTIN'. When he knocked on the door, he had a smile on his face.

"Kel! Hi, I wasn't expecting you."

"I should have called first."

"No, we're just having a little tea party before bedtime. Come on in."

In the center of the family room was a miniaturized dining room table complete with chairs. He didn't know his furniture that well, but he thought it was French Provincial. The table was set for four. A large Winnie the Pooh and an oversized doll that looked very pricey occupied two of the chairs.

"Her grandparents ordered the furniture in Europe and had it shipped. We just got it today. Would you care for some tea?" Laura flashed a wide smile and gestured with her hand for him to take Winnie's chair.

"Oh, I'd be delighted," he said and was rewarded with a huge grin from Kayla.

"We have crumpets!" she exclaimed.

"Well, that's just wonderful, I adore crumpets," he said as he took his seat and Kayla reached for the teapot to serve him.

"Milk?" she asked, when he declined she frowned so when she offered the sugar cubes, he took three in his lukewarm, very light brown tea.

Laura whispered, "caffeine" and he understood why the watered down version. It was getting close to Kayla's bedtime.

The plate of "crumpets" was formally passed and he helped himself to dainty little pieces of a Thomas' English Muffin.

They play acted with Kayla until bedtime and Laura

took her upstairs to bed.

When she came down, Kel asked her if she'd found time to ask Kayla what she remembered about the night she was taken, and to ask if the "really smelly smell" could have been dirt and grass. He wanted to know specifically if she thought she could have been put into an oversized golf bag.

"She doesn't remember that part Kel, or at least not yet. She only talks about the sirens and the breathing noises and how hungry she was and that she was afraid she'd ruined her new overall pajamas by going to the bathroom in them."

Kel shook his head. The poor child had been through so much. He was just going to have to let this part go. He'd gone back to all the children, but none could remember the specifics he'd asked about. The trauma had just begun for them and they had been too terrified to lock in things to remember. Now, they were all trying to forget the whole horrible ordeal and not remember the details.

"But she did say she remembers smelling yucky poop, if that helps any."

"That actually helps a lot. I believe that might be the smell of fertilizer. Thanks."

Kel helped her clean up the mess from the tea party and then on impulse blurted out, "My mother died several months ago and I have been straightening out her affairs."

"I'm sorry. It must be hard losing your mother."

"Yeah. I just came from her house over in Benton. I've been working on getting it ready to sell. That's were I spent my vacation this year. That's where I was when all this stuff with The Voyeur started happening. I cut my bereavement time short to get back to work."

"Do you want to talk about it, over something a bit stronger than this?" she held up the tiny teapot.

"Yeah. What have you got?"

"Coffee, some wine. I can make you a cocktail as long as it contains vodka or tequila, and I think there's some brandy in one of the cabinets."

"Some wine sounds good. Will you have some with me?"

"Sure." She took a bottle of Riesling out of the refrigerator and he opened it and poured some into the glasses she held. Then they walked over and sat on opposite ends of the sofa.

"So spill it, why did you go to Benton today?"

He explained about Snow's Cut, the little girl, his feelings of inadequacy, his mixed emotions when it came to his childhood home, and then the discovery of the copycat.

"My father really screwed up my mother's life. I'm still trying to deal with the anger I have about it. I just wish so much that things had gone differently for them."

"Why don't you start at the beginning," she said as she tucked her long legs under her. He remembered those legs brushing alongside his in the motel bed and a frisson of heat went through him.

"I've never talked about it, to anyone. But, I guess there's no harm in the telling now that they're both gone. It's hard to believe that they are sometimes. Their love was so special once. Everyone used to comment on it. For over twenty-five years they were the most devoted couple you can imagine.

"Then one day my Dad found out that he had cancer. It scared him and he started doing things he'd put off for years. And trying new things. Suddenly he was all up for trying new things, some of them pretty risky. I guess he wanted to live life to the fullest, experience it all.

"Well, that's what caused the whole problem between him and Mom. He wanted to try everything, at least once.

"Here's where it gets a little weird. One night some

fellas at the local bar were getting a bit raunchy and telling off color stories about oral sex. Well, it seems my Dad had never had the good fortune of feeling a woman's mouth on him that way, so he went home to mother and tried to coerce her into it. Well, she wouldn't have anything to do with it. She flat out refused him. And no matter how he argued, she wouldn't relent.

"So, he told her that if she wasn't going to do it, he'd find someone who would—that he wasn't going to the grave without experiencing what these fellas had described at length as the ultimate orgasm.

"She told him, 'Fine! You just do that. But don't come back here if you do.' She was furious with him and as far as she was concerned, they were finished in the bedroom department.

"Well, it didn't take dear old dad long to find a willing woman. He began seeing this young floozy pretty regularly, but as he still loved my mother, he tried to keep the affair secret. He didn't want to lose my mother and he didn't want to give this woman up either, as he was having wild, incredible sex. But he did something really stupid and got found out by the woman's red nail polish."

"Her red nail polish?"

"Yeah," he bit out harshly. "Her nail polish."

"What did he do, let her paint his nails?"

"No. What he did was bring her to the house. My mother volunteered for a lot of things. One day she was committed to work at the library all afternoon. This woman wanted to see the house my father lived in. I think she was trying to figure out how well off he was. Well, he took her there and when she saw the Jacuzzi tub in the master bathroom, she just had to get him in there for a little dalliance. While she was in there, her acrylic nails scraped the sides of the tub leaving little telltale streaks of red.

"Mother, meticulous housekeeper that she was, saw the marks the next day and knew exactly what they were and how they had gotten there. She had acrylic nails herself and knew that the darker polishes left those kinds of marks. However, she'd had French tips for the last few years and they didn't leave any marks on the fiberglass. She knew that another woman had been in her tub. She called my dad on it, and he either wasn't a very convincing liar, or he didn't even try. That part, I never knew.

"Mom sent him packing and he wound up moving in with the woman with the red nails. Only now the woman wasn't satisfied with just the bedroom romps, she wanted the whole deal. She'd seen our house, figured there had to be more money than my father had alluded to, so she insisted that my dad get legally separated. Then she used every trick in the Joy of Sex book to get my father to file for a divorce from my mother so he could marry her.

"While my dad was waiting until the time he could file for a divorce, he saw several different doctors. One gave him some hope of recovering from his cancer, so he started undergoing treatment and began racking up huge medical bills. Meanwhile, mom got herself a really good attorney and she ended up with most of dad's retirement. When the woman realized there wasn't going to be any money in this for her after all, she dumped my father.

"A few years after that, the cancer flared up and he got too sick to take care of himself. He had hardly any money left so he asked my mother if he could please come home to die. She let him back. She took care of him until he died a few months later. But nothing was ever the same again. He had killed their love. She never forgave him for what he did to her, or at least she hadn't meant to forgive him. Shortly after he died she developed Alzheimer's and as it progressed she forgot he'd had the affair and left her. She lived the last fifteen years of her life alone, so madly in love with him that she wouldn't look at anyone else with any serious interest."

"Wow, that is so sad. Geez, the fingernail polish. Mmm, mmm, mmm, you just never know do you?"

"No. No, you don't. And that's why I feel the way that I do. I've seen a great love die. If theirs could, anybody's can."

"They let it die, Kel."

"What do you mean? My mom didn't let it die!"

"Yeah, she did."

"How can you say that? She didn't do a damn thing wrong!"

"When he came to her and asked her for special sexual favors, couldn't she have at least tried it?"

"Laura, think about what you're saying! What if I wanted to try it with whips in front of an audience. Am I supposed to think my wife will be all right with that?"

"Well, you have to draw the line somewhere. Oral sex that way is pretty, well, normal though, isn't it?"

"As glad as I am to hear you say that, I have to disagree with you. You draw the line where one or the other is uncomfortable. She was uncomfortable with it. He should have done without."

"Yeah, I guess you're right. It's just a shame they couldn't work it out. Maybe counseling would have helped."

"I can't see either of them agreeing to that."

"Well, except for their last year together, they had a pretty good life, right?"

"Yeah, but she had ten miserable years alone after her memory forgot the bad stuff."

"Then she must have loved him, even then."

"Why do you say that?"

"Well, she didn't see anybody else again, did she?"

"She dated a little, but no, she never saw anybody seriously."

"She didn't think she could ever love that way again. I'll bet if her memory hadn't changed she still would have loved him."

"No, she wouldn't have."

"It's a shame we can't ask her, 'cause I think she might have."

"You didn't even know her."

"I know you. And I don't think the acorn falls far from the tree."

"Meaning?"

"Meaning that I'll bet when you finally fall hard for someone, it'll be for keeps. For always."

"Then I mustn't ever let that happen. It puts too much control in someone else's hands."

"When you love someone Kel, you trust them. It's a package deal."

"You loved someone."

"Yeah, but it wasn't the kind of love we're talking about. I always knew I was settling."

"Why? Why would you do that?"

"I got tired of waiting for it to happen. I wanted to be a wife and a mother. All my friends were getting married and it seemed to be the thing to do. So when Ryan proposed, I convinced myself that this would probably be as close as I'd get to my dream. I snatched the golden ring and then I watched as it slowly turned to brass. But I know one thing."

"What's that?"

"I'd do it again."

"What, get married?"

"Fall in love. I want what your parents had once upon a time. If I had what they had, I wouldn't let it die."

He took a big gulp of his wine and just stared over at

her. *What would it be like to be loved by a woman like her,* he thought. *What would it be like just to have an affair with a woman like her?* But he knew that Laura was not the type to have a casual affair. He suspected she was an all or nothing kind of girl, and she deserved to have someone faithful and true. But marriage wasn't for him. It was too painful. He'd never forget how two people who had really loved each other hurt each other so badly.

"I'd better go. I have a full day tomorrow. Thanks for listening to my sob story."

"I'm glad you came over," Laura said as she gracefully unwound from the sofa and walked with him to the door.

With her body language, she tried to show him that she wouldn't mind if he kissed her goodnight. She stood close. She tilted her face up to fully meet his. She smiled winsomely and damned if she didn't even bat her eyelashes. But either he was impervious, or this thing with his mother had really affected him in a bad way.

"Well, goodnight!" she called after him as he walked down the front steps.

He turned and waved, then gave her a cursory smile. "Make sure to set the alarm."

Then he was gone, driving away in an old purple car that reminded her of a Cutlass. Purple. That just didn't seem like Kel.

She turned back just in time to hear the phone ring. She shut the front door and locked it before running for the phone.

"Yes? Oh, yes. I did ask Kel to have you call me. Yes, we should. I would like that very much. Okay, I'll see you then. I'll look forward to it."

She replaced the phone gently in its cradle and tilted her head in wonder. Paige Lawson wanted to meet with her. She agreed that maybe they could help each other. She had

270

tried the number Kel had given her for Meggie Ryan many times, but there was never anyone at home. But at least Paige wanted to talk.

She turned off the lights and went upstairs. She had been asleep for two hours when she remembered the alarm. She wasn't sure what had caused her to wake up, but now she wasn't sure whether she had set the damn thing or not. She patted Kayla on the back and smoothed the covers over her shoulders, then went downstairs to check. The lights were flashing, showing that it was set. She pressed the display panel just for kicks to see what time she had set it. Twelve-thirty. That couldn't be right, it was only one o'clock right now. Maybe she hadn't been asleep as long as she'd thought. She hadn't looked at the clock when Kel left, maybe it hadn't been as early as she'd thought. She shrugged and went back upstairs. Well it certainly wasn't anything to worry about, no one would come into a house and set an alarm that had been off.

Chapter Twenty-eight

*H*arold Satterfield walked the beach, staying close to the dune line and ignoring the couples strolling at the water's edge. He tossed the key ring into the air and caught it repeatedly, enjoying the heft of it and listening to the keys clink together. All his girls' keys were here, he had collected them over many months. He had keys to all of Laura's houses, even to some of her daddy's beach houses.

He hadn't been able to resist using the key. He wanted to see if he had been right, the keys had been tagged and he had been careful to copy the tags when he had copied the keys. He'd had six places to check, but he had finally found her. But tonight wasn't the night, he had to find a way to get more of those little blue pills. He wouldn't do well by her without them. He had a source, but the man hadn't shown up this week. He'd be there tomorrow though, he was always there at the high school for the home games, and he'd get more Viagra. These days he needed help in the romance department, each day it was getting harder and harder to accept the fact that he was getting older, but it was becoming a hard, cold fact. His body was not what it used to be, but as far as he was concerned it was still pretty damn good.

Once he had been quite the catch, tall and handsome with a thick head of hair and twinkling eyes, as all the girls

272

had said. He'd had plenty of wavy hair into his thirties, but then it suddenly started receding and getting thinner. And the rangy, youthful physique he'd taken such pride in was considerably diminished, he supposed the beer might have had something to do with that. His stomach was no longer flat, and his waistline had grown considerably. But he still had that twinkle, and he knew that it would still work its magic on the ladies, and one in particular. He smiled and tucked the keys into his pocket. Laura was going to be one well-fucked lady when he was through with her.

Chapter Twenty-nine

*P*aige used the keys Cayce had given her to open the door and was surprised to find Cayce sitting in a big overstuffed chair, his chin propped on his turned-in fist, just staring into oblivion.

It had been two days since he had insisted she and Joshua move in with him to avoid the media camping out at her apartment building. He had promised her at the time that he would not touch her, and every day his promise was getting harder and harder to keep.

"Cayce?" It took a moment for him to register her presence, blink, and turn to look up at her. "Are you okay?"

He simply nodded.

"Joshua asleep?"

He nodded again. "Upstairs in his room and the monitor's on."

"What were you thinking?" she asked as she lifted her briefcase strap from her shoulder and placed it with her purse on the floor against the wall. She walked into the room and stood staring down at him, more than mildly concerned by the haunted look in his eyes.

He put his arms on the sides of the chair and effortlessly lifted himself out of it. She was standing just inches from him and he was touched by the worry lines wrinkling her brow.

274

"It's nothing. Don't worry about it."

"No, really. Tell me. What's on your mind?"

"Do you really want to know, Paige? Do you really want to know what's on my mind?" he said, his voice suddenly gruff.

"Yes," she said, trying not to draw out the word despite her sudden hesitancy. The way he was looking at her was reminiscent of a wolf circling his prey.

"It's your breasts. That's what's on my mind. Your beautiful, full breasts. Crested by the most tantalizing pink-tipped nipples I've ever seen." His eyes looked pained when he met hers. "And I want desperately to see them again," he whispered. "It's all I think about."

Her eyes held his as she drank in the pools of lapis blue. She watched them slowly darken to a rich, deep sapphire. Slowly her hand went to her blouse, and she began unbuttoning it. He watched as her fingers undid the center clasp of the lacy bra she wore and the cups fell away from her breasts.

Lovely white globes stood firm while pink nipples ruched and hardened.

He gave a low groan and bent to caress them with his hands, then his mouth. Within seconds she was on fire, burning so hot that she could barely stand it.

His hands moved to her face and he cupped it, kissing her wildly on her lips, her cheeks, and her eyelids. He backed her up against the wall, and with his large hands, he lifted her hips so he could press his pelvis into her and immobilize her against the wall. He reached down and grabbed a fistful of her skirt and momentarily paused while shutting his eyes and clenching his jaw. The decision finally and irretrievably made, he pulled her skirt up past her thighs to her waist. Strong hands molded her body to his as he caressed her thighs, her hips, and gripped her buttocks. She was wearing thigh-high stockings and he let his fingers toy with the smooth flesh at the edges. He was stroking her in ultra sensitive areas as he worked toward his goal, the place from which a heady muskiness was already emanating. When his fingers stroked her wet warmth, she gasped and buckled, and had it not been for his support, she would have crumpled onto the floor at his feet. He braced her with his knee long enough to remove her panties and unzip his pants. He hoisted her higher, spread her thighs so she straddled him and thumbed himself to her opening. He was inside her, fully sheathed before she could protest. God, it felt wonderful. His loud groan attested to the sublime pleasure he felt at just being inside her. Then the thought came to him that no one had been here, in this way, enjoying her like this for over six years. It was a heady feeling and he became so utterly possessive that he couldn't control himself.

He thrust into her, taking her hard against the wall and reveling in the feel of her tight slickness and the hot, incredible softness of her. Her vagina felt like fine velvet that had been left to warm in a sunny window. Total mindlessness came over him and he primitively gave in to the needs that had been battering him for almost a week. To say he took her would have been accurate, if not understated. He took her like a crazed demon, stroking in and out of her while he gripped the backs of her thighs; he took her to the precipice, and when she arched her body against his, he reached between them and touched her where they joined. When she collapsed against him and fell over the edge, he followed. They remained in their own private world until her gasps and pants eclipsed his consciousness and he allowed her legs to slowly fall to the floor on either side of him.

"Sweet Jesus," he muttered under his breath against her neck.

"Yeah," she whispered, still stunned by all that had

happened between them in the few short minutes since she'd come through the door.

They were silent for long moments while he kissed and licked her neck. Then he removed his hands from her hips and separated from her. She turned to move away, but he grabbed her by the wrist.

"Hey," he whispered, his voice husky against her ear. "I finally succumbed, and justified or not, if you think I'm not going to repeat this breach of trust, faith, or whatever the hell it is, you're mistaken. I know I can't stop now, not now that I've had you. You were addictive before, it's only going to be worse now. Let me stay the night in your bed. I'll beg forgiveness in the morning, whether it's once or a hundred times, it won't matter, so I'd rather have the hundred times if you don't mind. I know I did wrong by you, but by God and all that's holy, I'm not sorry. Not right now at least." His mouth covered hers and he crushed her to him.

When he pulled away and looked into her face, her liquid, sated eyes met his and she smiled. She gave him a tiny nod and said, "It's actually your bed, but I'd love to share it with you." He bent and scooped her off her feet, took her mouth greedily, and carried her to the Master's bedroom— his, then hers, now theirs.

❧❧

He was standing at the foot of the bed, between her splayed legs, looking down at where they had just been joined. He had separated from her because he wanted to watch her come this time. And, he wanted her to know how skilled he was with his fingers alone. For some reason, he felt as if this night was an audition of sorts, and he was trying out for the role of a lifetime—that of her lover, and he was desperate to get the part.

He reached under her and with just the tip of his

middle finger, he stroked her anus. She moaned no, pulled away and slid further up on the bed. He grabbed her ankle and gently pulled her back down.

"Please let me," he urged as he continued to press against the tiny opening of her orifice, not venturing inside, just putting the right amount of pressure on a certain nerve ending he knew was secretly begging to be activated. Most women didn't even know that they had a very erogenous nerve hiding there, unless a thoughtful man cared to show them. She stilled and he continued the steady pressure. With his thumb he rubbed her labia, gently circling the tiny nub that intermittently surfaced until he had coaxed it out completely. When he leaned forward and added plucking on a nipple, she shattered. Her face fracturing with such intense pleasure was the sweetest thing he had ever seen.

When she got up to make a phone call an hour later, he wondered who she could possibly be calling at a time like this, but he wasn't going to ask. Thank God he didn't have to, she volunteered the information when she came back to bed. He wrapped her in his arms as she slid in beside him and said, "I just called Laura Wyndham. I think I need to talk to somebody and maybe she does too." He kissed her on the temple and told her that was a nice thing to do. But inside his head he was high-fiving himself. This lady definitely had the making of a pastor's wife. *How did I get so blessed?*

Chapter Thirty

Kel stood outside Cayce's office for twenty minutes waiting for him to finish talking with a parishioner. When the door finally opened and Cayce ushered the frail old man out, Kel quickly slid into the office behind them. He wasn't waiting for anyone else to unburden themself before he got Cayce's attention. A few minutes later Cayce returned from walking the old gentleman to his car. He took one look at Kel and firmly closed the door.

"What can I do for you detective?"

"I need to ask Paige a question and so far I haven't been able to find her."

"She moved."

"I gathered that. I was hoping you could tell me where she went."

"I'm not inclined to, what do you want her for?"

"I need to ask her a question."

"What is it, I'll ask her for you."

"You're making this a bit difficult."

"That's the idea."

"You're protecting her from me?"

"I'm protecting her from everyone right now."

"Why, has anything else happened?"

"She just can't deal with it all. The media, the boy,

279

his problems, the fear someone's going to find pictures of her on the Internet, the nightmares, that it could all happen again."

"Is she getting help?"

"Yeah, me. I'm helping her."

"I mean a professional."

"I am a professional! This is what I do!"

"Look Cayce, I don't mean to butt in here, but I think you might be too close to the situation. You could be a part of what she's trying to forget. Don't you think someone else might be better for her under the circumstances?"

Cayce did not like hearing that the detective thought he could be part of what Paige wanted to forget. "No! I can take care of her just fine. And please do butt out, I have a handle on this. And I'm not stupid, I've talked to specialists, I'm getting good advice."

"Okay, fine. In the meantime, I have to talk to Paige. Just for a minute."

Cayce looked at Kel with narrowed eyes, then he shifted on his hip and put his hand in his pants pocket. He pulled out a small cell phone, flipped it open, and with his thumb punched in a series of numbers. Then he put it to his ear.

"You'd better not upset her. Man to man, you don't want to tangle with me on this." Then at the sound of a voice on the other end, his stern, set jaw softened into a bright smile and it transformed his face.

"Hi sweetie. Josh home from school yet? Yeah? How'd he do? That's wonderful. Tell him to be sure to save it for me, I want to see it. Paige, Detective Vain is here. He has a question he needs to ask you. Yes, I know. I will." Then he handed the phone over to Kel.

"Paige, I need to know if you've had a chance to go over that list of questions with Joshua yet. Yeah. Uhhuh. I understand. Okay, I will. Uh, by the way, remember I talked to you about that counseling service?" He heard Cayce mutter "Shit," and watched him as he sprang forward. Kel stood and moved with the phone to the other side of the room. "Yes. Yes. Oh good, I'm glad you connected because Laura could never get anybody at the other number. Yes, I'll give her your new number in case something comes up. Well, actually I can't. Cayce won't give it to me. Yes, I will. Thanks."

He closed the phone and tossed it back to Cayce.

"What the hell was that counseling service shit about?"

"Are you supposed to be talking like that, you being a pastor and all?"

"I don't know what I'm supposed to be doing anymore! Excuse me," his voice lowered to a whisper, "I don't know what the fuck I'm supposed to be doing any more!"

"What is your problem?" Kel asked, in shock.

Cayce ran long fingers through his thick hair. "I don't know. My emotions are on a seesaw. Ever since I met this woman, I don't have a clue whether I'm coming or going!"

"Join the club. I'm in the same boat."

"Pardon?"

"You are a real pastor right, not some fly-by-Internet praise jockey?"

Cayce stood and magnanimously bowed as he gestured to his credentials on the back of his office wall. "Help yourself, I think you'll find they're legit. Duke University."

"Then I can tell you things that you can't repeat, right?"

"Absolutely."

"Then let's go have a beer. You do drink don't you?"

"Hell yes."

Kel stood, rubbed his jaw, and looked around the office. "What denomination is this, anyway?" The look of chagrin on his face was priceless and Cayce let out a loud hoot. Then he grabbed his blazer, took some keys out of the drawer, and opened the door for Kel.

⚭

They sat in a booth at Henry's sipping on their drinks and eating a double order of loaded potato skins.

"I think about Laura everyday. Most days, most of the time. There are some days when I manage to put her out of my mind for a few hours, then someone walks past wearing a scent reminiscent of hers and I remember. Or I see a couple walking hand-in-hand or kissing, and I start to burn for her. But the nights are the worst. Those, I spend tossing from side to side and twisting the bed linens into huge knots."

"If you're asking me, I'd say you're a man who's in love."

"No, I'm sure I'm not that far gone."

"Hey, just two days ago, I was a basket case myself. I was at the computer, prepared to delete the pictures, but the temptation was just too great, I had to view them one more time. I was fascinated and titillated, and just plain overcome with lust. I could think of nothing else but her and as I sat there looking at the pictures that had hurt her so much, I was disgusted with myself, disgusted beyond belief. I was crying as I dragged and dropped each one into the trash can. Then after I had deleted them I curled into a fetal position on the sofa in my study and cried. Then I asked for forgiveness. But the lust I had for her was overpowering. And last night when she came home from work—in case you hadn't figured it out, she's living with me—I overpowered her. I took her Kel, I just took her. I didn't even know if she wanted to be taken.

I just took her. Now what kind of a man does that after what she's been through?"

"Well that's just the thing. At what point is it love? When does lust turn to love?"

"I think that one's going to take another beer."

"Yeah. Me, too."

"So when are you going to realize you're in love?" Cayce asked.

"Oh, I'm still in the lust stage. Definitely."

"Take it from me, don't be so sure. It sneaks up on you."

"So you admit it? You're in love with Paige?"

"I don't know what I am. But I do know that I am going to marry her." Cayce tipped his bottle and drained it, then he signaled the waitress for another round.

Chapter Thirty-one

Kel was sitting in his car, deciding where to go next when he heard the radio crackle. He normally didn't listen to the dialogue, it was the dispatcher talking with the beat cops. They had portable radios, but since he was a detective, if they needed him they paged him or called his cell phone. But this particular conversation was hilarious. An officer was citing a woman for throwing litter out of her car. After pulling her over he was flabbergasted to discover that the litter she had left on the side of the road was a used tampon. The young officer was completely dumbfounded and had no idea how to handle the situation. Kel could hear the sergeant on the squawk box trying not to lose it as he advised the officer. "If there's no danger, make her get out of the car and go pick it up. Then write her a ticket. But don't you dare bring that thing back here as evidence."

Comments, and every kind of zinger you can imagine came over after that and Kel could just imagine how red-faced the officer must be. Even he had to know he'd just earned himself a new nickname for the squad room.

He chuckled and turned the volume down and started the car. Then an odd thought occurred to him. A very odd thought and he was surprised it hadn't occurred to him or anyone else up to this point. None of the women had been on their periods.

He made a mental note to call each one and verify that, except Laura of course—he knew without a doubt that she hadn't been. But, if that were true, how would The Voyeur have known that?

He turned off the car and sat there in Henry's parking lot, watching people go in and out of Port City Java, and mulled that thought over. How indeed? From a doctor's office? Through a nurse? Using medical records and extrapolating? A hidden camera? He'd had his tech team do a complete electronic search of all the homes and no hidden cameras or bugging devices had been found anywhere. What other ways were there? Checking their trash? What was it that women did consciously or even unconsciously that could let on that they were menstruating? He pulled out his notebook and started making a list:

—buying sanitary products? Could this guy simply be a clerk in a drugstore? But that wouldn't necessarily mean that the women were menstruating at the time, some were organized and planned ahead, some probably stocked up when there were sales.

—disposing of the used product? Where? How? In a bathroom, possibly in a public restroom?

—emitting the pungent telltale odor that accompanied the discharge of blood and ammonia from the body? He once knew a kid in college who swore he could always tell when a woman was menstruating. He'd always had phenomenal luck in the bars. Was it possible The Voyeur got that close to his victims before targeting them?

—being astute enough to notice the subtleties a woman's body went through, like bloating, the tummy paunching, the irritability? Or were those symptoms experienced just before the onset?

He decided he needed to talk to a woman, so he dialed Laura's number. How the hell was he going to talk to her about this, he asked himself as the phone rang. He was actually relieved when she didn't answer. He decided not to leave a message about this subject on her machine.

He started his cruiser again. He sure had plenty of things to check into now.

Chapter Thirty-two

Laura was at Dillard's Department Store browsing around the cosmetic counters and towing a restless Kayla in her firm grip. "Don't you like looking at the lipsticks and polishes sweetheart? I love to try all these new things. When I was your age I even had play makeup made by a company named Tinkerbell. Then I graduated to Bonnie Bell."

Kayla wasn't paying a bit of attention. She didn't like this smelly stuff. In preschool she dressed up with her friends, and sometimes she even wore some of her mom's lipstick, but she could never sit still long enough for nail polish to dry, so it never stayed on. "I want to get some cookies."

"We will, just let me look around for a few minutes." Then she looked down and smiled at Kayla, "and sniff, too. This is where I buy my perfume."

"I like your perfume. You smell nice."

"Thank you sweetheart," Laura said as she led her over to the men's fragrances section. Something about Kel's smell intrigued her. Her mind had made a scent memory of him and whenever it returned it made her knees week. Now she wanted to know exactly what his essence was comprised of—a little male sweat for sure, some spicy scent from his deodorant, but then what? She sniffed the tops of several

287

testers trying to find one that might be similar. She picked up others, one at a time, from the back row of the display and brought the spray nozzles to her nose. She was on the second to the last one when her nose twitched and memories of burying her face in his neck came hauntingly back to her. She could almost feel his skin against her lips. She turned the small white bottle around and read the name on the aftershave bottle: Kouros. Mmmm, this was definitely it. She sniffed it again and smiled. Then she motioned to the salesclerk. "I'd like to buy this please."

"We have it in a larger size if you'd like,"

"No, this is fine." How much do I need if I'm just going to put it on my dresser and pathetically sniff the top, she thought with chagrin. But she couldn't help herself. She wanted reminders of him. She didn't know why, but it was comforting to be taking a piece of him home with her. His fragrance was something she could wallow in when she needed to feel him close. Sometimes the memories of her behavior with him that first night in the motel room were so embarrassing that she wanted to die, but when she remembered how excited she had been, how thrilled she had been by his touch, she had to marvel at life's ironic twists. She had been taken unaware to a place of pleasure that was not of this earth. He had made her feel wonderful and now she finally understood what it meant to be a woman.

The saleswoman took her charge card and rang up the sale. When she handed Laura the bag and her card, she said, "I really admire you Mrs. Wyndham, I'm glad your little girl is all right."

Laura smiled at her and graciously said, "Thank you. I appreciate you saying that."

Laura turned to Kayla and said with a big smile, "C'mon baby, let's go get some cookies."

"Yeah! I want chocolate chip. Three of them."

"Two. They're big. I'll eat the other," she said with a chuckle.

The man sitting at a table in the food court watched her pay for the cookies the little girl picked out, then watched as they sat down at a table to eat them. She was even lovelier than the last time he'd seen her.

Chapter Thirty-three

*H*arold Satterfield followed the little mother and her charge from the food court to the parking lot. He stayed thirty feet back and tried not to stare. He was spiraling away from all the precautions he normally took. He knew he shouldn't be stalking her like this, he knew it was dangerous to even walk on the same side of the mall as she was. But he couldn't help himself, he wanted to be close to her. He wanted to be so close that her pheromones overtook him. To smell her musky fragrance would be Heaven, to see her soft, warm flesh quiver for him, would be sublime, to taste her, he couldn't even imagine the thrill that would be, as she had captivated him so completely. This waiting was agony, he wanted her as badly as he thought he'd ever wanted a woman, and that was saying something, because at one time, his Gloria had owned him body and soul. As he watched Laura strap Kayla into her car seat, he cursed the man who controlled his destiny with her, the man who supplied the fuel for his insatiable lust, those tiny, powerful, little pale blue pills. Tonight, maybe he'd have some for him tonight.

❧⟡

Before going home, Laura stopped by her parents' house in Landfall. They fawned over Kayla and insisted on

290

keeping her for the night. When their maid took Kayla to the kitchen to have her help make a cake, they told Laura that they wanted to discuss her future and the effects the kidnapping were having on the upcoming charity events. Laura stopped them cold.

"Mother, Father, please hear me out first. This whole mess has made me do some serious thinking about my future, and Kayla's, too. Now that the media has been somewhat appeased and everything has calmed down a little, I've decided that I want to try my hand at actually doing some volunteer work instead of doing the fundraising all the time. I have an appointment with one of the doctors on staff at the hospital to discuss helping out on a few of the hotlines. It will keep me out of the public eye for a while and Kayla can come with me. Anyway that's what I'm going to do. I'm going to counsel women who have been raped or abused, after I've had some training of course. You two can do the symphonies and the theater and all the events in between. I need a break. Kayla needs me with her right now, and I need her."

"You aren't doing this just because you don't want to leave Kayla are you, because we're always happy to baby-sit."

"No Mother, I'm not. I just want to do something different, something significant to help people. In fact, later tonight I'm meeting one of the mothers who also had her child taken. Sort of a group therapy session if you will, only with two of us."

"Oh, Laura, are you sure that's wise?"

"Yes, Mother. I'm sure, very sure. We can help each other get over this."

"I hear Ryan's being a jerk about all this," her father interrupted.

"So what else is new?"

291

"Is he causing you trouble?"

"Nothing I can't handle, Dad, but thanks."

"I had a talk with your brother today."

"Oh? What did he have to say?"

"He says he wishes you'd return his calls."

"I will."

"He's not mad at you anymore. He understands what you did at the Hilton and why you had to do it."

"Well, he should have had more faith in me. Really! How could he possibly think I'd do something like that just for the fun of it!"

"He's sorry for the things he said, the messages he left on your machine."

"He is?" You could hear the wistfulness in her voice.

"Yes. He wants you to call him. Here," her father said as he picked up the phone on the end table and dialed his son's number. He handed the phone to Laura and then they both left the room to give her some privacy.

A few minutes later a teary-eyed Laura found them in the study. "We're okay again. It's just been a hard time for all of us. Apparently his fiancé isn't sure we're a fit family to marry into now."

"Her loss," her mother said, then mischievously she whispered, "I hear her tatas are enhanced."

"Men who've apparently seen both, say yours are much nicer, my dear." After the initial shock of what her father had just said passed, they all laughed.

It was the first time since Kayla had been taken that she knew everything was going to be all right again.

੧੪੬

When Laura arrived home there was a message on her machine from Meggie Ryan. Kel had given Meggie

Laura's number in case she needed someone to talk to. On the message, she sounded like she had been crying. She quickly punched in the number Meggie had left.

Meggie was crying when she answered the phone. "Meggie this is Laura. Honey, what's the matter, other than the obvious, of course," she added with exaggerated sarcasm. They had not met, but there was already a bond. Laura could feel it.

"It's my ex. He's being horrible. He's talking about going in front of the hospital review board and bringing Rand up on morals charges."

"Can he do that?"

"I don't know," she wailed.

"Have you told Rand?"

"No!" she sobbed. "I'm afraid Rand will kill him."

"Honey, you're going to have to tell him. It's his career that will be affected."

"I know." This time there was a long, drawn out sigh. "I know," this time a low whine. "I'm in trouble Laura."

"Worse than this?"

"Yes. I think I'm in love with Rand."

"Jeez Meggie, that was quick. I thought you had just met."

"Where'd you hear that?"

"From Kel. Isn't it true?"

"Yeah, it's true. I just didn't know how much you knew."

"I guess since we're kind of in the same boat, Kel shared some of your story. Hey, you want to come over to my house tonight. Paige, one of the other mothers whose son was taken, is coming over. We could, uh . . . ."

"Compare notes?"

They both laughed.

"Yeah," Laura said breaking into a big smile.

293

"Sounds like fun. Where are you staying? The papers say you moved out of your house."

"I'm staying on Wrightsville, a place my parents own. It's really easy to find. Bring your bathing suit, and we'll take a dip." She gave Meggie the address and told her to come over whenever she liked.

Chapter Thirty-four

Paige and Meggie showed up at the same time. They met coming up the walk. Laura was waiting for them and eagerly opened the door. The three women tentatively hugged each other, then the tears began to flow. Laura led them into the house and to the family room. Then she took the bottle of champagne she had put in an ice bucket into the room and placed it on Kayla's tea table that was still set up in the room.

"I hope Kayla doesn't mind that I'm using her table for something other than tea tonight," she joked.

Laura popped the cork as only a true debutante can, quietly and slowly, so as not to waste a single drop. Then she filled a flute for each of them. She handed one to Paige, then one to Meggie before lifting her own in a toast.

"To the best mothers in the world!"

"Here! Here!" They both seconded. They all drank it down and Laura refilled each glass.

"Paige, I know Cayce is with Josh, Kayla is with her grandparents, is Toby with Rand?"

"No, he's with his father," Meggie said between sips. "Hey, Laura this is good stuff."

"Thank you, I take a bottle or two from my dad's wine cellar whenever I'm there. He never says anything so

I guess he doesn't keep inventory. Today, I took four," she said with an impish grin.

"Woo-whee!" Paige exclaimed. "Time to party! I sure could use a nice long happy hour."

"Well ladies, we don't have to go anywhere, the kids are safe and being taken care of, and I have plenty of bedrooms if we drink too much. Let's celebrate us! We deserve a big pat on the back."

"Yeah, not the disdain we're getting . . . ."

And so it began, three hours of letting off steam, sharing stories and fears, baring raw emotions, and drinking. Lots of drinking.

After the second bottle Laura put a pizza in the oven. She had ordered it from Michaelangelo's off of Eastwood Road but asked them not to cook it all the way. They ate their fill of pizza while continually guzzling champagne. Then they put on their suits and went out to the pool. Laura had forgotten to call Paige back to tell her to bring one, so she loaned her one of hers.

Together they sat on the ledge in the shallow section, talking and sipping their drinks from plastic cups. The camaraderie was wonderful and the women found they had a lot to talk about outside of their recent experiences.

Laura was smiling and watching the women laugh and taking pot shots at each other when suddenly something occurred to her.

"Paige, Meggie, I think I've seen you somewhere before. In fact, I'm almost certain of it. And Meggie, I think I've even seen you in that bathing suit before."

They both turned to stare at her. Then it clicked for all three of them.

"Oh . . . my . . . God," three separate voices intoned at the same time.

"Jesus, the spa," Meggie whispered.

Then no one spoke for a full minute as their minds raced to connect the dots.

"He saw us there! It all makes sense now," Laura breathed. "That's how he knows so much about us, where we live, about our kids. The women are always talking!"

"Except there was no he," Paige said. "Men aren't allowed there. Never have been."

"But still, that's the tie that binds. That's the connection Kel's been looking for." Laura jumped out of the pool, stumbled a little on her wobbly legs, and made her way to the kitchen where she'd left the phone. But it wasn't there, and she couldn't remember where she had left it.

Chapter Thirty-five

Kel was dozing in front of the TV when his pager went off. The desk sergeant told him that there were two gentlemen at the desk looking for women.

"Well, aren't we all?" Kel quipped.

"Specific women sir, Paige Lawson and Meggie Ryan. I thought you'd want to know.

He sat up straight in his seat. "Who are the men?"

"Dr. Cheswick and the Reverend Cayce Braxton. They say you know where these women are."

"Give me one of them." He waited until one was put on the line.

"Kel?" It was Cayce.

"Yeah?"

"Paige and Meggie were supposed to be at Laura's tonight for a support meeting. We haven't heard from them and no one's answering at the number they gave us. It's past midnight. Can you give us Laura's address? It's been a bitch trying to get anybody in this town to give it to us."

"I'll be right there. I'll take you to them."

He hung up the phone and grabbed his keys and badge, tossing the remote back to the sofa.

He connected with Cayce, who had a sleepy Joshua on his shoulder, and Rand in front of the station and they formed a convoy. He was in a strange mood, and just to make it interesting, he ran his blue lights until they crossed the bridge to Wrightsville Beach.

It was dark on the beach and along the main boulevard. There were only a few lights on in some of the houses, but when they pulled up in front of Laura's, you could tell from the road that the backside of the house was lit up. As the three men exited their cars, Kel said, "They must be outside by the pool."

The sight that met them when they walked around the house to the pool shocked them all. The three women were asleep in their wet bathing suits, sprawled on the padded loungers, snoring.

"Well, doesn't this beat all?" Rand said as he walked by each one, stopping to take their pulse. Shaking his head ruefully, he said, "My professional opinion is that they are intoxicated."

Kel bent over Laura, and gripping her jaw, he moved her head back and forth, trying to wake her. "Laura, wake up," he called. "C'mon babe, open your eyes." She made soft mewling sounds of protest, then blinked and gave him a lopsided smile.

Cayce, with Joshua still sleeping in his arms, straddled the chair Paige was on, in effect, straddling her also. He made a circling motion with his hips and whispered so only she could hear, "Well, now that your inhibitions are down the tube, baby, ride this cowboy!"

"Are you sure you're a real pastor?" Kel asked with a wide grin as he looked over at Cayce while he was doing his little pelvis thing. Apparently he'd overheard.

Rand chuckled at Cayce's antics, then turned and gave a big, "Aha! I found the culprit." He reached under Meggie's lounger and brought out the empty bottle of champagne he had seen lying on its side under her chair.

"There's another one over here," Kel said lifting the bottle he found under a damp towel beside Laura's chair.

"Here's another!" Cayce whooped.

The three men laughed and then just shook their heads at the state the women were in. "Well, they certainly deserve a little, shall we say, down time?" Kel said. Then added, "C'mon we'd better get them out of their wet bathing suits and into bed."

"Spoken like a true cad."

"You know what I mean."

"Yeah, I suppose we do," Rand muttered. "Each one take the one that belongs to them and carry them back to the cave."

Kel lifted Laura high up into his arms and walked to the open patio doors. "You two take whichever one you want, I've got mine," he joked and then he disappeared into the house with Laura.

On the way up the stairs, her head lolled against his chest and she belched. For a minute he thought she might be getting sick, and he turned mid stride to take her in the opposite direction, toward the bathroom, but her steady breathing assured him that the crisis was over. He carried her into her bedroom, placed her on the bed, and then debated whether he should remove her wet suit or not. It wasn't much of a debate. He knew he couldn't leave her this way. He stripped off her suit telling himself not to take in her lovely breasts and incredibly long legs with the fury thatch at their apex, but he didn't listen to himself. He took a few seconds to admire her lovely skin before covering her with the comforter. Then he took the wet bathing suit into the bathroom and hung it over the bathtub. He heard her moan his name. Uh, oh. She was going to be sick after all. He ran back to the bed and knelt on the floor by her head.

"Laura?" he whispered, "are you okay?"

"Yes. Tried to call you."

"I didn't get a message that you had called."

"Couldn't find the phone, then I couldn't remember what I needed it for."

"Do you now?"

"Yessss!" she said emphatically, still quite drunk and slurring her consonants big time.

"What? What did you need to tell me?"

"I think I'm falling in love with you. But I mustn't."

He smiled, his heart careened and his blood warmed. "Why mustn't you?" he asked.

"I don't think you believe in happily ever after anymore. And I do."

"Oh, is that so?" he challenged, then he leaned over and kissed her cheek. "I have to go lock up and make sure the guys get the girls in their cars. Call me if you need anything. I'll just be downstairs. I'll turn on the monitor, so I can hear you."

The men were gone, so were the women, but Joshua was camped out on the sofa. "What the hell?" Kel began, then Cayce came through the front door.

"What? Did you think I could carry them both at one time? And mine got sick on the way."

"Sorry, no exchanges."

"Hey, before I forget, Paige keeps saying that there's something very important you need to know."

"And what's that?"

"Danged if I know, every time I ask, she passes out."

"Great."

"I'll call you if I get it out of her." He hefted Joshua into his arms and headed for the door.

"Seems like you have an instant family."

"Yeah, and I couldn't be happier," he said with a big shit-eating grin.

No sooner had Cayce disappeared before Rand came back through the door. "You got some paper towels?"

"She was sick, too?"

"I think she heard Paige and thought it was a good idea."

Kel went to the kitchen and got some wet dishtowels and took the roll of paper towels off the holder and handed it to him.

"Thanks. By the way, Meggie keeps saying there's something you oughta know, but I can't get her to tell me."

"Great. They all had a brainstorm, now no one can remember what it was. Let me know if you need more help."

"Nah, I think I've got it under control."

"You two an item?"

"Trying to be, but the ex won't let us."

"You lettin' that stop you?"

"Hell no!" he said with a big grin as he ran out the door.

Kel closed the door behind Rand, waited until he saw him pull away from the curb, then locked the door. He went out to the pool area and cleaned up, then worked on the kitchen. It appeared that three woman had polished off four bottles of vintage champagne.

He fixed himself a vodka tonic and went into the family room to find out how the game he had been watching had ended. He picked up the remote and spoke out loud, "Well, this certainly turned out to be a fun evening." But interestingly enough, he was quite content to be here in Laura's home, knowing she was safe and tucked in upstairs.

Chapter Thirty-six

$\mathcal{H}$e jerked awake when his brain registered a low moan; he was on his way up the stairs when he heard the ear-piercing scream. The monitor downstairs had been turned all the way up, so he heard it in stereo as he took the stairs two at a time, reaching the landing in only seconds. *Laura!* His blood was pounding and his heart was beating frantically as he ran into her room. She was sitting up in bed, white as the sheet she was clutching at her breasts, her tousled hair frizzed in places, and still damp in others. But it was her eyes that gave her fear away. They were huge and unblinking. If he hadn't known better, he would have thought she'd seen a ghost. The fear that she suspected someone was in the room became evident as her eyes flitted to each corner of the room. He quickly scanned them himself and then checked behind the door.

"Laura, did you see someone?" He asked as he walked toward her. There was something about her posture that made him take things slowly. "What is it? What woke you, honey?"

She blinked then and her head bobbed with the effort. "I saw him. Or at least I think I did."

"In here?" he croaked, terrified that the killer could have been this close without him even being aware.

303

"In my dream. An awful dream." Then she broke down and started crying, soft little sobs that shook her shoulders. Her hands were trembling when she covered her face and sobbed harder.

Kel sat on the edge of the bed and pulled her into his arms. He held her close to his chest and rubbed her back and stroked her long hair. "Shhh, it's okay. It was only a dream, none of it was real. Just your imagination, sometimes alcohol does that. It makes things seem real even when they're not."

"It was horrible Kel. He was the most despicable man. He made us do things. It was—" her voice broke on a sob and she had to fight to get a breath.

"Breathe, Laura. Concentrate on bringing one breath in, then letting it out. Deeper," he coached and he breathed with her until she had her rhythm back.

"It was the worst nightmare I have ever had Kel, and over the years I've had some doozies. This one was really horrible."

"Well, my mother used to tell me that if you turned on all the lights and shared the bad thoughts, that they would go away and never bother you again."

"I wouldn't want to wish this dream on anyone else."

"C'mon, tell me all about it. It'll make you feel better. The monsters seem smaller and more manageable when there's a united front." He got up and turned the overhead light on and then the two lamps on the nightstands. The room was glaringly bright, but Laura had to admit that she instantly felt better.

Then Kel found her bathrobe on the hook behind the bathroom door and handed it to her. "Let's get you warm first, you're shivering."

She hadn't even noticed. But now she even had goose

bumps. He turned his back and she slipped the robe on and tied the belt. "Okay."

He turned back and slid into the bed with her, settling his back against the headboard. Then he drew her back against his chest and held her close. "Okay, tell me about your dream. And don't leave out anything or it'll come back to spook you. Time to purge."

She took a deep breath and he could feel her chest rise and fall as he snuggled her back even more securely against his chest. Her breasts, resting on his arm, felt soft, full and warm under the fabric of her robe. When she didn't say anything he, prodded, "It began . . . ."

"I was in Lifeguard Class. I actually was in my junior year of college. It was late at night; we were all there for testing for our certification, seven of us. I can actually see the faces of every person who had been in that class, four girls and three boys. Our instructor never showed up. In the dream we had all received an e-mail to be there at ten o'clock if we wanted to be certified. So there we were in our bathing suits waiting for the teacher. But the man who showed up wasn't the teacher. He was evil. He was despicable. He was ugly and vile."

"What did he do?"

"He showed us a gun and fired it into the water to show us that it was loaded. He told us he had no problem with the idea of shooting us and throwing us in the pool to see how red he could make the water. In fact, he said he rather liked the idea, that it sounded like great fun. He had a horrible laugh—eerie and high-pitched, like the Joker in Batman.

"He made us line up in front of the pool. The girls had to drop the straps on their suits and bare their breasts. It was horrible Kel, everybody was looking at me. Even the boys who were just as scared as we were couldn't help looking, and he was leering. Then he walked down the row fondling us, pulling hard on our nipples. It hurt. It hurt really badly. I can almost feel it now, it hurt so badly in the dream, I think I moaned."

He watched as she moved one hand over both her breasts palming the nipples through her robe, testing them for soreness. He should not be getting hard at a time like this!

"Then he walked down the line pulling out the waistbands of the boys' trunks and looking down at them. He made crude remarks about their size. He laughed at one boy who'd been in the pool earlier whose penis had shrunk from the cold water. He said we all had to see this tiny thing and he pulled the boy's trunks down and made us all look at his shriveled penis. His name was Kevin, and I remember he started shaking and crying.

"Then he said he wanted to watch us all have sex together. He paired us up, but we were one boy short, so he picked me for himself. He looked me in the eye and said, 'It would really be nice if you were a virgin, because I haven't had one of them in a long, long, time.' Then as he took out a knife and cut off my suit, he leaned in and whispered, 'Or are you a tramp? Time will tell, time will tell,' he hissed. Then he laughed and rammed a finger inside me. I think that might have been when I screamed."

"Good God Laura, that's awful! Your recall is astounding though. Are you sure this isn't some kind of repressed memory?"

He felt and saw her shake her head. "No, just a bad dream. I can never seem to recall the good ones this well, but the bad ones," she shuddered, "well the bad ones, they're vivid, aren't they?"

"Yeah," he agreed as he pulled her even closer and stroked her from her hip to her shoulder. "I can see why you're so upset. But let's take this logically. Your subconscious takes a big hand in these kinds of things. You're obviously still thinking about the Hilton thing, and you might as well face it, you're probably going to be thinking about that off and on for the rest of your life. You need to find a way to deal with it. If nothing else, be proud—you're a beautiful woman. If half the women in that ballroom had breasts like yours, they'd have all been up on that stage strutting and showing themselves off. And take it from me, when men talk about you and that incident, it'll only be because they were pleased with what they saw. When the women talk, it'll be out of jealousy. Trust me on this babe, few women have what you have, that have come by it naturally. So turn the table, don't be embarrassed, be brassy and proud of your body. For the rest of it, you probably hate the idea that a man, any man can have control over your body. You're never going to get over the revulsion of the things you had to do that night at the Jefferson. No matter what goes on in your life, that night will always haunt you and give you nightmares. You gave up all your control, and you hate that. But remember, you did it willingly for Kayla. Never forget that. You always have the control, you just have to decide if you want to give it up for something more important. And for whatever it means to you, I think you did the right thing all around. I'm very proud of you. You should not entertain any thoughts of shame. You did what you had to." Then he chuckled and squeezed her hard. "And you did it remarkably well!" He kissed her at her hairline, on her temple.

"Thanks, Kel. I feel much better. The light thing really helps. I'll have to remember that with Kayla."

"Yeah, she's going to have some doozies over the years, too."

"I wish you could be around to handle them."

"That can be arranged," he said with a grin. But when

307

he turned to look into her face, she didn't have the look he expected her to have. She looked sad, and desolate.

"I'm not the type to have an affair, Kel."

"I know," he whispered into her hair.

"And you're not the type to consider marriage." She'd said it as a statement, and he couldn't argue with it. He had never considered it and probably never would. And since he couldn't refute it, he didn't say anything.

"So, where does that leave us?" she asked.

"I'm not sure."

There was silence for a few minutes, then Kel whispered, "Are you sure you're not the type to have an affair, a very, very discreet one?"

She chuckled. After another minute of silence she finally spoke. "Remember I once asked you if you were one of those men who needed variety?"

"Yes. I remember."

"Well, are you? Are you one of those men, Kel?"

"No. I think I've had enough variety. I'm ready for a steady diet now, something that can grow and get better with time."

"Well, that would be hard for us, wouldn't it?"

"Why do you say that?"

"Because I don't think it can ever be better than it was that night, even with all the stress. That night at the Jefferson has to be as good as it gets. It was the best I've ever had."

"Oh, you'd be surprised," he said as he turned her into his body. He cupped her neck and drew her close. As his lips descended to hers, he murmured, "Let me show you just how much better it can be when my mind's on nothing but pleasing you."

She allowed the scorching kiss. Who could resist those lips that parted hers so softly or that tongue that circled and dipped and lapped? But when his hand went between the opening folds of her robe and lightly stroked her belly, she had to stop him.

"Kel, we can't."

"Why can't we?" he breathed, in a devil-may-care voice as his lips moved from her lips to her throat. "It's not like we haven't already done it before."

His lips were working their way lower when he heard her say, "I need more than you can give me, and we both know it."

"When I removed your bathing suit," he murmured as he continued toward her breast, "I wanted so badly to do this." A split second later she arched and gasped as he captured her nipple in his mouth.

When he released her, he whispered, "I want you, Laura."

"Kel?"

"Yes?"

"I think I'm going to be sick."

He leapt off the bed and ran for the bathroom trash can, but he didn't make it in time. With a great deal of sarcasm he said, "So you've stumbled onto one of my favorite pastimes, changing a woman's bed linens in the middle of the night when I didn't have anything to do with getting them soiled."

He lifted her off the bed and deposited her by the bathroom.

"Where are the fresh linens?" he asked.

"You don't have to do this Kel."

"Yes, I do. You take care of yourself," he said using his hand to shoo her toward the bathroom, "and I'll take care of this." He bent to strip the bed.

"Thanks, Kel. The sheets are in the closet in the main bath at the end of the hall."

He made it to the doorway before she called him back. She was behind the closed bathroom door.

"I remembered the thing I was supposed to tell you. Paige, Meggie, and I discovered the link we have to each other. We went to the same spa."

Kel dropped the dirty linens and stared slack-jawed at the closed bathroom door.

Chapter Thirty-seven

"*M*eggie, you can't keep avoiding the issue. Not anymore. You're going to have to tell him point blank that there's absolutely no chance for him. He thinks as long as he can use these little machinations against me that I won't want to have anything to do with you. And it's not true. I won't give you up, so stop fighting it. I'm tired of his little games, I want to see you."

"Rand, I'm afraid if he sees us together—or God-forbid if he's hired some kind of private detective to keep an eye on me—that he'll come to the hospital and get you in trouble, or that he'll find a way to run into you somewhere and hurt you."

They were on the phone. And they were getting absolutely nowhere with this argument.

"I've told you I don't give a rat's ass if he comes to the hospital. I don't care what he says or whom he says it to. I'm a damn good surgeon, one of the best in the country, and no one can say anything about my morality that could possibly hurt my career as long as there's a waiting list for my specialty. Do you have any idea how long the waiting list is for neurosurgeons? Besides, even if he does show up, with one press of a button, security will have him in irons. And don't worry about me running into him on the street. I'm a big boy, he's the one who's going to come out on the bottom of a wrestling match."

"I just wish he'd find somebody else and give up on the idea that I might still love him."

"Is he still badgering you about what you had to do?"

"Yes. And it's only a matter of time before he hears about what happened on Topsail Island."

"How would he find out about that?"

"I think one of the beach patrol cops who came to leer was one of his buddies. I thought he recognized me, but I wasn't sure."

"Yeah, that glint in his eye couldn't have been because of something else," he teased. He couldn't believe he was taking this so well. The thought that she was practically naked in front of other men drove him crazy, but she absolutely, positively, could never, ever know that.

"He was wearing sunglasses. It was the way his head tilted that concerned me."

"Just angling for a better view."

"Rand, cut it out will you?"

It sickened him, and he was unaccountably jealous of all the men on that beach who had seen her topless, jutting her perky breasts out for all to see, but he knew if he didn't keep teasing her about it and acting like it didn't matter that she'd fall apart. And heaven help them both if Thomas did find out that she'd been on a beach topless and in a thong bottom.

"I want to see you. I miss you. Come to my office today."

When she didn't answer, he said, "Lunch time. Be here." Then he hung up.

Meggie put the phone in the cradle then flipped onto her back and stared at the ceiling. It was almost morning and

312

the only light came from the lamp on the night stand. After Rand had brought her home he'd been called to the hospital. She hadn't thought he would call. The ceiling fan took lazy turns and cast flickering shadows around the room. It was mesmerizing, and as she continued to stare at the rotating blades, she let her mind unwind and drift back. It was hard to believe that just a few days ago she had actually been topless and virtually bottomless on a public beach being leered at by both men and women. When she'd finally made it to a secluded area, the beach patrol officers with their binoculars had continued to torment her with their obnoxious leering.

And for the hundredth time, that horrible ransom note came back to her battered brain. As she recalled the condemning words the madman had written, expounding on how she was going to exchange sexual favors for her son's life, the mortifying shame of what she had done came over her again. It was this way every night. Alone in her room, she relived the terrible things she'd had to do until she just wanted to crawl up into a ball and die.

Rand had taken care of everything. He'd been a gentleman taking great care with her while doing the least gentlemanly of things. Rand had gotten her through that awful night, settled Thomas down when he was deranged, taken her to the library when the police had found Toby, and then followed the ambulance to the hospital so he could be there for her if she needed him. Then he'd stayed at her apartment until everyone had left, and at two-thirty in the morning, he'd taken her into his arms on her sofa and held her until she'd fallen asleep, her exhausted son in her lap.

At five he'd fixed coffee in the kitchen. When she'd joined him there, he'd taken her back into his arms and tenderly kissed her. Then he had taken her by the hand and led her into the bathroom where he'd stripped her and himself before turning on the shower.

313

She had been so raw, her emotions so frayed, she would have done anything he wanted, led as the zombie that she was. And he'd known it. With the capable hands of a deft surgeon, he'd gently washed her from top to bottom, then he'd used the removable spray shower head to carefully cleanse and soothe her soreness. He'd painstakingly dried her and then he'd bundled her into a robe. He'd tucked her into her bed, brought a sleepy Toby to lay beside her, and kissed her thoroughly before leaving to go to work.

"Thank you," she'd whispered.

He'd turned back from the doorway, "Don't thank me now. I have some wicked plans for you when you're recovered." He'd tossed her a smile over his shoulder and gone to the front door to let himself out. Then he'd walked right into Thomas, and had ducked just in time to avoid getting hit in the jaw. Thomas, on the other hand, had hit the brick full force and broke a knuckle.

Now as Meggie continued to stare at the ceiling, and the fan that was perpetually circling, she laughed. Just two weeks ago one of the nurses had told her that she'd heard Dr. Cheswick was gay and that his lover was his tennis partner. Not hardly!

Chapter Thirty-eight

*W*hen Laura came out of the bathroom, Kel just stared at her.

Then he found his voice and asked, "How could you have possibly forgotten to tell me something like that?"

"I don't know Kel, I'm sorry. I was wasted. We all were." She chuckled. "I'm not sure we would have put it together at all if we hadn't been drinking. It just came out of the blue."

"So what spa was this?"

"The one on South College, Exclusively for Women. He couldn't be a member there, maybe he saw all of us from the parking lot. Anyway, that's a connection the three of us have. Maybe you should check and see if the other mothers were members."

"I'll do that on my way to work. No one's up yet. How are you feeling? How's your head?"

"I'm fine, a little woozy still and my tongue feels like a Brillo, but my head's okay. After all the years of toasting with champagne, I'm not at all affected by the bubbles. I rarely get a hangover, but then again, I rarely drink as much as I did last night."

"Yeah, what got into you girls?"

"Just had to get away from it all I guess. It felt good.

315

I like both of them."

"Well, if I were you, I'd check on them, but not until later this afternoon. Both of them got sick on their way to the cars."

"You let them drive?"

"No! Cayce and Rand came to get them. Actually, I had to meet them at the station and bring them here."

"Oh Kel, I'm so sorry."

"Nothing to be sorry about. It was a hoot seeing the three of you passed out on those loungers, without a care in the world. But you do need to be more concerned with security. The front door was unlocked and the patio door was open. Anybody could have walked right on in and taken whatever they wanted."

"That's odd. I know I locked the front door after Paige and Meggie came in. No one went out of it again, I'm sure of it."

"Laura, the way you were last night, I doubt you could have been sure about anything." He walked over to her and kissed her lightly on the lips. "I'll call you later. Give Kayla a hug for me." Then he was gone.

Laura stood staring at her reflection in the double mirror over the dresser. *I am sure that front door was locked.*

Chapter Thirty-nine

*T*hree of *his* women in one place, all passed out drunk. He needed a camera, he needed some rope, and he needed blue pills, lots of blue pills. He couldn't believe his good fortune. Laura, Paige, and even Meggie, sturdy, Meggie. But then he heard car doors slamming, several of them. He had just made it over the sea grass and to the sand beyond when he heard men coming around the corner of the house. The men all looked vaguely familiar. As he crouched in the sand looking between the fronds of the vegetation, he had to bite his tongue to keep from exclaiming out loud. Each man there had been involved in satisfying his ransom demands. *What was this shit? Don't tell me that they're all involved! What were those men doing here?* His stomach clenched and so did his fists. These were his women! What were these men doing here carrying them off? They had no right! He fell back in the sand, clasping his hands to his head, and trying not to scream from the frustration he was feeling. All he'd needed was more time. They were his!

※

That afternoon Laura went into Kayla's room to hang up some laundry. Since Kayla had been at her parent's house she hadn't had occasion to go in there since yesterday morning. When she opened the closet door to hang up some dresses, Samantha, Kayla's American Girl Doll fell off the top shelf right into her arms. When Laura looked down at the doll she gasped. A note was pinned to Samantha's plaid jumper. On it was written:

Frank

Frankie

Francis

Frances

&

Laura

Laura

Laura

Laura

Laura dropped the doll and ran for the phone.

Chapter Forty

Kel was on his way to the Exclusively for Women Spa. It had been a crazy morning and it was only eight. He had the answers to a lot of his questions now, but damn it all, there were still a lot of unanswered ones. The most prevalent was, who and where was that fucking bastard! All of the mothers had been members of the spa at one time or another. None were still going regularly. None were on their periods at the time of the kidnappings. None of them had ever seen a man in the gym. One woman had even told Kel that when the air conditioning units had needed to be worked on, the repairs had by done by women. If workmen were needed they had to come late at night when the spa was closed.

But Kel was beginning to have an idea about how a man could infiltrate such an obviously gender-specific enterprise. And it was ridiculously simple.

Being around women in a locker room situation, it would be easy to track women's cycles, easy to discover patterns and habits, and to find out about their children. And their lovers, or their lack of them. And it would be child's play to find out where they lived, what they drove, when they'd be home, where they kept their keys. It was just too easy. The man must be laughing his fool head off at how easy everything was.

Then he thought of Laura and how this man had seen her there, in that gym, exercising, using the hot tub, dressing. Watching her shower. He felt himself begin to tremble with rage. His Laura, his beautiful Laura, being leered at and lusted over while she was unaware she was even being watched. At least by a man.

He parked in front of the spa, but before he could get out of his cruiser his phone rang. Noting the caller I.D. number of one of his team members, he flipped it open.

"Vain here."

"Kel, you're not going to believe this but guess what we found."

"What?"

"That big touring golf bag you keep talking about."

"Where'd you find it?"

"That's the odd thing. A few of us met at IHOP this morning for breakfast. When we came out it was on the roof of one of the cruisers. The officer whose car it was on wanted to throw it away, but a couple of us were kind of suspicious. So we took it over to Wilmington National — where you told us the one you were looking for had originated — and the pro there verified that it was the one they'd had in the showroom for display a few months ago."

"So why would he do that?" Kel said more to himself than to the other detective.

"Beats me. You gotta figure it could have a lot of forensic evidence in it."

"He wanted us to find it," Kel hissed. "But why?"

"I don't know. But it's on its way to the lab right now."

"Thanks. I'll be in the office in an hour or so." He flipped the phone closed.

What in the world? He sat there thinking for a minute, then flipped open the phone again. He punched in the number for Ben Atkinson, the profiler who was helping him on the case.

"Atkinson."

"Ben, what do you make of our serial killer leaving the carrying case he's been using to transport the kids in out in the open for us to find?"

"Oh, that's not good Kel. Not good at all."

"Well that's what he's done." He told him about the touring bag and where it was found.

"Kel, you and I both know that when a serial killer breaks pattern that it's just about the worst thing that can happen. He definitely wanted you to find it and my guess is that it's his way of telling you that the rules have changed. He's probably not going for the kids anymore. He's upping the stakes if you ask me. You must be getting close. Or something has changed in his personal life and he doesn't know how to deal with it."

"Any recommendations?"

"Yeah, work around the clock. Something's coming down."

"Shit!"

"He's got a new game Kel."

"And we have no idea what that is, right?"

"This is just a wild hunch Kel, and I wouldn't put any stock in it except that he's really been playing a sexual game. But I think he may be looking for a woman. We could be watching a serial kidnapper/killer morphing into a serial rapist/killer."

"Fucking wonderful," Kel breathed.

"Round the clock bud, you must have something. Work it."

Kel closed the phone. He stared up at the big spa sign and turned on his radio. Within minutes the spa was surrounded by police officers. There were at least ten cruisers and twice that many uniforms.

An hour later the department's female officers had processed all the clients. All were truly women. Truly mad women. The indignant owners were spouting threats of lawsuits and he was at a dead end—until one of the officers returned from the janitor's closet with a bucket filled with women's clothing and a wig. At the bottom of the bucket were twenty wax disks containing impressions of keys. A name was carved into the back of each disk. Kel put on a glove and turned each one over. Alice, Deborah, Connie, Melanie, Susie, Wendy, Anna, Emma, Heather . . . but there were no disks for the women whose children had been taken.

"Jesus!" he whispered. Then, "Collins, get the magistrate. We need a warrant for the client records and we need it now!"

Collins turned on his heel and ran for the door.

"Bill, line up the customers who are here and see if any of these disks have their names on them. If they do, see if any of their house keys match up. And make sure anyone who handles these uses gloves. They gotta have his prints all over them. Get a kit, let's print them first."

He walked over to the owners, the mother-and-daughter team who had been so righteous just a few minutes ago. Now they sat silently while officers rushed in and out of doors and began to cordon off the area with yellow tape.

"Ladies, do you know anything about this bucket?"

"All I can tell you is that I bought it about two years ago. Haven't seen it since."

"How about the clothing or the wig?"

"It's Frankie's. But I never knew it was wig," the mother answered. "She always wore some kind of scarf over her hair."

Kel picked up the dress and shook it. A multicolored scarf fell to the floor. "This one?"

"Yeah."

"So, Frankie's a woman?"

"Yeah. What else would she be? Men ain't allowed. Especially back there."

She pointed to the dressing rooms, the locker rooms, and the bathrooms. Kel put his hand in his pocket and rubbed his thumb over the plastic palm tree fronds. This was killing him. The man had stalked Laura, seen her naked, fantasized about her. How many times, over how long a period?

"So Frankie is your cleaning lady?"

"Yeah. She mops the floors, cleans the bathrooms, picks up the towels, you know all that janitorial kind of stuff. Women are messier'n you'd think. It's a full-time job picking up in there."

"Do you provide locks for the lockers?"

"Sometimes. The women can bring their own if they want as long as they don't leave 'em on the lockers."

"Do most bring their own?"

"No. Most don't even use a lock. Some get them from us, but not many."

"Does Frankie have access to the combinations, or were they keyed?"

"Combination. Not that I know of. We keep them in the office."

"Does she clean the office?"

"Yup. She does. She cleans the whole place."

"When was the last time you saw her?"

" 'Bout a week ago. Came in for her check and said she had to take a few days off. Her momma's sick."

"Well ladies, you'd better call your attorney, because unless I miss my guess, Frankie is a man."

"Can't be! We hired her away from that cleaning company. We have her records on file."

"I'm sure the records you have are bogus, but we're

going to need to see them anyway."

A man called to Kel from a back room.

"This lady says her name is Emma and her house key is an exact match for the impression."

"Bingo. Now all we have to do is find him. Ma'am," he said turning back to the woman he had been speaking with, "would you mind getting those records for me and anything else you may have on Frankie? It sure would save time if we didn't have to wait for a warrant."

The woman reluctantly stood and went into the office.

"Well maybe he felt secure enough to use his real phone number and address if not his real name," Kel said after looking through the file. "Hopefully, he was confident that we'd never make the connection."

"Yeah, he must think we're stupid." Officer Davis said.

"Well actually we wouldn't have made the connection if it hadn't been for the mothers," Kel said wryly, "we *were* stupid."

He picked up some client files and thumbed through them. "You guys stay here and sift through this, I'm going to go check out his address. Reilly, call S.W.A.T. Get them set up and ready to roll. I'll call you when I get there."

Chapter Forty-one

On the way up the stairs Kel noted the boards nailed over charred windows on the building across the street. Kayla's fire, he thought and smiled. They knocked, then broke into the apartment. No one was inside. The apartment had a funky smell, it made him think of a dirty diaper pail. The nauseating overlay of Febreeze permeated the heavy, dank air. In the closet in the largest bedroom were women's clothes, plus-sized women's clothes. In the second bedroom there were a few pairs of men's pants and a ratty old sweater. One wall had smudged scuffmarks close to the floorboards, someone had tried to clean them and just smeared them, and the carpet was stained in several areas. There was no electronic equipment, no computer. No porn, no videos, nothing but old furniture. Kel thought they had the wrong place when a woman named Gloria showed up dragging a suitcase on wheels through the door.

"What are you doing in my apartment?" she screamed at the policemen who were dragging her sofa away from the wall. An officer walked over to Kel and opened his hand for Kel to see the minute grass clippings he had found on the carpet in the smaller bedroom.

Kel flashed his badge, took her by the elbow and led her inside. When he told her what they were there for, she just shook her head. She was not shocked that they were there, and not at all surprised that they were looking for her husband.

"This doesn't surprise me. It should, but it doesn't. Nothing he does shocks me anymore."

"And why is that?"

She sat down heavily on the sofa that the officers had checked and left in the middle of the room. It bowed gradually as it took her weight and Kel prayed he wouldn't have to help her up off the floor when it maxed out. He pulled up a padded vinyl ottoman and sat with his elbows on his knees in front of her. He was going to need her to spill her guts about her husband, so the more he appeared a willing and unhurried confidant the better—before she realized she should be calling a lawyer.

"Why doesn't it shock you that your husband could be a serial kidnapper, a murderer, and a voyeur?"

"Well you got the voyeur part right for sure," she said with disdain. Had she spat it out between her front teeth? He had felt a spray of something—he reached up to wipe his cheek.

"Fill me in."

"Yeah, I'm sure you're gonna want to hear this." She separated her chubby fingers and ran them through her brittle-looking bleached hair, then she settled back against the sofa cushion causing the framework to groan.

"Eight years ago I found out about my husband, and his perversities. We had been married for six years. I still can't believe it, six years and I didn't even have a clue what he'd been up to." She shook her head sadly and let out a big sigh before continuing.

"My computer was down, the internal battery needed replacing. I needed to check something on the Web, so I went into the den to boot up his computer. He was still logged on, so I found what I was looking for and was preparing to shut down when a few icons caught my attention. The files were quite graphically titled, things like: cunt shots, tit shots, ass shots. Needless to say I was more than intrigued, so I opened them.

"They were pictures of me. Pictures of me naked and artfully posed. He had been taking pictures of me while I slept! Disgustingly vile pictures.

"As I read captions and clicked between programs, I realized that he had been sending naked pictures of me to his friends. I checked his e-mail account and was floored to find comments they were sending him about me, about my specific body parts. Crude messages had been passed back and forth and it was obvious that he was thrilled with their reactions to the pictures. He was eating up their comments about my body and their praise for his sexy, hot wife." She shrugged when inadvertently, he raised an eyebrow in question.

"I was a lot thinner then, I really did have a nice body in my early thirties."

He wasn't going to say a thing one way or the other. He nodded and murmured, "Continue."

"I was furious. I couldn't control my rage. The pictures he had taken showed me spread wide open. I couldn't believe that as I slept, that fucking bastard posed me, then sent pictures of me to his friends! When I stumbled onto a missive that mentioned his web site, I cried. With rage pounding in my head and tears of humiliation pouring down my face onto the keyboard, I went to the web site. That's when I found out that he was sending my pictures all over the world, and had been for quite some time. There had to have been over two thousand pictures of me, categorized and sorted with bulleted titles that would take you to pages headed 'Gloria's massive tits,' 'Awesome cunt shots,' 'My wife's splendid ass,' 'What's a dildo for?' He even had a section entitled, 'Gloria's friend is here,' with pictures of a tampon string dangling down my thigh! I couldn't believe it. This man who I trusted was showing my body to anyone who had a computer!"

She was wiping tears from her eyes with a crumpled wad of tissue and Kel couldn't help but feel for this woman who had been betrayed in one of the worst ways he could have ever imagined.

"How could you have slept through him doing all that?" he asked incredulously.

"I have always had trouble getting to sleep. I've been using sleeping pills since high school. But once I get to sleep, I'm dead to the world, nothing wakes me except time."

"So he knew this and capitalized on it?"

"Yeah. A few hours later when he came home I threw everything I could get my hands on at him. Then after I'd had a few drinks, I started asking him questions. I had to know how it had all started and why. He told me that he'd been doing it since we were in college. When I'd fall asleep on his bed in his dorm room, he'd undress me, pose me, and then go open the door so anybody walking by would be able to see me. He'd pretend to be asleep himself so he could hear the guys coming in and commenting on my body. He fed on the attention I was getting, and the things these guys were saying about my body caused him to swell with pride. He couldn't get enough of it. Eventually, he made pictures of me available to anyone who asked. And for a fee, he allowed men he met in bars to come into his room while I slept and see me firsthand. He confessed that many were allowed to touch me and that he opened me for inspection to as many as ten men at a time.

"When we were married, we had ten groomsmen in addition to his best man. He told me that one of the happiest moments in his life was when I walked up the aisle to join him and he had swelled with pride knowing that all those men had seen his new bride naked and completely exposed. During the reception when I had danced with some of them, I had felt a bit weird about the odd way they looked at me and some of the smirks I saw being passed around were a little unsettling, but I had no idea, no idea that he was sharing me with his friends. I had a really hard time hearing that. I clawed his face and screamed at him for almost an hour. Then the cops showed up. They insisted on seeing proof of my allegations, and he leapt at the chance to pass out pictures before they arrested him. I was mortified as they looked at me, then back down at the pictures. They didn't know what to charge him with; apparently he hadn't broken any laws! They took the pictures as evidence. The magistrate looked at them, then the attorneys, then the judge. It didn't look like this nightmare was ever going to end. I was beside myself and humiliated beyond belief. He was in heaven. He loved watching them hand my pictures back and forth and was excited when they invited yet another expert or consultant to be included. I finally dropped the charges, and moved out of the apartment.

"But then he kept calling and apologizing and begging me to come back. He promised he'd never do anything like that ever again. I finally gave in, but I insisted we sleep in separate rooms and I locked myself into my room before going to bed at night. Things were getting better and we were getting along. For our tenth anniversary, he took me to Jamaica and I agreed that I would share a room with him, and that we could try to establish a sex life again. The first night he slipped a Mickey into my drink, took me back to the room, and invited all the bellmen to come see my charms. When I awoke, I thought it was odd that I had red marks on my ankles and wrists. When I mentioned it to him, he said I had gotten a little drunk on rum punch and insisted on some light bondage. He said he'd practically had to gag me as well as tie me up to keep me quiet because I was so horny. I admitted that I had been quite a bit horny lately, as it had been almost four years since we'd been together that way, so I didn't think too much about it until the men in the bars and the male staff members at the hotel kept giving me these long leers and knowing smiles.

"That night I pretended to drink the Bahama Mamas he kept ordering for me, but I kept sloshing most of the spiked drink out of the glass or pouring it into the sand when he wasn't looking. And sure enough, when we got back to our room and I pretended to sleep, he stripped me of my clothes, laid me across the bed and spread my thighs wide. When he had me the way he wanted me, exposed toward the beach, he slid open the drapes of our patio door. There were already several men waiting to come into our room, most of them had heard about me from the locals on the beach. I jumped up off the bed and screeched at him until I was hoarse. I left him again.

"Months later, after I had filed for a divorce, he begged me to reconsider, he even agreed to counseling. I had started a new job that required a lot of traveling. He agreed to stay at home, take care of all the housework, do all the laundry and the cooking and go to counseling. By this time I was putting on so much weight that I thought no one would ever want me and I was scared to be alone, so stupidly I came back, again. The locks went back on the doors. And hey, it worked for me. I got a free maid and he left me alone. I never knew what he got out of it. I refused to have sex with him from that point on. When I was home, my door was locked every single night. A few times he threatened to break the door down, but he never did.

"Meanwhile, I was a mess. Because of the divorce

proceedings I'd started, my coworkers had found out the things I'd been trying to hide. Rumors started circulating. Pictures some of his friends had of me resurfaced, and people began to look at me oddly again, said strange things, men I didn't know winked, leered, propositioned. He hadn't done it, but he hadn't bothered to stop it. By this time, I knew that it was never going to end. Never. I started drinking, binge eating, even doing drugs now and again. And finally, I couldn't take all the innuendoes, all the stares, and all the tongues wagging. When I was out of town, I took on all comers. If someone winked or raised an eyebrow, I did the same. Soon I was agreeing to meet business associates in bars. I was sleeping with a different man every night. When one asked if he could take some pictures, I even let him. Can you believe that? I let a man take vulgar pictures of me.

"Then I got pregnant. And I had absolutely no idea whose it was. Harold was furious when I told him. I hadn't had sex with him for years, so he definitely knew it was someone else's. He told me I had to get rid of it. I begged him to let me keep it, but he refused. He said he was not going to raise somebody else's snot-nosed bastard and neither was I. I was trying to figure out what I was going to do, making plans to find a place of my own when he changed his mind. He said if I promised to start losing weight and we slept together again like we used to, that he'd help me raise the baby. I went on a diet and let him back into my bedroom.

"For a few months we were really pretty happy. Then I lost the baby. I know he was happy about that, it solved a problem for him, but it put me into a severe depression. I went off the diet and started having indiscriminate sex with strangers again. Whenever I was out of town on business, I would go trolling in the bars. It was one sleazy affair after another. I think, subconsciously, that I might have been trying to get pregnant again. But it didn't happen. When I topped three hundred and fifty pounds, the ready line of sex partners began to drastically taper off. These days businessmen don't have to settle for a heifer like me, there's plenty of young, nubile stuff out there, more than willing to take them on.

"I still fly all over the country fixing everybody's broken computers, but nobody ever wants to have sex with me anymore. Can't say that I blame them." She shrugged her massive shoulders and sighed heavily. "I used to love computers, now I can't stand the sight of them. Those Internet pictures ruined my life. I never was able to regain my self-esteem. Eight years ago, men flocked to see naked pictures of me, now I couldn't pay someone to look at my unclothed body. And it's all his fault. He did this to me!" she sobbed, her hand indicating her obesity. The hard, gritty look may have been because life had dealt her a blow, but the bitter bile running through her veins that made everything about her blotchy and ugly had been caused by one man, one very depraved, selfish and disgusting man. The same man who had hurt Laura, and Paige, and Megan, and many others. He had to stop him. He couldn't ruin more lives. He had to get him before his calloused disregard for women ruined another woman or child's life.

"So you can see why I'm not at all shocked by what you've told me. Except for the killing part. I don't find it at all hard to believe that he'd make women strip so he could ogle them, but it never occurred to me that he could kill anyone, especially a child. I often wondered if he had poisoned me when I was expecting, if what you're saying is true, he could have done just that, he could have killed my baby." Her voice broke and he could see she was having difficulty swallowing. For a moment he thought she might be having a heart attack, then she sniffed and sat upright, causing the sofa to groan again.

"Where is he, Mrs. Satterfield? Where is your

husband?"

She gave a sideways leer and grunted. "I have no idea. I haven't cared a wit about that disgusting scumbag in years. As long as he does the laundry and keeps the place halfway decent, I really haven't paid a whole lot of attention to what he does."

"Where does he work?"

"To tell you the truth, I have no idea about that either. Last year when we filed our taxes, I found out that he'd only made four thousand dollars for the whole year. He was working as a telemarketer then. I don't know what he's up to now. We don't talk, we despise each other. We have for a very long time."

"Do you have a recent picture of him?"

She laughed bitterly. "Me, have a picture of him? Not hardly. I don't even own a camera. He's the one into photography!" The way she spat out the word showed her contempt for the hobby.

"Well what does he look like? Describe him and his habits. And does he play golf?" Kel fired a barrage of questions at her and she managed to answer most of them. He ended with: "Does the bra size 38 D mean anything to you?"

"Yeah, it was the size I was wearing when we married. Sometimes Harold would wear my bras around the house as a joke. A few times he also put on my dresses. I think he might have even taken one of them. I'm missing a red one."

"Is he good with computers and electronics?"

"That's what he studied in college. He was some kind of electronics whiz. He could do all kinds of things with computers."

"How about alarm systems?"

"He used to design them, but he lost his security clearance and got blacklisted."

"How did that happen?"

"A woman found a miniaturized camera in her bathroom a few days after he had installed an alarm system at her house. He couldn't get work for the longest time after that little incident."

"Hmmm," he said as he wrote in his notebook. Then looking up, he asked, "What do you know about his mother?"

"She was raped by her brother when she was fourteen, when she started showing, it was too late, the state wouldn't let her abort. So far as anyone knows she never let another man touch her. She resented Harold for the way her life turned out. After he was born she ended up working as a shoe salesman at a department store six days a week to support them. When Harold was seventeen she kicked him out of the house. He had just been accepted at State on a scholarship. She caught him doing the deed with his cousin and told him to never come back. She was real religious, said she'd never be able to forgive him for that. Some religion, huh? No forgiveness."

"Did he talk about it a lot? Did it seem to bother him?"

"No, he didn't talk about it much. But I think it did bother him. He always said she should have been a better mother, that she should have loved him if for no other reason than he loved her. She died a few years ago. He didn't bother going to the funeral."

When he had asked all the questions that had come to mind, he closed his notebook and stood looking down at her.

She looked up at him with puffy, tearful eyes. "You know the really sad thing about all this is that he was a pitifully inadequate lover. I could have done better, a lot better. But I thought he was special, that he cared about me. He worshipped my body, loved looking at it, and was always

334

complimenting me on it—he made me feel so good about myself. Like I was the most beautiful thing in the world. Ironic isn't it?"

Kel didn't say anything; he couldn't think of anything to say to that.

"My psychiatrist once told me that it probably would have been better for me if I had never discovered his dirty secret."

And Kel couldn't help agreeing. Several other women and their kids would certainly have been better off if she'd never found those pictures of herself.

"I hope you catch him," she said as he walked away, "he's ruined enough lives."

He only nodded as he walked down the hallway to join the other detectives. Fragments of her bitter words swirled around in his head as he unconsciously put one foot in front of the other. The words *He was a pitifully inadequate lover,* kept running like a banner across his mind, and finally he made the connection. His friend, Ben Atkinson, the profiler had said pretty much the same thing. *The guy you're looking for is probably pathetic in bed.*

They had him. They knew who he was—Harold Francis Satterfield. Now they just had to find him. Another thought occurred to him and he turned back to her. "Did your husband own a boat or have access to one?"

She nodded. "Yeah, a jon boat. He kept it at a friend's house on the Waterway. Their house is for sale and they don't live here anymore, so until it sells, he keeps it beside their house under a tarp."

"Do you know where that is?"

She gave him a house number on Masonboro Loop.

Dear God, that was just a couple of houses down the waterway from Laura's house.

ॐ

335

Kel watched as the small boat was loaded into a van. It was being taken to a garage where crime scene techs would go over it, looking for anything that would give them a clue about where they could find this disgusting son-of-a-bitch. The ground underneath had been all but vacuumed as they tried to capture anything that might have fallen from the boat when it was turned upside down. He fingered the small plastic bag that contained the one thing they had managed to find, wedged as a shim under the seat. A flyer, folded the maximum times an 8 1/2 x 11 sheet of paper could be folded—six. It was a promotional flyer, the kind you'd find under the windshield of your car after spending three minutes in the grocery store. It was promoting the *Exclusively for Women* gym on South College Street.

He felt for the tiny palm tree in his pocket and thought of Laura. He wondered how she was feeling, wondered if she was thinking about him. He looked at his watch. She should be picking Kayla up from her parents' house right about now. He'd wait until he got back to the office before calling her. Meanwhile, he had to find Harold "Frankie" Satterfield.

Chapter Forty-two

*R*and was sitting at his desk when Meggie opened the door and walked into his office. He hadn't been sure she'd come. He dropped his pen on the open patient file and stood to greet her.

"You looked surprised to see me," she said with a laugh.

"I am."

"What did you want to see me about?" she asked, feigning innocence. She was perky and happy and it did his heart good to see her that way.

He smiled and walked over to where she stood by the door, then reached behind her to lock it. "This," he said as he placed his hand on her jaw, cupping her head behind her ear with his splayed fingers. Ever so slowly, he bent his head and took her parted lips with his. As he savored the feel of her soft lips against his, his other hand snaked out, circled her waist, and pulled her tightly to his chest. Then the plundering began in earnest as his lips molded themselves to hers and his tongue delved into her soft, moist recess, tasting and taking her essence with a fevered passion.

She shouldn't be allowing this, this was highly unprofessional. But she had no choice. The feel of his lips pressed against hers, his tongue tracing every nuance of her mouth, and his warm, hard chest pressing against her breasts attested to the fact that she had absolutely no control of this situation. He could have lifted her up, placed her on the desk, and climbed on top of her and she would have been unable to stop him, he had so affected her senses.

Fortunately, he had more decorum than she at this moment and he pulled back to stare down at her wet lips. "I don't know if you know it or not, but you've been ruining my sleep and interfering with my work since the day I met you."

"At Eddie Romanelli's?"

"No, in the operating room. Three weeks ago, the Marchetti resection."

"You were attracted to me then?" she stammered.

"From the moment I saw your eyes over your mask. I waited until you came out of recovery just so I could see your lips." He kissed her again, lightly this time, savoring the feel of her lips against his. "I noticed how every once in a while you'd pat the patient's hand or shoulder, even knowing he couldn't feel it. And you stand without moving for hours as if it's effortless. Everyone else is constantly shifting back and forth on their feet and it drives me crazy."

"Mountain pose."

"What?"

"Yoga. It centers you perfectly. You fit into your pelvis and you settle, it takes the weight off your spine."

"You'll have to show me that sometime." He bent and took her mouth with his and softly used his lips and tongue to feel every curve of hers.

"I only have twenty-five minutes before I have to pick Toby up from school," she breathed as he continued kissing her.

"Then you have to agree to see me tonight."

"I'm not ready to get a sitter for Toby."

"I'll come to your house."

"I don't think that's a good idea. Thomas watches everything I do."

"Then bring him to mine."

"I can't, he has school tomorrow."

He took a deep breath and she could hear the frustration he was experiencing when he let it out. "Okay, let's do this. I'll call Kel, we'll see if he and Laura and Cayce and Meggie want to get together with all the kids for a barbecue at my place this weekend. How does that sound?"

"Doable, very doable."

"Good. This is the hardest I've ever had to work for a first date."

"We are so beyond a first date."

"You don't know how happy am I am to hear you say that,' he said with grin. Then he kissed her on the nose and set her away from him. "You'd better get going or you'll be late getting Toby."

But before he let her leave, he pulled her back for one more deep, soul-melding kiss.

∂ℬ

At nine o'clock that night, Rand knocked on her door. When she looked through the peephole, then opened the door to him, the shocked look on her face was priceless. "I thought we agreed that this wasn't—"

He cut her off by placing his fingers over her lips. He stepped inside and closed and locked the door behind him. "I had a buddy of mine ask Thomas to play poker tonight. We're clear until at least two or three in the morning."

She just stood there staring at him.

"Aren't you going to invite me into the living room?"

"Oh. Yeah, sure. Man you are one determined man

aren't you?"

"When it comes to you, yes." From behind his back he produced a bottle of wine, a spray of fresh orchids, and a box of Godiva Chocolates. "The beginning of a proper first date."

She laughed. "That's the equivalent of more than one date — more like six or seven in my book."

"Good. Then we're beyond the randy sex of our first date and can move on to the real deal — the lovemaking. Go put a dress on, and some heels. I want to dance with you."

"I can't go out dancing with you tonight, Toby's asleep in his room."

"Who said anything about going out?" His hand dipped into his pocket and he brought out a CD. "Put on something soft and sexy. Show me where your stereo is and I'll do the same."

The clock in the dining room chimed then sounded off twelve bongs. They had danced through the CD twice, her hips swaying into his, his hands wandering and arousing her with their light sensual touches.

"It's late, I've got to get some sleep. I have to get Toby up at seven."

He stopped dancing and lifted her chin with his fingertips. "I don't want to go," he said simply. And then her world spun as he captured her lips with his and didn't let go. His hand came up to hold her head as he pulled her face closer to his and his tongue breached the barrier of her teeth. He lapped at her tongue, twining in and out, chasing it while he alternately sucked and nibbled on her bottom lip.

"Meggie," he breathed against her lips, "I don't know what you're doing to me, but I can't seem to get enough of you. Just the taste of you is driving me wild."

His words were driving her over the edge. She felt the heat of their embrace, the desire pooling in her center, and she timidly touched her tongue to his, causing him to groan as if he was in pain.

His lips seared into hers and his tongue parlayed with hers, and then he dropped his head and kissed the long column of her neck, showering her with one hot, burning sensation after another. When his lips found their way to her bare shoulder, he used the palm of his hand to ease her shawl collar down to her elbow, exposing a full, ripe breast to his waiting hand. His palm curved and he cupped her under her breast, hefting the weight of it in his hand while his thumb grazed the peaked nipple. It was her turn to groan and he thought he would die from the sheer pleasure of hearing it. He bent to take her nipple in his mouth and she swooned against him, unable to support herself from the sudden collapse of her legs. He caught her in his arms and carried her to her bedroom, never once taking his mouth from her breast.

As tenderly as he could, he laid her down on the soft linens of her bed. Then he kicked off his loafers and levered his body down to hers. As he stretched out beside her, he heard her mumble something and, desperate not to have her deny him, he covered her mouth again with his. He plundered her mouth with his rolled tongue, thrusting and retreating repeatedly into her until the rhythm was so compelling that she reached her hands up to hold his head to hers as she followed his lead. He had one hand under her shoulders holding her to him, while with the other, he stripped her dress all the way down past her knees. When he felt rather than heard her gasp against his mouth, he slid his hand back up along her outer thigh, grazing her hip and hugging her waist before caressing her breast again. Instinct took over as he subtly read every nuance of her body as it responded to his.

A woman with breasts this large and responsive

was every man's dream, and as she moaned to every type of caress he used on them, his body grew hard and more demanding. Moving his lips from one fully distended nipple to the other, he used his hand to caress her waist, her flat abdomen, and then to delve down into the region between her thighs.

He cupped her as his middle finger fluttered against her labial lips, beckoning them to open to his touch. They flowered open like the full ripe petals they were, and he groaned at the silky, slick wetness he found. "You are so wet," he murmured into the cleft between her breasts. He licked her cleavage and the mounds of flesh under her nipples as he moved his tongue lower and lower with a definite target in mind.

When his mouth grazed her furry mound, he felt her hands reaching down to stop him. He knew he had to act quickly or all would be lost. She couldn't come to her senses now, he couldn't stand the agony of it if she did. His lips joined his fingers where they opened her wide for him and he kissed and sucked on her slick lips while he insinuated his body between her legs. He had taken her dress all the way down her legs and it was bunched at her feet. Had he known all night long that she'd had no underwear on, he would never have been able to stand it. His tongue joined the action as his hands spread her legs even wider.

"Rand, no. We mustn't . . . ." Too late, he now had her legs spread completely open, bent at the knees, his forearms holding her inner thighs down as he licked and kissed and lapped at her. Running his tongue up and down inside her slit, he probed deeper, enjoying the taste and feel of her against the grain of his tongue and curl of his lips. Expertly he tongued her and fingered her, backing away to look at her glistening, gaping opening. Greedily he went back for more, this time concentrating on the top of her slit where a hard bud was starting to tremble and throb. He took the small, full nub against his lips, and as he felt it shudder, he grasped her buttocks to lift her higher, giving him even more access to her. He felt her convulse against his lips. Her cry of ecstasy echoed in the room, and the sheer satisfaction of giving her such pleasure caused him to feel the urgency of his own much-desired release. He quickly stood, undid his pants and dropped them to his knees, but not before removing a condom from one of the front pockets. He tore it open with his teeth, pulled it out, and rolled it down onto his pulsing erection. Then he mounted her, positioned himself at her opening, and entered her.

He reveled in the incredible feel of her tight sheath surrounding him, and he thrust forward repeatedly, pinning her to the bed. He knew he was only going to be good for a few more short thrusts and maybe one or two deep ones since he'd been so consumed with passion and his incredible desire to have her for several days now. Gripping her buttocks while he thrust into her, he exploded with the most incredible orgasm he'd ever experienced. It left him weak and completely drained as his head fell alongside hers on the pillow. Propping himself up on his elbows to keep the bulk of his weight off of her, he gasped, "Jesus, Meggie! I'm so sorry."

"That's not exactly what a woman wants to hear a man say when she's just given herself to him."

"You didn't give yourself to me, I took you. I used every trick in the book to keep you senseless and I plain took you. I am so sorry."

"I wish you'd stop saying that. Couldn't you just tell me you couldn't help yourself and that it was the most wonderful feeling you ever had? That would at least make me feel better."

"Oh, Meggie, it goes without saying that I wanted

you. I've wanted you since the moment I saw you. But you were Thomas' wife."

"I'm no longer Thomas' wife. I haven't been for a very long time."

"He's always made it sound like you were getting back together."

"No, I'll never be his wife again. Never."

"Would you consider being mine?"

There was absolute silence while he stroked her back and waited for her to reply. A full minute passed before she said, "I think that's fourth or even fifth date stuff."

"Gotcha. First we have anal intercourse, then we make out like teenagers in my office, then I practically rape you, then we get engaged. Do I have the order right yet?"

"Somewhere in there is flowers, champagne, and chocolate."

"You had plenty of champagne last night, but I did bring flowers and chocolates."

"And condoms."

"Yes, we don't want the pregnancy to come before the actual ceremony, now do we?"

"Pregnancy?"

"You are going to have a few babies for me, aren't you? I moved back to Wilmington to find a wife, to settle down and have some kids. It just wasn't happening in Chicago. After years of dating I simply could not fall in love. I can't believe that it's happening so fast now. But hey, I did bring you flowers. And orchids at that, they're not so easy to come by this time of the year you know."

"Why do you want to marry me Rand?"

"Because sometime between you saying, 'Clamp, retractor, we need more gauze here,' and crying into my shirt at Romanelli's, I fell in love with you. That's why."

"You're in love with me?"

"Desperately."

She ran her fingers lightly over his face, stroked his eyebrows and lips, then softly ran her fingers through the hair at his temples. "Show me."

"Gladly," he said with a big smile. His arms wrapped around her and he covered her soft, pliant body with his hard, demanding one. Her moans joined with his until they were in such a fevered frenzy that neither one heard when the front door was unlocked and Thomas came into the apartment.

❧

Rand was kneeling on the bed holding her centered on his erection, her back was bowed as his hand caressed her breast. And they were both screaming their release when Thomas saw them from the doorway.

He had never been in this kind of pain before. Sure, he'd been jealous but never like this, and the fury sped through him until his rage became so great he wanted to lash out, and lash out with a vengeance that was lethal. He wanted to hurt as badly as he was being hurt. But even though his fists were balled and the cords on his neck were strained, he knew he would not be the victor this way. Rand was bigger, faster, and right now he had more to live for. Thomas stepped back from the doorway before he could be spotted and leaned on the wall between Meggie's room and Toby's.

He heard them chuckle and whisper and murmur things about love. He heard Rand tell his wife that he loved her breasts. Those same breasts that he had just discovered she'd been showing to the whole fucking town of Topsail. Along with her ass! Three of the officers who had seen his wife all but naked had been at that damned poker party, and were just too happy to tell him all about her penchant for nude sunbathing. He had to come directly here and call her on it, because he didn't want to believe it. She wouldn't do that!

But then he remembered Toby and that there were things she'd had to do that no one would tell him about. And now, he had used a key he wasn't supposed to have, and walked in on this!

Quietly, he slid down the wall and went into Toby's room. He hesitated for just a second before he made his decision. Yes, he definitely wanted to hurt her. He wanted to hurt her as much as she'd hurt him. Taking the son she adored would hurt her. It would kill her. And Rand? Well, she would never forgive him for being there and being the reason she was so distracted that she hadn't heard someone come into her house and take her son. Again.

Chapter Forty-three

Kel couldn't find Laura and he was frantic. By the time he'd made it to his office, he'd had four messages from her on his voice mail. The first said she'd try his cell number. The second said the cell number had been busy. The third said she was moving out of the beach house that afternoon, and the fourth said she had something very important that she had to show him. He realized that he really needed to get call waiting installed on his cell phone.

He tried the beach house number, then he tried to reach her at her parents', but the person who answered was only able to tell him no one was at home. He'd asked about Kayla and had learned that Laura had picked her up at two. He decided on the spot that he was going to get that woman a cell phone whether she wanted one or not!

He finally had a description and an old photo of Satterfield and it was now being circulated through the media. His car had been found just a few blocks from the house Laura and Kayla had just moved out of. The whole city was on alert as cops were being called in to help canvass the area.

He was holding onto the palm tree stirrer in his pocket so tightly that he snapped it in two. Where the hell was she? Where would she have gone?

He called her father's realty company. No one had seen her all day. He finally tracked down her brother's number and he said he had no idea where she was, but that she had known there were renters coming to stay at TIDES AWASTIN' tomorrow, so she must be moving into another place.

Yeah, he already knew that part! But where? Where the hell was she moving?

On a hunch he drove to her house on Masonboro Loop. When he saw her car in the circular drive, he slumped and put his head back against the headrest. He closed his eyes tightly and actually fought tears.

His mind flashed to a memory of Laura eating an ice cream cone with Kayla on the deck and he remembered having a dickens of a time keeping his eyes off of her trim legs showcased by her camper-style shorts. She had been so busy talking to Kayla that she hadn't noticed her ice cream start to drip down her thumb. She had stuck her pink tongue out and licked it along the length of her hand. He had wanted so desperately to feel that tongue on him. Anywhere, but mostly . . . . He saw her when she'd been sitting on the sofa across from him sipping wine while he had talked about his mother. He saw her as she'd looked in the pool, her hair slicked back from her face as she'd looked up at the stars. He saw her holding Kayla and crying with her about her nightmare. He saw her face just before he'd entered her in the sleazy motel room.

Damn! Why couldn't he keep his mind on his work? Thoughts of her were making him crazy. He had always told himself that he would not get involved with a woman like this. If it ended badly, he would be the one in pain. Well, what the hell was the difference? He was already in pain. And he didn't like the feeling one damned bit.

He reached for his cell phone and punched in the

number for her house. And since when had he been able to do that? Numbers weren't his thing, half the time if he remembered them at all, the numbers were usually reversed. While it rang he fingered the piece of the palm tree in his pocket. The sweet, breathy and cultured voice of the woman who was never far from his thoughts came on the line.

"Hello?"

"I've been looking all over for you. Couldn't you have told me where you were going?"

"I didn't know for sure where I was going. I was hoping to reach you after I finished working out."

I could give you a workout, certain muscles would think they were in Heaven.

"I've been on my cell phone a lot today, I'm sorry I've missed your calls."

"Any luck at the spa?"

"Yeah, that's where it all started. He was watching all of you, disguised as a woman. I've interviewed his wife and we found the boat he used the morning he came back to find your underwear." The tone of his voice had hollowed. He hated thinking how he had let her down and what could have happened to her and Kayla that night.

"Who is he?"

"His name is Harold Francis Satterfield. He's been using his middle name in both a male and a female version. At the gym he was known as Frankie."

Goose bumps crawled along her flesh as she remembered the note and made the connection to the sweet old lady perpetually cleaning the locker room and bathrooms at the spa.

"Frankie? The cleaning lady?"

"Yeah. What do you know about her, rather him?"

"I saw her all the time. I even spoke to her, er him a few times."

"Definitely a him. His wife verifies it, although she does say that he likes to dress up as a woman on occasion."

"Arrrgh! That really frosts me! The only reason I joined that club is because I don't like men watching me when I'm working out. Not that I'm shy or anything, but some of the positions are . . . well, pretty suggestive."

He envisioned her doing bench presses on her back, straddling the bench, thighs spread wide—he'd often seen the line of sweat marking a woman's opening when he'd been stair stepping just scant yards from they were working out and knew exactly what she meant. It was the main reason most guys worked out at a gym instead of at home.

"I'm sorry, honey. From now on, I guess it's better to just work out at home. I think we're close to catching him though. How's Kayla?"

"She's sunning on the deck outside of the work room, reading one of her books."

"Can I come see you?"

"Yeah, I wish you would in fact. I have something I need to show you."

"Okay. I'll be right there."

He got out of his car and walked up the steps. When he rang the bell scant seconds later, he saw the surprised expression on her face through the side panel when she came to open the door.

"What, you didn't believe me?" he quipped.

She shook her head. "It just never occurred to me that you'd call from your car, in the driveway. Why didn't you just come in?"

"I didn't want to see you."

"Why not?"

"You're starting to affect me rather badly." He ran a finger down her cheek past her jaw line. "I want you," he whispered. Then pulled her close for a mind-numbing kiss.

When he pulled away her eyes were glazed. "Now, what did you want to show me, and I am fervently hoping that it's something under your sweat suit."

She blushed, and looked down at her damp shirt. "I'm afraid that you're not going to like what I have to show you, or the reason that it came to be in the house."

She told him about the doll falling out of the closet and then showed him the note. She watched him cringe as he realized the meaning it conveyed. "He wants you," he said simply.

"That's what I kind of thought it meant, too."

"What's this about how it got to be in the house?"

She told him about the night that she hadn't been sure the alarm had been set, and how it turned out that it had been, but not at the time she thought she'd set it, and about the night she had been sure the front door had been locked when he'd said it hadn't. Then all hell broke lose in terms of his tongue. He just couldn't hold it in any longer.

"Are you crazy! Do you think this is some kind of a game? Why aren't you being more careful? This is serious! Deadly serious! I cannot believe you were not constantly checking those alarms! You need a keeper! You should have taken your father up on his offer—you need a bodyguard more than anybody I know! Do you want to be his trophy!"

She just stared, eyes wide as his mouth spewed out one thing after another. The tirade did not appear as though it was ever going to end.

Then he started pacing and more came out, only these were anguished. "He could have had you, he could have taken you. You could be his prisoner, doing any number of his perverse demands. You could be dead right now!" She saw his shoulders shake and then he whispered, "You could be dead. Kayla, too."

She touched his shoulder and made him turn back to

351

her. His face was wet, his jaw clenched. She walked into his chest and his arms wrapped around her and held her tight.

"I'm sorry, Kel. I'm so sorry. But I had to tell you the truth."

"That's twice that he's been in your house after Kayla was returned. Twice that we know of!"

"You know who he is now. I'm sure you'll catch him."

"Yeah, but I don't want to use you as bait!"

"Well, Kel what do you want me to do?"

"Why don't you go live with your parents for a few days? Landfall is very secure and your parents have servants."

"This house has a whole new alarm system."

He held her at arm's length and looked down at her. His mouth opened. But she stopped the expected comment with her fingertips on his lips. "I know, I know, what good does it do if I don't engage it?"

"His boat was found just three doors down. Less than half a mile from here! You can't stay here. Not with him on the loose. He's changing, he's morphing."

"What?" she asked.

He told her about the conversation he'd had with Ben Atkinson that morning. Finishing with, "You can't stay here."

"Okay, if you feel that strongly about it, I'll leave tomorrow."

"No. Tonight."

"I can't move Kayla again today, it upsets her each time we move. Tomorrow we'll go to my parent's, I promise."

"Then I'm staying here tonight. And in the meantime, I'm sending over a few officers."

"Is that really necessary?"

"Read that note again, Laura. What do you think?"

He was angry again and she didn't know how to handle it. She did know that it stemmed from his feelings of inadequacy when it came to protecting her.

"Whatever you say."

"I've got some things I have to do, I'll be back shortly. But I'll definitely be staying here tonight. Before I leave, I want to say hi to Kayla." He walked through the room to the French doors that opened onto the deck. He saw her nestled in the hammock as he stood framed in the open doorway. He could tell by her breathing that she was asleep. Laura came to stand beside him. He turned and gave her a cursory kiss on her temple. Stopping to hold her cheek in his palm while he shook his head, he muttered, "You're killing me Laura. Tying me into all kinds of knots. I've never felt like this. You scare the daylights out of me." He dropped his hand, turned, and went back into the house.

He left to go back to his office. What was going on with him, he thought as he drove through rush hour traffic. He would have used his lights to move through it faster, but he needed some time. Some time to think.

I am losing it. I am not handling this very well. He had to admit that the reason was Laura. And the fact that he was in love with her. Shit! He'd told himself that this was not going to happen!

Laura watched him leave from the front window. How was it that now, whenever she thought of that night, she didn't remember the seedy, dusty, damp-smelling room or think of the streaked television screen with the camera hidden behind it, but thought instead of Kel and where his lips had been and the wonderful place he had taken her with his talented lips and tongue.

Was it the same reason she had taken to putting a drop of Kouros on her bra so she could be around his smell all day? She went to the back of the house and out onto the deck to check on Kayla. She was asleep in the hammock under the eaves, her book and Winnie the Pooh tucked under her arm. She bent and kissed her on her sweat-dampened cheek. Then she walked over to the railing to admire the flowers in her garden below and the Waterway beyond. She loved living here. It was her home. It had been in the family for generations. But, if it wasn't safe, she knew she had to leave. She looked down the Waterway trying to envision three doors down and the place where Kel had said they'd found the boat, and she shivered. Could he really be this close?

❧

The man hidden in the tall grasses of the marsh was fixated on the woman leaning over the railing looking down into the water. He knew she couldn't see him, but even if she could, he looked like any other fisherman camouflaged and in waist-high waders. He even had a rod in his hand and a creel on his hip, but he wasn't at all interested in the fish swimming around his legs.

The rod in his hand shook as anger pulsed erratically through him. That fucking bitch! The man she had just been on the deck with, the man whose unmarked cruiser had just been parked in front of her house, was the exact same man from the motel room! The man she had taken into her body. At his bidding!

He was incensed and the jealousy that flared through him heated his blood. He told her not to involve the cops! How dare she? How dare she enlist that cop to be a whore to? Letting that man see her, touch her, lick and kiss her as part of his fucking job! Ohhh! He was livid. And on top of that, they took his fuckin' boat!

Chapter Forty-four

Kel was exhausted by the time he got back to Laura's. He had arranged for off duty personnel to be with Laura and Kayla whenever he wasn't there to protect them. He set up patrols for the houses on the Waterway around hers, and he had the shore patrol continually cruising that stretch of the Waterway. At his office he had checked and double-checked a huge pile of lab reports. They had plenty of evidence against Satterfield, if only they could catch him.

He still had no idea where that deviant douche bag could be. He'd called Cayce and Rand and alerted them to what was going on in case a note turned up for Meggie or Paige. They both assured him that they were going to stay close to home and watch out for their women until Harold Satterfield was caught. Rand had said that he was on his way over to Meggie's now for what he hoped would be an evening of romance and debauchery.

He and Laura had a late dinner and Kel feel asleep reading Kayla a bedtime story. Laura had let her stay up late just so she could see him.

Three hours later his cell phone rang. Toby had been taken from his bed. The Voyeur had struck again and Meggie was beside herself. He grabbed his gun and badge case, kissed Laura on the lips, and ran for his car.

He was mystified. He had thought Laura was the target. This had caught him completely off guard, and he knew that Rand had been stunned too.

❧

Something wasn't right here. There was no note. And even though he had been making love to Meggie and totally focused on that, he found it hard to believe he wouldn't have heard someone opening and closing the front door, unless they'd had a key. Since Meggie had just had the locks changed, how was that possible?

He asked her if she'd made any copies. She said no. He asked her where the copy was that had come with the lock set. It didn't take him long to discover that it was missing from the key ring in her kitchen drawer.

When Kel got there, he told him what he suspected. And the two of them went off in search of Thomas. An hour later they found him drunk on the first hole of Wilmington National Golf Course, smashing the swing camera to smithereens.

When Thomas saw Kel and Rand coming up the slope he bolted, but he was too drunk to put one foot in front of the other fast enough and Rand easily overtook him and tackled him. Then Kel had to jump into the fray to keep Rand from choking Thomas to death.

They found Toby asleep in Thomas' truck. By the time they had everything sorted out for the night, Kel was impatient to get back to Laura. He had officers lock Thomas up for the night. Meggie and Rand had some major decisions about how all this was going to be handled in the morning— decisions that didn't involve him, thank God. Poor Thomas, he had whacked the swing camera until it was no more than a handful of metal pieces, surely as the assistant pro, he knew it had been broken for weeks and unable to record Meggie and Rand?

356

Chapter Forty-five

$\mathcal{T}$he tree frogs suddenly stopped their incessant chirping and something about it unnerved Laura. She had only moments to react before the door to her bedroom silently swung open. She thought that maybe Kel was home, but something about the stealth of the movements in the hallway alarmed her. Kel would not have wanted her to be afraid, he would have called out or boldly entered the house when he returned.

"Who's there?" she called and she gasped when a man's form filled the shadowed doorway.

"It's Frankie, Laura. The man who idolizes you." A tall man stepped into the room and she saw his face. The eyes and lips were familiar but the unshaven jaw line confirmed that Frankie the cleaning woman, was indeed Frank, The Voyeur. He was slovenly in his appearance, wearing rumpled, dirty chinos and a sweat-stained shirt pulled tight over his big gut.

"I'm here to finally enjoy my fantasy woman. I've seen you, now I want to touch you."

Laura sat perfectly still against the headboard despite the frantic pounding of her heart. Try to stay calm, she told herself. Try to keep him away from Kayla.

"How did you get in?"

"I have a key. Even when you changed the locks, I got a key."

"How? I know you're clever, but how did you manage that?" She was going to keep him talking in hopes that the officers patrolling would come to check up on them.

"Oh, that was easy. I know the company your father's rental agency uses. I simply called and canceled the service call and instead, I came and installed the new locks myself." He waved a shiny gold key. "I kept one for me."

"How did you know I was changing them?"

He raised his brows and gave her a quelling look. "Come on Laura, don't be naive, after what happened, of course you'd change the locks."

"You set the alarm that night and came into the house when I had Meggie and Paige over, didn't you?"

"I wanted you that first night, but I lost my last pill. I had it in my pocket, but I lost it. I knew I had to come back. I can't perform, take care of your needs, if you get my drift, without my pill. I watched you sleep for a while though. You are so beautiful. I set the alarm before I left so nobody else could have you until I returned for you. The other night when I found all three of you drunk and asleep by the pool, I thought I had hit the lottery, all my favorite girls in one place. But the damned phone kept ringing and then I heard cars pulling up out front. I watched the men find you and take you all inside from the beach. I didn't take the time to lock up, I'm sorry." He flashed her an evil smile.

"I promise I'll lock up after I leave tonight though. Now why don't you just come with me to another room so we don't wake up the precious little one?"

She watched as he took a filet knife out of a sheath in his waistband. "We wouldn't want to wake her. She probably already has enough trauma to deal with. By all rights, Laura, I should take her again. You disobeyed me. You went to the cops."

Laura's anger flashed through her and exited out of her eyes with heated fury. But she wasn't going to lose this opportunity to get him away from Kayla, so she slowly slid over to the edge of the bed.

"Actually, I didn't, he came to me."

"What an assignment he was handed," he said, his voice laced with sarcasm. 'I know he enjoyed himself, I saw the proof. You must have enjoyed yourself too, since you've invited him back. But once you've had me, no one else will do. Come on Laura, let's go. I can't wait for you to show me those beautiful titties I used to admire while you were showering." The man stepped forward and pulled the cover off the bed.

❧

Kel pulled his cruiser into the circular drive and stepped out. The night was still except for the rustling of the sea grass and a few orphaned tree frogs. The officer who had been here had just radioed him that all was clear and that he was going to walk the main road one more time before leaving. Kel had waved to him just moments ago when they had passed on the long lane. It was a beautiful night and he sincerely hoped that one day, he and Laura could just sit out on the deck and enjoy it. But right now he was definitely ready for bed, or in this case, the sofa.

He had not gotten a key from Laura, but knew she would be awake, there was no way she would have gone to sleep without knowing how Meggie was and if they'd found Toby. He was about to ring the doorbell when he saw that the door wasn't pulled all the way to.

Without the connection why wasn't the alarm ringing and waking the dead? Oh don't tell me she didn't set it again! And instantly he knew that would not have happened. Not tonight. Not after their argument. He pulled out his gun and quietly pushed the door open, then he pushed it to but didn't let it latch. He looked around and saw that it was dark on the first level. He climbed the stairs slowly straining to hear any noises in the house. When he got to the top of the staircase, he saw light coming from under Laura's door. Kayla's door was closed and no light shone underneath. He doubted that Kayla would be anywhere but in her mom's bed tonight. They would both be in Laura's room. And if Laura had left the alarm disengaged, and the front door unlocked, he was going to be absolutely livid!

Just as he made it to the door, and was about to push it forward, he heard a gun go off. His reflex pushed the door open and he saw Laura with a gun in her hand and a man with a knife swaying in front of her. Kel fired. He double-tapped the man in the head. As the man fell to the floor, Kel looked to Laura for any sign that she was hurt.

Kayla screamed and Laura, her face as white as a fine porcelain plate, stared at the body on the floor. Then she whispered, "I promised myself that if I ever had the chance that I'd never let him do this to anyone else."

He walked over to her side of the bed, skirting the body so he could take the gun from her. She had shot him in the balls. "You did real good, honey. Real good. Now I only have to figure out how to explain how you had a gun that's registered to me," he quipped.

"I'll tell them you left it here and that I stole it from you, I already have a record for shoplifting."

He grinned and put the gun in his waistband before bending down to reach for Kayla who had her eyes tightly closed.

"We need to see to her, let's get her out of here. And I need to call this in." He hefted Kayla into his arms, cooed something into her ear, and waited for Laura to climb over the bed so he could hand Kayla to her. Then he walked back to the body. He had to see the face of the man who had affected so many lives.

The man had probably been good looking once. Now he would have been called nondescript, easily overlooked in any crowd, and maybe that had been a part of his problem. He didn't look like a man who leered at women. But then, what did that kind of man look like, he mused.

The man lying at his feet had certainly changed his own life. This man was the reason Laura had needed him.

He looked down at the man's crotch where a pool of blood was soaking his pants and the carpet all around the bed. *The woman's a good shot, he thought. A damn good shot!*

Chapter Forty-six

*H*e hadn't been able to find her anywhere. He wasn't sure if it was the media or him that had made her run. But run she had. He'd waited a few days, thinking surely when everything settled down, that she'd call him. But she hadn't.

He was stretched out on his sofa, staring out the window at the summer day, watching the birds fly back and forth in his back yard. He fell asleep with the image of her in his mind. The image of her as she'd looked just before she had reached down and led him to her body. He even remembered groaning as he fell asleep.

When he woke, he sat up, rubbed his face and said out loud. "Okay, it's time. Time to go find her."

༄༅

Torcello, In The Lagoon of Venice

He'd finally found her. It had taken almost a week. She was staying in a tiny villa just outside the town square.

She saw him get off the small boat from the open window and watched as he came toward her little house. The sun was setting behind him and he had an eerie, ethereal glow. He was so tall and formidable that he looked like some kind of medieval conqueror. She was standing in the wide doorway when he walked up to her. He fingered the tiny palm tree in his pocket, marveling at how sturdy that little piece of plastic was. He had worn it smooth while flying over the Atlantic.

He put his suitcase on the ground and stood gazing at her for a moment before he whispered, "Laura, mi amore." His hands cupped her cheeks. He looked down into her face, watching the tears well in her eyes. "Will you be my love?" he asked.

"For as long as you'll have me," she managed to sob before his head bent and his lips brushed lightly over hers.

"Forever. I'll take you forever."

He kissed her with the turbulent passion he had carried across a seemingly never-ending ocean.

When he broke the kiss, his fingertips stroked her cheeks as his lips lingered at the corners of her mouth. Then he shoved his suitcase into the house and bent to gather her into his arms. "Where's our bed?" he asked as he kicked the door shut behind him. She didn't need to tell him where her bedroom was, he instinctively moved toward the light at the end of the hallway. Entering the rustic country bedroom, he placed her gently on the bed. "Kayla sleeping on her own again?" he asked. She simply nodded.

Situating himself bedside her, he stretched out his long body and ran his palm down her torso. His hand rested on her flat belly and he gently rubbed little circles over the silk of her dress. "By the way, how's my baby?"

"You know?"

"When I couldn't find you, I went to see your ex, figuring he'd have to know where you took Kayla. He didn't, but he did manage to tell me you had prepared him for your next breaking scandal, that you were pregnant by the man who had helped you get Kayla back. Unless there's another, I figured that had to be me."

"I told my doctor that I didn't know how I could have gotten pregnant since you pulled out before ejaculating, and he said the pre-come lubricant on a male's penis has a very heavy concentration of sperm."

Her hand reached up and her fingertips grazed the stubble she found there. "You're okay with this?" she asked timidly.

"I am more than okay with it. I am ecstatic, delirious with joy in fact. How about you?"

"I'm thrilled. And you don't know how happy it makes me to know that you're okay with it. I didn't think you would be since you didn't even want a wife." Hastily changing the subject, she asked, "How did you find me?"

"Interpol. They ran your passport, found it had been stamped in Florence, and then pulled your immigration record and found you had listed this little hamlet on the island of Torcello as your place of residence in Italy. Piece of cake."

"And here I thought I was running away and hiding from everyone."

"You never need to hide from me. Ever," he whispered as his head lowered and his lips caressed the side of her neck. "Marry me, Laura. Let me take care of you and Kayla and this little one," he said as his hand moved in an ever-widening circle on her abdomen. He remembered the first time he had rubbed her here, when he had taken his ejaculate from the hollow of her backside and rubbed it into her belly. Pregnancy by osmosis, he thought with chagrin.

"I love you and I need to be with you. And more than anything, I need to be inside you again," he murmured huskily as he took her hand and showed her just how badly he was aching for her. "I'm praying that you desire me just as badly."

"You wouldn't believe how my body has yearned for yours. Ever since that night at the Jefferson, I keep reaching for you in my dreams."

"Believe me, I know exactly how that feels. My nights have been filled with only thoughts of you—a naked you."

"I knew that until I slept with you in my arms, nothing would ever be right again," she whispered.

"Well, we're a long way from sleeping, yet I can hardly wait." He breathed in her sweet floral fragrance and something else, an underlayment of spice and wood.

"Has there been a man in here?"

"Not since I moved in, why?"

"I smell my aftershave."

Laura laughed delightedly. "It's the smell of my man, Mi Amore."

His mouth took hers and he crushed her velvety lips beneath his firm ones. Life was good. Evil had come full circle to make something wonderful happen. Lust and love interchanged and fought for dominance as he made love to her that night. It was wonderful to have both, as they tended to work really well together.

www.ingramcontent.com/pod-product-compliance
Lightning Source LLC
Chambersburg PA
CBHW050909250626
47155CB00001B/166

9781424310197